THE BRONZE LEGION:
To Tread
Obsidian Shores
VOLUME ONE

**BAEN BOOKS by
JASON CORDOVA & MELISSA OLTHOFF**

THE BRONZE LEGION
To Tread Obsidian Shores

**BAEN BOOKS
by JASON CORDOVA**

Mountain of Fire
Monster Hunter Memoirs: Fever with Larry Correia
Chicks in Tank Tops edited by Jason Cordova
Dancing with Destruction edited by Jason Cordova
Chaos and Consequences edited by Jason Cordova, forthcoming

**BAEN BOOKS
by MELISSA OLTHOFF**

Rise from Ruin

To purchase any of these titles in e-book form, please go to www.baen.com.

THE BRONZE LEGION:
To Tread
Obsidian Shores

VOLUME ONE

Jason Cordova &
Melissa Olthoff

To Tread Obsidian Shores

This is a work of fiction. All the characters and events portrayed in this book are fictional, and any resemblance to real people or incidents is purely coincidental.

Copyright © 2026 Jason Cordova and Melissa Olthoff

All rights reserved, including the right to reproduce this book or portions thereof in any form.

A Baen Books Original

Baen Publishing Enterprises
P.O. Box 1403
Riverdale, NY 10471
www.baen.com

ISBN: 978-1-6680-7306-3

Cover art by Pierluigi Abbondanza
Title page art by Rabbit Boyett

First printing, January 2026

Distributed by Simon & Schuster
1230 Avenue of the Americas
New York, NY 10020

Library of Congress Control Number: 2025039175

Printed in the United States of America

10 9 8 7 6 5 4 3 2 1

DEDICATION

Jason: This one is for my dad, Max,
who died after Melissa and I finished the first draft of this novel.
I miss you.

Melissa: To my INCREDIBLY NOISY children.
You made coworking with "Uncle" Jason so much more interesting.
Like the Chinese curse. I love you both!

THE BRONZE LEGION: To Tread Obsidian Shores

VOLUME ONE

DRAMATIS PERSONAE

BRONZE LEGION, BRAVO COMPANY

COMMANDING OFFICER—Capt. Oren "Tripwire" Truitt

4TH SQUAD, FIRE TEAM ONE LEADER—Sergeant Afton "Claw" Klau
    Specialist Timothy "Stickboy" Hanz
    Corporal Tom "Ratman" Coonradt
    Private Alec "Loosey" Luta
    Private Josh "Crusty" Kruschke

4TH SQUAD, FIRE TEAM TWO LEADER—Specialist Ryan "Pigeon" Pridgeon
    Specialist Alan "Vixen" Voecks
    Corporal Ray "Krawdaddy" Krawczyk
    Corporal Vindahar "Jabber" Jabbalogoeczeski
    Private Diego Tavi

4TH SQUAD, FIRE TEAM THREE LEADER—Sergeant Emmette "Ordo" Ord
    Corporal Jim "Muster" Masterson
    Specialist Oscar "Banger" Kolbinger
    Specialist Wally "Walleye" Davis
    Specialist Adam "Toejam" Thompkins

5TH SQUAD, FIRE TEAM THREE LEADER—Sergeant Travis "Duck" Cox
    Sergeant Eddie Munoz
    Private Hector Gomes
    Private Streicher

✧✧✧

BRONZE LEGION, BRONZE RAVEN SQUADRON

COMMANDING OFFICER—Major Nikki "Voodoo" Ellingwood
DIRECTOR OF OPERATIONS—Captain Stephanie "Ditch" Baxter

BRONZE RAVEN FOUR COMMAND PILOT—Captain Makenna "Twister" Latham
    COPILOT—Lieutenant Astra "Blue" Eliassen
    LOADMASTER—Sergeant Miguel Carvalho
    GUNNER—Corporal Emi "HeyHey" Hayashi
    GUNNER—Corporal Iolana "HeyHey" Hekikia

BRONZE RAVEN FIVE COMMAND PILOT—Captain Wanda "Witch" Sanderson
    COPILOT—Lieutenant Serella "Killi" Killowen
    LOADMASTER—Sergeant Malcolm Tinnesz

BRONZE RAVEN ONE COMMAND PILOT—Captain Brandy "Medusa" Newkirk
    COPILOT—Lieutenant Heather "Ruby" Ridolfi
    LOADMASTER—Sergeant Tim Morrison
    GUNNER—Corporal Justin Tyson
    GUNNER—Corporal Andrew Jacobi

✧✧✧

PNV *PERSEVERANCE*, PROTECTORATE OF MARS NAVY

COMMANDING OFFICER—Captain Eric Esper
EXECUTIVE OFFICER—Commander Beth Lobdell
SENIOR OPS OFFICER—Lieutenant Darin Stahl
JUNIOR OPS OFFICER—Ensign Garrett Campbell
SENIOR COMMS OFFICER—Lieutenant Commander Remy Logan
JUNIOR COMMS OFFICER—Ensign Adrian Grimes
INTEL OFFICER—Lieutenant Commander Liam Hart

✧✧✧

SURVEY CORPS

CHIEF EXPEDITER—Dr. Charles William Joseph Schmoyer IV
XENOBIOLOGIST—Dr. Mitzi Wingo
GEOLOGIST—Dr. Huyan Xi-Smith
METEROLOGIST—Dr. Albert Childs
METEROLOGIST—Dr. Rodrigo Morales

✧✧✧

AURORA RESEARCH OUTPOST

PLANETARY SUPERVISOR—Sir Percival Norwood III
ASSISTANT FACILITY SUPERVISOR—John Delany
PILOT—Captain Marx Fischer
PERSONAL ASSISTANT—Quinn Warrow

PROLOGUE
The Lost Boy

THE OVERDARK, MYRKYMA

Even the water was poisonous in Overdark. The people hunting him, though, would kill him quicker.

The boy stood outside the small granite building, his hands clenching and unclenching rhythmically as he struggled to find the courage to step inside. He'd been standing there for ten minutes, watching, wondering. The only course of action that might keep him alive would be to walk through those doors, yet he hesitated. There were two guards in some sort of armor just inside the doors, while a man in a dark uniform was seated behind a desk further in. He was doing something on a notepad and seemed to be deliberately *not* looking up. Unlike the rest of the Overdark, the man seemed unaware of the boy's existence.

Which made sense to the boy. Blatant overtures and brashness might scare people away. As he'd learned from watching his mother pull tricks into the brothels when he'd been much younger, it was the coy, almost shy looks which drew in the customers. Why be forward when the customer already knew what they wanted and merely lacked the courage to ask for it?

Yet he hesitated. Was it really better to stand outside in the acidic, poisonous rain?

He needed to do something. Anything, really. Eventually, those looking to murder him for his genetics would track him down. Then they would kill him and burn his body like they had all the others who shared his modified bloodline. *After* mounting his head like some war trophy for everyone to see. All in the name of revelry and freedom.

With just the slightest smidge of revenge tossed in.

The steady condensation which collected then dripped from the stalactites above gave Overdark its rain. The toxic atmosphere outside the underground hive city gave it the poison. The ruling Tyrants, who had only been cast down and executed the day before, were the very reason he'd been forced to flee, courtesy of his blood. Not because he was afraid of dying, no. It was the *manner* of his death which gave him pause.

He was pushing the door open before his conscious mind actually realized he had moved.

With that simple action a new life began.

"Good morning," the man behind the desk greeted him, standing up. He stuck out his hand. After a moment of confusion, the boy simply bowed. The man tapped his chin thoughtfully as he regarded the boy. "Hmm... interesting. Are you from Syngaard?"

"Yes, lord." His use of the official name for Overdark marked the man as an outsider, a *farjain*, one not to be trusted. The boy had no other choice, though. He had to put his faith in this man. There would be no other options. Those hunting him would track him down soon enough.

"Please. Not a lord at all. My name is Sergeant Hager Buckholz. Not lord, sir, or anything like that. You understand?" the man asked.

"Yes, Sergeant Hager Buckholz."

The sergeant smiled at him. It was pleasant, not condescending or threatening in the least. The facial expression was almost unfamiliar to the boy. Usually there was a glint of greed or want in the eyes of those who would smile at him.

"You're going to be a tough nut to crack, aren't you? Make my life as a recruiter difficult?" Sergeant Buckholz chuckled and shook his head. "I'm assuming the reason you stood outside in the toxic pseudo-rain for ten minutes is because you were unsure about joining the Legion. Not that I blame you. It's a radical change of life. If accepted, you'll more than likely never set foot on this world again."

"I'm fine with that, Sergeant Hager Buckholz," the boy responded, keeping his eyes down and his features properly schooled. He'd known too many men—and quite a few women—who would beat him for daring to match their gaze. If the boy knew anything, it was subservience.

"Call me 'Sergeant,' if you're going to be that stubborn. Did you mean to walk into my recruiting station, or are you lost?" The boy didn't know the answer, so he shrugged. The muscular recruiter pursed his lips and nodded. "Who're you running from, boy? And are you even old enough to register?"

"Running..." The boy shivered as unbidden memories less than a day old came to the forefront of his mind. Other kids from Overdark being killed because of who their fathers were, slaughtered simply because they carried the genetic material of the Tyrants. He was one of those cursed spawn, bastards who lived in the Overdark, whose mothers made their livings on their backs. "I'm seventeen, lo— Sergeant. I'm a legal adult."

"By local law, yes," Sergeant Buckholz said before blowing out a breath. "We have requirements of those who wish to join the Foreign Legion. You did know that's what this place is, right? You understand what a recruiting station is?"

The boy knew. When he'd been ten years old, a few others had braved the doors and walked inside. Other kids his age told of how those few had left the world to live on a paradise planet away from the Overdark, where they were fed two whole meals per day and given new clothes to wear. They also never returned.

Or not. Since they never came back, there were whispered stories of horrible things that happened to them. Theories. Myths.

The boy was fairly certain that the amount of food given to them was a lie—after all, who could afford to eat so much? But the other stuff? Not having to sleep under refuse so someone didn't try to knife you and steal your shirt? Actual shoes? Being allowed to leave and never having to return? A chance at something else? Those parts of the story appealed to him more than anything else. It might be possible, and that was all he had going for him now—the promise of a chance.

"I know what this place is, Sergeant."

"Do you have a name?" Sergeant Buckholz asked, then held up a palm to forestall an answer. "Actually, let me do you one better. If you're accepted into the Legion, you can pick your new name, new identity. Martian law. So, what would you like your name to be?"

The boy shrugged. "I have only one name, lo—Sergeant. Diego. My mother named me that when I was born."

"Ah, so you *do* have a mother. Is she around still, or did she pass away?"

"She . . . died." How could he tell the recruiter the truth? How would he respond to knowing his father, a Tyrant, had killed his mother one night because he'd grown bored of her? Would the sergeant reject him as the brothel manager had once his mother's corpse had been bio-reprocessed? "I have no one else."

"I figured that part out," Sergeant Buckholz told him. "So . . . do you want to keep your name as Diego?"

He nodded. "Yes, Sergeant."

"Okay, Diego. It's very nice to finally meet you. Why don't you have a seat in the chair there and we can get started."

The chair was comfortable, far more so than anything Diego was used to. For the first time his eyes darted around the room, taking it all in and understanding very little of it. It wasn't decorated like any room he'd been in before. There were three flags hanging on poles behind the sergeant's desk. Off to the right of the flags there was a single digital photo of a much younger-looking Sergeant Buckholz in some sort of armor. Around him were a group of similarly dressed men, each holding in their hands what Diego guessed to be a weapon. Above them, a ringed planet loomed in the background.

For a moment Diego thought it was fake. He knew of the Outside, of course. The Outside was death on Myrkyma. He was even aware there were other worlds out there which were inhabited. People lived there, in constant danger of death and ruin, with Myrkyma being one of the more successfully colonized worlds. But a planet with rings around it, in the sky, for all to see?

Yet . . . nothing else in the office seemed false. Why post a picture of something which could be easily disproved? It was confusing and made his head swim.

"The first thing we have to do, Diego, is run a quick blood screen," Sergeant Buckholz told him as he moved behind the desk and pulled out a small bio-scanner, very similar to the ones the local Enforcers used when they arrested someone. Or, more often than not, beat them until they were sufficiently bribed. Diego was familiar with the device, though he wasn't quite sure why the sergeant needed it. The recruiter explained. "We accept anyone who wants to be in the Protectorate of Mars Foreign Legion, but there are a few stipulations. No, we don't care about who you were in your past life. What we're searching for is if you have any outstanding Class One felony warrants for your arrest. Past convictions, time served? None of that matters. Basically, we want to know if you're running from the law *now*."

Diego swallowed nervously. The sergeant was on point about that. He *was* running, but for a very good reason. Taking a calming breath, he thought about it. Was there law anymore on Myrkyma? He wasn't too sure. There'd always been two types of law in Overdark itself—Tyrant's law, and the laws which were enforced on everyone else. With the tarred heads of the Tyrants decorating the spiked walls outside the Reina, the laws for everyone else had scattered into the dark. Blood was the law now, revenge its sweet judge, jury, and executioner. So who would decide the law next? He had a sneaking suspicion who it would be, and it made him shiver.

Those were the ones who wanted him dead. Of course he was running.

He stuck his thumb in the scanner and felt a small pressure, a slight pain. The scanner chimed once and Sergeant Buckholz pulled it away. Looking down, Diego spotted a small bloody streak where he'd been pricked. It wasn't much, but it did bring back a troubled memory of a spot of blood on a pearl cufflink, and a Tyrant eating a steak with the very knife Diego's mother had been murdered with.

There'd been nothing in his father's expression as he calmly carved the steak in practiced, measured cuts.

The device chimed and Sergeant Buckholz immediately began reading. After a moment his eyes went wide, and he looked back at Diego with a strange expression on his face. Diego felt his heart fall. The sergeant knew what he was now. He needed to leave. There was no way they would accept a bastard of a Tyrant.

"Everything...looks in order here," Sergeant Buckholz said after a slight cough. "There *are* warrants for your arrest, but there's a small caveat. It says there is an arrest warrant for anyone sharing this DNA, and not you specifically. Which means...jack squat to us. Unfortunately, the query I ran pinged whoever the local law enforcement is in these parts now. Fortunately, you're on Mars Primus sovereign soil, since this is a Foreign Legion Recruiting Station. Our laws are respected, but not necessarily binding, when it comes to blanket warrants such as these. We can ignore it, unless you have moral qualms about doing so... which, to be honest, I don't think you do, do you?"

"Does... that mean I can still join?" Diego asked in a cautious tone. The recruiter chuckled dryly.

"Definitely. But I need to break it down for you what your requirements will be, should you decide to enlist." Sergeant Buckholz moved around to the other side of the desk and sat down. He leaned back in his chair and contemplated Diego for a moment before continuing. "I don't think you'll have any problems accepting our terms, but I am required by law to state them before we talk about enlistment papers. You will serve ten years in the Protectorate of Mars Foreign Legion, henceforth to be known simply as the Legion. You will obey all orders given to you, and you will be expected to comport yourself to our higher standard of conduct. After ten years of service, which begins the moment you report to your first Legion—*not* Basic Training or Advance Combat School, mind you—you will be eligible for full Protectorate citizenship, either a small plot of land to farm on a colony world, should you choose for you and your descendants, or the monthly equivalent in monetary compensation for ten years after your time of service ends.

"Desertion is not tolerated. If you desert, when you are found— that's not an *if*, kid, trust me—you will be branded a traitor, flogged, marched in front of a firing squad, and summarily executed as a traitor to the Legion, and then your body tossed into an unmarked grave, your name stricken from Legion rolls. If you become physically unable to complete your term of service in the Legion due to injury or wounds suffered in battle, you will be moved to a support position and retrained. This will not 'restart the clock,' as they say. You will complete your term of service serving the Legion, one way or the other. You still with me?"

"Yes, lord... Sergeant."

"Good." Sergeant Buckholz leaned forward, and his voice changed subtly. "This isn't an easy life, Diego. We go where the Protectorate needs us to go. We've had peace for many years, which is why most people think they want to join. Free education, land, money, glory... whatever drives kids these days. But the truth of the matter is, training can be just as dangerous as real combat. You could die in an accident, in combat, in school—"

"Or in an alley here," Diego interjected. "I understand."

"That's one way to look at things," the recruiter said as he offered Diego a small smile. "Once you repeat the Oath of Enlistment before the duly-authorized representative—that being Captain Rhys, of course—and sign some papers, you'll officially be Legionnaire Recruit Diego ... uh, do you have a last name?"

Diego shook his head. "No, Sergeant. I wasn't given one. Neither was my mother."

"Well, the beauty of joining the Legion is that you can invent one, since you're an entirely new individual. Plus, having a surname allows the drill instructors to yell at you more properly while going through basic." Sergeant Buckholz steepled his fingers in front of him. "You don't *have* to have one, mind you. But it's one of those things that makes life easier in the Protectorate."

"I can pick any name?" Diego asked slowly. The sergeant nodded. "Can I use Tavi as my last name?"

"Why not?" Sergeant Buckholz grinned. "Why that one?"

"It was the only name of my mother."

"Sergeant?" a voice interrupted from behind Diego. "Problem."

Diego turned in his chair to see what the guard was talking about. It took him less than a second to recognize the small crowd gathered outside for what it was. His heart dropped as he recognized two of them from the group who had chased him down an alley the hour before. They'd almost caught him then, but Diego had managed to slip between two large trash bins and escape. He'd almost let himself build up hope that they would give up their pursuit.

The revolutionaries were passionate and full of zeal. He should have known they would never give up on their hunt for him. Especially since he'd given them the slip not once, but three times already since they first rose up and started murdering anyone with Tyrant blood coursing through their veins.

"Corporal Aires? Alert the captain. Tell him the situation," Sergeant Buckholz ordered as he stood from behind the desk. "Corporal Jeffe—secure the entry. No one in or out without authorization. Can't have the riffraff pushing through and dirtying up our lobby. Might hurt recruitment efforts."

"Lord? Are you going to turn me over to them?" Diego asked.

"Turn you over... what? And miss my monthly quota?" Sergeant Buckholz looked at him incredulously. "I think *not*!"

"Sergeant?" Corporal Aires asked from the door after locking it from the inside. On the other side of the glass, Diego could see the small crowd growing agitated. There was muted shouting, most of which he couldn't make out, though "Tyrant's bastard" was clear enough. He could guess at the rest.

Sergeant Buckholz frowned. "Corporal? Grab your gear."

"Nonlethal only," a new voice said from the back room. Turning, Diego saw a broad figure walk into the room. His face was young but stern, and he was taller than Diego by almost an entire foot. He was more muscular than any of the others as well. For a moment Diego wondered if the stern giant was kept around for head-bashing purposes, like bouncers at some of the seedier clubs in Overdark. The other three men braced to attention as the large man gave Diego a curious glance before continuing.

Everything snapped into place for him. This was something he knew. Diego nodded to himself, understanding. Of course the biggest and strongest would be in charge. That was how things worked in Overdark. Why wouldn't it be similar everywhere else?

"Sergeant? You've been here the longest. How do you see the locals reacting to this?"

"Lethal, sir? They'll run, sure, but eventually they'll be back. Syngaard is not a gentle burrowtown, sir," Sergeant Buckholz said, a thoughtful expression on his face. "If we wait and let them protest, sir, more will come. Eventually one of them will get all full of himself—always a young guy trying to impress a girl, sir—and then it'll explode and get really messy. Nonlethal and abrupt, before it can get going? Sends a message, Captain Rhys, that we don't want their trouble. But they might not listen, sir."

"Indeed. Well, Sergeant, let's not waste any time in dispersing this group. I'll take the young recruit... Recruit, what's your name?"

"Diego, lord. Diego Tavi."

"Huh. You're from Syngaard. Interesting. In the future, 'sir' will more than suffice. Recruit Diego, come with me so you can swear your Oath of Enlistment. Step lively now."

"Will that make a difference, sir?" Diego asked, confused.

"Of course it will. Your oath is your pledge to the Protectorate, and the Protectorate owes you once your Oath is given. Ours is a two-way street. You serve us, and the Legion serves you. Sergeant Buckholz?"

"Sir?"

"Riffraff. Get rid of them. Recruit Tavi and I will be along in a minute. You've run his blood sample?"

"Yes, sir," Sergeant Buckholz said. "He's clear." The captain nodded.

"Instruct them to disperse, begin extraction protocols of this station—I expect difficulties in the near future—and send word to the ambassador in Klysgaard. Also, notify local law enforcement—if any are still in service. Remind the local force that this is sovereign Martian soil, and if this is violated, it is an act of aggression against the Protectorate of Mars itself, and an affront to the Legion. If the protestors decide to get froggy before the police arrive, then we stop them fast and hard. Ensure the watch commander at the embassy is aware of the situation as well. And remember"—the officer paused, holding up a single finger—"nonlethal doesn't necessarily mean painless."

"Yes, sir!" Sergeant Buckholz grinned from ear to ear. "Jeffe, Aires? You heard the captain. Suit up. I'll get on the horn with Klysgaard."

"Come with me, Recruit Tavi." The captain turned and walked towards the three flags on the poles behind Sergeant Buckholz's desk. Unsure, Diego followed, and stopped a few feet away from him. The captain coughed and shook his head. "Normally we have a little more pomp and circumstance with these, but time is precious. Since everything in this room is recorded... This is Captain Armando Rhys, Commanding Officer of Legion Recruiting Station Sininen, Syngaard District, Myrkyma. Standing before me is Legion Recruit Diego Tavi, of Syngaard. Time and date stamp for reference is on file with this recording. I solemnly avow as a citizen of the Protectorate and as a commissioned officer within the Mars Foreign Legions that the following oath is given with free consent and free will of Recruit Tavi. Recruit, are you here of your own free will and volition?"

"Yes, sir."

The captain nodded. "Please turn and face the Protectorate flag—that's the red-and-white one in the middle—and place your right hand over your heart. Good. Now, repeat after me.

"I, state your name, make this Oath of Enlistment of sound mind and body..."

"I, state... I mean, Diego Tavi, make this Oath of Enlistment of sound mind and body."

"To uphold the laws of the Protectorate..."

"To uphold the laws of the Protectorate."

"And follow any lawfully given order..."

He repeated everything the captain said. It was brief and to the point, which Diego appreciated. Part of him had been afraid it would be a long and tedious ordeal. At the very end, the captain nodded before offering him the final line in the oath.

"...and lastly, I promise to comport myself to the highest standard possible for as long as I serve in the Legion..."

"Sir?" Diego paused, uncertain.

"Problem, Recruit?"

Diego swallowed nervously. "I...I don't know what comport means, sir. I'm sorry, sir."

"Ah. Comport means to conduct or behave oneself in a given manner. I expect you, as a legionnaire, to be an example of just what the Legion is, and is meant to be. To protect the weak, defend the innocent, and follow Protectorate law to its fullest. Does that explain it?"

"Yes, sir." Diego understood the words, though he suspected there was a deeper meaning behind them, something he couldn't quite grasp just yet. Still, promising anything was better than being torn apart by the mob outside. "I promise to comport myself to the highest standard possible for as long as I serve in the Legion."

"So help me God..."

"So help me God."

"Congratulations, Recruit. You are officially enlisted in the Legion." Captain Rhys nodded briskly. "As soon as this issue here is sorted, we'll get you on a shuttle and sent to Mars Primus for Basic Training. From there you'll be sent to Advanced Combat School, and then you'll be assigned to your legion. Now, let's go outside and talk with these... hooligans."

Diego followed the captain back to the front of the office, where both Jeffe and Aires had quickly dressed in some sort of strange armor. Parts of it reminded him of the gear the police and enforcers wore in Overdark: ballistic armor designed to thwart most attacks. However, there were strange gaps in the armor which would allow a knife or bullet through, with the only thing protecting the wearer being some sort of thin material beneath. While it looked flexible and soft, there was an underlying mottled gray pigmentation to it which made Diego's eyes drift away. After a second he realized the armor was adjusting to the wall behind them. Even the plates on top were shifting color slightly to better match the surroundings. He'd never seen anything like it before.

At the front door, Sergeant Buckholz was in similar armor, though there was a red "VII" emblazoned on his left shoulder. Diego glanced at the other two and noticed they both sported a white "X" on theirs.

Seeing Diego's querying look, Captain Rhys took the time to explain.

"Those were their legions before they were pulled for recruiter duty. Corporals Jeffe and Aires were part of the 10th Legion, *Protectores Legio*. The sergeant was in the 7th Legion, *Serpens Bellator Legio*. I myself served in the 5th Legion." His chest swelled with pride. "*Sol Custodes*."

None of the words meant anything to Diego, but clearly they were important to the legionnaires. He would ask them to explain later... if they survived this mess, he decided.

"The duty watch officer at Klysgaard has been notified, sir, and our ambassador is making a formal protest with whoever is running the show now on the planet," Sergeant Buckholz reported upon seeing the captain. He offered Diego a comforting grin before continuing his report. "The crowd is restless, no firebrands yet. We might see a few eventually as word spreads, sir."

"Well, there are only legionnaires in this building now, so they'll need to disperse," Captain Rhys said. "Quickly."

Any nervousness Tavi might have had was instantly quelled by Rhys' calm demeaner.

With Corporal Jeffe leading the way, the trio of enlisted exited the building and stood in front of the door in the warm, poisonous rain of Myrkyma. Sergeant Buckholz looked around at the gathered mob and snorted derisively.

"Unless you are here to join the Legion, you are ordered to disperse from these premises," he called out in a tone which brooked no argument. His voice easily carried over the assembled crowd of a dozen or so men and women. Flanking him, both corporals remained motionless, as still as stone. If not for the slight movements of their chests, Diego would have thought them statues. "This is sovereign soil of the Protectorate of Mars Primus."

"Land stolen from us to bribe Martians to do the dirty work of the Tyrants!" a woman's voice cried out from within the crowd.

"Odd... I would've thought it'd be one of the men," Captain Rhys murmured. Diego said nothing. He really didn't know if he was supposed to respond, or if the large officer had merely been thinking out loud. Guessing wrong in the past when dealing with men in charge had oftentimes led to beatings. Better to say nothing and be forgotten then to speak and remind someone a thrashing was due.

"The Protectorate does not interfere with local politics," Sergeant Buckholz responded. The angry crowd, Diego noticed, was getting more and more worked up with each passing second. His sharp eyes spotted at least three knives, a blackjack, and a cheap-looking pistol which appeared older than Klysgaard itself, one which he doubted would even fire. "We don't even care—"

"Give us the Tyrant bastard!" a man screamed and pointed at Diego. "That one! His father was the Butcher of Archangel! The Revolutionary Tribunal Council has decreed that anyone with Tyrant blood is to be executed to prevent their taint from spreading any further, trueborn or other! He might not be a trueborn son of a Tyrant, but he has their blood! He'll be a monster like them!"

Diego swallowed nervously and looked up at Captain Rhys. How could four men handle such a mob?

Only the captain appeared... *bored*?

"I won't ask you again." Sergeant Buckholz raised his voice slightly, his tone colder than anything Diego had heard or felt before in his life. The switch from pleasant yet firm to dangerous had been abrupt. He wondered if anyone else in the crowd had noticed. Would it even matter at this point? "Please disperse, or *be* dispersed."

"His kind are evil and need to be killed!" the first woman screeched again.

"Ma'am?" Sergeant Buckholz paused and adjusted his uniform slightly. "You are free to test the Legion's resolve in this matter at your leisure, but be forewarned that our response will be quite... robust. You shall not enjoy it."

One man screamed, a cry filled with hate and passion, and charged Corporal Jeffe. The legionnaire twisted slightly and planted his rear foot. With one hand, he held up his palm, a seemingly wasted gesture to force his would-be attacker to halt. However, Diego watched as Jeffe's other hand made a peculiar twisting motion. A two-foot-long metallic baton snapped out and lashed forward, a brutally fast strike which caught the revolutionary square in the jaw. Before the man could ever register he'd been struck, Jeffe brought the baton in for a follow-up blow. The baton struck the man's knee, and he was falling face forward, unconscious and more than likely permanently crippled, before anyone else could even react.

Jeffe slid forward two feet, his momentum carrying him, before he froze. Slowly he raised his head and looked at the stilled crowd. Barely two seconds had passed from the moment the attack had begun. Diego couldn't believe it. He'd never seen anyone move so quickly or fluidly in his life. There was no way the human body could do that, and yet he'd seen it with his very own eyes.

"That's one test of our resolve," Sergeant Buckholz said into the silence. There were uneasy glances shared between those in the mob. "I think your man failed. Would anyone else like to try?"

"Murderers!"

"Not yet," Sergeant Buckholz replied coolly. "He still lives. He'll be eating through a straw for the next year, and I doubt he'll walk normally without major reconstructive surgery on his tibia, but he breathes. He survives at our discretion now."

Four men from the group rushed in to attack. Beside him, Diego heard Captain Rhys sigh and mutter under his breath.

"Hot-blooded zealots always have a hard time learning..."

The two corporals moved simultaneously. Aires caught a punch from a skinny kid in one hand, and then brought his elbow down violently across the forearm. It snapped audibly and horrible screaming filled the air. He then twisted his hips and threw the broken young revolutionary, who barely looked older than Diego, to the ground before dropping a knee on his solar plexus. The kid's eyes bulged like a fish, and he struggled to breathe, his mouth making strange motions in a vain attempt to suck in any oxygen he could.

Jeffe continued to use his baton with brutal results, dropping two of his attackers the moment they drew within range. His strikes were quicker than Diego could follow, but he could hear the crack of metal upon skin and bone. One man lost all his teeth while another ended up on the ground, clutching both his knees and howling like a madman. Diego wasn't too sure about human anatomy, given that he'd never attended school, but he was fairly certain knees were not designed to bend that way.

The fourth attacker held a pistol, and he raised it to shoot. "Fuck you and the Tyrants!"

The shot was loud in the confined quarters. The round struck Corporal Jeffe in the shoulder, causing him to stagger back. Diego's eyes widened in fear as he waited for the legionnaire to fall to the ground, bleeding. Instead, Jeffe rolled his shoulder and cursed under his breath. Aires moved to cover him instantly, shattering the kneecap of a man trying to take advantage of Jeffe's lapse in concentration.

"We use an armor that... well, you'll discover how it works at Advanced Combat School," Captain Rhys explained calmly to Diego. "The corporal is going to feel that tomorrow, though. The armor will keep you alive, but it's not necessarily... pleasant."

Sergeant Buckholz moved forward. He was fast, and managed to snatch the pistol out of the revolutionary's hand, then proceeded to backhand him contemptuously. The man yelped and tried to flail back, but the sergeant slapped him again, and again, each blow more demeaning than the last. With a split lip and tears in his eyes, the shooter fell onto the group and curled into a fetal position, his begging sobs loud enough for all to hear.

For good measure, the sergeant slapped the man a few more times to drive the point home. Diego, ever the survivor in Overdark, understood the message immediately. He hoped the crowd understood it as well.

Through it all, Captain Rhys had remained standing at the doorway, his face a carefully neutral mask as the beatings had commenced. Diego, wide-eyed and shocked at how quickly the legionnaires had dismantled the main aggressors, could barely breathe. The men had moved with purpose, unity, and as a team watching each other's backs.

For the first time in his short and sad life he wanted to be part of something bigger than himself, larger than surviving. The sudden drive for more than his next meal almost terrified him. He wanted to be the *best*, like the men protecting him. Not just a legionnaire, but *the* legionnaire.

Sergeant Buckholz flicked a stray bit of blood from his hand, as though it was a contaminant not worthy of touching his flesh. He looked down at the mewling puddle of would-be revolutionary and spat on the ground, effectively dismissing him as any future threat. Jeffe, still rubbing his shoulder where he'd been shot, looked around at the downed men while Aires simply stared, unblinking, waiting for the next person to move at them. Captain Rhys remained motionless as well, daring someone to say something wrong.

"You have been ordered to disperse." Sergeant Buckholz's voice cracked like a whip through the toxic air. "Don't make me repeat myself again."

Diego had never seen people flee so fast in his life. He turned to speak to Captain Rhys, but Sergeant Buckholz seemed to anticipate his next question.

"That? That was nothing," Sergeant Buckholz said as he grinned. "Not even a worthy warmup. You'll handle worse things in your career and not even remember things like this. Plus, local politics aren't anything we ever pay attention to. Not like we're going to start now. Leave the politicking for politicians, you know?" His grin turned conspiratorial, and he winked at Diego. Behind him, Jeffe and Aires fist-bumped. Gently, in Jeffe's case. It was clear his shoulder was still sore. Even the captain looked less stern than before. Only mildly, but it was better than the granite face he'd had prior. The sergeant continued after spitting on the rough pavement of the street.

"Eh, fuck 'em all anyway. You've sworn the Oath. You're one of us now. Welcome to the Legion, Diego."

CHAPTER ONE
The Hotshot

LAUNCH TERMINAL DIACRIA, MARS PRIMUS

If everything had gone to plan, Lieutenant Astra Eliassen would never have joined the Legion. She never would've been a dropship pilot, never been saddled with the callsign "Blue," never had to catch a transport shuttle and return to active duty after her leave was cut short. No, if everything had *gone to plan*, she would've passed the Survey Corps' rigorous entrance exam and been accepted into the Explorer ranks like her grandmother, the legendary Shava Turnien.

A wry smile tugged at Blue's lips as she hitched her heavy duffel bag higher on her shoulder and wove her way through the crowded terminal. She absolutely *would* still be living in fear of her mother showing up at her gate with some hapless eligible bachelor in tow, though.

Diacria was the oldest spaceport on Mars Primus. Built by the founding families after they'd fled the Sol System and the destruction of Mars, they'd used it to establish a new homeworld. Mars Primus was a paradise compared to that dusty red planet, but the survivors—now known as the Five Hundred—had never forgotten their lost home, and they'd paid tribute to it here. Expansive murals adorned the walls, sweeping panoramas of red deserts and vast canyons and intricate habitat domes, and arched ceilings boasted a breathtaking view of the old Martian skies. The view shifted throughout the course of the day until darkness fell and travelers could look up and see the old stars that had once graced their ancestors' night sky.

It was busy today, the terminal echoing with countless conversations as people rushed down the gently curving corridors like a river of humanity. The air purifiers were top-of-the-line though, only the faintest traces of food and body odor lingering beneath the clean desert-orchid scent perfuming the expansive facility. It took longer than Blue wanted to get to her gate, and when she'd finally battled her way through the crowd, she found someone had beaten her there.

Relief punched her in the chest, because it wasn't her mother waiting for her—it was her friend Sylvie Gallagher. The taller woman stood near the gate, arms crossed and all but tapping her foot. She wasn't dressed in the traditional gray uniform of the Survey Corps, opting instead for loose civilian clothes by necessity.

Unlike Blue, Sylvie had passed the entrance exam. While Blue had been going through the Legion's basic training and flight school, Sylvie had gone through her own training and had been a full member of the Survey Corps for over a year now. Blue might desperately want to be accepted into their ranks, but she'd never once held it against her oldest friend for succeeding where she'd failed.

At least everything had gone to plan for *one* of them. Her gaze dropped to the other woman's rounded belly. Mostly.

Blue bit back a smile. "What are you doing here, Syl?"

Sylvie grinned. "Did you think I was letting you sneak out without a proper farewell?"

"You know it wasn't *you* I was sneaking away from," Blue muttered, but her own smile finally broke free. "I'm glad you tracked me down."

They moved out of the flow of traffic and stood against the wall, a mural of a sleek black atmospheric shuttle sweeping across a staggeringly deep red canyon behind them and a hazy butterscotch sky above them. For the most part, her black Legion duty uniform was enough for people to give them space, but one family was too distracted by their boisterous children to notice them, and Blue had to drop her bag and move quickly to shelter her friend from getting jostled. Sylvie arched a manicured brow, the other woman just as athletic, curvy, and gorgeous as ever despite being heavily pregnant.

"My hero," she said dryly, ice blue eyes twinkling in amusement. "I'm pregnant, not breakable."

"Hey, that toddler looked dangerous," Blue said, only partially joking as she gently kicked her bag against the wall. "I've seen legionnaires charge forward with less determination than that kid!"

Time flew past as they caught up on all the things and made plans for her return, Blue delaying the inevitable as much as saying her goodbyes. Then the *ping* of her wrist comm cut through their conversation, a pitiless reminder that final boarding was fast approaching. She was out of time.

"Aw, don't look so *blue*," Sylvie teased, tucking a raven-dark strand of hair behind her ear. "Just a few more years in the Legion and you can join me in the Survey Corps. Then you'll get to see what's *really* out there."

Her friend smiled, but something dark flashed in her ice blue eyes. Blue wondered just what Sylvie had seen before she was sidelined back to Mars Primus with her unexpected pregnancy. A pregnancy she refused to elaborate on, and an absent father she refused to discuss. Blue couldn't help but tease her back, if only to banish the shadows in her gaze.

"It's hot men, isn't it?"

"Of course. It's literally the unofficial motto: Join the Survey Corps, explore new worlds, see the galaxy's hottest men." Sylvie flashed a look over Blue's shoulder, nothing but appreciation in her eyes now. "Though I don't think you'll be lacking for those on this deployment."

Blue twisted around to see who had caught her attention but only managed a glimpse of a Navy uniform before the man boarded the transport shuttle. Her wrist comm pinged again, and she had to resist the urge to rip it off and fling it across the spaceport.

"It's not just the deployment, it's the *timing*," she growled as she slung her bag over her shoulder again. "I'm going to miss the birth of my godson!"

"You'll be back soon enough." Sylvie winced and rubbed a soothing hand across her rounded belly. "And from what I've been told, you're better off missing that part. To be clear, you *better* make it back."

Blue rolled her eyes. "Syl, there hasn't been a *battle*, let alone a war, in over fifty years. It's just another escort mission to an outpost world. If I didn't have my checkride prep to keep me busy, I'd probably die from boredom."

"I'll hold you to it." Sylvie pulled her into a hug made awkward by pregnancy. "Get going, Blue. Kick all the ass and then come home and meet little...whatshisname."

"You better pick out an actual name soon."

"I'm working on it."

Blue gave her an innocent smile. "How about after his father?"

"Nice try." Sylvie shoved her toward the gate with surprising strength. "Get on board before your mother really does show up with potential husband number twenty-three."

With a shudder, Blue hustled through the gate and onto the shuttle, resisting the urge to look back for fear that her mother would magically appear.

"Cutting it a little close, LT," the stocky loadmaster muttered as he took her bag and secured it with the rest of the cargo.

Blue shrugged sheepishly and settled herself at the rear of the passenger compartment. A few moments later, the hatch was sealed in preparation for takeoff. The reassuringly deep *thrum* of the troop transport engines rattled her bones as she strapped into her chosen seat. Reassuring, because it meant nothing had broken on the old ship and they wouldn't have to reschedule their departure due to endless maintenance delays. Reassuring, because it meant she wouldn't be stuck on Mars Primus and miss her rendezvous with her unit before their deployment. Reassuring, because it meant she had once again successfully escaped her loving yet *incredibly overbearing* mother.

Blue's relieved smile barely had a chance to form before a dissonant note interrupted the siren song of the engines. Tension whipped through her lean frame, and her nails dug into the seat cushion, the padding flattened to near uselessness after countless years in service. She shifted her weight, attempting to find a position that didn't hurt her tailbone, all while listening to the keening cry of an engine about to fail. Or explode. Either was a possibility.

Legion ship or not, the ATS-8 Mule transport had been old *before* the Andradé War. Fifty years of peacetime operations hadn't exactly led to increased budgetary spending on military assets, so they were stuck with an aging fleet. When she'd been assigned to the 13th Legion last year, fresh out of pilot training and very much wet behind the ears, watching the maintainers keep her ALS-71 Rhino assault shuttle in flying shape had been an education in creative swearing. Her mother, the daughter of generations of proper Martian citizens, would be appalled at the expansion in her daughter's vocabulary. Her father, the son of a legionnaire who'd earned his citizenship in the Protectorate the hard way, would be amused.

A litany of Blue's favorite new curses ran through her mind as the off-pitch note climbed higher. She gave it another three seconds before the pilots initiated an emergency shutdown. Then she'd be stuck, her mother would be delighted, and she'd end up in prison for matricide before the week was out.

Three ... two ... one—

A shudder ran through the airframe. The engine pitch dropped, right along with her heart, but then it stabilized. Her gut tightened in anticipation as the twin engines slowly ramped back up.

Come on. Come on!

She held her breath, but the dissonant note didn't make a reappearance. The engines roared, a sound she felt as much as heard. Abruptly, she was pressed down into the uncomfortable seat as the transport ship gave gravity the middle finger and reached for the stars. She settled back in her seat as much as possible but didn't relax. There was still plenty that could go wrong in the thick atmosphere. The ship rattled and groaned, but even though the pilots held it steady, Blue's fingers twitched and her gaze remained fixed on the forward hatch.

It wasn't that she felt she could do a better job, or even because she was the kind of pilot who *needed* to be in the cockpit. No, it was pure, unmitigated desperation that had her hands twitching for the flight controls. If her mother had mentioned Blue's ticking biological clock one more time, or lamented her lack of grandbabies, or thrown one more cookie-cutter businessman at her, Blue would've screamed. Right before the aforementioned murder. Honestly, all she needed to do was present a fraction of her mother's persistent, entirely unsubtle messages in court and no jury would convict her.

A final shudder rocked through the ship, and the brief kiss of the weightless void washed over her. As the thrusters kicked in and gravity returned, profound relief swept through her *soul*.

She'd escaped.

Blue slumped as much as the straps allowed and was grateful she'd been able to grab a seat in the rear of the passenger compartment. The dozen or so Legion and Navy personnel sharing the space were all at the front, leaving her relatively alone and with nobody nearby to observe her less than professional bearing.

Her wrist comm *pinged* to alert her to new messages, and she glanced at the screen.

MOTHER: IF YOU RUN INTO ANY DELAYS AT THE SPACEPORT, COME BACK HOME. WE'RE HAVING COMPANY OVER FOR DINNER!

Oh, Blue knew exactly what her mother meant by *company*. Some semi-successful businessman named Frederic, or Robert, or John, with a fat retirement fund, diversified stock portfolio, impeccable breeding, and zero personality. No, thank you.

DAD: YOUR MOTHER MEANS WELL. THAT BEING SAID—*RUN*. RUN FAR, RUN FAST. DON'T LOOK BACK.

A smirk pulled at her lips. She could always count on her dad to diffuse any situation with humor. He also meant every word.

AERIC: TAKE ME WITH YOU! PLEASE DON'T LEAVE ME ALONE WITH HER...I'M BEGGING YOU, ASTRA!

Her smirk widened into a true smile. Her little brother better watch out, or their mother would be playing matchmaker with *him* the second he came of age. Blue had suffered through the Legion's drill instructors in basic training, harsh flight instructors in pilot training, and highly critical evaluators on active duty. None of them held a candle to her mother's determination to shape and mold her children into what she desired. Lovingly, of course.

Blue casually swiped through the messages, but straightened up abruptly when she saw the last one was from her grandfather. She honestly hadn't expected to hear anything further from the old man, who was notoriously reclusive and somewhat of a luddite when it came to using technology.

GRANDFATHER: STAY SAFE OUT THERE, SPROUT. REMEMBER, KEEP YOUR HEAD ON A SWIVEL, EARN THOSE RAVEN WINGS, AND WATCH OUT FOR YOUR BOYS.

Blue flexed her shoulders. She'd flown twelve successful missions over the course of her first year of service, completed twelve months of upgrade training and mission quals. Peacetime didn't necessarily equate to peaceful, and there had been more than a few close calls and learning experiences along the way, but she was still considered a newbie. She glanced down at her black shipboard uniform and brushed her fingers over the silver wings above her nametag. She smiled.

She wouldn't be considered a newbie for much longer.

While pilots earned their official wings when they graduated the Legion's flight training program, each Legion had their own customs. The 13th Legion—called the Bronze Legion by its legionnaires—was stranger, and definitely more superstitious, than most. When pilots successfully completed their thirteenth mission, their thirteenth drop, they earned their Raven wings—a gorgeous set of tattooed black wings across their upper back and shoulders.

Many pilots added feathers to the tattoos with every mission they completed, every year served, and sometimes, with every legionnaire lost. Some of the older pilots had feathers stretching down their shoulders and upper arms. Her commander's feathers reached the back of her hands.

Her mother had been appalled, but it wasn't as if Blue couldn't have them easily removed later if she wished. The Survey Corps certainly didn't give a shit if their members had tattoos, and at the end of the day, that was all Blue really cared about.

Blue was about to mute her comm when another message from her mother popped in.

MOTHER: OH DRAT. I JUST SAW THE DEPARTURE NOTIFICATION FOR YOUR SHIP. STAY SAFE, SWEETHEART. I'LL INTRODUCE YOU TO JAMESON THE NEXT TIME YOU VISIT. ASSUMING HE'S NOT ALREADY MARRIED BY THE TIME YOU FINALLY COME HOME AGAIN.

"Way to be passive aggressive, Mother." Blue rolled her eyes. "Dad was right. It was definitely time to run away bravely."

How her grandmother had ever produced her staid, boring mother was beyond her. Shava Turnien was a gods damned *legend* in the Survey Corps. Over the course of her long career, she'd explored countless planets and traveled to the far reaches of known space. She'd identified potential colony and outpost locations, located resources, found new lifeforms and strange phenomena that occasionally defied the current understanding of physics.

Shava Turnien had been the first to *see* so many things.

Blue had spent much of her childhood sitting at her grandmother's feet, listening to her stories, pestering her with endless questions, wanting nothing more than to follow in her footsteps. As she grew older, those stories changed, or rather, Shava had stopped editing them for a child's ears. The dangers and deaths, the loss of teammates and friends, the injuries that never quite healed right...they made the stories real in a way they hadn't been before.

It didn't deter Blue one bit. If anything, the real stories only made her desire to join the Survey Corps burn brighter.

Blue had never seen the point of hiding anything from her family—every last one of them had a way of ferreting out secrets—so she'd declared her intentions over one memorable dinner. Above the sound of her mother's hysterics, she'd locked eyes with her grandmother and told her *she* was going to be the first to see things one day too. Shava had barked a laugh and said at least somebody in the family had inherited her itchy feet and gypsy soul.

Every step Blue had taken since that day had been to secure her future in the Survey Corps. She'd graduated primary school with honors, obtained a Masters in Atmospheric Science, earned her civilian shuttle pilot's license, and spent years studying for the grueling entrance exam.

And then she'd failed.

It didn't matter who her grandmother was. The Survey Corps was above nepotism. All that mattered was that her scores weren't quite good enough for her to make the cut. Soul-crushing disappointment had weighed down her shoulders when she'd trudged out of the testing facility with the other failures.

A Legion recruiter had been waiting for them.

Blue gave the man credit for a smooth delivery and a compelling argument for joining the Legion as a stepping-stone to what she really wanted. Four years of service as a dropship pilot and she could transfer into the Survey Corps. Because she wasn't an idiot, she'd verified his claims. All it took was a simple message to her grandmother, who enthusiastically supported the idea. Blue had signed on with the Legion that same day.

Shava Turnien had passed away before Blue graduated flight training, but she'd left a final message for her granddaughter.

You were meant for great things, my little gypsy. Whatever you choose to do in this life, go after it with everything you've got. Never settle for less.

Blue had no intention of settling. One year down in the Legion, only three to go, and then nothing would stop her. Not the plan or the path she'd envisioned for herself, but it would work—all she had to do was survive her years of service.

A grimace twisted her face. She'd downplayed it for Sylvie's benefit, but rumor had it the outpost they were heading out to support had active volcanoes. One of which was currently smoking.

Idly, she wondered if they could toss one of her more annoying comrades into the volcano as a sacrifice...

The rattle of reentry broke into her bloodthirsty daydreams and her hands tightened on the seat once more. They'd barely broken orbit over Mars Primus, so why were they dropping back in? More importantly, if they were landing because they needed repairs, would her mother somehow ferret it out and attempt to drag her off the transport?

"What the hell?" she muttered.

Not quietly enough, apparently, because the closest Navy officer twisted around in his seat. Blue knew without a doubt that *this* was the man who had caught Sylvie's attention. She hadn't recognized Ensign Garrett Campbell from behind, but there was no mistaking that ridiculously handsome face. Perfect cheekbones, soulful dark brown eyes, and a smile that had probably gotten him out of all sorts of trouble—or into it.

He gave her that charming smile now, amusement dancing in his eyes. "Flight crew said we're making a quick pitstop to pick up a legionnaire recruit fresh out of the Advance Combat School."

Heat washed over Blue's face. She'd been so stuck in her own head, she'd completely missed the announcement.

"Wait..." Her brow furrowed. "We're getting a raw recruit for the *Bronze*?"

"Must be some kind of hotshot," he said with a casual shrug.

As an officer in the Protectorate Navy, Campbell wasn't a member of the Legion and might not grasp the implications. The Bronze Legion specialized in force recon missions, and its ranks were typically filled by experienced legionnaires transferring in from other legions. It was why the Bronze was smaller than the typical Legion. For a recruit straight out of training to get assigned to the Bronze was highly unusual.

Campbell, who the Ravens had nicknamed "Ensign Hotness" on their last deployment together, gave her a slow, interested once over.

"He's not the only hot thing around here." He winked. "We should catch up."

Blue eyed him in consideration. The man was an incorrigible flirt off-duty, but because he was the junior Operations officer, he knew all sorts of interesting things. They'd met during the Bronze Legion's last deployment, and he'd proven a good source of scuttlebutt. While she had the official and highly sanitized mission brief, she'd been on leave long enough that she'd missed out on all the pre-mission gossip. It would be good to know what she was walking into before she hit the flight deck.

The corner of her mouth curled up. "I might take you up on that."

After the initial turbulence of reentry, the rest of their drop was smooth. Blue barely felt the ship touch down on the tarmac. The pilots didn't fully shut down the engines, probably concerned that previous dissonance would creep back in if they didn't keep them running hot. She wholeheartedly approved. Should they have the misfortune to run into maintenance issues out here, she wouldn't put it past her mother to show up.

The loadmaster quickly got their newest passenger and his gear on board. As the engines ramped back up, the recently graduated legionnaire took a seat near Blue.

Curious, she turned to give the young man a once-over—and nearly had a heart attack. But no, that wasn't her little brother in the black uniform of a legionnaire. She huffed out a sharp breath and tried not to stare as she let her heart rate settle back to something close to normal. For just an instant, she'd thought Aeric had grown a pair and defied their overbearing mother in an even more dramatic way than she had. Which made zero sense since she'd seen him on the other side of the planet not even ten hours prior.

The young legionnaire was fumbling with his straps, and Blue took the opportunity to observe him with a slight frown. The resemblance was uncanny. Same dark hair, same dark eyes and bone structure. There was a hard edge to this young man that her sheltered little brother lacked, however, something she'd seen in the legionnaires who'd dealt with the Janus City riots on Gemini. Her brow furrowed as she realized that hard edge had fooled her, mentally downgrading him from a young man to a kid barely into adulthood.

When the engines reached the telltale pitch of imminent takeoff and he *still* hadn't managed to strap in, Blue's patience snapped. She threw off her straps and marched across the narrow aisle between their seats.

He looked even younger up close.

"Good lord, have your balls even dropped yet?" she muttered as she roughly straightened the mess he'd made.

A scowl flickered across his face before his gaze landed on her rank. His expression blanked and his right arm twitched as if restraining a salute.

"Thank you for your assistance, ma'am," he said cautiously, "but I've got it from here."

"Sure you do, kid." Blue snorted as she dropped back into her seat and strapped in. A few seconds later, she heard the *click* of his straps properly snapping into place.

"I'm not a kid, ma'am," he said stiffly. "I'm eighteen."

They were pressed back into the threadbare cushions as the aging transport ship rattled and groaned its way into the air. When they'd broken free of atmo again, Blue turned back to the fresh recruit.

"What's your name, kid?"

Blue mostly called him "kid" because he clearly *was* one, but also because she occasionally gave into her urge to poke people with sticks to see what kind of reaction she could get out of them. Pointing out his age, or lack thereof, was an obvious sore point, one he'd better get over quickly before the experienced legionnaires ate him alive.

"Private Diego Tavi, ma'am." Tavi lifted his chin with a hint of pride. "Distinguished graduate, ACS Class of 711, assigned to the 13th Legion, Bravo Company, 4th Squad."

Blue bit back a grimace. He really was going to the Bronze. She'd half hoped Campbell was wrong, because the 13th was no place for noobs. Either someone *really* hated this kid, or he really was that good. It would be interesting to find out which, and she'd have a front row seat along the way. The Bronze paired squads with dropship pilots, and the 4th Squad was her responsibility.

The thrusters kicked in, giving them an approximation of gravity as the small transport boosted for the orbital shipyard where they would rendezvous with the *Perseverance* and the rest of the Bronze Legion's task force. From there, they'd head to the system's jump point. Blue tossed off her straps and stood with a low groan.

"Stupid seats."

The only reason she didn't rub her abused tailbone was because the kid was staring at her, and she figured he didn't need to see an officer rubbing her own ass, no matter how badly it ached. She settled for twisting her back until it popped. As she did so, the young private's insignia caught her eye.

"Oh, for fuck's sake," she muttered and stalked back over to Tavi.

Mister Distinguished Graduate had managed to mess up his rank pins while wrestling with his straps. Rather than the comfortable standard black duty uniform Blue was wearing, he was in the formal dress uniform some upper-level staff weenie had mandated for reporting into a new unit.

"Stand up," she ordered with an impatient gesture.

His expression remained impassive, but a hint of wariness touched his eyes as he swiftly unbuckled his harness. Blue backed into the aisle to give him room to stand. When he rose to his full height, she didn't even have to tilt her head back to meet his inquisitive stare. They were nearly the same height, though she wagered he had at least one growth spurt to go before he was done growing.

"Permission to touch?" Her request came out as more of an impatient demand than a question, and Tavi frowned at her.

"Ma'am?"

Blue took that as permission. Brusquely, she properly angled his rank pins and straightened out his stupid dress uniform until everything fell into crisp lines again.

"Um, what are you doing, ma'am?"

Blue gritted her teeth at the carefully hidden alarm in his tone, more irritated with herself than anything else. She'd clearly spent far too much time around her mother if she was babying this kid. No, this *legionnaire*. Despite his relatively small size, his frame was packed with lean muscle that her little brother absolutely did not have.

She gave his uniform one last, narrow-eyed glare and nodded. "Now you're squared away."

"Thank you, ma'am?" Tavi cleared his throat. "Can I ask you a question?"

Blue bit back her urge to tell him he just did and nodded permission.

"Is there a spot on the ship where I can see the stars?" A faint wash of color swept across his face as he glanced around the bare-bones passenger compartment. The narrow, elongated space was nothing more than gray metal bulkheads and battered old seats. The designers hadn't seen the need to give troops a view portal or even a screen. "I'm still getting used to seeing the sky."

Blue stared, completely taken aback by the odd statement. "Where the hell did you grow up that you're not used to seeing the *sky*?"

"Overdark... er, Syngaard, ma'am."

A frown marred her brow as she struggled to place the name. Something about poisonous rain?

"On Myrkyma," he added helpfully.

Her expression brightened as the knowledge slid to the forefront of her memory. One of her atmospheric science classes had covered that planet in detail, as the professor had used the unique composition of the atmosphere for his doctorate dissertation. They hadn't spent a great deal of time on the planet's cities, by necessity all situated underground, instead focusing on the excruciatingly slow terraforming process that would one day enable humanity to colonize the surface. They weren't part of the Protectorate and, from what she could recall, had no interest in ever joining. Something about overzealous revolutionaries...

"Huh, I suppose you wouldn't be used to it yet, would you?" The rear hatch of the passenger compartment clanged open, and Blue snagged the loadmaster's attention as he ducked through. Her gaze dipped to the name tape on the upper right breast pocket.

"Hey, Sergeant Murphy, can you check with the flight crew and see if there's room for two jump-seaters up front?"

The stocky man gave her a friendly grin. "Plenty of room, LT."

Blue tilted her head toward the front hatch. "Let's go, kid."

She gestured for Tavi to go first, and he froze for half a heartbeat before his expression firmed. He marched down the aisle, chin up, back straight, and she followed at a more leisurely pace. As she walked past Campbell, she put a little extra sway in her hips. She glanced back in time to see his eyes focused considerably lower than her face. He slowly dragged his gaze up to hers with a lazy grin, completely unashamed to have been caught looking. Considering the fact that Blue had *wanted* him to look, she didn't mind in the least. She winked and caught up to Tavi.

Something strange caught her attention before she ducked through the forward hatch. At the very front of the passenger compartment, partially hidden thanks to a pair of massive legionnaires, was a gaggle of civilians. One older gentleman with gray-streaked black hair, deep wrinkle lines along his brow, and a haughty tilt to his chin was holding court, three of the younger civvies hanging on his every pompous word. A fourth young woman sat slightly apart, her expression a polite mask that mostly hid her annoyance.

Blue glanced back at Campbell and tilted her chin toward the civilians in silent question. His lips curved into a smug, knowing little smirk. She made finding him after they docked at the orbital shipyard a priority. He knew things, and she wanted to know the things.

The fact that he was hot and appreciated her ass was a bonus.

With one final, puzzled glance at the civilians, she ducked through the hatch and nearly ran into Tavi. He'd frozen one step into the cockpit, his gaze riveted to the vast sweep of stars shining bright against the infinite black of the void. Blue took a moment to appreciate the view as well. It had been a few weeks since she'd last seen the stars without the wavering interference of atmo, and Tavi's awe reminded her of her own.

No matter how many times she experienced it, she never got tired of seeing just how big the universe really was. It didn't make her feel small or insignificant. It filled her with a wild longing to see everything she possibly could, to get out there and explore it all.

One of the Mule's pilots, a grizzled older man, twisted around and nodded a greeting. "Have a seat. We're only ten mikes out."

"Appreciate you letting us come up front," Blue said with a friendly grin.

"Anything for a Raven." As he twisted back around, the sleeve of his black flightsuit pulled up slightly, revealing the tattoo on his inner wrist. The bronze outline of a skull and crossbones still stood out sharply against the black spade. He'd served as a legionnaire in the Bronze before he'd retrained as a Navy pilot. Blue wasn't surprised. Many legionnaires who completed their ten years of service stayed in the Legion in a support function or cross-trained into the Navy.

Blue clapped Tavi on the shoulder to break his trance and showed him how to pull down the narrow jump seat and strap in. As soon as he was settled, his gaze went right back outside the cockpit.

"Thank you, ma'am," Tavi breathed out.

"Lieutenant Eliassen or LT is fine," she said firmly. When he looked as if he would protest, she added, "You're one of mine. Fourth Squad flies on *my* bird, so we'll be working together on missions."

"Yes, ma'am."

Blue rolled her eyes and let it go. The kid would figure out how things worked in the real world soon enough.

Less than ten minutes later, the orbital naval shipyard came into sight. Tavi's eyes widened ever so slightly, but it was a subtle tell, as if he'd long been trained in suppressing his reactions. There was certainly an impressive collection of ships currently in dock, and Blue gave him a moment to take it all in before she quietly pointed out the PNV *Perseverance*.

"She's not the biggest or the prettiest, but she'll get us where we need to go." Blue pointed out the corvettes docked on either side of the Legion transport ship like a pair of fierce guard dogs, smaller but more heavily armed. "And they'll make sure we make it in one piece."

The Mule slowly spun around as the pilots lined them up for docking at one of the smaller slips. In the distance, Mars Primus slid into view. They were close enough to make out the green and reddish-brown landmasses, the deep blues of the oceans, and the thick gray swirls of cloud cover. The larger moon was currently behind the planet, but the smaller was visible. The rocky red surface of the moon was almost completely obscured by the multitude of habitats and orbital stations. Mars Primus was the most heavily populated of the Protectorate planets, and it showed. Some colonies were more suited to sustaining human life than others, and with the population rapidly growing thanks to decades of peace, the mission of the Survey Corps was even more critical.

Identifying a new colony world for the Protectorate was Blue's dream. She glanced at Tavi, still utterly enraptured by the view, and grinned. Preferably a colony world where humans could live *above* ground.

In short order, the pilots had the Mule snugged up to their assigned docking slip. As soon as the pressure seals locked into place, Blue left the aircrew working their postflight checks and exited the ship. She thought she might have to chase Campbell down, but the man was waiting for her at the bottom of the ramp, his duffel bag slung over one shoulder. Blue carried an identical one stuffed with her personal items. The loadmaster and dockhands would transfer the rest of their gear over to the *Perseverance*, but it was always smart to keep personal effects close.

As she strode down the ramp, Tavi trailed after her, his own duffel bag slung over his shoulder.

"Hey, Blue." Campbell arched a brow. "You seem to have gained a shadow."

"He's one of mine."

"Yours?" Campbell pinned Tavi with an inquisitive stare as he halted exactly one pace behind and to her left. "I thought he was a legionnaire, not a Crow."

Blue waved a dismissive hand. "By 'mine,' I didn't mean aircrew. I meant he's one of the legionnaires assigned to my dropship."

She wrinkled her nose as the familiar metallic tang of recycled air stung her sinuses along with the faint burn of industrial cleaning chemicals, and glanced around the shipyard. Not much had changed since her last time passing through. The shipyard might be rundown, but it was serviceable and ruthlessly maintained, because there weren't any funds flowing in to replace the aging facility. While the Navy could operate without certain aspects of the shipyard, troop transfers and supply loading were much easier, not to mention all the maintenance required to keep the ships in service.

Battered gray metal corridors stretched into the distance, the gradual curve barely noticeable. Shipyard personnel in various colored jumpsuits hustled in both directions in a steady stream of traffic, voices echoing off the walls and blending into incomprehensible background noise.

"Ma'am," Tavi said and gestured to a trio of gray-jumpsuited personnel marching their way with a sense of purpose. They all stepped to the side of the ramp so the cargo haulers could begin the unloading process.

The haulers had barely made it inside the Mule when a chorus of shouts and irritated cries drifted out. One outraged voice rose above the rest, and the haulers hastily backed down the ramp. The older civilian gentleman stood at the top for a moment, haughty stare panning around the shipyard before he strode down the ramp. His civilian suit was perfectly pressed, and his shoulders were unencumbered by anything so mundane as a bag. He was closely followed by three young civilians, two men and a woman, each carrying a single small bag. Their bright and eager gazes darted everywhere as they scurried after Mister High and Mighty.

There was a brief pause, and then the last civilian staggered into sight. The young woman was weighed down with a backpack that seemed nearly as large as she was in addition to a smaller bag hanging off one shoulder. Her earlier annoyance was now tinged with grim determination, and she stomped after her companions with murder in her eyes. Blue silently applauded her spirit... though she would've been more impressed if the young woman had managed to avoid getting loaded down like a pack mule in the first place.

Eager to get all the juicy details on the civvies, and fairly certain Campbell wouldn't talk freely in front of a private, Blue glanced at Tavi. "Do you know where to go?"

"No, ma'am, but I can figure it out. Thank you for your assistance."

"Oh, for the love of... just follow us." She rolled her eyes again, something that seemed to be developing into a habit around the young legionnaire. She firmly grabbed Campbell's arm and tugged him into the flow of traffic. He allowed the manhandling with an amused grin, and she tilted her head toward the gaggle of civilians expectantly. "Well? What's the deal?"

As she marched down the corridor, the strap of her bag slipped, and she yanked it back up with an annoyed grimace. Tavi quickly caught up, once again placing himself at her left, and held out his hand.

"I can carry your bag for you, ma'am."

Campbell shot him an irritated look. "I've got it."

"Boys!" she barked. "I can carry my own shit, thank you very little."

Tavi stiffened, and she sighed. She'd forgotten how fragile male egos could be at his age. Her little brother was just as touchy at times.

"If you really feel like helping someone," Campbell said gruffly, "go see if the civvie needs a hand."

Campbell pointed to the young woman struggling down the corridor a short distance ahead of them. She was a tiny little thing, and despite her murderous determination, she'd fallen well behind her companions.

"Please tell me you're not threatened by a kid," she muttered as Tavi took his suggestion as an order and hustled off to help.

"Of course not." Campbell smirked when her bag slipped again and deftly relieved her of it before she could protest. "I just wanted you all to myself."

Blue rolled her eyes again and decided the new habit had nothing to do with baby legionnaires and everything to do with men. Just before Tavi reached the young woman, a hulking man in the red jumpsuit of a maintainer bumped her shoulder as he brushed past her, and she sprawled to the cold deck with a frustrated cry. The burly man looked at her disdainfully before starting to move past without so much as an apology.

And Blue got a front row seat to why an undersized Legionnaire like Private Diego Tavi had made it into the Bronze straight out of training.

Tavi's expression snapped into a hardened mask, and in the time it took Blue to blink, he had the hulking maintainer in a painful armlock. The kid certainly knew how to use leverage to his advantage, and he quickly had the bigger man pinned up against the wall. Blue wasn't close enough to hear what Tavi said, but a moment later he released him, his expression still locked down tight as he helped the young woman to her feet.

The maintainer flexed his arm a few times, his ruddy complexion pale, and apologized profusely before he hurried away. The young woman stammered at Tavi, her face flushed and her eyes huge behind thick-rimmed glasses with the telltale markers of slate linkage. Blue mentally downgraded her age to twenty at best and bit back a smile as Tavi gallantly shouldered the girl's heavy bag and escorted her down the corridor.

"Oh, that was *very* interesting." Blue tore her gaze off the Bronze's newest legionnaire and arched a brow at Campbell. "So what's the deal with the civvies?"

"They're the entire reason for our deployment."

"Say what?" Blue frowned at Campbell, certain he was joking, but his expression was serious.

"There's something weird going on with the native fauna on Aurora. Some kind of oversized reptilian species threatening the science outpost. One research assistant went missing, along with her guards, all presumed dead. The Council tasked a Survey team with figuring out the new aggressive behavior. It'll be the Bronze's job to keep them from getting eaten."

"And as always, you guys are the taxi service," she teased.

"Happy to give you a ride anytime."

Campbell winked obnoxiously, but with just enough playfulness that Blue wasn't tempted to put her fist through his face. Instead, she shoved him just hard enough that he had to sidestep to recover his balance. His husky laugh pulled a grin out of her, and they trailed behind Tavi and his new friend in companionable silence.

As they caught up to the rest of the civilians, she compared Campbell's scuttlebutt to her official mission brief. It had said nothing about a science team but sure enough they, too, stopped at the *Perseverance*'s docking slip. She hummed thoughtfully as she noted Campbell's smug grin.

"What aren't you telling me?"

"Plenty." He dropped his voice low. "But I'll tell you this part for free. We're not heading to Aurora first."

Campbell fell silent, amusement dancing in his eyes as he waited. Blue huffed an annoyed sigh, but she couldn't stop her slow smile.

"What will the rest of it cost me?" she asked as they drifted to a halt at the back of the small crowd waiting to board.

"Your soul." He chuckled at her exasperated glare. "But I'll settle for a night out drinking with you."

Blue pretended to think about it, but really, she would've gone out with him for free. Judging by his confident grin, he knew it too.

"You're on."

"Can't wait." Campbell leaned close, his voice a quiet murmur in her ear. "We're going to Sagetnam first. I can't tell you what the Survey team needs, but I *can* tell you we'll be there for at least forty-eight hours."

Anticipation curled low in Blue's belly. Among other things, Sagetnam was typically used by the Legions as a training ground, which meant she'd get at least one flight under her belt to knock the rust off before the mission. Even better, if they were going to be there for a few days, they'd almost certainly be granted liberty call—and Yortugan Bay was famous for its bars.

Somehow, she doubted the Survey team was interested in either of those things.

"Yortugan, huh?" Blue muttered as her gaze drifted back to the haughty scientist impatiently waiting for the airlock to open, his eager little helpers, his mousy assistant, and one short, dangerous legionnaire. "This ought to be entertaining."

CHAPTER TWO
To Protect the Weak, Defend the Innocent

PNV* PERSEVERANCE, *MARS PRIMUS SYSTEM

Protect the weak, defend the innocent. Every single day Tavi did his best to live by that specific part of his Oath. Helping someone was to be expected of any legionnaire. Tavi wasn't just going to excel at being a legionnaire, but exceed all expectations.

He... just wasn't exactly sure how to do that just yet. Until then, though, he lived the Oath as best as he could.

The *Perseverance* was the largest ship he'd ever been on, and was one of the biggest ships the Legion had at its disposal. While technically owned and operated by the Protectorate Navy, the Vosagus-class carrier was built for one specific mission—to carry legionnaires wherever the Protectorate needed them.

Fortunately for Tavi, the young civilian seemed to know where to go once they were forward of the airlock. Carrying her heavier bag, he was happy remaining silent as she marched determinedly after the professor, her shorter legs struggling to keep up with him and the sycophants tailing him like dogs after a treat. The professor was regaling them with stories of his days pioneering out in uncharted worlds and the trio keeping pace was hanging on his every word. Tavi did notice, though, that the young assistant the Navy officer had ordered him to help wasn't paying as much attention to her boss as she was their surroundings.

"Pay attention to the markings on the walls," the young woman told Tavi as they passed another cluster of glowing numbers. "See?

3—5F—Level 4? That means we're port side, fifth section forward, on the fourth deck level."

"How do you know?" Tavi asked, genuinely curious. Knowledge was good, and he didn't want to get lost. Years of surviving the streets had taught him to know all the escape routes possible, just in case. It'd kept him alive when the revolutionaries had come for his head.

"The first number you see always tells you what side of the ship you're on," she explained. "Odd is port—left, if you're looking forward, and even is starboard, or the right. Don't say that in front of the Navy people. They get... irritated. They're old nautical terms that stuck when spaceflight became a regular thing, all the history books say, and Navy personnel are very superstitious and like their old, outdated traditions. The second number tells you if you're forward or aft. Uh, front or rear. The indicator is if there's if it's an F or an A after the number. We're five sections from the bow of the ship. If it had been an A, we'd be five sections from the stern, or aft. Level 4 just means we're on the fourth deck. There are seven decks—levels—on the *Perseverance*. It gets a little different the deeper you go belowdecks, but I don't know if legionnaires are allowed in the engine compartments."

"How do you know all this stuff, though?"

"Child prodigy."

Tavi had no idea what that meant, but it sounded impressive. "You're very smart."

"Yes. That's what child prodigy means."

"I understand now, ma'am." He nodded, pleased. One mystery solved, at least. He still felt like a fool for letting his uniform become fouled during the lift from Mars Primus. He'd *known* the straps would screw it up, yet he'd been caught off guard when it had, and it'd taken an officer to point that out. Worse still, apparently she was assigned to his squad. Hopefully nobody would hear about it and he silently vowed to never let it happen again. "I just learned to read while I was becoming a legionnaire. It's really fun."

"Oh! I'm reading *Reptiles Across the Stars*," she said brightly. Her smile softened as she looked at him. "It's a rather dry read, more academia than anything else. It's impressive that you are trying to learn to read. Truly."

"Thank you."

"You know... I think you actually mean that," she said and gave him a strange look. Even the heavy weight of the bag was nothing compared to the intense scrutiny he was under. It made him more than a little uncomfortable. "I think you're going to do just fine. And here we are."

He looked at the numbers of the compartment: 3-4F-Level 4 was expected, since they had been moving forward. The actual hatch number—*1005*—was situated above a glowing security lock. There was no other indication this room was important at all. The woman quickly punched in a code and the door swung open. She stepped inside, then motioned for him to follow.

"Well, come on. The stuff you're carrying can go on the table over there."

The room was larger than he'd expected. There were piles of boxes stacked along one wall, while on the opposing one someone had taken the time to construct a small shelf to hold actual, physical books. There were three doorways leading into other rooms at the far wall. A comfortable-looking sofa, three cushioned chairs with personal crash webbings, and two large tables filled the main room. Of all the things he'd expected to find on a Navy vessel, this had not been one of them. It almost looked like something out of a vid drama.

"Thank you again," the mousy little woman said, bobbing her head as he set all the heavy gear on the larger of the tables. He shifted his own duffel bag so it wouldn't slip. "Mister...?"

"Private Diego Tavi, ma'am," he responded instantly, six months of training reflexively kicking in. "Thirteenth Legion, Bravo Company, 4th Squad."

"That's a bit of a mouthful."

"Yes, ma'am." He'd never been comfortable around pretty girls. Especially older ones. It hadn't helped his embarrassment one bit when the pilot had actually touched him to straighten his uniform. "As you say."

"Thank you, Diego. For all your help. I'm Mitzi."

"Nice to meet you, ma'am."

"Ma'am? Please, you can call me—"

"*Miss Wingo!*" a male voice shouted from a side room off the common area. "I can't find my book on the linear genetics of *Carassius harbingus auratus*! That is a rare leather-bound edition autographed by

Doctor Benson herself! Miss Cunningham here has never seen it before, and I wanted to show it to her! Why is it missing *again*?"

Mitzi blushed and ducked her head a few times apologetically, an almost instinctive movement, before looking at Tavi.

"Thanks again for all your help, Legionnaire," she whispered. She shooed him out of the common room, and he abruptly found himself in the corridor. A quick smile from the young assistant and the hatch was shut, leaving him standing with his duffel bag over his shoulder and feeling rather stupid. He could hear her voice inside, feigning cheerfulness. "Coming, sir. I have it right here, Professor!"

Tavi turned and started walking down the corridor back the way he'd come. He had only a slight idea where he was going but figured eventually someone would steer him in the right direction. As much as a rivalry existed between the Navy and the Legion, it wasn't as bad as both sides made it out to be. A few minutes later, a helpful petty officer ("Not a sir, Private, and for the love of God don't salute me") directed him along the proper way and he found himself in legionnaire country.

From there it was smooth sailing. Tavi found the Bronze Legion's XO—or more accurately, the lieutenant found him. After a brief introduction to the 13th Legion and an "attaboy" for making nice with the strange civilian group from the Bronze's Commanding Officer, Captain Oren Truitt—a man whose stark resemblance to Captain Rhys had floored Tavi into silence almost immediately—he was turned over to Sergeant Emmett Ord and officially reported to Bravo Company, 4th Squad.

As he trailed the sergeant down the narrow, metallic hall which would be his home for the foreseeable future, he finally was able to exhale everything he'd been holding in since setting foot on the transport shuttle. He'd done it. His official term of service had begun. He was officially a legionnaire.

"I know they gave you the rundown on how the Legion works in Basic, and again at ACS," Ord was saying, bringing Tavi's attention back to the here and now. His eyes took in the surroundings, as well as the various deck and levels marked along the walls so he wouldn't get lost again. He'd been warned that there was a little bit of "hazing" he'd be subjected to, but nothing cruel. At least, that was what Sergeant Buckholz had told him. Ord stopped and looked down at him. One thing Tavi was quickly realizing was that, by Legion standards, he was small. *Very* small. The sergeant continued.

"We here in the Bronze are different. Most legions take months to stand up and deploy. Since it's just the Thirteenth and our escorts, we can deploy anywhere needed within forty-eight hours. No other legion can do that. But because we're always on standby and rapid deployment, we get a different berthing setup. Instead of barracks, you are assigned to a pod with your fire team, three pods to a squad.

"There's a shared common area in the middle of a pod, two latrines per pod. Work out the shower rotation with your fire team. You will have a personal sleeping area that will be DNA coded to you. We still do inspections like in Basic, but that's mostly to make sure you don't bring sailors into your bunk. If you do, we will find out about it, and it will not be pretty. You get me, Private?"

"Yes, Sergeant!" Tavi responded automatically, his head swimming.

"I don't care if you prefer boys or girls, Private. No. Sailors. In. Your. Berthing. Space. Are we clear?"

"Crystal, Sergeant."

"Don't want Navy down here screwing things up..." Ord muttered and shook his head. "The XO and Master Sergeant Jun decided you needed a battle buddy from a world similar to yours, to avoid unwanted cultural shock. I suggested someone else, but Top said Jabber was the best fit for you. Plus, he was available and his fire team had a slot open anyway... those bastards."

"Jabber?"

"Drop name," Ord explained. "Corporal Vindahar Jabbalogoeczeski. Once you make your first successful drop without pissing yourself, you'll get your callsign, your drop name. Mine's Ordo, because originality is not key to the Legion's mission."

"Jabber, Sergeant?"

"You try calling out his name in a firefight. Plus, he won't shut up." Ord sighed. "Ever. Like, fucking *ever*. You get to call him 'corporal' until told otherwise. Gird your loins and put that Distinguished Honor Graduate badass mental armor on, because we're going to be throwing a lot of shit your way in the coming days and weeks. You'll absorb it and make it through your ten, or you won't, and die messily somewhere, hopefully without killing a fellow legionnaire along the way. And we're here."

Tavi looked at the markings on the wall and committed them to memory. Relying on others to simply show him the way all the time was a recipe for disaster. If he learned anything from surviving in Overdark, it was self-reliance. The Legion was almost as tough, and while they'd taught him to trust his teammates, they expected every legionnaire to be self-sufficient as well.

"Press your thumb on Pod E's pad there, then get your gear stored and your personal effects squared away," Sergeant Ord said, pointing at one of the small doors in the pod. Tavi did as ordered and the door unlocked immediately. He pushed it open and peered inside. There was a thin mattress with crash webbing, two blankets, a pillow, and a cabinet squeezed into the tiny space. There was just enough room for him to enter, turn around, and get dressed without bumping into anything. It was bigger than anything he'd ever had before in his life. Ord continued. "This is your space, Private. Keep it squared away. Jabber is a slob, and I better not hear we picked up another one."

"No, Sergeant." Tavi privately swore right then and there that his berthing space would be the cleanest in the Legion, perhaps the cleanest in the history of mankind as a whole. "No slobs."

"Okay." Sergeant Ord nodded. "We've got a quick pre-jump introduction with the squad for you in ten. Get organized and meet me out in the pod."

"Yes, Sergeant."

Sergeant Ord closed the small door. Tavi set his duffel bag on the thin mattress and gave the bed a push. It was secured to the floor and wall, which meant it wouldn't move during transit when the ship jumped through space and into a new system.

While he'd done a jump before, it'd been a quick one, from Myrkyma to Mars Primus, and he'd been partially sedated thanks to his minor panic attack upon seeing the sky for the first time in his life. It'd been weeks on Mars Primus before he really got used to seeing clouds, the expansive blue sky of everything and nothing beyond them, and almost to the end of ACS before he'd come to love it all. Now? He yearned to see every sunrise and sunset.

Tavi knew he would see thousands more of each, but never would he grow tired of them.

Exactly five minutes later Tavi was out in the common area of the pod. Gathered around Sergeant Ord were four other legionnaires, all in the standard black day uniforms, which were simply jumpsuits with a bronze "XIII" on their collar lapels, and name tags above their left breast pocket. It was a complete contrast to his Class "A" he'd been told to wear when reporting. Tavi was uncomfortably aware that he was in the wrong uniform, though none of the others seemed to care. Sergeant Ord waited until Tavi was situated before he began.

"We'll be doing a squad briefing tonight at 1900 hours once we jump. I want Private Tavi here squared away before then. Jabber? He's your battle buddy, and assigned to Fire Team Two."

"Aye, *bossjna*, can do," a tall, muscular man with a wicked scar running down his left arm said, nodding. "The *tasawa* from poison world, *ke*?"

"Yeah, Private Tavi is from Myrkyma."

"Oh, damn. That's where everyone lives underground and shits poison water, right?" a smaller man asked, his dark face creasing into a grin. "Navy's always pissed about our water usage, Ordo. They're *really* going to start complaining now."

"Stow it, Krawdaddy," Ord growled. "They don't shit poison, only drink it."

"Fuckin' hardcore, man."

"Introductions," Ord said as he rubbed his temples, a pained expression on his face. Tavi wondered why. "Left to right. The big man with the funny accent is the aforementioned Jabber. Next to him is Corporal Ray Krawczyk. Call him Krawdaddy. Specialist Alan Voecks, goes by Vixen."

"I still say Violence is a better drop name for me," the tanned legionnaire standing next to Jabber complained, running his hand across his smooth scalp. "I bring violence with me."

"You named your rifle Violence, *tollejo*. That don't count," Jabber snorted.

"If drop names were supposed to be cool, we still wouldn't call you Violence, you idiot." Krawdaddy laughed. "Veedee is more apt."

"Shut the hell up, man."

"Yellowstain, Jockpox, Clappy... those are good, too. Hey, is there one you haven't gotten yet?" Krawdaddy continued, still laughing. "You're like the testbed for antibiotics."

"You know, *balara*, Jockpox make a decent drop name," Jabber added helpfully. "But Veedee is good. *Real* good. Knew a *pojata* when I was little young thing with name like that. Poor girl."

"No. No, Vixen's fine. Really..." the specialist muttered.

"And Specialist Ryan Pridgeon, AKA Pigeon, is your fire team leader," Sergeant Ord said, nodding to the older man as tall as Jabber but skinnier, sporting a rather impressive mustache. It was the first time Tavi had seen any legionnaire with facial hair. While he remembered someone saying it was allowed, the tight confines of the legionnaire combat helmet would make one that bushy uncomfortable on the best of days. "If you have any problems Jabber can't fix, Pigeon'll help you. Anything he can't handle, he'll come to me and we'll get this shit squared away. You understand?"

"Yes, Sergeant!"

"Excellent." He gave the rest of the fire team a look which Tavi could only describe as *dangerous*. "Go easy on him."

"Sergeant! I am *appalled* you think that we would abuse the innocent young private," Vixen said, clutching his chest in an exaggerated manner. "My poor old heart can't take such heinous insinuations!"

"We hurt, *bossjna*. Truly," Jabber added.

"You little shits drove Morty over to 1st Squad," Ord reminded them. "You in particular, Vixen, are the reason we had a spot on this fire team in the first place."

"Morty was *balara*, Sergeant. *Keiche?* Not a team guy. All about him. He had it coming," Jabber countered, though he said it with a grin. The sergeant sighed.

"We're doing a squad briefing in ten, but scuttlebutt travels fast, so I'll tell you what's what now so you will keep your trap shut later, Jabber. Direct order from the Old Man. Work-ups in the Anat system, simulated combat drop, then sunrise liberty call—unless someone fucks it up." He pointedly glared at Vixen, who looked away. "Then the *Perseverance* is moving onwards to more interesting points of space. Bravo Company only. Alpha, Charlie, and Delta will be doing work-ups elsewhere. No, I don't know where, or what their destination will be. I know it won't be with us, though, so don't ask, Krawdaddy. Jabber! After the briefing, take Tavi to the Armory and get him suited up. Claw is expecting him. Once that's done, give him the five denarii tour of Legion country. Show him the mess deck and everything."

"Is he authorized to have a well deck key, Sergeant?" Vixen asked, an innocent smile on his face. Ord considered for a moment before he shrugged.

"Up to your fire team leader."

"We'll see," Pigeon said as he stroked his magnificent mustache thoughtfully. He eyed Tavi up and down for a moment before grunting. "Seems like the type who doesn't need to carry one around, but I've been fooled before. Let's hold off."

"You're no fun, Pigeon."

Meanwhile, Jabber was grinning and poking Tavi with an elbow in the ribs. "Hell yeah, *bossjna*! We going to Sagetnam!"

"Is that...good?" Tavi asked quietly, cocking his head. Jabber nodded eagerly. The rest of the fire team was smiling as well, even Vixen.

"Oh yeah, *tasawa*. You gonna love it there!"

Tavi had a sneaking suspicion this, was in fact, a bald-faced lie.

The briefing was short and sweet, to the point, and completely unlike anything Tavi had sat through during ACS back on Mars Primus. It would be a full drop for Bravo Company, with 4th and 5th Squads being selected to be on what the CO of Bravo Company termed "civvie duty." During the training drop on Sagetnam, they would be carrying a full loadout, including hauling around one-hundred-pound rucks to simulate the civilians they would be babysitting. This would help them prepare for any and all eventualities, including moving the civilians to safety whether they wanted to be moved or not.

The lighter gravity on Sagetnam was identical to their actual mission site, another reason the Legion had chosen it for its training exercise locale. Tavi had never been on a low-grav world and was interested to feel the difference.

Once the briefing was concluded, Jabber took Tavi to Bravo Company's armory. It was here he met arguably the most important person on the ship—the armorer, Sergeant Afton Klau.

"Call me Claw," the armorer said once introductions had been made. He held up a prosthetic hand, whose metallic fingers were slightly curled, and smiled. "For obvious reasons. Lost the hand...six years ago? Training accident. Tried to cook a grenade before tossing it, but it had a short fuse. Oops. Hamatic combat suits are good, but not good enough to prevent them from having to amputate my hand when every bone in it was broken and pulped because of my stupidity. Still, two years left and I'm a citizen. Because it's my off hand, I can do combat deployments."

"Also a *valkan* good armorer," Jabber added. "Great at his job."

"I appreciate the sentiment, Jabber." The armorer turned an appraising eye on Tavi. "Hmm. Smaller than I normally kit out. Still, I have an HCS somewhere in here that'll fit you for now."

"For now?" Tavi asked.

"According to your chart, you're predicted to hit a few more growth spurts before your term of service is completed. I've got a feeling I'll be seeing you a few more times before my own service ends."

He'd been told as much back at ACS, but he really hadn't believed it at the time. Tavi had always been smaller than most, thanks to malnutrition as a child. Now that he was in the Legion and eating regularly, as well as working out constantly, he was supposed to be growing. He hadn't seen anything yet, though. He hoped this supposed growth spurt would kick in soon.

Tavi eyed the suit as Sergeant Klau began taking his measurements. They'd covered the suit, and more importantly, the non-Newtonian ballistic gel which existed inside, during his intense six months on Mars Primus. There was so much science behind it that Tavi had a hard time remembering everything he'd learned, especially considering everything else he'd had to learn since leaving Overdark— like reading. One thing that did stick in his head had been the most important thing drilled into them by their instructors—if one broke, take it to the armorer. That was their job. Case closed.

However, the version he'd worn at ACS had been older. This version had a wavy pattern in between the gel chambers of the skin-tight ballistic suit, as well as a different texture. It felt grainy, not smooth, reminding him of concrete or pavement. He asked Sergeant Klau about the differences.

"Well, those older suits are worn by everyone cycling through ACS," Sergeant Klau responded as he began pulling out the kinetic plates for the suit. "The friction gets worn down over time, understand? Plus, these newer suits have the regenerative camouflage, which means they *have* to have the rougher texture. If not, the camouflage looks flat and wrong against a backdrop, and draws the eye to it. Plus, this model has a diffused battery system in the back. The ones you trained in at ACS still have the circular packs in the small of your back, don't they?"

"Yes, Sergeant," Tavi answered.

The armorer motioned for him to grab the suit. "Put that on so I can figure out what size plates you're going to use."

Tavi looked down at his dress black uniform, then around at the dirty workshop of the armory before shrugging and ditching the outfit. At a guess he figured there would be some sort of way to clean them, though back in Overdark Sergeant Buckholz had told him that he would rarely, if ever, wear his dress blacks anywhere outside of award ceremonies and when reporting to a new command.

"Don't worry," Sergeant Klau said, guessing at Tavi's initial hesitancy. "There's a detergent that'll get everything from oil to week-old blood out of anything. Won't even harm the fabric, either. Just toss your stuff on the bench over there and let's get rolling."

In short order he had the hamatic combat suit on. The suit was snug, a much better fit than the one he'd had to use at ACS, as he had suspected it would be. The higher quality was also evident, lacking the frayed edges and microlesions of the older model. The suit also felt *right* on him somehow. Tavi couldn't explain it, so he asked.

"First step of a legionnaire is getting their hamatic on and fitted right." The armorer grunted as he began to adjust the ballistic kinetic plates. Thanks to his actually paying attention at ACS, Tavi knew these plates would be attached by the armorer and remain sealed to the suits themselves without fear of accidentally falling off during movement. Tavi hadn't precisely understood what the instructors had said about the electromagnetic energy of the suit keeping the kinetic plates in place, but he'd gotten the gist of it relatively quickly.

First, two narrow ones went directly down his front and back, protecting his breastbone and spine. Two plates then went on his chest, another over his stomach. Two larger ones went to cover his back. Tavi twisted as commanded, testing the flexibility of the suit while the armorer made adjustments as needed.

"There. Only missing gloves, but I don't have any your size. I'll need to special order them. We should get them before the actual op, though. But otherwise, that should just about do it," the armorer said as the last of the kinetic plates was attached to the suit. The undersuit remained form fitting and snug, yet he barely felt the additional weight of the kinetic plates. They didn't seem to impede his movements, either, which was a good thing. Sergeant Klau nodded, apparently satisfied. He tapped numbers into his personal slate. "Kinetic plates are assigned. You lose them, it comes out of your pay. Don't lose them. They're almost impossible to detach by accident, so don't try and claim they 'fell off,' okay?

"Also, we're going to adapt your suit as you grow. So try not to become a giant, got it? Don't grow too big. All right. There's a hermetically sealed drawer in your bunk, lower left corner at the foot. That's your storage bin. There is only enough room in there for your plates and your undersuit. Your boots will not fit in there. If you try and make it fit, the drawer will jam. Ask me how I know. Your squad leader—Sergeant Ord, in case you haven't figured that out yet—will verify your suit is in your locker *without* your boots during semiregular armor inspections. You *will* practice getting your suit on, by yourself, until you can do it in the dark, hung over, in less than a minute. Your fire team is usually quick, so don't slow them down, or they'll Morty you. Don't get Morty'd. Trust me. That shit was disturbing. Otherwise, you should be good to go."

"Sergeant?" Tavi cocked his head, confused, the armorer's previous words still ringing in his ears. "Why shouldn't I grow more?"

"Hung up on that, eh? Interesting. Well, kid, the bigger of a target you are, the easier you are to shoot."

Tavi nodded. Wise words, indeed. The armorer would have fit right in back in Overdark.

CHAPTER THREE
Seriously, It's Only Tacos

PNV **PERSEVERANCE,** *ANAT SYSTEM*

Blue was nearing the end of her limited patience. The short jump to the Anat system had gone without incident, and she'd spent most of her time reviewing the aircrew notices that had come out while she'd been on leave, ALS-71 Rhino Emergency Procedures (EPs), and the local airspace procedures.

The rest of her time had been spent fending off the nosy as fuck Lieutenant Serella "Killi" Killowen.

Blue braced her elbows on the battered metal table bolted to the deck in the center of the mission planning room and glared as the other woman slung herself into the chair across from hers. Killi's grin was nothing short of smug, and it took everything Blue had not to throw her slate at her. She'd been so careful sneaking out of their shared bunk and had figured she'd have at least another hour of studying before she was discovered.

Supposedly, Killi was her best friend, but if she didn't stop pestering her about Campbell, she was going to be in the market for a new one.

"Oh come on, is that really all he told you?" Killi gave her an arch look. Short, curvy, and with a tumble of black curls barely kept in check and bottomless green eyes, Killi had the innocent look down. Too bad it was a lie. "Can't you pump him for more gossip?"

Killi made a crude gesture with one hand and cackled at Blue's sour expression. She hadn't noticed the shorter woman in the crowd waiting to board the *Perseverance* back at the orbital naval shipyard, but Killi had most definitely noticed *her*. More specifically, she'd noticed who Blue was with and had decided to entertain herself by making Blue's life miserable. Killi was lucky there weren't any good options for a replacement best friend. *Yet.*

Grumbling under her breath, Blue closed out the single-engine EP checklist she'd been reviewing. Memorization wasn't the point. The point was to refamiliarize herself with the various checklists so she could find what she needed quickly in the event of an emergency—real or simulated—for her upcoming eval flight. She had another dozen to review before they started mission planning for tomorrow's training drop, but it was obvious Killi wasn't going to let her.

"Don't give me that look," Killi said teasingly, accurately interpreting Blue's annoyance. "You've got that shit locked down. You're going to do great."

"I'm going to do great because I'll be properly prepared," Blue shot back.

"I'm sure Campbell will appreciate that you're *prepared*."

"You're ridiculous," Blue said in an exasperated growl, but she couldn't hide her amusement.

"You mispronounced jealous." Killi's grin promised she wasn't actually serious. "I mean, who wouldn't be—you're with Ensign Hotness!"

Blue managed not to roll her eyes at Killi's exaggerated dreamy sigh, but only because she was trying to break the new habit.

"I'm not *with* him. We're just going out drinking tomorrow night at Gunrunner's." Blue shot her friend a sly smile. "The only question is whether we end the night in his bunk or mine."

Killi's eyes widened. "Oh no you're not."

"Relax." Blue snorted a laugh. "I'll give you warning if it's ours."

They'd long since worked out a system if one of them needed the room for *reasons*, but Killi pinned her with a horrified stare.

"Girl, you *cannot* keep a guy like Campbell on the hook if you don't play the game a little." Killi shook her head as if disappointed in Blue. "You can't just go for it."

"The hell I can't."

Irritation shot through Blue, and she set her slate down on the table slightly harder than necessary. The sharp *snap* echoed off the metal bulkheads.

"I'm not playing any games, Killi. Besides, who says I want to keep him long term? The man's a fuckboy. There's nothing wrong with that, but he isn't relationship material." Her nails bit into her palms as her control frayed a little more, and she drew in a deep breath of recycled, sterile air to calm down. "And for that matter, I don't *want* a relationship. You know I'm not sticking around any longer than I have to, and there's no future with a Navy guy like Campbell. Not when the Survey Corps will keep me in the far reaches of the known galaxy."

"Right." Killi bit her lip and glanced down, her delicate fingers tracing random patterns on the scuffed surface of the old table.

Blue's gut twisted and she felt like the worst friend ever. She'd met Killi at Legion inprocessing, and they'd been inseparable ever since. They'd survived Basic Training together, pulled through flight school together, flown their first year of service in the Bronze together... but Killi had commissioned into the Legion via the standard track. She had nine more years to go, whereas Blue only had three before she could shift over to the Survey Corps.

To her credit, Killi always tried to be supportive of Blue's dream, but she also flat-out admitted to being a selfish bitch. She wanted Blue to stick around, and she hated it when Blue talked about leaving.

With a low sigh, Blue reached across the table and took her hand. There were still traces of glittering green nail polish around the edges, evidence of Killi's tropical vacation. In hindsight, Blue really should've spent her precious leave with her best friend on the beach rather than being harassed by her mother. *Missed opportunities.*

"You listen to me right now." Blue tightened her grip. "It's you and me, ride or die. Whether we're breathing the same stale recycled air or messaging each other like crazy from different systems—you're never getting rid of me."

Killi flipped her hand over and squeezed her back, eyes shining with a touch of moisture.

"You're damn right." In the next instant, her mercurial friend flipped a mental switch and was all mischief again. "But so am I. Trust me on Ensign Hotness. He can get all the tail he wants, but you brushed him off the last deployment. Now he's chasing what he couldn't get. So, girl, *make him chase.*"

"Copy chase." Blue snorted a watery laugh, and then checked her wrist comm as it pinged an alert. "Come on. We've got just enough time for chow before mission planning. Tragarz said they've got tacos today."

"Oh, heck yes!" Killi shoved back from the table and smirked. "Just remember—no *tacos* for Ensign Hotness."

Mission planning for their training drop had been fairly standard, with one interesting exception. They had to prep for the possibility of volcanic ash operations. A long-ago quirk in Aurora's terraforming had resulted in a planet with volatile tectonic activity, and the area they were dropping in was littered with volcanoes, both dormant and very much not dormant.

While the Rhinos were heavily armored, volcanic ash was incredibly abrasive and could cause all sorts of issues for the assault shuttles. Engine damage, pneumatic and hydraulic system problems, windscreen scarring... and ash, much like sand, was invasive and got *everywhere*. The last thing Blue wanted on a drop was a contaminated oxygen system or cascading failures in her instruments.

Volcanic ash ops boiled down to one very simple concept—avoid if at all possible, and if it wasn't, get the fuck out of the ash cloud like your tail was on fire.

The locker room was packed with everyone gearing up before preflight, and Blue was grateful that her locker was at the front of the room rather than buried in the middle of the chaos like Killi's. Her fingers flew nimbly over her body armor, checking the connections as her ears rang with the clanging of battered metal doors slamming and the bantering of two dozen pilots. Even if they didn't all need to drop on Aurora to play babysitter to one little science team, the Bronze Legion wasn't about to pass up a training opportunity. Everyone in Bravo Company would participate in the day's exercises, which meant the full wing of Rhinos was needed.

Blue waited just long enough for Killi to join her, and then the women headed for the dropship bay. As copilots, the bulk of the preflighting duties for their respective ships fell on them.

The raucous shouts of maintainers hard at work drifted out into the corridor, and Blue breathed in the familiar pungent scents of fuel, grease, and oil as they strode through the open hatch. The bright lights of the cavernous bay shone down on the swarm of maintainers hurriedly finishing up their tasks, maneuvering with practiced grace around the two rows of six ALS-71 Rhinos lining either side.

Sparks cascaded from the ceiling as a maintainer repaired a panel, the stocky man made tiny by the height and those orange embers dying long before they came close to reaching the deck. On either side of the hatch, the bay stretched into the distance, taking up a considerable portion of the *Perseverance*.

The massive dropships made the cavernous space look small.

At an impatient grunt from behind them, Blue and Killi quickly cleared the hatch, because they weren't the only copilots hustling. They absently waved at Lieutenants Tina "Tiny" Tragarz and Heather "Ruby" Ridolfi as they trotted past them for Bronze Raven Three and One respectively. Ruby paused long enough to wave back, her eyes bright with excitement. She was one of their newbies fresh out of training and viewed everything through the lens of enthusiastic inexperience.

Blue stopped at Bronze Raven Four, eyes eagerly drinking in *her* dropship.

"Missed your baby, did you?" Killi nudged her side. "Girl, you can love your ship, but don't *love* your ship. Or do! Whatever keeps you here with us. I won't judge."

Killi easily dodged Blue's lazy swing and trotted off to Bronze Raven Five, laughing under her breath the whole way. Blue shook her head at her incorrigible friend and turned back to her ship.

A possessive smile pulled at Blue's lips as she started her external walkaround. Measuring twenty-five meters from nose to tail with a thirty-meter wingspan, the ASL-71 Rhino was a *beast*. A true assault shuttle rather than one of the sleeker fighters the Legion used in aerial combat, the Rhino favored bulky armor and sheer power over maneuverability and speed.

Slightly concave wings stretched out to either side of the armored fuselage. Fully ten meters above the deck, Blue had to crane her head back to inspect the underside of the wings and engines. While the powerful rear thrusters were critical for void operations, it was the rotating atmospheric engines on the wings that turned the bulky Rhino into a VTOL. Considering how often the Bronze was deployed to austere locations, that was a critical function, and Blue climbed up onto the wings and spent long minutes inspecting the system before she moved onto the next item on the checklist.

Auxiliary hatches on the port and starboard, currently sealed for void ops, hid the dual M268 GAU-18 Aries Miniguns. The six-barrel Gatling-style machine guns spat out 30mm depleted uranium rounds, high-explosive incendiary rounds, or anti-personnel rounds at a rapid rate of fire and were the cherished babies of her gunners. She ensured the hatches were secured and turned her attention to the recoil attenuation thrusters, or RATs.

Designed to mitigate recoil, there were four RATs per gun, equally spaced around the hatches in a square pattern. Any two by themselves could handle the recoil of the gun on the opposite side of the ship, but the Rhino's engineers were a fan of redundancy. If any one RAT failed, the diagonal thruster would automatically shut down for balance purposes. Even if the entire system failed, there was a manual backup and crew coordination that would keep those Aries Miniguns firing as long as their ammo lasted.

And the massive Rhino could carry a *lot* of ammo, along with twenty personnel including aircrew and a full-loadout of gear and supplies.

Blue left the actual inspection of those guns to her diminutive gunners and moved on to the chin-mounted railgun.

This was *her* gun, controlled from the cockpit by the pilots, and she carefully checked the six-foot barrel. It fired 20mm tungsten sabot rounds, but the smaller caliber didn't matter when those rounds were sent downrange at a blistering 7,000 feet per second. They usually practiced with dummy rounds, but in combat conditions she'd have access to the standard tungsten penetrator armor rounds, as well as frangible anti-personnel rounds designed to shatter on contact.

Blue was really happy she'd never had to use those on live targets.

In short order, she'd finished her external checks and affectionately patted the scuffed gray hull. The Rhino definitely wasn't the prettiest or the quickest, but she was fun as hell to fly, and Blue had missed hers. She might not be obsessed like some of her fellow pilots, but she really did love flying, especially in atmo.

Blue strode around the side of her Rhino and found Killi waiting for her. The other woman stood with one hand on her hip and her helmet in the other. Only Killi could manage to look adorable in their Legion-issued body armor.

Black with bronze accents, the dropship pilot armor lacked the adaptive camouflage and hamatic capabilities of the legionnaires' armor, but it would stop small-caliber rounds and was void-rated with a rebreather unit built into the suit. Though if a pilot had the misfortune to end up in the black, it wouldn't be enough to keep them alive for much longer than a quick farewell and a quicker prayer to whatever deity they worshiped.

"You ready?" Killi asked with a grin as dropship commanders and aircrew poured into the bay.

Blue winked and bumped her fist against Killi's.

"Let's rage."

"Here's our ride," Jabber said as 4th Squad entered the dropship bay. Around them was organized chaos as the other squads of Bravo Company were prepping to board their own lifts. For the first time, Tavi was able to see the ship which was supposed to keep him alive on the way down to the planet.

Tavi had never seen a more beautiful ship in his admittedly short life. It was Death Incarnate, an avenging angel waiting on high to smite any foes who dared stand in its way. The fuselage was a gray, mottled pattern which faintly resembled his hamatic suit. The blunt nose was painted with a black raven with wings outstretched down the sides, bronze trim etching the edges of the largest feathers. Bronze eyes gazed balefully in front of the massive aircraft. Plus, there were guns *everywhere*. Tavi could appreciate the firepower. He knew that one day it could mean the difference between life and death, and he wanted his ride to be that difference.

Tavi had seen a Rhino before, of course. But never one which looked like *this*.

He'd dropped from a designated training Rhino at ACS, a larger version which was capable of handling thirty recruits and their instructors easily. Every legionnaire recruit was required to experience a full-on atmospheric drop in one before they could graduate. Those who screamed, begged for it to stop, or threw up their toes, were forced to do a second drop, and a third, and a fourth... as many as it took to ensure they could do a drop without a word of complaint.

Tavi had managed to keep everything down and not emit so much as a peep on his first drop, much to the chagrin of the pilot who'd been determined to make every single recruit in his class vomit. While every other recruit had been forced to wash the interior of the vessel before going back up for rounds two and three, Tavi had been standing at attention on the tarmac waiting for them to return.

And waiting...

...and waiting some more...

He would have rather been on the vomit comet. At least in there he could have been doing something other than standing.

But seeing the raven's profile on the tail and the bronzed "IV" emblazoned below it for the first time made his heart swell with... pride? Joy? Or was it excitement? He couldn't decide. His own armor sported "XIII" in bronze on his shoulder, but seemed to be lacking the logo on the Rhino. He didn't necessarily mind. It only made him a little more curious.

One of the things they had neglected during Basic and later, ACS, was the history and traditions of each legion. Which made sense. They were being taught *how* to be legionnaires at Basic. Let the legions themselves train the new recruits on the *whys*.

Tavi followed his fire team to their spots in the hold of the bird while a grumpy-looking older legionnaire wearing a flight crew uniform and sporting the distinctive step of a man with a prosthetic leg walked around cracking weird jokes at the flight crew as they boarded the Rhino. The sergeant glanced at the squad, then back onto the loading bay, then over at Sergeant Ord.

"Fourth Squad! Your civilians look reluctant to board!" the man barked. There was a smirk on his tanned face. Tavi didn't understand why. "Motivate them!"

Tavi looked back over his shoulder at the loading dock and grimaced. Weighted bags were piled there, waiting for someone to load them into the ship. The briefing had covered this, and he'd forgotten already. He mentally chided himself. Nobody had thought to ask their squad leader which fire team was going to be hauling around the "civilians."

Sergeant Ord leaned forward in his seat and glared at Pigeon. "Team Two! Why aren't your civvies on this ship yet?"

"Sarge?" Vixen asked from her seat, confused. "Why are they *our* civilians?"

"Do I really need to explain it, *Vixen*?"

"C'mon, *tasawa*, let's grab a bag and get them in their spot," Jabber said, pulling Tavi along behind him. "You think that getting rid of some *balara* would be good for the squad and everyone be happy, but no. Ordo never happy, *keiche*? That man was born bitter, angry, and old."

"I swear to the gods if Morty talked, I will fucking end him," Krawdaddy muttered as he swung the heavy bag over his shoulder. He coughed once and looked at a bag still on the deck. "Right this way, my good sir. We'll get you safe on board this bee-*yootiful* bird without problems, and we'll keep your dumb civvie ass safe from all manner of wildlife—"

"*Krawdaddy!*" Pigeon snapped. "Stow your shit before you get us KP duty. You're almost as bad as Jabber!"

"For once it's not me, *bossjna*," Jabber crowed as he easily picked up and handed Tavi one of the bags. The ungainly thing had been weighted poorly, with the majority of the heavier weights at the top. Tavi swung it over his shoulder and nearly fell on his face as something inside the bag shifted. He managed to keep from making a complete fool of himself by swinging a leg around to rebalance himself, making what should have been an ugly and embarrassing fall a graceful and purposeful maneuver. Jabber, unaware of the almost stumble, whistled. "You act like you done this before, *tasawa*."

Tavi kept his mouth shut and instead hauled the bag into the back of the bird. There were designated seats forward with extra padding and cushions for the civilians, so he dropped his bag into one of the seats and looked around. He spotted the loadmaster and waved to get his attention.

"Do I need to secure the civilian, Sergeant?" he asked.

"Naw, I got this, cherry. Grab your seat and fix your harness. I'll be by for a check in a minute."

"Yes, Sergeant!" Tavi hurried back over to his seat and started buckling in, mindful of how the harness would work over his suit. It took him longer than he would've liked, but it was still easier than doing it in his dress blacks.

"Secure helmets and prepare to pressurize," the loadmaster instructed the rest of the hold once the last "civilian" was secured in their seat. The rear loading ramp closed, and the interior lights shifted from regular to a dim red. With quick professionalism he went to each legionnaire and checked their straps. When he reached Tavi, he double-checked the harness and nodded with satisfaction. His eyes then moved to Tavi's hands. "Private? Where are your gloves?"

"They didn't have my size at the armory, Sergeant."

"Didn't have... shit. Rectify this before your next drop. Your hands are gonna get chewed up otherwise." As he moved on to Jabber, he called out, "Hey, Ordo! Your cherry doesn't have gloves!"

"Confirmed," the sergeant said as his helmeted head turned Tavi's way. "Carvalho! When we hit the surface, can he borrow a pair of gloves from one of your door gunners? I'll owe you one."

"Got it, Ordo. Kid-sized gloves for the kid. I'll check with HeyHey and see if they have an extra pair."

Tavi flushed but bit back a sharp response. He knew doing so would be asking for trouble. After promising to never speak a word of it, Jabber had sort of explained to him what had caused Morty's transfer to 1st—more accurately, what had been the driving force behind it—and he didn't want to be on the receiving end of *that*.

"Comms check," Sergeant Ord said as Tavi finished securing his helmet. One by one the fire teams went through their customary checks, with Specialist Oscar "Banger" Kolbinger from Fire Team Three being the last to respond. "Comms confirmed. Loadmaster, 4th Squad reads clear. Ready to depart."

"Copy, Sergeant. Load is secure. Prepare for departure."

Tavi swallowed as the Rhino lifted from the deck of the *Perseverance* and, with a gentle tug, was out in space. Using the suit control on his wrist, he began filtering through the HUD settings to cut down on some of the extraneous data feeds coming in until only Fire Team Two showed. Since he wasn't the team leader, there was no point in paying attention to the data feeds of the other teams for the time being.

"Here we go..." Tavi whispered as the Rhino abruptly dropped into the atmosphere, his hands holding on tightly to his straps as he schooled his features into an expressionless mask. There was no point in letting anyone else know just how much he was looking forward to this. Too many people back at ACS had been upset when he'd whooped for joy during takeoff for his first drop.

"Entering atmosphere, on target for DZ Juliet in fifteen mikes," Blue said over the ops channel so both her aircrew and the legionnaires loaded in the back could hear.

Tension wound up her spine and across her shoulders, tightening her muscles to the point of pain, but she kept her hands light on the controls as she guided the Rhino into the optimum reentry angle. Her gaze flicked from the flightpath projected on her helmet's HUD to her instruments and back out the cockpit in a practiced rhythm. Sweat trickled down her back and dampened her undersuit, and she dragged in measured breaths of the slightly metallic oxygen mix pumping into her helmet.

It wasn't that the drop wasn't going well. Her skills hadn't rusted all that much from her extended leave, and she was actually happy with how quickly she'd fallen back into flying. No, it was because while her dropship commander Captain Makenna "Twister" Latham sat in the left seat, she'd assumed the copilot duties and placed Blue as pilot in command for the sortie. It changed nothing from their mission planning session but for one key detail—the command-and-control decisions were in Blue's hands.

Blue wasn't stupid. She understood the more experienced pilot was prepping her for her upgrade ride, but a little warning would've been nice.

Maybe that was the point.

Twister, only a few years older than Blue but with silver already threading through her white-blonde hair, verified their course.

"Entry angle checks good," Twister said crisply before she switched over to the airspace control channel and made the appropriate comm calls to get clearance.

A tremor ran through the tough assault shuttle as they slipped into the upper atmosphere, and Blue firmed up her grip on the controls. Another, harder tremor hit, and she grinned as the vibrations rattled her bones. She was so damn grateful the Legion had long ago done away with those annoying—and highly ineffective—AI cockpit systems. Nothing more than decision tree matrixes, most AIs couldn't handle the rapidly changing environment of a combat drop. And the ones that *were* advanced enough calculated the odds and refused to drop.

Only humans were dumb enough—*brave* enough—to do the job right.

Blue's tension fell away, all of her focus given over to flying her ship. No time to worry about any simulated EPs Twister might throw in to trip her up, no time to stress over being in command. The only thing that mattered was the feel of her ship beneath her hands and completing the drop safely.

They were shedding altitude a touch faster than Blue wanted, and she pitched the nose up to bring their airspeed back within the target range. A glance at her scope verified Bravo Five was still in formation several hundred meters off her right wing, and she briefly wondered if Killi was flying the drop or if Captain Wanda "Witch" Sanderson had it.

"Airspace Control cleared us to DZ Juliet," Twister said as an alert pinged on their weather radar. Bright green outlined an alarming amount of yellows and reds, indicating a rapidly building storm system off the coast. The older woman arched her brow. "And they passed along an advisory on that thunderstorm."

Blue felt the weight of the other pilot's gaze as she rapidly assessed the unexpected weather and its projected path. If she did nothing, the edges of the storm would brush up against their route by the time they were over the ocean. While the Rhino could handle a little rain, lightning and atmospheric turbulence were another matter entirely— especially when it was avoidable.

"Adjust our flightpath so we're approaching the DZ from the northeast and update Bravo Five."

Twister smiled and bent her head over the console, her fingers dancing over the screen. A few seconds later, a new flight profile flashed in Blue's HUD.

"Bronze Raven Five, Bronze Raven Four, transmitting updated profile due to anticipated weather," Twister said.

Blue verified the flightpath would keep them well clear of the vicious storm and turned the Rhino onto the new heading. The second dropship followed.

"*Bronze Raven Five, updated profile acknowledged,*" a low contralto voice purred over the comms as the second dropship followed their lead.

Blue grinned.

If Witch was on the comms, Killi was flying.

Twister waited until she'd leveled the wings and resumed their steady descent before she traced one finger on the weather radar scope.

"What would you have done if the storm was tracking in this direction instead?"

"RTB," Blue said immediately.

If the storm was going to hit the DZ, there was no point in continuing the drop. The system was too big, too slow rolling to clear the area quickly, so going into a holding pattern to wait it out wouldn't work. Returning to base (RTB) was the only proper course of action.

Twister nodded as if she'd expected that answer, flipped on the cargo compartment camera, and pushed the feed to the auxiliary viewscreen. Fifteen legionnaires, including one undersized, underaged newbie, were strapped in. Most were relaxed, a few looked as if they were napping, and only one or two seemed nauseous. Tavi's expression was stoic, but she noted his white-knuckled grip on his straps and couldn't tell if he was nervous or excited.

"And if they were on the ground, operating in hostile conditions, and needed an immediate extraction?" Twister asked quietly.

Blue hesitated. Risk the ship, risk her aircrew, risk her life... or leave the legionnaires high and dry. Like any other aircraft, the ASL-71 Rhino had published regulations and standards for safe operations.

Those regs went out the cockpit during combat ops.

Her gaze locked onto Tavi's painfully young face, shocked all over again at the resemblance to her brother. Her hands tightened on the controls, and she had to let out a slow breath before she could soften her grip once more.

"We'd get them out."

The silence stretched between them, and Blue's gut clenched. Had she gotten it wrong?

And then the corner of Twister's mouth curled up.

"Good answer."

As they continued to drop altitude, Airspace Control vectored them around a live-fire training exercise. Blue's HUD automatically filtered the bright flashes of high-yield ordnance off her left wing. A few minutes later, she banked the aircraft thirty degrees left in a descending turn that dropped them down to their cruising altitude.

The high desert training area, all twisting canyons and narrow rivers, passed by beneath their wings. Envy stabbed into Blue's heart. The rest of Bravo Company would be conducting their training session there today, which meant low-level flying, possibly within the canyons themselves. Those were the best sorties, even if the Rhino wasn't the most agile bird in the sky.

Unfortunately, 4th and 5th Squads had somehow drawn the short straw and would be the ones actually on scientist babysitting duty on Aurora. Since the Legion always trained how they fought, their exercise for the day would mimic the upcoming mission parameters and local conditions. Sagetnam was blessed with a variety of ecosystems, so Blue reluctantly left the canyons behind for the jungle training area located on a large island off the coast.

Blue had a sneaking suspicion that the Morty incident had something to do with her legionnaire squad getting tagged with babysitting duty.

Ravens might not get the legionnaire scuttlebutt directly from their boys, but their Crows, or enlisted aircrew, was another matter entirely. Blue's gunners had been only too happy to share the latest gossip with her while they'd been inspecting their babies. Nobody was entirely certain what the 4th had done to "convince" Morty to request a transfer to 1st Squad, but it had spawned a new game as everyone tried to guess. Sergeant Miguel Carvalho, her loadmaster, was running the betting pool.

Blue had quietly transferred fifty denarii to Carvalho and told him to put it wherever he wanted. Despite losing a leg during his ground pounder days, the man had an ungodly lucky streak. It was probably the only reason he'd survived to retrain as a loadmaster.

Up ahead, the greenish-blue horizon resolved into the vast expanse of a tropical ocean. At their current altitude, Blue couldn't yet see the jungle island training area, but the massive thunderstorm on their weather radar was visible as ominous dark clouds to the south, with the brilliant flicker of lightning flashing every few seconds. Thanks to their new route, they were flying through clear skies with only the occasional puffy cloud, but even this far out the ocean was unsettled, with white-capped waves rolling beneath their wings.

A hard gust of wind rocked the Rhino, but Blue easily corrected. As they left the coast behind, the turbulence increased, and Blue grinned as the dropship dipped and swayed. A low level over the ocean wasn't the same as canyon flying, but it was still fun. Her hands automatically made the tiny adjustments necessary to keep them on course.

After a few minutes of bumpy flying, a miserable groan filtered over the comms, and Blue flipped over to the aircrew channel. "Carvalho, how's our newest legionnaire doing back there?"

"*Near as I can tell, just fine,*" he said cheerfully. "*He's not our groaner.*"

At another groan and a watery belch, Blue hurriedly switched back to the ops channel. "Sergeant Ord, kindly remind your boys of the rules."

"*You puke, you clean the ship, boys.*" Sharp amusement infused the legionnaire sergeant's voice. "*The* whole *ship.*"

"Bronze Raven Four could use a good scrubbing, don't you think?" Twister asked with an innocent smile.

"Why yes, yes it could." Blue smirked, nothing but the devil in her own smile. "I bet Five could use a scrub down, too."

Twister chuckled and got on the comms. "Bronze Raven Five, how would you feel about a little extra maneuvering?"

"*Bronze Raven Four, Killi says the flight controls feel just a little… stiff. Can't have that. I bet a few aggressive maneuvers will solve that problem right quick.*"

That was all the agreement Blue needed, but while she wanted to mess with the legionnaires, her aircrew was another matter entirely. "Standby maneuvers, Crows."

She only waited long enough for her gunners and loadmaster to double-click acknowledgment over the comms. With a little warning waggle of her tail for Killi, she dropped the nose and pushed the Rhino into a hard right bank. Keeping a close eye on the altimeter, she abruptly leveled the wings, gave it a two-second count, and threw the sturdy dropship into a left bank.

Out on her right wing, Killi mirrored her before she abruptly popped up several hundred meters and spun her Rhino into an impressive snap roll.

"Oooh, someone's playing to win," Blue murmured in appreciation at the sharp maneuver. With a grin, she pushed the throttles to max and launched into a series of twists and the quick right and left breaks designed to get a dropship clear of any ground fire. There were a few groans over the ops channel, but a couple of *whoops* as well, proof *some* of her legionnaires enjoyed flying. "Hmm, no winners yet. Let's try this."

Blue threw the Rhino into a defensive spiral, dropping altitude in a dizzying spin that whipped the view outside the cockpit into a colorful blur of turquoise ocean, blue sky, and gray storm clouds. She leveled out barely fifty meters over the ocean, so close to the waves the salt spray kissed their belly.

As they raced across the water, the dropship bucked beneath her hands. Blue pulled back on the controls, pointed the nose up, and pushed the Rhino back into the sky, chasing the altitude she'd lost on the last maneuver. She was pressed back into the padded seat and tightened her abdominals in response. A sidelong glance at Twister, a sly smile, and she abruptly pitched the nose low, trading in all those positive Gs for weightlessness.

And one of the legionnaires retched miserably, while the rest cheered.

"*And we have a volunteer!*" Sergeant Ord bellowed.

"But Sarge," Vixen protested. "*I puked in my helmet, not the ship!*"

"One, that's disgusting, Vixen, and you will be thoroughly cleaning your armor after the training ex. Two, is your helmet on the ship?"

A brief pause, then a very miserable, "*Yes, Sarge.*"

"*Then you're cleaning the ship.*"

Blue opened up a private line with Sergeant Ord as she leveled out and soared above the waves. "Does Vixen need a battle buddy? I'm sure I can get another one to puke before we hit the DZ."

"No, ma'am. He needed a little character building anyway. This'll do nicely."

"Copy character building," she said with a laugh.

Killi had also apparently scored at least one winner, because she'd leveled out and was flying on her wing as steadily as any passenger shuttle. And just in time too. The jungle training area was less than twenty miles away and closing fast.

The island was an irregular square in shape, with wide sandy beaches and thick jungles. There was a tiny, timeworn mountain range cutting through the middle like the spine of some ancient beast, more rolling hills than anything else. The island was large enough to boast three different drop zones, all painstakingly carved out and maintained by Sagetnam's training center, but their two squads had the run of the entire island today.

What her legionnaires did once they were on the ground was up to Sergeant Ord. If the aircrews were lucky, they'd get called back in to play a little too, but per the current mission plan, their involvement ended at the hot drop.

Blue pulled back on the throttles and decreased their airspeed to within an acceptable range. She dropped one wing low in a smooth turn and circled over DZ Juliet, ensuring the wide clearing was a go for their training drop. Just because nobody was supposed to be out there didn't mean accidents never happened, so while Blue conducted the visual scan, Twister verified the area was clear on their scopes.

Blue leveled out at one hundred meters. "DZ clear, confirm?"

"Confirmed clear," Twister said briskly.

"Gunners ready?" Blue tossed a quick glance over her shoulder into the gunner compartment, which was located directly behind the cockpit through an open hatch. Corporals Emi Hayashi and Iolana Hekikia were strapped into harnesses at their Aries Miniguns.

Collectively known as HeyHey, the diminutive door gunners could have been twins, though they weren't even from the same system, let alone the same planet. Tiny, blue-eyed, and dark-haired, with matching attitudes and all the savage joy when they got to shoot things. They had been less than pleased to miss out on the main training exercise until Blue had briefed them on the necessity of clearing the DZ of any "hostile native fauna." The instant they learned they'd get to put dummy rounds on target, they'd been all smiles.

HeyHey gave her a simultaneous thumbs up and a verbal, "Ready on the guns."

A fierce grin spread across Blue's face. It was time for the fun part. As she lined the Rhino up for a low approach, she felt a slight drag and verified the gunner hatches had fully opened.

"Get some, ladies."

As Blue flew the Rhino in a fast pass over the DZ, HeyHey opened up with the Aries Miniguns in tight one-second bursts.

Brrrt! Brrrt! Brrrt!

Blue felt as much as heard the guns spitting training rounds. The pilots' helmets acted as adequate ear protection, but the gunners wore specialized earpieces to ensure they survived their service with their hearing mostly intact.

Mostly being the operative word.

Brrrt! Brrrt! Brrrt!

Twister pushed the external camera feed to one of the viewscreens and nodded in satisfaction at the puffs of dirt and vegetation erupting in wide arcs on either side of the dropship's path. Blue had offset her approach so they were covering the southeast side of the DZ, while Killi flew several thousand meters in trail and on the northwest side to ensure full coverage.

"Looking good." Twister let out a low chuckle and put a few dummy rounds through their chin-mounted railgun. The crown of a towering, vine-covered tree at the far end of the clearing exploded in a shower of wood chips and greenery. "Railgun checks good."

Blue smirked. "You know, I thought that tree was looking at us funny."

"Don't get cute." Twister arched a brow. "Drop ain't over yet."

"Says the woman blowing up innocent trees," Blue muttered as she pushed the Rhino into a sharp climbing left turn. She needed to set down in the center of the DZ where 4th Squad would be simulating protecting the science team, while Killi would do a double hot drop on the north and south side of the DZ to allow 5th Squad to set up a perimeter watch. As she set up her approach, she activated the rotation on the engines and smoothly shifted into VTOL mode. Clouds of dust kicked up from the field as they descended, and Blue kept running down the checklist in a practiced rhythm. "Engines locked into vertical position, rate of descent good, gear...shit."

Twister grimaced at the yellow alert flashing in their HUDs but waited for Blue to make the call. Blue cycled the gear again, but the alert didn't clear. The rear gear had locked into place, but the nose gear refused to deploy. It left Blue with two options. She could abort the landing and circle the field while they ran the gear malfunction checklist, delaying the drop.

Depending on how long it took to sort out their gear issue, it could impact the whole training schedule, which would be less than ideal. It would also impact the promised shore leave, which would not endear her to her legionnaires or Crows.

Her other option was to hot drop her legionnaires, keeping the engines engaged and the nose up and off the ground. Trickier, but well within both the limits of the Rhino and her skillset. Then they could run a diagnostic on the nose gear while flying overwatch above the training area. With any luck, they could clear the issue. If not, they'd simply repeat the two-point landing maneuver when they picked their boys back up at the end of the exercise.

Either option was perfectly legal and acceptable. All of that ran through Blue's mind in an instant. In the next, Blue made her decision.

"Nose gear malfunction acknowledged, proceeding with hot drop."

"Copy hot drop." Twister nodded, her expression giving nothing away, and cleared the alert from their HUDs.

"Carvalho, Ordo, we're hot dropping," Blue said over the ops channel. "Got a gear malfunction. I'll keep the Rhino steady, just get those boys off my ship like it's last call at the cantina. Copy?"

"Carvalho copies."

"Ordo copies."

Landing in VTOL mode was strikingly similar to attempting to balance on a beach ball. Twister monitored their descent, while Blue kept the wings level and the nose at a slightly higher angle than normal. A jolt traveled through the sturdy dropship as the rear wheels hit the ground. Almost before the impact faded, the "ramp opening" alert flashed in her HUD. Carvalho was on his A game today.

Blue focused on keeping the Rhino's nose in the air, a balancing act aided by the ship's automatic stabilizer system. Less than a minute passed before Carvalho resealed the ramp and double-clicked over the comm to indicate he was properly secured again.

Blue slid her gaze toward Twister. "Verify cleared for liftoff."

"Cleared," Twister said calmly after she'd verified the legionnaires were well away from the Rhino's engines.

Blue wasted no time in getting them back into the air. As soon as she'd gotten them into an overwatch pattern opposite Bronze Raven Five, the two pilots went through the gear malfunction EP checklist. By their second circuit around the island, the nose gear was working again, though the action was far from smooth.

"Enter a note for maintenance to service all of our gear," Blue ordered as they closed out the checklist. "If the nose gear is having issues, I want all of them thoroughly checked before we fly again."

"Done." For the first time since the gear malfunction alert, Twister smiled. "Good job on the EP."

Blue tore her gaze from the tossing greenery passing beneath their wings. The horizon split into a partial blue sky and greenish-blue ocean as she nudged them into a wide turn.

"A test?" she asked Twister with a wry grin.

"Nope, but you handled it perfectly."

Blue flexed her shoulders to shed the tension. Killi had been right. She was ready for her upgrade ride.

CHAPTER FOUR
Just Need to Knock a Little Rust Off...

HONEN DISTRICT, SAGETNAM, ANAT SYSTEM

"*Gooood morning, Sagetnam!*" the loadmaster screamed into 4th Squad's comms the moment the nose of the bird flared. Tavi was jerked in his seat as the Rhino's momentum changed abruptly. The ship shuddered as power roared through the fuselage. The rear loading ramp dropped onto the ground mere moments after the rear wheels touched down. The howling of the engines was quickly dampened out by Tavi's helmet as it adjusted to the sudden noise increase. "*Welcome to the lovely jungles of the Honen District, Sagetnam! Where the air is wet and the water tastes like recycled piss! 4th Squad! Get the hell off my bird! Move! Move!*"

"Team Two! Get your civvies and unass!" Sergeant Ord commanded as the other two teams hurried out of the Rhino and formed a small security perimeter. Nearby, another set of engines could faintly be heard as 5th Squad dropped nearby to establish a larger perimeter. Like their final destination, Sagetnam had an abundance of wildlife in the native jungles, some of which could potentially injure and kill their civilians. The security of the civilians was paramount to their mission parameters—weighted bags though they may be at this particular moment.

Tavi slapped his quick-release harness and stood as soon as the straps had fallen aside, then grabbed his weapon off the rack next to him. It took him less than a second to reach the seat where he'd parked his "civvie" and unstrap the weighted bag. Before he could pick it up, though, someone grabbed his shoulder. Turning, he recognized the loadmaster.

"Make sure I get these back in good condition!" the sergeant shouted over the howl of the engines, shoving a pair of gloves into Tavi's hands.

"Thank you, Sergeant!"

"Don't thank me, thank HeyHey. Now get off my bird!"

Tavi had no idea who or what a HeyHey was but slid the gloves on gratefully nonetheless. He secured the wrist straps before flexing his fingers to test them out. They were comfortable and padded, though they had clearly seen some use, but they fit well. He didn't care. Not shredding his hands on some native fauna was going to be a nice change of pace. The abrasions he'd suffered during ACS had left small but noticeable scars across the backs of both hands.

"Thanks again, Sergeant!" he called out.

"Why the *fuck* are you still on my bird, cherry? Do you want to be a Crow or something? Move your scrawny ass!"

Even though it felt like forever, the entire extraction of 4th Squad from the bird had taken less than a minute. Tavi, the last off, barely had his feet on the ground before the rear load ramp was closing and the engines of the Rhino ramped back up to full power. All of 4th moved outside of the danger area of the Rhino's powerful thrusters. Within seconds the dropship was climbing and quickly disappeared from view, leaving them alone in the vast wilderness with their clueless "civilians."

Ordo wasted no time. "Claw, move north one hundred yards and establish a perimeter. Three, we're headed south, doing the same. Two, grab your civvies and prepare to move them. Points of interest are marked on your HUD maps...now. By the way, your civvies have weak bladders, and flying disagrees with them. Pigeon, keep your team in position until told otherwise. Copy?"

"Pigeon copies. Hold here while our civilians potty," Pigeon stated as Fire Team One moved north and Team Three headed south after confirming their orders. His next words came in the team channel, for their ears only. "I swear, Vixen, if this is because of you..."

"Maybe he's just in a bad mood? I'm sure this has nothing to do with Morty," Vixen suggested. Tavi shifted his bag on his shoulder and looked around, curious.

He'd never seen such dense foliage before. Even at ACS, the forest floor had been open and easily traversable. Here on Sagetnam, the jungle floor was filled with small bushes threatening to choke out everything, and various types of flora littered the ground. With the exception of a few easily identified game trails, it looked impossible to make it through.

"All right, first point on the map is two-two," Pigeon told them. "Jabber, take point. Krawdaddy, rear guard. Wait... damn. Belay that. Gotta protect the whiny civvies. Damn it. Stick together in one group. Claw, Pigeon. Moving to marked point two-two, copy?"

"*Claw copies.*"

"*Tollejo* civvies, making things harder," Jabber muttered as the team began to painstakingly work its way through the dense underbrush. "I don't see why it has to be us, *ke*? What we do wrong? Okay, my bunk is messy, but this is bullshit. Team One scored lower than us on readiness reports. They should have to hump these bags through this jungle. Nope, Ordo hates us, and makes us his bitch every single time. You think he hates the number two? I think he hates it. Hates me. Hates Pigeon. Likes Krawdaddy, but you kiss his ass. Don't know about Tavi yet. Too new. I *know* he hates Vixen. Diseased motherfu—"

"Come *on*, Jabber. Give it a rest," Vixen snapped, which caused the others to laugh. "Sulfatum chloride cures all."

"Makes you sterile, *keiche*."

"No, it doesn't."

"Does so."

"No way."

"Pigeon knows I'm speaking truth."

"No way... Pigeon?"

"I ain't getting involved in your lover's bitchfest. Keep moving."

Tuning out the argument, Tavi kept his eyes scanning the dense jungle as he'd been taught. Occasionally he would see glimpses of clearings, but every time they seemed to be approaching one, it would disappear. The shadows created shapeless forms, broken up by random beams of sunlight from above.

The going was slow because of the thick underbrush. For once, though, Tavi's slighter frame and smaller size worked to his advantage as he was able to navigate the trails easier than the others. While the others had to constantly duck beneath low-hanging branches, Tavi was able to breeze beneath them with nothing but a stray leaf occasionally brushing his shoulder.

Back at ACS, his training squad had jokingly called him Smoke due to his ability to waft through the roughest terrain without making a sound or being impeded by the environment. It was a cool nickname, but he knew it wouldn't carry over. Drop names, like Ordo had said, always seemed to be both a knock on the legionnaire and fitting at the same time.

The trek through the sweltering humidity was backbreaking work. The bag on his shoulder shifted with every step he made. The suit, designed to keep him alive, did nothing for the extra bag over his shoulder. The CCR-95 (Close Combat Rifle Version 95) bumped constantly into his hip, the strap out of place courtesy of the simulated civilian. Again, no permanent damage, but irritating nonetheless.

"Point two-two," Pigeon announced as they rounded a small cluster of undergrown trees. Tavi looked around but saw nothing interesting. Why the civilians would even be remotely interested in such a place was beyond him. Shifting the bag on his shoulder again, he inspected the flora.

Most of the plants featured broad leaves and hung low to the ground. Here and there a random sapling grew, struggling to find a gap in the trees above to grow large. Ancient imported Spanish moss covered most of the downed logs and trees, a testament to mankind's long ago colonization and terraforming of the planet. Tavi knew a little of this thanks to Jabber's obsession with history, but most of the details were just boring enough to make him turn his brain off.

"*Tasawa*, I think your civvie is gonna puke, *ke*?" Jabber said, nudging Tavi's elbow as he walked past and set his heavy bag on the jungle floor. Stretching his back, even the suit couldn't diminish the loud *pop!* as Jabber tried to loosen his joints. "*Fech*. Everything hurts. This bag shouldn't be so heavy. What they pack in them anyways?"

"Ordo, Team Two," Pigeon transmitted. "Arrived at marked point two-two. Awaiting orders."

Tavi slid the bag off his shoulder and gave his back a rest. Maneuvering around, he tried to find a better position to hang his weapon from its sling. Unfortunately, thanks to the ungainly and awkwardly placed strap of the "civvie," there was no way he could comfortably carry both. He had a suspicion the bags had been done up for this precise reason.

"*Copy Team Two. Hold position. Civvies need another potty break,*" Ordo's voice came over the comms a moment later. Pigeon sighed before responding.

"Two copies. Holding position."

"This is pretty," Tavi admitted quietly to Jabber as Vixen began complaining about the humidity to Krawdaddy, while Pigeon did his best to ignore them both.

"Yeah. Reminds me of home sometime, *tasawa*," Jabber murmured as he turned his helmeted face around to look at their environment. "More plants trying to eat you there, but still... pretty. Feral, but pretty. My world has many plants. Trees grow tall there, tall and wide. Smaller plants trap you and eat prey with honey or sweets. Others are like trap doors... prey wanders in, gets eaten. Took me long time to believe not all plants eat men."

"We didn't have plants in Overdark," Tavi admitted as he reached out with a gloved hand to touch one of the broad leaves. It was soft, spongy, yet resilient. It flexed between his fingers but didn't break nor bend. "Other cities had them, I think. Rigged lights to give plants something to grow by. But Overdark didn't have that. It had nothing."

Not even hope dwelled there, his inner thoughts whispered. It oftentimes amazed him just how much his perception of life had changed in the months since leaving his homeworld. Would he even recognize the streets he'd grown up on? Would he be able to survive those dark and shadowy labyrinths? He shoved the thoughts away. A legionnaire didn't waste time on self-pity.

"Is it true about the poison water, *tasawa*?" Jabber asked.

Tavi thought about it for a moment before nodding.

Jabber whistled softly. "So why they call it Overdark? Is that the district name?"

"It's what we called it," Tavi replied, his mind drifting back to the world which had birthed him. There were many painful memories there, ones he hadn't known would hurt him later. He simply had been too ignorant of how horrifying his life had been before the Legion. Leaving Overdark, Myrkyma as a whole, had changed him more than he ever would have believed before. "Outsiders called my city Syngaard. That's how we knew they were from somewhere else.

Everyone local called it Overdark because... well, the cities are built to go down into the planet's crust. Just beneath the surface, the water is tainted, poison. Water seeps through the rock and drips down onto the cities, like a rain. But the deeper down you lived, the better life gets, the wealthier. It was safer. Water purifiers worked better. Geothermal energy was more abundant deeper down. It was... the Tyrants ruled there, but... in some ways? It was better. Others, not so much."

"Better?" Jabber shook his head. "Too deep for me, *ke*. I need trees, sunlight. No sky?"

"First time I saw the sky, I panicked." The memory was one of the few shameful moments in his admittedly short life. He'd never imagined anything so big and endless in his entire life, yet staring up at the poisonous green skies of Myrkyma, where the roiling clouds went on for as far as the eye could see, and the constant, tainted rain smacking incessantly on the windows of the launch shuttle, had caused him to grab the arm of Sergeant Buckholz to help steady himself. To his credit, the stalwart sergeant hadn't said a word about it, nor had he brought it up once they were safely ensconced inside the transport ship which would return the entire Protectorate's embassy staff and Legion recruiters to Mars Primus. For that alone, Tavi owed him everything. "It was too much. It took me a long time to get used to it. But now I look up and see beauty. Life. Different than what's in Overdark."

"Death everywhere," Jabber stated, though he did so with a smile.

"Death everywhere," Tavi agreed. "But still, beauty."

"You scare me a little, *tasawa*. You're not afraid of dying."

"No," Tavi responded with a shrug. "I've never been afraid of dying. Growing up, I wasn't afraid of anything because I didn't know I was supposed to be. Not until they came for me, the revolutionaries. The new *protectors* of Myrkyma. Now? I'm afraid of everything I do being meaningless. I didn't realize it until I joined the Legion, but I don't want to be forgotten. So... I want to be the best legionnaire possible. I want to matter. I want to be *remembered*."

Jabber opened his mouth to respond, but Sergeant Ord's voice cut off the discussion abruptly.

"*Team Two, Ordo. I just received word from reliable sources that your civvies need to move deeper into the jungle one klick due east to look at... flower samples. Proceed to marked point two-five on your* maps. You need to be there within seven minutes. Clock's ticking, Team Two. Don't dawdle along the way. Ordo out."

"Team Two copies. Shit." Pigeon looked at the weighted bags piled up next to the tree. "All right, you heard the sergeant. Grab your civvie and let's haul ass."

"This here some bullshit, *tasawa*," Jabber muttered to Tavi as he scooped up his heavy bag and looked around. The bag was *still* perfectly positioned to make carrying his rifle uncomfortable. No matter what he did, nothing changed this. "He's punishing us for something that was for the best of the squad, *keiche*? But oh, we need to be on some shit list because *somebody* didn't know how to work with us. Stupid *balara* piece of worthless garbage. I hope his pecker falls off if he ever gets a woman."

Tavi just shouldered his bag. Once again the CCR-95 banged painfully against his hip. The armor absorbed most of the impact, but he still felt it. The non-Newtonian fluid which was the basis of the armor's individual cells stopped a lot, but one still felt the impacts. Lessons learned while at ACS reminded Tavi that at least he wasn't getting shot at.

"Well, they're not as heavy as the real civilians probably are," Tavi pointed out. "The professor is not a small man."

"You seen the civvies?" Krawdaddy asked.

"All five of them," Tavi confirmed. "Their boss is some sort of professor or doctor or something. I don't know. I thought doctors were all about medical stuff."

"Ah. You met an academic," Pigeon said as they tromped as fast as they could through the jungle. Around them, they could hear faint animal noises as birds and other creatures lingered in the lower branches. Tavi had to resist the urge to remove his helmet to take in the air. The canned air of the suit grew boring over time, even if it was safe for weeks on end.

"Academic?" Tavi asked as he pushed aside a branch and held it so Jabber didn't get smacked with it when he passed. The big man, though, released it the minute he was clear and the branch slapped Vixen in the stomach.

"Hey!"

"Sorry, *tollejo*. Didn't see you there."

"An academic," Pigeon continued, ignoring the byplay behind him, "is usually someone who teaches at a university. Medical doctors go to school to become doctors who treat sick people, usually. Academics usually go to school to continue studying a specialization in something that is... hmm, how to put this? Random studies?"

"I don't understand," Tavi admitted.

"I'm doing a poor job of explaining this," Pigeon stated. "Think smart guys who study obscure things, I guess."

"*Tasawa*... them academics demand you call them doctor, but medical doctors usually want you to call them by their name, *ke*?"

Tavi's head swam. The more they tried to explain, the worse it became. Fortunately for him, Vixen saved the day.

"So who else was with the academic?"

"Four people," Tavi replied instantly. "Two men and two women. They were his assistants or something."

"Sounds like a right pompous sort of academic, probably used to his stuffy office and not actual work," Krawdaddy muttered as he kicked a stone. It bounced along the small game trail and rolled under a bush.

"Any of the women single?" Vixen asked, suddenly more interested than before.

"Any of them *cute*?" Krawdaddy pressed as he climbed over a fallen log. "Shit. Careful. Almost stepped on a nettlebush."

"I don't care if they're cute," Vixen countered. "Are they single, or about to be single, or really not caring about their relationship back home, or do you think they simply have daddy issues which need to be worked out with a young, enterprising, and rakishly good-looking legionnaire?"

"*Fech!* Dial it back, *balara*," Jabber snapped. "Don't go scaring the kid before he gets to the good stuff."

An image of the professor's younger assistant flashed through Tavi's mind. Embarrassed, he shoved the memory away and focused on not stepping on the nettlebush. The prickly leaves were known to shoot needlelike projectiles hundreds of feet when disturbed. The HCS *should* protect them from the worst of it, but Tavi didn't want to borrow trouble. "I guess they're pretty?"

"Pretty-pretty, or good-personality pretty?" Vixen asked. Seeing Tavi's confused look inside his helmet, he smiled. "I speak chick talk. I know things."

"Except how not to catch the Grendel fungal..." Krawdaddy muttered *sotto voce* as he walked past and took the lead.

"Pick up the pace. Still have a half klick to go and we only have four minutes left," Pigeon interrupted. "Vixen, stow the fake creepy shit. We know you're just trying to make the cherry nervous. Besides, you're not allowed that far forward on the ship. You stay away from those civvies, Vixen, or Ordo's gonna make your life hell. Well, more than he already does."

"Is that possible?" Jabber asked.

"Ah, but what if they can't stay away from me?" Vixen crooned.

"Then we tell 'em about that time at Bimini Bay," Krawdaddy replied, chuckling. "And how much you paid... three times. And what you walked away with. Heh. The doc sure was *upset*..."

"You guys are *fech*."

In spite of the suit's stay-cool design and functionality, Tavi was starting to sweat profusely. The HCS was great for fighting and maneuvering in the heat, but in humidity like Sagetnam offered... he was sweating in places he didn't even know he could. None of the others seemed bothered, though, so he kept his mouth shut and continued to move through the brush, keeping a careful eye on his bag to ensure his "civilian" didn't get a stick or something stabbed through it. He had a sinking feeling they'd be graded not only on if they made it in time, but on the condition of the bag as well.

"You good, *tasawa*?" Jabber asked as he sidled up beside him. "Your civvie looks chunky."

"I'm good," Tavi responded as he shifted the bag on his shoulder to the other side. His right shoulder was starting to ache. Once again the rifle slammed into his hip. Ignoring the jolt, he focused on the path ahead. "Just hard to balance this thing with my rifle. You think the sergeant's going to mark us on the condition the bags'll be when we get there?"

"*Pokerro*. I didn't think about that. Pigeon, you hear that?"

"Yeah," the team leader acknowledged. "Didn't think about that myself. Should have. Sergeant's sneaky that way. Team Two, quit your yakking. Tertiary concern—take care of your bags. Don't let them get punctured or cut or anything."

"Pigeon, at point two-five now," Krawdaddy said from up ahead as he stopped in the middle of a small clearing within the jungle. "No sign of... flowers?"

"Ordo, Team Two." The team leader shifted his bag and set it down next to a small tree stump. "At point two-five now. Civvies are unharmed but relatively unhappy about having their fat asses hauled across the jungle on the backs of magnificent legionnaires. Copy, over."

"*Ordo copies unhappy civvies. Maybe in the future, other teams will learn a valuable lesson about other ways to get someone out of their fire team at the hands of those magnificent legionnaires,*" Ordo said, amusement in his tone evident over the comms. "*Hold position there. Your civvies are complaining and need another potty break, over.*"

"Copy potty break, over," Pigeon said, his voice strained. Switching frequencies, his next broadcast was for the team only. "Vixen, you piece of shit. He's using us to make an example for the other fire teams."

"Hey! How was I supposed to know Morty would go screaming to the old man?" Vixen whined as he set his bag down next to Pigeon's. "We never take problems directly to the LT! It's called the chain of command for a damned reason!"

"Morty must have missed that memo when you put itchy powder in his HCS!" Pigeon snapped.

Tavi set his bag down and stretched out his back. Grateful the oddly weighted bag was off his shoulder, he began to inspect his and the others for any sign of tears or punctures. The others continued their debate—which, to Tavi's ears at least, sounded almost rehearsed.

"He totally deserved it though!" Vixen protested.

"What about the reticulated Marsworm in his bunk?"

"Little bitch earned that one..."

"Filling his mattress with lard you stole from the mess deck?"

"Oh, come on. After what *he* did? What I did was at least funny."

"I'll give you that. It *was* pretty damn funny. The smell? Not so much. But...you knew the *real* reason he left would come back to bite us eventually," Pigeon reminded him. He turned and looked at the bags gathered on the ground. "Tavi! How're the civvies?"

"Looking good, Specialist. They're not complaining at all."

"Stow that rank shit for when we're back on the ship, Tavi. We have drop names for a reason. Down here in the mud we use them. Get me?"

"Got you...Pigeon."

"Good lad. Vixen! Scout the surrounding area. I have a feeling we're going to be asked to 'assist' the civilians in their search," Pigeon ordered. "Fire Teams One, Three, this is Pigeon. Confirm perimeter around point two-five, copy?"

Silence was the only response. He tried a second time with the same result. Grunting in annoyance, the team leader looked around. "Shit. Sergeant's gonna make us work a little harder today. Everyone fall back on their bag. That means you too, Vixen. Tavi? Time to show me just how good an ACS Distinguished Graduate really is. Recon out, fifty yards, expanding circle patrol. Tell me what you see. Krawdaddy, watch his civvie. Everyone else, eyes out."

"Copy," Tavi grunted and looked at Krawdaddy. The older legionnaire smiled at him.

"I'll protect her with my life," he said in a solemn tone as he gently patted the bag. Tavi snorted, trying not to laugh, and moved back into the jungle just beyond their little clearing.

In the jungle without his cumbersome bag weighing him down, Tavi finally was able to put to use his training to sweep the area, his rifle pointed down but at the ready as he moved. Surviving in Overdark had taught him to tread carefully through dark alleys to avoid blades or worse. Making it through ACS had honed his survival skills to a fine point. The shadows, the near-space between light and death, were his preferred moving grounds. With the full capabilities of the hamatic combat suit at his disposal, Tavi was a ghost as he moved around point two-five in a slow, careful circle.

Each step was measured. Only the noisy ones walked heel-toe, and noisy legionnaires were dead ones. Any dried or dead leaves he carefully avoided, sticks on the ground were stepped over. Instead of pushing low-hanging branches out of his face, he twisted under them. The birds and animals barely noticed his passing as he ranged around point two-five, looking for anything suspicious or out of place. His small, slight form was perfect for moving through thick foliage without being seen or disturbing the surroundings.

As he moved carefully through the undergrowth, he began to understand just what Jabber had meant when he called his world a beautiful but feral place. Much of the jungle of the training grounds had been imported from elsewhere during terraforming, but not all. In spite of the heat and humidity, Tavi supposed he could live on a world such as this after his time in the Legion was served.

Then he saw the trap.

It wasn't much of one, a simple tripwire with a mine resting at the base of a tree and a smoke grenade beneath it, but it would have been enough to completely wipe out the small fire team had they come this way. While the mine was a dummy and was set to simply pop red smoke had they tripped it, it would have been enough to cause their team to fail the exercise. Somebody was being devious.

"Pigeon, Tavi." He commed in over the team's private channel, then paused. He looked back down at the dummy mine, unsure. Was it a leftover from a prior training exercise? The Legion *did* regularly use Sagetnam for training purposes. However, a legionnaire *never* made assumptions. It was one of the sacred tenets of the Legion—assumptions made an ass out of everyone. "Found something. Tripwire, dummy mine, with training grenade. OpFor in area?"

"Not that I'm aware," Pigeon muttered. *"If there is, Ordo must really be pissed off at us. Okay, let's assume we're dealing with oppositional forces and not simple, mindless wild animals who happen to have opposable thumbs and a working knowledge of combat engineering for a second. Fire Teams One and Three are nonresponsive. I'm open to suggestions."*

Tavi looked around. He couldn't see anybody, but that meant nothing in an environment like this. The hamatic suits had been designed for precisely this sort of environment, where their skin could molt and shift in color and light to perfectly blend into a surrounding area where sunlight changed within a few steps. In the clearing, he could see the patrol fanning out, keeping their weapons on standby. They were filled with training rounds, so while someone felt it when they were shot, it was still no more than taking a hard hit.

The "civilians" were safely in the center of their quasi-protective ring near the downed logs. If someone—or something—came for them, they'd have to face down the entirety of Team Two in order to achieve their goal. The position wasn't great, with lots of cover and concealment for any opposing forces, but the downed logs could provide some cover.

Which suggested the trap wasn't just a random leftover. They had been herded here by Sergeant Ord, after all.

"Can we . . . I mean, are we allowed to call in CAS?" Tavi asked in a quiet voice. Someone giggled. He wasn't sure if it was Krawdaddy or Vixen, because both of their indicators lit up simultaneously on his

HUD. Struggling for words, Tavi continued. "Um...Bronze Raven Four's up there anyways, and nobody said we couldn't during the briefing..."

"*Heh. I like it. Your idea, Tavi. You get to call it,*" Pigeon said after a moment. Tavi swallowed nervously. This was definitely outside the expected wheelhouse. Yet at the same time, he would have to do it eventually. Might as well be during his first training exercise with the Bronze.

He changed frequencies. "Bronze Raven Four, Bronze Raven Four, this is Fire Team Two. Copy, over."

"*Fire Team Two, Bronze Raven Four copies. Go ahead.*"

"Bronze Raven Four, requesting close air support around point two-five, one hundred yards out. Simulated potential hostiles surrounding Team Two's position."

There was silence on the comms for a few seconds, and Tavi began to wonder if he'd screwed something up. Were they breaking the rules of the exercise? Really, nobody had ever said they *couldn't* use their Rhinos as close air support, and he'd seen the door gunners of the airships. The dropships were up there, just circling, idling away. Before he could really start to worry, though, the smooth voice of Bronze Raven Four responded.

"*Confirm close air support on point two-five, Team Two. ETA one-five seconds. Clear the area.*"

Tavi backed away from the trap and headed back to point two-five as quickly and quietly as he could. Overhead he could faintly hear the roar of the Rhino's engines as power was poured into them. Looking up, Tavi got a glimpse of black and gray as it descended from on high.

"*General broadcast, general broadcast,*" Bronze Raven Four's call went out to every single comms device in the exercise area, the smoky contralto of the radio operator at odds with the fury the Rhino was bringing to the table. Every head on Team Two turned and looked skyward as the Rhino screamed low overhead, barely clearing the treetops, before banking sharply to the left and disappearing from view once more. "*Simulated strafing run around point two-five, one hundred yards out, and circling. Any and all OpFor in the area are considered dead. Real live-fire exercise commencing in one minute on grid one-one-seven-four-four-five. Repeat, live-fire exercise commencing in one minute on grid one-one-seven-four-four-five. Clear the area.*"

"*Motherfucker!*" an unfamiliar voice screamed over the comms. "*You cheated!*"

"There is no cheating in war... only the will to do what it takes to win," Tavi muttered quietly under his breath. The Tyrant responsible for his genetics had said that to him many times. Unfortunately for him, the comms easily picked it up and broadcast it across the entire exercise for all to hear.

"Damn, Tavi. That was *cold*." Pigeon chuckled once the laughter died down. "I like it, though. A lot. Good call on the CAS, by the way. That should make Ordo's day. Let's sit back and watch the rain."

Tavi found a small log to sit down on and watch as the Rhino above began to spit fiery death down upon a nearby section of the dense jungle, the tracers from the gunners rounds appearing like lasers as they fired. The noise split the air, ripping through the space between them with purpose and hate. The Rhino began to smoothly maneuver in a figure eight pattern, with each door gunner taking turns laying down a steady stream of fire while the dropship's chin-mounted railgun seemed perfect for tree trimming and general destruction.

After two passes the nose of the Rhino abruptly pitched up and the ship clawed for altitude. Behind it, white flares so bright they defeated the helmet filters were ejected from the rear of the Rhino, creating a winged pattern. Blinding strobes of light filled his eyes. The flares dissipated and, when Tavi's vision finally returned to normal, there was no sign of the Rhino anywhere.

"Not sure who was flying that bird, but that was one badass bitch," Vixen murmured happily. Tavi nodded in agreement. "Smart money's on Blue, though."

"*Team Two, Ordo. Terminate exercise. Good work. You might earn your way back into my good graces yet—if my civilians are undamaged and unharmed. I will be inspecting them. Using the Rhino was the right call. Extraction in five minutes on your location. Don't forget to bring your civvies home. Debrief at FOB Four at sixteen hundred hours. Ordo out.*"

"Team Two copies extraction," Pigeon confirmed. "Two, out."

"Hell yeah! Good work, Tavi!" Vixen crowed and smacked him on the shoulder, nearly knocking him off his log. "We're going to be out of here in a hurry, and we can enjoy the nightlife of Sagetnam!"

"Early?" Tavi asked as he rebalanced himself. "What do you mean?"

"Debriefing before chow means we're getting all the love, *tasawa*, and early liberty call," Jabber explained. "Question is whether we get a muster liberty, or only midnight."

Tavi nodded, not really caring when they had to report back in. Liberty call meant potentially getting to stay topside on a planet, to breathe the air, not worry about toxic water dripping onto his bare skin, and see another sunset. Best of all? It would be a sunset on an entirely new world. Even if they had to be back by midnight and all he could do was watch the sunset, he would be happy.

Which was something he'd never really thought about before the Legion.

Happiness, that is.

CHAPTER FIVE
Ill Met by Whiskey and Moonlight

POTEYAN DISTRICT, SAGETNAM, ANAT SYSTEM

Sitting quietly near the end of the pier, Tavi felt at peace as he watched the sun begin to kiss the very edge of the horizon, his eyes shifting between the sunset and the slate in his hand. He was reading the book the young woman had mentioned previously, *Reptiles Across the Stars*, and was thoroughly enjoying it. There was just something fascinating about the prospect of *learning*.

It was also a small distraction. He found it disconcerting to be staring out at the endless expanse of the sea, especially with the wide-open sky above, but the sight was too alluring for Tavi to quit and walk away. Flashes of purple, oranges, and blues caused the sky to look aflame as the light reflected off distant clouds.

He knew he would never grow tired of watching a sunset, no matter where it was. Nor would he ever grow weary of the calm such beauty brought him.

One of the more interesting features of Sagetnam was the low-lying salt marshes which dotted the area around the training grounds and the Legion base attached to it. Like all places throughout human history when a constant military presence had been established, a small city had sprung up around the base. The salt marshes were a byproduct of ground at the edges of both the base and the city district where he found himself at. There were more bars in this particular district than the rest of the planet combined.

And that was before the other various nightlife activities offered magically appeared...

None of this intrigued Tavi, though. None of the women who pranced around him garnered his attention for more than a few moments. Growing up in one of the worst areas of Overdark, he'd been quickly inured to the salacious offerings of various brothels and nightclubs. He'd avoided the worst, found the few which had offered scraps after closing to the orphaned and homeless kids living on the streets, and had stuck close to the places his mother had worked before her death. Given what his mother had done—and how he himself had come into being—there was almost zero chance of him enjoying that sort of entertainment.

Plus, as much as he liked his new squadmates, sometimes he simply preferred to be alone with a book. The end of a dock, jutting out into the bay and facing west, gave him the peace and solitude he was searching for.

"Tavi? Private Tavi?"

So much for peace and solitude.

Withholding a heavy sigh, he half turned to see who was interrupting his moment alone. He blinked in surprise. The diminutive civilian he'd helped back on board the *Perseverance*—had it only been a day, he wondered—Mitzi Wingo, was standing ten feet behind him, her hands behind her back. She was standing awkwardly, as though she had been aware of his desire to be alone but, at the same time, wanted to speak with him.

Her eyes drifted to the slate and a brief flicker of something—*surprise?*—flashed across them. She gave him a smile.

It was odd. Why would she bother with him?

"Ma'am?" Tavi said, pulling himself to his feet quickly and sliding the slate into his pocket. Though not in uniform, he had to force himself not to brace to attention. Both Basic and ACS had been adamant about how to treat civilian superiors. Uncomfortable, he tried to smooth his shirt and slacks. He hadn't really thought about purchasing new clothes since joining the Legion—something he never would have considered a year before—but Sergeant Ord had demanded he buy basic civilian clothing for liberty calls. He had, albeit with great reluctance, picked up some of the cheapest and most basic button-down collared shirts he could find—black slacks and a simple, sky-blue button shirt.

He'd refused to purchase new shoes. His service boots would do just fine.

"Why are you out here, alone?" she asked, her voice filled with concern. Tavi cocked his head.

"I'm sorry, ma'am. I... my shore buddy is in the bar, and I just wanted... not a fan of bars... I like sunsets," he finished, feeling rather silly.

She smiled kindly at him and brushed her hair away from her face. For the first time he realized her glasses were *techie* glasses, capable of connecting directly to her slate and displaying information only the wearer could see. They were uncommon in Overdark—or anywhere on Myrkyma for that matter.

"I was just wondering why you were alone."

He nodded. "You're right, ma'am. I should be with Jabber. I'm sorry—"

"Stop, please." She held up a hand, palm out. "Stop apologizing. And please, call me Mitzi, not ma'am. I'm not that much older than you."

"Yes ma—ah, Mitzi. Miss? Miss Mitzi."

"No, just... *argh*. Never mind. I've met legionnaires before," she said in a quiet voice, her gaze drifting out towards the sea. "Our village on Mars Primus is popular with legionnaires who've earned their citizenship, and half the population are military vets, either legionnaires or otherwise. They all act like normal people. But you? You act different."

"Yes, ma'am," he responded automatically.

"Mitzi."

"Yes... Mitzi." The word felt wrong in his mouth.

"Better." She stepped closer. "Weird isn't the right word I'd use, though. Young. Definitely young, younger than me. But you seem... I don't know. Older? Where are you from? You're not from any of the Protectorate worlds, are you?"

"No, miss."

She waited expectantly for him to continue, but she was rewarded only with silence. She had asked him a yes or no question, after all. Tavi was not one to volunteer information, something which had endeared him to his drill instructors not too long before. After a minute she exhaled.

"Nothing more? It's like pulling teeth with you, isn't it? Fine. Private Tavi, what world are you from?"

"Myrkyma, miss."

"Well, *miss* is definitely better than ma'am," she said before pursing her lips, a thoughtful expression on her intelligent features. "Myrkyma... toxic-rainfall world, stage-two terraforming, another forty years until stage three is attained and people can live topside, underground hive cities make up the majority of the settlements, colonized almost a century ago, ruled by the Tyrants until about a year ago. Not a member of the Protectorate. Interesting. You joined a year ago, didn't you?"

Tavi nodded, his mouth dry. She knew more about his homeworld than he did. "Less than that, miss."

"Are *you* a Tyrant?" she asked, curious. He recoiled suddenly, caught off guard.

"Yes, miss." His voice came out in a bare whisper. "Half. A bastard of one, at least."

Mitzi didn't seem put off by either his Tyrant or bastard status.

"Interesting. Tyrant blood has fascinating properties. They've experimented with so much genetic tinkering that some studies argue that they aren't even baseline human anymore, but something else," she said, as she stepped closer and lifted his chin with her hand. She began to slowly inspect his features, seemingly unaware of how uncomfortable the inspection was making him. "Huh. You have aquiline features like people from Lorraine, but your eyes and nose are reminiscent of Teutonwelt. So you're a terrific clinical study of the transitive properties of Tyrant genetics and regular, boring old human. Fascinating. I wonder what traits you'll develop and exhibit as you grow older."

"They said I'd grow taller, miss," he stated lamely. He had no idea why she'd stopped and talked to him in the first place, and her presence filled him with a growing nervousness. She nodded.

"As expected. The shortest Tyrant on record is almost seven feet tall."

"How do you *know* all this stuff?" Astonished, he forgot to add on the honorific. However, either Mitzi hadn't noticed, or didn't care.

"Child prodigy, remember? I read *everything*."

"Oh. Right. You said that before, miss."

"You joined the Legion to avoid the riots, didn't you? Or rather, the fallout during the revolutions," she continued, letting his face drop once more. "It's okay. I would have, too. Dying is scary."

"I'm not afraid of dying, miss."

"Want to know a secret?" she asked him. "It's not death anybody is afraid of. It's reconciliation with how they lived their life. Whether it's in their bed, facing death as an old and feeble person, or alone on a battlefield, or in some misbegotten back alley with a knife in their back. Religious or not, doesn't matter. At the end, when staring Death in the eye, we always wonder... did we live a life worth living?"

Tavi shrugged. He didn't know what to say, so he said nothing. The Legion had simply enforced his own hard-learned belief that it was better to be silent and thought a fool than opening his mouth and confirming it.

"So what do *you* want, Tavi?" she asked him, her piercing gaze lingering on him for a moment before it slid away and off into the distant horizon. "What do you want out of this life?"

"To be the best legionnaire possible," he responded immediately as his promise to Sergeant Buckholz came to mind. "To defend the weak and protect the innocent, to obey all lawfully given orders, and uphold the ideals of the Legion. I made an oath. I intend to live by it, miss."

"Admirable. But unfulfilling, I think. There's more to life than that."

Tavi shrugged and bit his cheek, not sure where she was trying to go with the conversation. Many times at Basic he'd been questioned by seemingly irate drill instructors who'd been doing their best to try and rattle him. After growing up in Overdark, however, the drill instructors really hadn't managed to rattle him much. Sure, the push-ups and running had been hard work, but the mental toughness the Legion demanded of him in Basic had been easy enough to achieve.

Mitzi, however, continued to rattle him. He didn't understand why she had that effect on him.

"How, miss?" He idly scratched his chin. The bugs were starting to come out in force, and he felt as though their menu consisted of only him. "I get fed, they give me a bed to sleep in, and they took me out of Overdark, away from Myrkyma. I never have to go back. Seems pretty fulfilling to me, if the word means what I think it means."

"I'm just saying that there's more to life you should experience before you shuffle off this mortal coil," she said, frustration evident in her voice. Tavi wondered why. She wheeled on her heel and started back the way she came. Halfway down the pier, though, she stopped and looked back at him. "If you go through life simply existing, are you really making the most of the chance you were given? You wanted off your world, and you got it. When you're old, do you want to look back at your life and regret? Or do you want to see the amazing adventures you had, the friends you made, the people you came to love? I know what I want...and I think it involves a drink. I don't know. Never drank before. Not old enough on Mars Primus. But out here the laws are different. People are different. I've never been in a bar before, actually. But still...I want to meet people and become friends, maybe see the universe, and make important discoveries which can help humanity. But what do *you* want?"

With that, she continued on her way.

Tavi was torn. He knew an invitation when he heard one. Still, the salt in the air and the flashes of colors in the sky called to him. Loneliness had been his life for so long that being close to someone was a terrifying thought. But at the same time, what if it wasn't so bad? Did he want to be alone at the end, or did he want to be surrounded by people who liked him?

He watched as the very last remnants of Sagetnam's sun dipped below the horizon, the sight once more filling him with a steadying calm he'd been lacking before joining the Legion. Perhaps Mitzi was right. She had, after all, already seen more places than he ever could hope. The woman was also smarter than he was by an insurmountable margin. Perhaps he should go inside and be with the others.

He might even enjoy it.

He blinked as a sudden blue flash rippled across the horizon. It was gone almost as soon as his brain registered the strange light. Smiling, he recalled when the dripping poisonous rain in Overdark would sometimes catch an exposed power conduit, creating a light very similar to what he'd seen. In Overdark, this was a good omen. Why shouldn't powerful omens carry over to other planets?

Another insect bit his wrist. The last flicker of indecision disappeared in a bloody welt.

Heaving a sigh, he walked down the pier and headed toward the bar it was connected to. He would go and see for himself if there really was anything more than just being the best legionnaire possible—even if it was inside a bar he really had no interest in. He doubted she was right, but Mitzi had seemed pretty insistent.

Hopefully this effort at... whatever *this* was, wouldn't end too horribly.

Blue was having a *great* night.

Her debrief with Twister had gone well and left her feeling confident in her abilities. The more experienced pilot had broken down the things she could've done better, explained *how* to do them better, and went over a few EPs with her that she might run into on her upgrade flight. And then Twister had cut her loose to go enjoy Sagetnam's nightlife. Cut them both loose, really. The silver-streaked blonde had ridden down on the same shuttle before disappearing into the twisting streets of Yortugan Bay with Witch and their best friend, Captain Brandy "Medusa" Newkirk.

As with any place where the economy was centered on entertainment and fleecing as much money out of the Legion and Navy as possible, there were safe places and not so safe places. Jam packed with bars, restaurants and street vendors, and dance clubs of every type, Yortugan Bay was not for the unwary.

The older Ravens were a formidable trio though, and well armed. Blue pitied any locals who got in their way. Locals they didn't want in their way, that is, because those three were definitely on the hunt.

Blue smirked. *And more power to them.*

It wasn't like she wasn't hunting too—though in Blue's case she knew exactly who her prey was. Before she'd bounced off to drink with a handful of other Raven copilots, Killi had given her a pointed glare. Blue had just winked, and Killi had rolled her eyes before slinging her arm around Ruby and promising her a fantastic first time at Yortugan. Chuckling, Blue hoped their young companion knew what kind of night she was in for and headed to Gunrunner's to meet up with Campbell.

Popular with both the Legion and the Navy, Gunrunner's had reasonable drinks, good music, and surprisingly outstanding food. Half of it was an open patio, with party lights strung over the expansive area and old-fashioned torches casting a flickering glow across the picnic-style scarred wooden tables. With its strategically placed palm trees, rum barrels, and skull-and-crossbones motif, the place leaned heavily into the tropical-island theme popular in this section of the city. Inside followed the same decorating scheme, with the addition of dark wood paneling, high ceilings with lazily spinning antique fans, and a bar that stretched across the entire back wall.

As she walked through the open doors, the roar of countless conversations hit her like a wall of noise. She didn't pause to adjust. Even here, where she expected there were plenty of legionnaires to back her up should she need it, she wouldn't show weakness. Hesitation was an invitation for trouble, even as well armed as she was. So she kept her shoulders back, her eyes up, and strode inside like she owned the place.

Blue breathed in the layered scents of spicy rum, rich food, and warm bodies and let a smile tug at her lips. Out of every bar she'd been to in Yortugan Bay, this was her favorite by far. She sauntered across the slightly sticky wood floor and threaded around the packed tables, allowing her hips to sway to the hypnotic beat of the music as she searched for Campbell.

She wasn't so lost to the hunt that she failed to maintain situational awareness as she worked her way through the crowd. Or failed to notice *her* legionnaires bunched at the far end of the bar. She heard Jabber first, that distinctive accent of his cutting through the noise as effectively as the battlefield bellow of a sergeant. Vixen was in the thick of things, and she wondered how the man had managed to clean her Rhino so quickly. Then she noticed Tavi wasn't there. Now thoroughly distracted, she scowled at Vixen. If that shit had stuck Tavi with his cleaning duties, she'd have a word with Sergeant Ord.

Full of righteous fury, she cast a quick look around and found Ordo at a table adjacent to the bar, a piping hot steak in front of him and a frosty beer mug next to the wide plate. She'd known the sergeant for a year now, and she could never predict what he'd do on shore leave. Sometimes he casually drank with his boys, at least to start the night before leaving them to their own devices. Sometimes he tore it up with the other NCOs. Most nights out, he was doing exactly what he was doing now—enjoying a meal not cooked by the Navy mess chefs and observing the festivities without joining in directly.

His gaze briefly met hers, and she caught a flicker of the steel hidden beneath the lazy mask. She dipped her chin in a respectful nod and amended her thoughts as if he could hear them.

Privately. She'd have a word with him about Vixen *privately*.

A rush of warm air laden with brine swirled inside as somebody opened a side door, the one that led to the back deck and the long dock stretching out into the tropical waters. She caught a glimpse of small figures at the end of the dock and wondered if one of them was Tavi. For Vixen's sake, it better be.

And then Krawdaddy noticed her and roared a greeting echoed by the rest of the squad.

Inwardly, she groaned, but just as quickly she shrugged it off and gave them a casual wave as she strode past without slowing. Since they weren't in her chain of command, it didn't matter in the least if they saw her having a good time.

And she intended to have a *very* good time.

Dismissing her legionnaires from her thoughts, she resumed the search for her date. A boisterous mixed group of legionnaires and local girls abandoned their table for the scuffed dance floor, and she finally found Campbell, or maybe he found her. His gaze locked onto hers. He'd secured a table in the quieter section adjacent to the rowdy bar crowded with thirsty legionnaires and scattered bar stools, not too far from Ordo, in fact. A warm thrill shot through her when he braced one elbow on the table and gave her that charming smile, the one that promised *all* the trouble and no regrets.

Those soulful dark brown eyes held her attention as she sauntered over to his table. Killi's admonishment to make him chase her rang in her ears as she slid into the empty chair across from him, but Blue had never been great at playing those kinds of games, long or otherwise. Her grandmother had taught her to go after what she wanted, and both Blue and her libido were in absolute agreement that what she currently wanted was Garrett "Ensign Hotness" Campbell.

Blue had planned to wear a skirt for *reasons*, but Killi had vetoed the idea before she'd done more than held up the silky material. Her bestie had snarled something about "no easy access for Ensign Hotness" and thrust a pair of skintight jeans into Blue's face. She had to admit, they did great things for her ass and paired perfectly with her favorite pair of black low-heeled boots. They were her favorite because while they might look fashionable, they were as comfortable as her combat boots and just as effective if she had to run... or kick someone in the balls.

She raked an appreciative gaze over Campbell. Not that she planned to *kick* him in the balls. The man was far too hot for his own good, especially out of uniform and in a black button-up with the sleeves rolled up to expose muscled forearms. He also seemed to appreciate her choice in off-duty clothes, especially her low-cut blue crop top. She'd thrown a gauzy short-sleeved blouse on top and left it unbuttoned.

"I was beginning to wonder if you stood me up," Campbell murmured, amusement dancing in his eyes as if the thought of anyone standing him up was hilarious.

There was a half-full whiskey glass in front of him. He slid a second glass to her with a challenging grin.

"Debrief ran late. Should I be insulted that you ordered for me?" Blue raised her glass and swirled the rich amber liquid gently. Her eyebrows rose at the familiar earthy scent undercut with the perfect amount of vanilla and butterscotch. "Or impressed you know my favorite whiskey?"

Campbell shrugged easily. "It's crowded tonight, and I was taught never to leave a lady waiting—not even for a drink. I figured at worst I'd have an extra whiskey."

The table was small enough that their legs brushed together. Blue bit back a smile and leaned her elbows on the table. His gaze dipped exactly where she wanted it before he dragged it back up. And took his time about it.

"And at best?" she purred.

His voice dropped low. "I'd have impressed you."

Blue straightened back up and allowed her smile to break free. "It'll take more than a little stalking to impress me, Navy boy."

Over Campbell's shoulder, the side door to the back deck opened again and the little mousy assistant to Mister High and Mighty scientist crept inside the bar—and did everything wrong. She hesitated, she looked around with a helpless expression, she jumped when a rowdy group of legionnaires roared in laughter. Scuttling past them, she hesitated again next to a group of drunken locals. Blue tensed, but then Tavi walked in after her. The little mouse would be fine.

"I'll have to try harder then," Campbell teased.

"That's what he said." She raised her glass with an impish grin as Campbell laughed.

The whiskey had barely kissed her lips when one of the locals slurred something unintelligible and grabbed the little mouse's ass. He then pulled her in closer and tried to kiss her. Instead of screaming obscenities at him and slapping him, the little mouse froze in terror. Nearby, fury washed over Tavi's young face as he saw the woman being accosted. It then snapped into that hard expression she'd seen once before.

"Oh, *shit*." Blue froze for half a heartbeat before she tipped her glass up and drained it, the alcohol burning a path straight to her belly. Slightly sacrilegious to treat good whiskey in that manner, but she had a feeling if she didn't drink it now, she wouldn't get the chance later. She carefully set her empty glass back down with the smokey sweet taste lingering on her tongue and a strange mix of dread and anticipation rising in her gut. Slowly, she licked the last of the whiskey from her lips and met Campbell's curious and very heated gaze. "This ought to be good."

Five seconds later, all hell broke loose.

CHAPTER SIX
I Just Came for a Good Time

GUNRUNNER'S BAR, POTEYAN DISTRICT, SAGETNAM, ANAT SYSTEM

The pier-side entrance gate to the bar Mitzi had disappeared through—a place called Gunrunner's, Tavi noticed—was clear of the usual homeless kids who'd lurked outside the back entrances of similar places back in Overdark, which was a bit of a surprise. Nor were there any signs telling people not to linger without buying things. There was a vibe here he'd never really felt before. Curious, Tavi swung the gate open and stepped inside.

And was promptly slammed in the chest by the sheer *energy* of the place.

He spotted Mitzi, who'd paused in the middle of a cluster of bar top tables, staring around at the mass of humanity crammed into the bar. Tall tables with men and women standing around them seemed to be the norm, though there were a few with stools around them scattered throughout. The lighting was very bright, with actual torches at strategically placed locations to give certain areas a rustic charm while allowing private spaces for those who didn't want to be seen or recognized. An open-air patio was on the far side, brightly lit with more torches and strings of party lights. While the picnic tables were a nice touch, he was far more interested in where the largest group had gathered—the bar.

It was long and crowded, with a few vaguely familiar faces lined up along it. There was a healthy number of Navy and Legion personnel mixed in with the locals, most of whom probably worked at the nearby Protectorate base. More than a few looked as if they were spoiling for a fight. He'd seen many such men before, in Overdark. It was the sort of place Tavi was willing to bet the local police and constables were only too familiar with.

Tavi watched as Mitzi jumped at the sound of some legionnaires from 5th Squad roaring with laughter. Her previous confidence was gone, and now she looked about as timid and unsure as he'd been outside. She slid past the legionnaires and moved deeper into the bar. He lost sight of her for a moment and followed, not sure precisely what else to do.

Mitzi had been wrong. There was no way anything like this could be enjoyable.

"Hey, little sexy. Ever been with a real man?" a drunken voice from a nearby group of locals asked as a hand snaked out. The calloused palm fully cupped Mitzi's ass, then turned into a squeeze as he tried to bring her in close. She froze and stood still, a terrified expression on her face. The local was emboldened by this and pulled her in for a wet, drunken kiss.

Tavi felt a familiar anger course through his veins as he saw Mitzi being accosted. As quickly as the rage came, it fell away, replaced by something entirely different. Cold, calculating *clarity* washed over him as the world around him seemed to slow to a crawl. He heard, saw, felt *everything* simultaneously. Striding forward, he slid between two of the larger men who'd been in the process of turning his way.

The local assaulting Mitzi was big, much larger and more muscular than Tavi by a wide margin. His hands and fingers were stained with a faint red color, and he reeked of fabricator oil, a sure sign the man wasn't military. His face was lean and hard, and in better days had probably been considered a very handsome man. Time and hardship, combined with years of heavy alcohol use, had dulled that rugged handsomeness. Now he simply looked bitter and angry.

Not that any of this mattered to Tavi. It was mere observation now, since his next course of action had already been determined. He was already inside the man's defenses before the drunk had noticed him.

A single strike dislocated the man's elbow and the follow up shattered the wrist of the same arm. Before the man had registered the pain lancing up his arm, two more blows destroyed a kidney. Just for good measure, Tavi snapped a kick at the drunk's ankle and was rewarded with the audible *crack* of breaking bone.

While at ACS, one of Tavi's instructors had been a short, wiry legionnaire who'd seen the young teen from Myrkyma as a personal training challenge. Instead of teaching the tiny recruit the standard hand-to-hand used by normal legionnaires, he'd instructed Tavi on various techniques which better suited his slight frame. Speed and accuracy, not strength, were his allies. Knowledge of where to place a blow, to find the weak points of the human body, and punish them accordingly had been the name of their game. By the time it came time for grappling and close-combat training, Tavi was far beyond his classmates when it came to delivering the maximum amount of damage in the shortest time.

The debilitating attack had been accomplished in less than two seconds. Instructor Moops would have been proud.

Mitzi stumbled to the ground as the hand holding her suddenly fell away. The man's drinking buddy, seated next to him and somehow not noticing the entirety of the attack, reached out to grab Tavi's arm just as the screaming began.

"Hey, y—!" the uninjured local managed to get out before Tavi jabbed him, hard, just below the sternum, paralyzing the diaphragm temporarily. The shout turned into a gasp as he struggled to breathe and he fell off his stool and onto the floor, where he joined his still-shrieking pal. Tavi, not wanting to draw too much attention to the mess he'd created, kicked the screamer in the face. Blood, snot, and teeth went flying as the man was driven into unconsciousness.

A pair of arms encircled Tavi from behind. He struggled against them, but the grip was too much for him to overcome. Cursing his own inattentiveness, Tavi slammed a heel into the man's shin. He heard a grunt and then was promptly tossed through the air.

It really wasn't as far as it felt, only a few feet, but it was enough to cause him to slam through a table filled with drinks. Wood was splintered by the force of the impact, and beer, alcohol, and food went *everywhere*. Shoulder aching, Tavi rolled onto his back and stared up at the ceiling. A very concerned and familiar face filled his visage.

"Eh, *tasawa*? Need some help?"

"Hi, Jabber. Can you help me up?"

"Hey! You fuck with a legionnaire, you fuck with Legion! 4th

Squad, to me!" Vixen screamed drunkenly and threw a beer bottle at the offending local. It missed and slammed into the face of a Navy enlisted. Infuriated, the enlisted turned and slugged someone else in the jaw.

Tavi inwardly sighed.

There went his quiet evening out.

Chaos ensued.

For a short time, the bar fight *was* good and highly entertaining. Blue and Campbell were far enough from the initial fight to be clear of the action, close enough for a front row seat. After Tavi had *thoroughly* dismantled the first offender and moved on to his buddy, Campbell had scooted his chair around the table so he could watch. She could feel his body heat, his arm brushing against hers with each inhaled breath.

Blue smiled. *I'm not sad about it.*

After 4th Squad had jumped into the growing brawl, and it became clear they weren't going to get refills any time soon, Campbell had offered Blue his whiskey. She'd taken a slow sip, and then they had shared what little was left and took bets on which drunken local was going down next. They both lost when two of the locals tag-teamed to take down Vixen, but only because the burly legionnaire roared a laugh and took them both out simultaneously and eagerly looked for his next opponent.

Blue had just taken the last sip of whiskey when one of the locals made the mistake of jumping on Pigeon's back. The fire team leader grinned and launched the drunk over one shoulder. He flew an impressive distance through the air and landed on their table with a startled grunt. Surprisingly, the old high-top held up to the sudden weight, though the wood creaked alarmingly as the table rocked back and forth.

Hazy eyes landed on Blue, or more specifically, Blue's assets. Looking wouldn't have been enough to elicit a response, but the moron also thought it was acceptable to touch. Or at least, he tried. Campbell snarled and shoved the table over before the grubby hand got anywhere near her, sending the man tumbling to the sticky floor. Campbell slid off his chair and kicked him away from their feet, his eyes hard.

"Hey, asshole! We don't touch women." He glanced over his shoulder at Blue and winked. "Unless they want to be touched."

A smile stretched across Blue's face, but a glint of light on metal sent a bolt of fear through her.

"*Check six!*"

Campbell twisted around as another local thug rushed him from behind, knife raised high overhead. One arm came up to block the blade's descent, but Blue could tell he would be too slow to stop it.

Jabber wasn't too slow.

A sinewy arm corded with muscle wrapped around the thug's throat and yanked him backward. The knife slashed down with several inches to spare from Campbell's chest, cutting nothing but air. The lean legionnaire did something too fast for Blue to see, and the knife clattered to the ground. His arm tightened, and the thug choked and flailed, desperate for air.

"Now now, we don't stab people from behind. We fight fair, not like some little Navy *balara*, you *fecher*." Jabber glanced at Campbell. "No offense, *bossjna*."

"None taken," Campbell said, the tension leaving his shoulders. He arched a brow. "Are you going to let him breathe?"

By that point, the thug's face had turned an alarming shade of purple.

Jabber shrugged but released him. "If the ensign insists... will do. Only because *bossjna* said to keep things nonlethal, *ke*?"

It was possible the lack of air had destroyed brain cells, because instead of catching his breath or bowing out of the fight, the dumbass immediately tried to punch the legionnaire. Jabber knocked him out with a single blow between the eyes and then ghosted back into the brawl without so much as a farewell or "you're welcome."

God bless legionnaires, she thought.

Blue met Campbell's gaze and allowed him to see her relief that he wasn't bleeding out on the floor. The overwhelming cacophony of the spreading bar fight faded for a heartbeat, and then his eyes shifted to a point over her shoulder.

"Down!"

She dropped without hesitation. And then got a front row seat to how well the Navy trained their officers. Or maybe it was all Campbell, because it turned out Ensign Hotness was a vicious fighter. He also apparently had some aggression to work out after his near miss with the knife-wielding thug. Blue watched in appreciation as Campbell laid into the local who'd tried to sneak up on *her*, not an ounce of mercy in his expression or blows.

The thug was curled up and groaning on the floor in under five seconds. A slow smile tugged at Blue's lips as she met Campbell's fierce gaze.

"Okay, *now* I'm impressed."

He shook out his fists and grinned. "Darlin', you ain't seen nothing yet."

A pair of locals, friends of the one groaning on the floor if their slurred shouts were any indication, charged over from the churning mess that had engulfed half the bar and spilled out onto the open patio.

"You messed with the wrong gang," a whipcord lean, heavily tattooed man growled. It would have been more menacing if he wasn't slurring his words into a nearly incomprehensible mess. "Let's dance, asshole."

He launched a clumsy swing of his fist at Campbell's face, while his buddy tried to tackle Campbell—and nearly caught his friend's fist in the side of his head for his trouble. Not seeing any weapons and judging Campbell's skill far above theirs, Blue just arched a brow.

"I'm waiting." She rolled one hand. "Show me what you got, Navy boy."

He gave her a cocky smile before he turned his attention to his dance partners.

Throughout the entire brawl, Sergeant Ord hadn't done anything more than call out "nonlethal" near the beginning of the fight. After that, he'd gone back to slowly eating his steak with the manner of a man thoroughly enjoying his meal. Right up until Campbell sent one of the thugs staggering into Ordo's table. He sighed and looked up with a bored expression.

"This rare, beautifully marbled ribeye cut is an imported, real beef slab from a Grade 1A Martian steer," Ordo said in a calm, clear tone. He angled his knife delicately and the light reflected into the thug's eyes.

Blue took a hurried step back. "God damn it, Sergeant, not again! At least wait for me to get out of the splash zone."

Ordo maintained eye contact with the thug, who stared at the Legion sergeant like he was a venomous serpent he'd accidentally stepped on in his living room—wholly unexpected and utterly terrifying. His face turned bone white, and he took several careful steps back before spinning on his heel and sprinting into the brawl rather than face the sergeant.

"Fresh meat!" Vixen bellowed and chased after him with a delighted expression.

Blue shook her head in amusement and turned back to Campbell. It looked like he was having fun playing with his remaining opponent and she crossed her arms and leaned against a high-top table, ready to enjoy the show Ensign Hotness was clearly putting on for her benefit.

"Well, now," a pleased, gravelly voice called out. "Aren't you a pretty little thing."

Blue snapped her head around. Apprehension sliced through her enjoyment as she assessed the large man stalking toward her, cutting through the brawl like a lion shoving his way through the jackals. He wasn't just too big for her to easily fight—he carried himself like a man well used to taking what he wanted from those smaller and weaker. Her hand dropped to the small carry gun holstered on her right hip. The man hesitated midstride, eyes suddenly wary.

"Nonlethal, Lieutenant," Ordo reminded her in a mild but carrying tone. With a grimace, Blue released her sidearm.

The man grinned as Ordo calmly went back to eating his dinner. "Looks like you're on your own, little girl."

Blue's eyes narrowed as that twist of apprehension sharpened and adrenaline buzzed. She *was* little. And while she'd been through the same Basic Training as any other legionnaire, pilots didn't go through Advanced Combat School. She was no Tavi, who could easily take on opponents twice his size without breaking a sweat. That was okay.

She didn't need to be.

Blue reached around to the small of her back, where her gauzy blouse had hidden the narrow metal cylinder she'd clipped to her belt. With a practiced flick of her wrist, she extended the stun baton to its full length and swung it full strength into the side of the bruiser's head. He staggered but didn't go down. Instead, he launched the sort of haymaker a raw trainee could've seen coming. She ducked the blow and thrust the end of the baton into his paunchy gut and squeezed the insulated rubber handle. Thirty thousand volts of electricity traveled through his body, and his expression froze as he twitched and moaned.

"Nonlethal doesn't mean painless." She gave the twitching man a savage grin and squeezed the handle again, sending another wave of fire and pain through his nervous system. "Bitch."

Campbell, who'd brutally finished his fight the instant he'd noticed she was facing the human version of a grizzly bear, went from a frantic run to a casual saunter.

"Okay, that was hot." Campbell stopped at her side, one corner of his mouth curled up in a smirk and his voice dropping low. "You ready to get out of here?"

Blue tilted her head, considering, and then the bruiser twitched a little harder, one arm rising as if reaching for her. Almost casually, she kicked his balls up into his guts. The man turned an unhealthy shade of green before he vomited, collapsed, and curled up with his hands cupped between his legs.

She nodded in satisfaction. "Now I'm ready."

A passing legionnaire gave her a wide berth and more than a little side eye, and even Ordo winced slightly between bites of his steak. Campbell just grinned.

"*Damn*, woman. Remind me not to piss you off."

Blue's chest heaved as that adrenaline continued to sizzle in her veins, the fight over and nowhere left for it to go. Campbell's gaze dropped. Heat swirled in her belly as his eyes flicked back up to hers, so much *want* in them her breath caught. As her adrenaline shifted to something else entirely, she looked for a way outside. The brawl had cut off the patio exit, and there was no getting anywhere near the main doors, but there was a relatively clear path to the deck exit. So long as they moved fast, they could make it out without getting embroiled in another fight.

A slow smile tugged at her lips. Killi *had* said to make him chase her. She knew her bestie hadn't meant that literally, but Blue figured it still counted. She met Campbell's heated gaze as she slowly backed away from him.

"Catch me if you can." She spun around and sprinted for the door. A husky laugh cut through the shouts and bellows of the bar fight, and she knew he was chasing her. She ran past Tavi—who had someone in a nasty arm lock—without slowing and burst out into the balmy night with a breathless laugh.

She made it halfway across the deck, the wooden planks thudding a hollow beat beneath her boots, before Campbell caught her. A warm hand wrapped around her arm and spun her around. She grinned up into Campbell's handsome face, the flickering torches casting his cheekbones into sharp relief while leaving those soulful brown eyes in deep shadow, but she could see well enough to know he was grinning back at her.

The cacophony of the bar fight was a distant thing, muffled by thick walls and eclipsed by the steady *hush* of the waves rolling into the sandy shore. An errant breeze tugged at her hair, heavy with salt and the memory of the day's warmth. Campbell's grin faded, swept away by something darker. He backed her up against the back wall of the bar and she went willingly.

His arms caged her in, and he dipped his head as if he meant to kiss her. She tilted her face up, but the damnable man bypassed her lips in favor of her ear. His warm breath washed across the sensitive skin as he murmured, "I want you to beg."

"That's cute." Blue laughed in his face even as she tugged him closer. "You're lucky you're hot, otherwise I might be tempted to stab you."

"I'd love to *stab* you."

"Play your cards right," Blue purred, "and maybe—"

"Hey! Get the hell off her!"

An undersized freight train hit Campbell and ripped him away from her. Small fists flew with vicious precision, and as good a fighter as Campbell had proved himself that night, it seemed it was everything he could do to keep from losing his head. The torchlight wasn't the best illumination, but Blue had no trouble recognizing Tavi, or the hardened expression on his young face.

"Tavi, stop!"

Tavi didn't seem to hear her, too intent on destroying her supposed attacker. Blood splattered on the decking, and Campbell let out a pained grunt. Both men were moving far too fast and violently for Blue to get near them, so she did the next best thing. She dragged in a deep breath and gave her best impression of Sergeant Ord at his most displeased.

"Private Tavi, STAND DOWN!"

At her roar, Tavi faltered just enough for Campbell to send him staggering back a step. As soon as he was clear of the young legionnaire, the Navy officer backed away, his hands up and empty.

"It's okay, kid," he said raggedly. "Take a breath."

Tavi snarled and snapped his fists back up, but Blue darted between them, flinging one arm protectively across Campbell's chest. He was breathing heavily, and every muscle under her arm was tensed, ready to act.

"Tavi, he wasn't hurting me!"

The young legionnaire faltered, fists drooping as he stepped back. Heat swept across her cheeks at the confusion on his face.

"But you were running away from him!" His expression hardened again. "And he had you pinned. And you were struggling..."

Campbell choked on a laugh, which didn't help matters in the slightest.

"Oh, sweet bear," Blue mumbled. "Tavi, he wasn't doing anything I didn't want him to do."

"I... I don't understand," the young legionnaire admitted, his own face darkening with embarrassment.

"I don't need you to understand," Blue bit out between clenched teeth, wondering if it was possible to die of embarrassment. Though if Campbell didn't stop laughing, she might not be the one who died tonight, because she might actually stab him.

At the hurt in Tavi's eyes, she sighed. *Stupid fragile male egos.*

"Tavi," she said as softly as she was capable of in that moment, "I very much appreciate that you thought I was in trouble and jumped to my rescue. Please trust me when I say I don't need rescuing at this time and would very much like it if you went back to your squad."

Campbell chose that moment to shift his weight just enough to bring his shadowed face into the torchlight. Tavi's gaze flicked over her shoulder, and he blanched. Apparently, the kid had a good memory for faces and rank.

"E-excuse me, sir. I didn't recognize you in the confusion."

Campbell's amusement died. "And if you had recognized me? Would you still have attacked?"

Tavi lifted his chin. "Yes, sir. If I thought you were assaulting a woman and a fellow legionnaire, I would've attacked you without hesitation."

The silence stretched to the breaking point. And then Campbell smiled.

"Good answer." He tilted his head toward the door. "Dismissed, Private Tavi."

Tavi glanced at Blue. When she nodded, he fled back inside. The roar of the bar briefly washed over them, and then the door was firmly closed, cutting off the racket once more.

"Thank you," she said into the awkward silence Tavi had left them in.

"For what?" Campbell let out a rueful laugh. "Getting my ass handed to me by a kid?"

"For not hauling him in front of Sergeant Ord and demanding he get written up for striking an officer."

Campbell gingerly wiped his mouth. His hand came away bloody.

"He was trying to do the right thing." He turned and spat more blood on the deck. "I can respect that. Damn. How does someone so tiny pack a punch like that?"

"Let me see how bad it is," Blue said quietly.

Carefully, she tucked her fingers under his chin and turned his face up to the light. Campbell allowed it with an amused snort, but Blue groaned in frustration and more than a little regret. Tavi had done a number on his poor face. They definitely wouldn't be having any *fun* tonight.

In the distance, sirens shattered what was left of the calm night, slowly moving closer.

"Come on, Navy boy." Blue sighed and patted him on his shoulder. "Let's go get you cleaned up."

With the Bronze Legion officially banned from Gunrunner's for the foreseeable future, the still-conscious and non-detained members of 4th Squad had been forced to find a new drinking hole for the rest of the evening. Much to Tavi's chagrin, though none of the others seemed to mind too much. Even Sergeant Ord had taken the banishment with good humor—*after* he'd finished his precious steak.

Not even the owner was willing to deprive the sergeant of *that*.

Fortunately for them, The Whiskey Noir was owned by a retired legionnaire who had his own security at the door. It was pretty much a military-only establishment, which kept most of the problems which invariably rose with drunk locals and drunker legionnaires to a minimum. Best of all, it featured a ferry service which would take an unconscious sailor or legionnaire back to the base for a modest fee.

Tavi and the rest of Fire Team Two were lined up at the bar, waiting for the owner/bartender to bring them their drinks. Tavi, in the middle of the group, was nursing his still-sore shoulder and trying to ignore the throbbing pain. Everyone else, though, was having a grand old time.

"Little Tavi fight like a demon, *ke*?" Jabber laughed and slapped Tavi on his back. He winced as more pain flared down his arm. "He kicked that *balara's* ass!"

"Both of 'em!" Vixen added in a slurred voice. He'd taken a bottle of Gunrunner's famed double-barreled vanilla rum with them when they'd been kicked out, and had not slowed down since. The bottle was already half empty and The Whiskey Noir's proprietor, while not one who typically allowed outside alcohol in, had agreed after a one hundred denarii bill had been passed over. "He dropped them quick, too! *Pow pow!* Done. Then *poof!* Disappear like smoke. Oh man...I think I'm gonna be sick."

"Outside, *balara!*" Jabber roared and shoved Vixen away. The drunk legionnaire stumbled to the side door, just made it outside, and promptly puked his guts out into the waste receptacle next to the door. A few moments later he returned to his place by the bar and set the half-filled bottle of rum on the counter.

"This was a bad idea," he muttered and wiped his mouth dry.

"To keep drinking?" Pigeon asked, mock horror in his tone. "Vixen, are you getting old?"

"Hell no. But...maybe vanilla rum and me are like my relationship with my high school sweetheart. A good memory, but toxic. Very toxic. Probably not a good idea to be more than a memory."

"You sure do wax poetic when drunk," Krawdaddy said with a chuckle. "Tavi, you okay?"

"Sore," he admitted as the owner of the bar returned with their drinks on a small tray. Small, black-stained glasses, each filled halfway with smoke wafting from the top, were set in front of the legionnaires. The owner stopped at Tavi and squinted.

"You old enough to be in here, son? We have a minimum age limit..."

"He's a legionnaire, Dragon!" Krawdaddy said. "Of course he's old enough!"

"Distinguished Honor Graduate at ACS right here," Pigeon added. "You know how hard that is, Dragon."

"Eh, good enough for me." The owner/bartender set the glass in front of Tavi and continued down the line. "If you're old enough to die for the Protectorate, your liver is old enough to die for you. ACS Distinguished Honor Graduate and not a self-righteous prick, or assigned to one of those bigger, fancier Legions? Interesting. This one's on the house, kid."

Tavi picked up the glass and inspected it. "What is it?"

"My special blend," the bartender replied as he returned. "Ginger whiskey is difficult to make right, and after waste and filtration you're lucky to get a bottle or two out of the still per week. You put a drop of Vosker oil on top for the smoke effect, serve it in a black-stained glass, and you've got the Noir Fatale."

"Never had anything like it," Tavi admitted.

"If you guys had started here, you probably wouldn't be nursing a bunch of injuries or puked your guts out thanks to synthetic rum," Dragon said, his eyes on the half-empty bottle next to Vixen. "And you wouldn't be out a hundred denarii to placate the owner of this bar for bringing that fake stuff in here."

"We go to Gunrunner's to blow off steam, *tasawa*," Jabber protested. He sounded mildly insulted by the accusation. "We come here to *drink*."

Pigeon slid another hundred denarii bill across the counter. "And we'll be using your delivery service at dawn, Dragon. Because you are a good and honorable man."

The bartender snorted and pocketed the bill. "I don't know about good..."

"Why do they call you Dragon?" Tavi asked as he took a sip of the dark-colored drink. The smoke wafting up from the liquid reminded him of something, but he couldn't put a finger on it. The taste was smoother than he expected, with a slight spice at the backend which suggested this could become a favorite drink of his. He smiled. "This is tasty."

"You ever had a Rhino pilot hate your guts?" the owner asked, leaning on the edge of the bar top. He rolled up his sleeve to expose a black "XI" tattooed on his bicep, with a skull framed with angel wings below it. "11th Legion, *Legio Leo Aquilonis*, 6th Squad. The Lion Legion, they call us. Defenders of the North. Anyway, our Rhino pilot was a madwoman, always out to get me. One time we were doing a training drop on... I forget the planet. Duram, maybe? Eh, doesn't matter. You know the rules of a drop, right, kid?"

"*You puke in it, you clean it!*" the entire group chorused, Tavi included. Dragon grinned broadly.

"Yep, that one. She hit us with a maneuver that caused *everyone* to throw up. But since I was the only one without their helmet on, I was the winner."

"Hey, that's not fair!" Vixen protested. "I had to clean our Rhino, and my helmet was on!"

"That's still disgusting," Pigeon murmured.

Dragon rolled his eyes and continued. "So I cleaned it front to back, like she wanted. Then she hit us with the same maneuver again the very next drop. Again, I scrubbed that ship down from front to back because, darn my luck, my helmet happened to be off again. Then again, and again. No complaints from me, she was always supervising and nearby. Seven years later, after I retired, we got married and settled down here."

"No shit?" Pigeon asked as he elbowed Vixen in the ribs. "Hey, maybe the lieutenant has the hots for you?"

"You think?" Vixen asked, perking up. "I don't normally go for blondes... well, okay, it's not their hair I'm looking at usually, but—"

"No, she doesn't," Tavi said miserably as the heated moment in the alley replayed in his mind. "She's got a thing for one of the Navy officers. The Ops guy."

"You know this, *tasawa*?"

"I, uh, might have interrupted them... and kicked his ass before they could... uh..."

More laughter erupted around him. Never before in his life had he wanted to disappear into the floor more than this. However, the laughter didn't sound cruel or especially mocking, but different somehow. He looked around as Jabber wrapped an arm around his head and squeezed gently.

"You *feched* up some prettyboy Navy *bossjna* and you're not in restraints? *Valkan!* You have to tell us how!"

"I need another drink first," Tavi said, shaking his head.

It didn't take long for him to relay what had gone down in the alley, including admitting his own embarrassment at interrupting the duo. By the end of it, after Tavi repeated his exact words to the Navy lieutenant, the entire team was laughing uproariously. Even Dragon was smiling as he poured them all another drink.

"So you beat the hell out of a Navy officer, was *thanked* for it, and then proceeded to cockblock your Rhino pilot?" Dragon asked incredulously as the laughter began to die down. "Fucking *legend!*"

"You don't think she's going to be a little upset and make us pay for it?" Krawdaddy asked, concerned.

"Ah, damn it. I just got the smell out of my helmet," Vixen added.

"Who cares? *Tasawa* done God's work tonight!" Jabber said, laughing.

"To Tavi! Our little demon protector of womanly virtues!" Pigeon roared and raised his glass in the air. "May you kick Navy officer ass without repercussion for the rest of your days, and make women swoon as you defend their honor!"

"*To Tavi!*"

Maybe Mitzi was right, he mused as he sipped his drink. *Maybe there was more to life than simply being the best legionnaire.*

CHAPTER SEVEN
The Things We Do...

PNV* PERSEVERANCE, *AURORA SYSTEM

By the time Blue got Campbell back up to the *Perseverance*, he was swaying just enough to be noticeable and favoring his right side, where Tavi had nailed him in the ribs more than once. His pupils were still tracking and he wasn't slurring, but in the harsh ship lights, it was obvious just how much damage he'd taken in that short fight. She insisted on taking him to Medical.

The corpsman on duty checked Campbell thoroughly, pronounced he'd "gotten his bell rung good," treated the worst of the cuts, and recommended observation for the next several hours to ensure his condition didn't deteriorate. Still too wired for sleep, Blue shrugged and offered to keep him company.

The uncomfortable exam cot was too narrow for them to both sit lengthwise, but Campbell solved the issue by turning it and shoving it against the nearest bulkhead. And there they sat, shoulder to shoulder, leaning up against the cool metal with their legs hanging off the edge.

An awkward silence fell. And then Campbell nudged her side with a lopsided smile. "Hey, beautiful, come here often?"

Blue snort-laughed and carefully bumped him back. "First time."

Amusement crinkled the corners of his eyes. "Tell me about your first deployment?"

"Oh man, that was a clusterfuck start to finish..."

The hours flew past as they talked. First, about past missions and their different training experiences, but then, in the deepest part of the night, they'd turned to more personal things. It turned out Campbell was no stranger to familial pressures. His parents expected him to serve a single term in the Navy and get into politics like his older brothers. Campbell had no intention of doing that. He was exactly where he wanted to be. Blue had hesitantly told him about her plans to sidestep into the Survey Corps after her initial service term was up. Reluctant because of how Killi and other Ravens had reacted more than because she worried about his reaction, but Campbell had just nodded.

He understood having dreams.

It wasn't the night she'd planned or wanted, but it was shockingly... fun. Relaxing even, not having to pretend to be something she wasn't.

The corpsman kicked them out sometime after dawn. Blue went back to her quarters to change into her duty uniform before hustling to the mess deck. The dull roar of countless conversations washed over her in a wave of white noise as she grabbed food and, more importantly, coffee before winding her way through the long rows of bolted down tables to where she normally sat.

Killi took one look at her exhausted face when she collapsed on the bench next to her and groaned. "I told you to make him chase you."

Blue cradled her head in one hand and took a long swallow of coffee. The only reason she didn't chug it was because it was still too hot.

"I mean, technically I did," she mumbled before she shook her head to clear her muzzy thoughts. "And it's not what you think."

Killi narrowed her eyes. "You honestly expect me to believe you didn't have a wild night of hot monkey sex with a certain ensign when you show up to breakfast looking like *that?*"

"Gee, thanks?" Blue paused. "Wait. You did *not* just say 'hot monkey sex.'"

"Just making sure you were paying attention." Killi snickered and wagged a finger at her. "And you did, you totally did. Fess up!"

Blue mentally said "fuck it" and chugged the rest of her coffee. "Did not."

"I don't believe you," Killi sang out gleefully.

"Believe her," a husky male voice grumbled. Blue snapped her head up. Campbell stood next to their table, tray in hand. He winked. "But it wasn't for lack of wanting. Room for one more?"

Surprise rippled through Blue. While the Legion and Navy personnel shared a mess deck, they didn't usually mix, though there was nothing in the regs forbidding it.

She gave him an exhausted smile. "Sit down before you fall down, Navy boy."

Campbell slid onto the bench next to her. While he was careful to keep a respectable distance between them, his leg casually brushed against hers. Blue didn't mind in the least.

Killi snorted and leaned around Blue to pin him with a disbelieving stare. "And why should I believe anything you—" She broke off with a shocked gasp. "Damn, girl! What did you do to Ensign Hotness' face?"

Killi was not a quiet person. A mixed group of Ravens and Crows sat further down the table, including Blue's own aircrew. At Killi's loud question, her savage little gunners snapped their heads around.

"Oooh, were you guys involved in that epic bar fight at Gunrunner's?" HeyHey called out.

Blue was so tired she wasn't even sure if it was Corporal Hayashi or Corporal Hekikia who spoke. The two younger women were sitting side by side, much like Blue and Killi were, eager eyes taking in Campbell's bruised face and scabbed lip.

"What bar fight?" Blue asked blandly.

"I didn't hear about any bar fights," Campbell added with a casual shrug.

Hayashi and Hekikia groaned in disappointment and no little disgust at their refusal to share the gossip. But Sergeant Carvalho, sitting on the far side of the tiny gunners, smirked down at his steaming coffee mug. Blue would bet good money he'd already heard everything from Sergeant Ord. The two had served together before Carvalho's transfer to aircrew and gossiped together like old women. It was the other reason she'd told Carvalho to put her money where he thought best in the current betting pool, because if anyone knew what had *actually* been done to force Morty out of 4th Squad, it was him.

"Spoilsports," HeyHey muttered.

Carvalho shot them an exasperated glare. "You'd know all about spoiling things on shore leave, wouldn't you, Crows?"

The two miscreants exchanged a wide-eyed glance and intently focused on their breakfast again without another word. Blue studied her gunners a little more closely. Bloodshot eyes and a slight tremble in their normally steady hands pointed to Asodephedrine use to sober up.

They'd had some fun last night.

And apparently messed with Carvalho's.

Blue bit back a grin. Her gunners were no doubt in for a world of trouble, but she was willing to bet her Rhino would be spotless as a result.

Killi waved a piece of bacon in Blue's face to regain her attention. "I leave you unsupervised for *one* night and you got into the biggest bar fight of the year, got the hottest guy on the ship's face messed up, *and* you clearly got less than zero sleep." She snickered. "At least tell me it was good for you."

Campbell shook so hard with suppressed laughter the bench vibrated. Blue glared at him and he put his head down on the table, shoulders still shaking.

"You're not helping." Blue stared mournfully at her empty coffee cup and her shoulders slumped. "And I'm not caffeinated enough for this conversation."

Then, as if by magic, a full, steaming mug slid in front of her. She jerked her head up, eyes wide with gratitude and more than a little surprise. Campbell, now sans coffee, shrugged awkwardly, though traces of laughter remained on his bruised face.

"Seems the least I could do after you kept me company in Medical all night."

Killi bit her lip. "Is that what we're calling it now?"

"Would you cut it out?" Blue sunk her elbow into her friend's side none too gently, though she couldn't help her snort of laughter. Still smiling, she looked up at Campbell. "Thanks."

He gave her that grin of his, though with the bruising it was more roguish than charming this time, and leaned just a little closer. "So, about our interrupted date—"

Calls of encouragement and poorly muffled laughter from a nearby table dominated by 4th Squad drowned out Campbell's quiet murmur. Tavi had stood up and was marching over with a determined expression. He carried a small pair of gloves in his hands that looked similar to what she wore in the cockpit, only they had reinforced sections hers lacked. Tavi crashed to a halt across the table from Hayashi and Hekikia and cleared his throat.

"Good morning, Corporals. I understand I have one of you to

thank for the use of these gloves during yesterday's exercise. Sergeant Carvalho said I could keep them, but I wanted to verify with you directly..." He paused and looked between the two dark-haired, blue-eyed corporals. "Um, which one of you is HeyHey?"

The gunners looked up with identical smiles and chorused, "I am."

Blue swore they practiced that shit in their downtime, because they were so perfectly in sync it was somewhat terrifying. Bewilderment flashed across Tavi's face before he pulled his professional mask back into place.

"Um, that's... not what I was expecting. I think." It was a cautious tone, one which bespoke just how young he truly was. Of course, the gunners were looking at him with a strange and terrifying mixture of amusement and something else.

After taking a quick sip of Campbell's coffee—followed by a longer, more appreciative sip because he'd put in just the perfect amount of cream and sweetener so that it didn't taste like bitter sadness—Blue decided to take pity on the young legionnaire.

"HeyHey, behave."

"Why?" Both gunners turned to her, again perfectly in sync, but then Hayashi dissolved into giggles, and Hekikia rolled her eyes before turning back to Tavi.

"You can call either of us HeyHey and we'll answer," she said. "The gloves were mine, but they were my backup pair. Keep 'em."

Hayashi eyed Tavi in appreciation. "Let us know if you need anything else." She leaned forward, lips curved in a blatantly inviting smile. "And I do mean *anything*."

Tavi looked politely baffled, but Blue shuddered. "No offense to Tavi, but please flirt with him when I'm not around. The kid looks way too much like my little brother."

Now she had her gunners' undivided attention. Hekikia jerked a thumb at Tavi. "Your brother looks like *that*? Dibs!"

"You can't call dibs!" Hayashi frowned. "We've got to flip for it."

"I thought you wanted that one," Hekikia protested, pointing at Tavi, who seemed uncomfortable, or maybe simply confused by the tiny but savage gunners. It could have gone either way.

Hayashi smirked. "Why not both?"

"You can't have both!" Hekikia paused, grinned, and declared, "We could always share."

Shuddering again, Blue tuned out her gunners. Under the cover of their squabbling, she leaned toward Campbell and murmured, "You were saying something about our interrupted date—"

"Excuse me, Lieutenant Eliassen? Ensign Campbell?" Tavi had escaped her gunners and was standing across the table from them, his expression so painfully earnest that Blue squashed her irritation.

Several tables behind him, the members of 4th Squad were enjoying the show, though their muffled laughter cut off at a glare from Sergeant Ord. He raised his brows as if asking Blue if she wanted him to intervene. Subtly, she waved him off, and he saluted her with his coffee mug.

"Yes, Private Tavi?" she asked evenly, when all she really wanted to do was bang her head against the table at his untimely interruption.

"Sir, ma'am." The young legionnaire drew in a deep breath and squared his shoulders as if bracing for his own execution. "I wanted to take the opportunity to apologize again for last night. I'm very sorry I interrupted . . . whatever that was."

Heat swept across Blue's face and lit it on *fire*, and Campbell groaned quietly. Killi, though, fixed Tavi with a pleased expression.

"Private Tavi, you have nothing to apologize for." Killi's voice turned sweeter than honey. "Nothing. At. *All.*"

"You don't even know what he did," Blue hissed under her breath.

"I know he kept you from doing what I specifically told you not to do," Killi murmured back in a singsong voice before she beamed up at the bewildered legionnaire. "Thank *you* for your service, Private Tavi."

"Um, you're welcome, ma'am?"

Blue was torn between laughter at poor Tavi's confusion and killing her entirely too smug best friend. She settled for pointless threats and glaring.

"I will murder you and find a new best friend."

"Good luck finding someone anywhere near my caliber." Annoyance flashed across Killi's face when Blue snatched the last piece of bacon off her tray. "You're lucky I love you. Nobody would convict me if *I* murdered *you* right now."

Blue savagely bit off a piece and aggressively chewed at her friend. Then she handed the rest of it to Campbell.

"Betrayal," Killi said dramatically. "He's not even that hot right now."

"I can hear you, you know," Campbell muttered.

Tavi stared at them like they'd all lost their minds. Poor kid probably had a very different image of officers in his head from training. Blue washed down her bacon with more coffee and was about to send him on his way when a ripple that had nothing to do with surprise or embarrassment washed over her in a line of cold heat, leaving her vaguely nauseated and decidedly uncomfortable.

The *Perseverance* had just completed a jump.

If everything had gone as planned—and it always did nowadays—they were now in the Aurora system. Most people weren't affected by a jump, couldn't even feel the discomfort or tell that anything had happened at all. Only roughly one in two hundred were wired the right way to feel it. Blue had described the sensation to Killi once, and she'd said the sensation sounded similar to how she felt when she'd dealt with airsickness at the beginning of flight training. If so, Blue almost felt bad for making Vixen sick.

Almost.

Campbell eyed her in a mix of curiosity and sympathy when she swayed just enough to bump against his shoulder. "You're jump sensitive?"

"Yeah." Blue took measured breaths until the sensation passed. "Not apparently as badly as the kid is."

Tavi had braced one hand against the table, his face washed of color, but at her words, he straightened up and lifted his chin. "Still not a kid, ma'am."

He stepped back exactly one pace, spun on his heel, and marched back to his own table, where the rest of 4th greeted him with whistles and jeering. Killi sighed and stood up.

"If we're in Aurora, we've got mission planning to do. Hope you got enough caffeine in your system to handle this."

Blue chugged the rest of her coffee and slammed the cup down. "I do now." She smiled at Campbell as she stood. "Thanks again for an ... interesting night. And for the coffee."

Before she could walk away, he caught her arm in a warm grip. "Don't forget, you still owe me a drink, Blue."

"Do I?" She raised her brows, unable to resist teasing him. "Our deal was drinks in exchange for information. You gave me information, I had drinks with you. I'd say I satisfied the terms of our deal."

She carefully concealed her anticipation and a warm flutter of excitement behind a bland expression. They were in the middle of the mess deck and it wasn't the time or place for flirting, damn it all.

"Technically, we each had one drink. The deal was for plural." Campbell's voice dropped into a low murmur. "You still owe me, darlin'."

For a heartbeat, all Blue could do was stare, captured by the amusement and blatant interest in his warm brown eyes. Then she gave him a slow smile. "You're on, Navy boy."

With a low laugh, Killi dragged her away. "Mission plan now, flirt later."

"Do you want the good news or the bad news first, ladies?" Major Nikki "Voodoo" Ellingwood asked with a grim sort of fatalism as she stalked into the mission planning room.

Blue and Killi shot to their feet, but their commander irritably waved them to at ease. Judging by the time, Voodoo had just gotten out of the command staff meeting. The fact that she'd come straight to them didn't bode well. Blue exchanged a glance with Killi, but her bestie shrugged one shoulder.

"The good news, ma'am?" Blue hadn't meant for it to come out sounding like a question, but displeasure radiated off Voodoo in near visible waves.

It wasn't often that their laid-back boss was in a mood, but when she was it was best to tread lightly.

"The good news is you both still get your upgrade checkrides. The bad news is the Alpha Company flight evaluator we were supposed to pick up back at Sagetnam got mixed up in a bar brawl at Gunrunner's. She ended up with a busted knee and is on the no-fly list for the foreseeable future. You wouldn't know anything about that, would you, Lieutenant Eliassen?"

Blue stiffened to attention. "No, ma'am."

"And the report from Medical that you kept a certain Ensign Hotness company all night for unspecified injuries?"

"An unrelated incident, ma'am," Blue answered truthfully.

"Hmm." Voodoo eyed her with a healthy dose of skepticism but fortunately let it go. Restlessly, she paced from one end of the mission planning room to the other. It didn't take her long. Not only was the room small, Voodoo was not a short woman. "The rest is a mixed bag, *ke*. The Aurora Research Outpost has a reactivated Legion pilot on staff who happens to be eval qualified, which is the good."

"And the bad, ma'am?" Killi ventured cautiously.

"I'm sure *he's* a competent pilot, but a reactivated officer who's been out of the Legion and a Rhino's cockpit for years would not be my first choice."

Blue and Killi exchanged another glance when her back was turned, this one full of understanding and more than a little exasperation. The squadron commander of the Bronze Ravens might be a fair leader and one of the best damn pilots in the Legion, but while Voodoo absolutely loved men, she did not love them in her cockpit.

She'd earned her callsign for good reason—she was excessively superstitious. Partly because she was Passovan and they were a superstitious lot in general, but mostly because she was one of the few survivors of the Abaddon Incident, the last in a string of disastrous Bronze Legion deployments over a decade ago.

During the rebuilding process, a quirk in the personnel system had seen only female pilots assigned to Bravo Company. It had marked the beginning of a run of incredible luck for the Ravens. After that, every time a male pilot had been assigned to their squadron, bad luck had followed like clockwork. When Voodoo had taken over command, she'd fought tooth and nail to keep only women assigned to the Ravens.

They hadn't lost a pilot to anything but retirement since.

Of course, if Voodoo hadn't been politically connected outside the Legion, there was no way a mere major could have prevailed over the notoriously bureaucratic and by-the-book Personnel department. However, Voodoo was a member of one of the ruling families of Passovan's predominantly matriarchal society, and while Passovan wasn't a Mars Protectorate planet yet, it was on the schedule to be made an official world during the next budgetary cycle hearing—and Mars Primus *wanted* Passovan. Not just because of the valuable minerals in their asteroid belts or their massive population, but because of the abundance of lupinium, the rare element critical to jump drives.

It gave Voodoo an unusual amount of political power.

And she'd used it to bully Personnel into assigning male pilots elsewhere, which was both amusing and somewhat scary.

"Regardless, I have every confidence that both of you will pass, otherwise I wouldn't have put you in for the upgrade." Voodoo flicked her fingers as she marched past. "Killi, you're up first. Captain Marx Fischer is going to hop up on a shuttle, and he'll ride with you on the first combat drop to the surface this afternoon."

"This *afternoon*?" Killi squawked before she regained her professional bearing. "I thought we weren't dropping until tomorrow morning, ma'am."

Voodoo came to an abrupt stop and swept her short brown hair out of her face, green eyes narrowed in irritation. Fortunately, it wasn't directed at Killi.

"The *balara* outpost supervisor is eager for the Expediter and his team to get to the bottom of the aggressive wildlife behavior and has requested that we *expedite* matters." Her lip curled. "He's in line to be the governor of Aurora if he can get it accepted as a Protectorate world in the upcoming budgetary cycle. We've been told to play nice."

There were times Blue was exceedingly grateful she wasn't in a leadership position. This was definitely one of them. Playing nice wasn't exactly one of her strengths.

"He's pushing for us to get in and out as quickly as possible, all without bothering his precious outpost personnel with our apparently offensive presence, *ke*. Unfortunately for *balara* supervisor, our orders and fuel conservation protocols supersede his wishes. You'll be operating out of the outpost as planned. I expect you both on best behavior, *keiche*?"

Voodoo's accent usually only thickened when she was agitated, and her pilots had learned to gauge her mood based on how much Passovan was sprinkled in. That was more than Blue had heard in a long time. Their commander braced her hands on the table and breathed out a slow, controlled breath before she spoke again, this time with a less noticeable accent.

"Blue, you'll have your upgrade in the next few days. It's anticipated that you'll need to take the team to multiple locations. Captain Fischer will ride with you when you do an orbital hop so he can fully evaluate your skill." Voodoo straightened and pinned them with a somber stare. "Keep your wits about you. There's more to worry about down there than just the hungry beasties, *keiche*? There's political undercurrents I don't want either of you getting caught up in. Follow Twister and Witch's lead, keep your mouths shut, and take care of your boys."

"Yes, ma'am," they chorused.

She gave them a sharp nod and left as quickly as she'd arrived. Blue collapsed in her chair with a long sigh.

"I was wrong." Blue closed eyes burning with fatigue. "I don't have enough caffeine for this shit."

Killi heaved a sigh. "You're lucky I love you, bitch."

There was a faint *crinkle* of plastic. Blue scrubbed her face before opening her eyes. Killi was holding out one of her carefully hoarded caffeinated chocolate bars.

"You are the best," Blue said fervently. She broke it in half, handed one piece to Killi, and inhaled the other. Killi gave her a smug grin.

"I know. Voodoo must really want our checkrides done if she was willing to bend that far," Killi mused as she took a delicate bite.

"Or someone higher up the command chain ordered it." Blue licked chocolate off her fingers. "Possibly both. Let's see what kind of political swamp we're wading into so we don't drown in the sludge."

Blue pulled up the Auroran file on her slate and swiped past the relevant atmospheric data and local flight regulations. She briefly paused on the entry detailing the volcanic mountain range which ran just off the westernmost black-sand coast—volcanoes which might be dormant for now, but Blue didn't need her old geology classes to tell her that could change in a heartbeat—and quickly moved on to the file detailing the local wildlife.

"Whoa..." Blue stared at the image of the predominant and currently very angry Auroran predator, reminded of the time her grandmother took her to the Earth zoo on Mars Primus when she was a child. The reptilian creature resembled nothing so much as a cross between an eight-foot-long Komodo dragon and an armadillo. "I don't think I want to run into an armadon on the ground."

"Armadon?" Killi peered over her shoulder and blanched. "I know I've said it before, but I'm really glad I'm not a legionnaire." She gestured to her curves and smirked. "Not that it was an option. No balls in the cockpit, no boobs on the battlefield."

"You read that in the regs?" Blue bit back a smirk because, while there were absolutely no women allowed in the combat legionnaire units, the "no balls in the cockpit" was more of a Bravo Company guideline than an actual rule.

"I'm paraphrasing," Killi said with a regal air, tilting her chin high.

Their eyes met, and they burst out laughing. Shaking her head, Blue swiped past the entry on armadons and finally found the data entry on the research outpost—and the personnel running it.

Blue whistled soundlessly and tapped a finger on the screen against an image of the supervisor, a refined man wearing a suit more appropriate to the civilized streets of Mars Primus than the jungles of Aurora. His face was lightly lined, and he had the perfect amount of silver in his dark hair, just enough signs of age to say "I'm experienced" without crossing the line into "too old." But even though he was smiling, his blue eyes were icy and cold.

"Now there's a name I recognize," she said softly.

Sir Percival Norwood III was a scion of the ruling family of Aries, the first colony world to be added to the Mars Protectorate, and the last man she'd expected to willingly be this far from the centers of political power.

"What are we looking at?" Killi tilted her head. "A wolf in sheep's clothing?"

"More like a snake," Blue murmured. "Norwood served for a time in the Survey Corps before he got into Martian politics. Grandmother Shava was *not* a fan. In fact, sport bitching about his pretentious ass with some of her old comrades during their weekly tea was one of her favorite retirement pastimes. What the hell is he doing out here?"

"He must have really pissed someone off," Killi said with a derisive snort. "Outside of Shava, I mean."

"Maybe," Blue replied doubtfully.

Her initial surprise at finding him in charge of a backwater outpost faded as she considered what she knew of him and combined it with what Voodoo had told them. Cold realization washed over her. *Power.* Norwood wanted power and a way to make his mark. When the Survey Corps had failed him—his exact words when he quit, according to Shava—he'd turned to politics, and apparently, politics landed him here. Planetary governors were not only a lifetime appointment, they wielded a great deal of power back on Mars Primus.

Unease stirred in Blue's gut. A man like Norwood would fight viciously to ensure his rise to power went smoothly . . . and he clearly didn't want the Legion around any more than necessary. Because he thought he was better than a bunch of scruffy legionnaires? Or because he was afraid they'd find something he'd rather remain hidden? Nobody who got into politics as deeply as Norwood kept their hands clean for long...

"He looks like a real *balara*," Killi said, borrowing her favorite Passovan insult.

Blue slowly lifted her gaze to Killi—an average citizen, born from an ordinary, middle-class family. A Legion officer with no connections, nothing and no one to protect her outside of the Legion itself. Her best friend, who had an endearing and at times unfortunate tendency to speak her mind regardless of who she was speaking to.

"You need to stay the fuck away from him." When Killi bristled, Blue shook her head and added a touch of steel to her voice. "Promise me. Promise me you'll keep your mouth shut around Norwood no matter what we see down there. Worse comes to worse, let me jump on any grenades." Blue forced a smile. "Being Shava Turnien's granddaughter occasionally comes in handy."

"Damn it, Blue—" Killi paused, her green eyes searching her face. "You're serious."

"As a legionnaire about to go on a three-day bender," she said grimly.

"Okay, I promise." She held out her fist, and Blue gently bumped it. "Now help me prep for my checkride. If we're flying this afternoon, we've got some work to do, and I am *not* about to fail my ride in front of some reactivated, dried-up, has-been pilot."

Hours later, they'd finished mission planning and briefed everything with Twister and Witch. Then they headed to the dropship bay to do the preflight checks. It was a hive of activity. All the Rhinos had actually been flightworthy for the Sagetnam exercise—a minor maintainer miracle—but they'd come out of it with five hard broke and two in need of minor repairs, including Bronze Raven Four's nose gear.

Damn, they're getting old. Hell, they were old when my grandfather served.

Blue checked the time as they dodged around a handful of maintainers. Everything was just a little too bright, a little too loud, and it wasn't simply because they'd gone from the quiet of the mission planning room to the chaotic dropship bay. Her sleepless night was catching up with her, and though she could function well enough to safely drop, a nap wouldn't be a bad thing either.

"If I can preflight fast enough, maybe I can catch up on some of that lost sleep in the cockpit before we drop."

"Good luck with that." Killi laughed and pointed at Bronze Raven Four. The ramp was already down, and the nonstop chatter of a certain pair of gunners was audible even over the background noise of dozens of maintainers. She popped a hand on her hip. "So . . . are you going to make your boys pay for cockblocking you last night?"

Blue gave her an evil grin, a match to the evil glint twinkling in her best friend's eyes. "What do you think?"

"Those *poor* damned souls." Killi slowly shook her head, a mocking smile stretching across her face. "Good thing those civvies are riding down with me on this trip."

If anything, Blue's grin turned even more evil. "Yes, a very good thing all we're carrying is their gear. It'll survive. My boys on the other hand . . ."

Both women cackled loudly enough to catch the attention of several maintainers, but those hardened crew members didn't bat an eye. One grizzled older woman saluted them with her wrench as she strode past.

Killi's laughter abruptly cut out and her face snapped into an expressionless mask. "Check six."

Blue twisted around. An older man in outdated dropship pilot armor strode across the bay, his humorless stare fixed on Killi. He could only be their evaluator. Captain Marx Fischer had the kind of face that would be handsome enough if he smiled . . . but it looked as if it would break before that ever happened.

"Good luck with *that*," Blue said, careful to keep the wince from her face, if not her voice. "Damn, that shuttle got up from Aurora fast."

"Crap. I thought I'd have more time to prep."

The evaluator halted in front of them, gaze flicking between them both before settling on Killi. To his credit, he held out his hand, though he still didn't smile.

"Lieutenant Killowen, I'm Captain Marx Fischer. I'll be riding with you this afternoon."

Killi clasped his hand. "Looking forward to it, sir."

"Are you? Hmm." He turned to Blue and shook her hand as well.

"Lieutenant Eliassen, I'll be seeing you in a few days. Now, if you'll excuse us, I have an evaluation to conduct. Lieutenant Killowen, walk me through preflight and then we'll go from there."

"Yes, sir," Killi said, visibly biting her tongue.

Again, Blue hid her wince. There was no reason for Fischer to monitor preflight for this type of upgrade. That was something you did with a trainee still in flight school. It was borderline insulting and didn't bode well for either of them. With one last sympathetic look at her best friend, Blue trotted up the ramp to see what had lit a fire under her gunners' asses. They were *never* this early to preflight.

Blue's rapid footsteps stuttered to a halt midway through the hold. She stared into the gunner compartment. The strong, slightly sweet scent of gun oil mixed with the pungent odor of permanent marker flooded her nose, strong enough to make her eyes water.

"HeyHey, what in the name of all the hells are you doing?" she demanded as she forced herself to march inside.

"Preparing," Hayashi said with a grim air at odds with her normally bubbly personality as she wiped down the barrel of her Minigun with a clean rag. "We have to protect our babies!"

She didn't even look up from her task, though Hekekia tossed her an absent wave from the other side of the compartment.

"Protect them from *what*?" Blue demanded, utterly baffled and just a touch irritated.

"Balls in the cockpit," Hekekia said with a hiss and a Passovan gesture meant to ward off ill luck.

Both of the Aries Miniguns had been ruthlessly cleaned and oiled, and they gleamed like they were new. Except for the barrel of Hekekia's gun. Her tongue stuck out from the corner of her mouth, brow furrowed in concentration as she adjusted her grip on the black marker in her hand. Black smudges stained her fingers and the tip of her nose. She'd covered the entire barrel in a strange mix of what looked like Passovan good fortune symbols, Heidron runes, and squiggles that were made-up nonsense as far as Blue could determine.

A black symbol in the corner of the gunner hatch drew her gaze. Slowly, her jaw dropped as she found another rune at the base of the Minigun and several more throughout the compartment. She took a single step forward and groaned. There were more in the cockpit. *Oh my god... Twister is going to kill us all when she sees this mess.*

"Enough!" Darting to the side, she snatched the marker out of Hekikia's hand. "No more voodoo bullshit!"

Everywhere she looked, she spotted more symbols and runes and nonsense squiggles. Tiny, almost hidden, but glaringly obvious once spotted. There would be no hiding this from Twister. She scrubbed her face and almost stabbed herself in the eye with the marker she'd forgotten she still held. Grumbling in exasperation, she turned to Hayashi.

"Give me the other one."

Nobody could do innocent like Hayashi, not even Killi. The tiny little gunner blinked big, wide eyes up at Blue.

"What other one?"

"The other marker," Blue said through gritted teeth. She wondered what the regs had to say about strangling a gunner. Just a little strangling, not even all the way strangled. It would be therapeutic for her and instructional for her gunners. Everyone would be a winner.

Hayashi must have seen the murder in her eyes, because she heaved a sigh and held up a second marker. Blue snatched it out of her hand before she got any more bright ideas. She checked the time and growled. The odds of her grabbing a power nap had just dropped to nonexistent.

"I need to get going on preflight," she snarled as she tucked both markers away. "Highly recommend you two clean as much of this up as possible."

"Spoilsport," they murmured in unison but it was far enough under their breath that Blue decided to pretend she hadn't heard them. As a lieutenant, it wasn't her place to discipline her junior enlisted. That was Carvalho's job.

She stomped through the gunner compartment and ducked into the cockpit, irritation simmering through her veins, and exhaustion and marker fumes burning her eyes. As she ran through the initial checks, an alert pinged, and she dutifully checked it.

"Of *course* we have a tropical system building to the south, why not add a volcanic activity alert to the mix while we're at it," Blue muttered as she viciously swiped the screen, acknowledging the alert. As if the universe heard her, a second alert came through advising of increasing seismic activity along the Portzelana coast where their Survey team needed to conduct their research. Her shoulders slumped. "I just had to jinx it."

She'd finished the last of the preflight checks when boots stomped up the ramp, paused, and then hurried closer. A second set of footsteps, the slightly uneven gait telling Blue exactly who it was, followed close behind.

"Gods damn it, HeyHey," Twister mumbled, rolling her eyes as she walked into the cockpit.

"What the hell did you do to my Rhino?" Carvalho roared.

Blue crossed her arms and settled back in her seat to enjoy the show. Once Carvalho was done venting his rage, she'd brief Twister on the tiny addition she wanted to add to their planned sortie. At the sound of boots marching across the bay, she flicked on the rearview camera. Under the direction of Sergeant Ord, 4th Squad was gathering outside the Rhino, deployment gear in hand.

A burst of anticipation flooded her system.

"Heh..." A savage grin crossed Blue's face. "Looks like I've got enough caffeine in my system for this day after all."

CHAPTER EIGHT
This Place Isn't as Pretty as Advertised

AURORA, AURORA SYSTEM

"I *told* you she was pissed off at you for cockblocking her!" Vixen whined pathetically as the Rhino violently twisted once more before falling into a sharp dive, then flared abruptly because the pilot simply *could*. Vixen hiccupped, then belched. "Damn it, Tavi!"

Tavi held onto the straps and ignored Vixen's incessant complaints, focusing instead on a weird black scribble above Sergeant Klau's head across the bay. Between them was all the civilian gear necessary for the deployment, safely strapped down. The civilians themselves would be dropped off at the first site—gently, he presumed—and they would link up with them so the scientists could begin doing whatever it was they were supposed to do.

Tavi sighed and closed his eyes as the nose of the Rhino suddenly pitched up, once again creating that weightless sensation which had previously caused members of Fire Team One to nearly lose their lunch inside their helmets. Fortunately they'd held it back, but only just.

Instead of lasting a few seconds, though, this time the maneuver seemed to go on and on. Tavi forced his eyes open and tried to clench his stomach to get rid of the feeling, but was only moderately successful. The nausea remained. It was manageable. Beside him, Jabber squirmed and began to shake his head violently.

"*Tasawa!* Me and you have talk later about timing, *ke*?"

Chewing on his inner cheek, he nodded and watched as a member of Team Three removed his helmet and proceeded to belch loudly.

Vixen groaned again and rolled his head back. The clear-glass facemask showed just how green the legionnaire's face had turned.

"GODS DAMN IT, TAVI!"

"*Prepare for landing,*" a brusque voice echoed in their ears. Gone was the comforting contralto they'd previously enjoyed. *Someone* in the cockpit was teaching a valuable life lesson here, and every single soul on board knew who it was directed toward, though not necessarily the reason behind it. "*Touchdown in five...*"

"I'm *sorry*!" Tavi screamed in frustration as the Rhino suddenly swung on its axis, gravity returning rather abruptly. The rear settled onto the ground, then the nose touched down. The engines cut back abruptly.

Sergeant Carvalho stood and slapped the ramp release. He stared at 4th Squad, clearly amused, with his eyes lingering a moment on Tavi before moving onward as daylight spilled into the dark interior. The chipperness in the man's movements and attitude was worse than the prolonged weightlessness they'd suffered through. "On your feet, legionnaires! It's a beautiful day and the sun is shining, and I'm getting an appetite! Get this shit off my bird!"

"Teams Two, Three! Undog those straps, get a work party together, and get those boxes out!" Ordo barked. "One, establish an inner perimeter. 5th Squad, 4th Squad. We're on the ground now, copy."

"Copy, Ordo. Outer perimeter established. Babysitting bodyguards at Checkpoint Alpha, over."

"Copy Checkpoint Alpha. Ordo, out."

Team One staggered out of the Rhino and popped their helmets. Tavi, carrying one of the larger boxes with Jabber, moved around Private Alec "Loosey" Luta, who was looking a little green. Tavi caught an angry glare out of the corner of his eye as they continued past.

"Don't worry about him, *tasawa*," Jabber muttered as they set the large box down in the soft soil. "Not your fault, really. Even if I hate you right now."

The landing area was remarkably clear of most vegetation. There were quite a few large, flat rocks which felt almost laid out by design. A quick glance around the area suggested that it had been artificially cleared once for this very type of landing, then later forgotten about. Who had cleared it, though, Tavi could only guess.

"Pigeon! Time for you and your team to go retrieve the civvies. It's only two hundred yards away, so try not to dawdle. *Gently* remind them that you are here for their security," Ordo instructed, his voice dragging Tavi's attention back to the task at hand. "I've heard some interesting rumors about our civvie from the LT, so try not to piss them off, okay? Vixen! Hands off the women! I'm not even fucking joking here! I will neuter you myself if I hear anything!"

"Vixen, you fuck this up..." Pigeon warned in a low voice.

"Not even going to talk to them," Vixen promised. "You said they had two male scientists with the evaluators? I'll stick with one of them. Maybe he has a cute friend back on Mars Primus?"

"That's probably the smartest thing I've heard you say this month," Krawdaddy muttered as he stacked another box on top of the rest. "We moving all these with every stop, Sarge?"

"Negative," Ordo responded as the last box was neatly placed with the rest. "Base camp is set up at the high point there." He pointed to a raised knoll at the end of the clearing. "Every single point of interest is within a mile in all directions of this location. 5th Squad is going to hate life, but they're gonna love not being us. Pigeon! Get a move on!"

"Yes, Sergeant! Team Two, grab your shit and let's roll."

After moving the last heavy crate, Tavi went back to the Rhino and got his rifle from Klau along with four extra magazines. It was the first time he'd been issued live ammunition since assigned his suit, and he noticed the slight weight difference immediately. It was, shockingly enough, lighter than the training rounds they'd used back on Sagetnam. He looked at the sergeant, who grinned and flexed his bionic arm at him.

"What? The loadout weight is almost the same, kid. Don't tell me you're one of those freaks who can tell the difference between training rounds and real ones?"

Tavi could, but kept his mouth shut. Once he was fully kitted up, he rejoined the rest of Team Two. Pigeon brought up the local satellite imagery on their HUDs. It wasn't real-time, but it was good enough for legionnaire purposes. He pinged a location to the west.

"That's Bronze Raven Five," Pigeon told them. "Tavi, point. Vixen, rear. Stagger patrol formation. You know the drill. Two hundred yards doesn't seem like much, but through the brush and jungle you can get easily turned around. Use your instruments. Magnetic north is also marked on the map. Keep it relative. Tavi, move out."

While the underbrush of the jungle environment on Sagetnam had been very much in line with what they were seeing on Aurora, Tavi knew the dangerous reptilian creatures here lurked throughout. Taking point, he led the team away from the small clearing and into the thick, overgrown jungle which separated them from Bronze Raven Five. It took him a second to find a small animal path they could use to move through but once found, he didn't hesitate and plunged into the jungle.

The jungle canopy overhead was thick, allowing very little light to push through the tangled greenery. Denied direct sunlight, most of the thick ground cover was either fernlike vegetation or some sort of spongy mass with branches growing out of the center, more moss than actual bushes. In some places there was a brittle-looking, dried black residue on spots of the lichen.

Other than the game trail, there were no other signs of animal life. The arrival of the Rhinos easily explained this phenomenon, but it still made Tavi a little uneasy. Birds had been common on Mars Primus as well as Sagetnam, and he'd expected something similar on Aurora. However, other than a few insects, there was absolutely nothing to be seen or heard.

Tavi drew in a deep breath of air rich with green growing things that wouldn't have survived in Overdark but detected nothing unusual. And if there *had* been anything toxic in the air, his suit would have detected it and automatically switched to filtered air.

"Eyes up," Pigeon warned them as they moved deeper into the dark. "Remember, they've got eight-foot lizards who want to eat you somewhere out there."

"Kind of quiet here," Tavi muttered as he stepped over a downed log. It was so covered with moss he'd almost mistaken it for a rock. "No birds."

"Can't even hear Bronze Raven Four anymore," Vixen added.

"That's because they powered down their engines, dumbass," Krawdaddy reminded him.

"Oh, right."

"*Tollejo balara,*" Jabber swore. "You get out here in the middle of a death jungle and wonder why things quiet. You act like you never been on a world with lots of plants before. Sagetnam ring a bell? You worse than a *pojata* on her first date and the *bucko* is smooth talker—"

"I hear engines," Tavi interrupted them before Jabber could gain a full head of steam. He stopped and swiveled his head to get a better bearing on the source of the noise. After a second, his systems homed in on the direction. "Tracks with where Bronze Raven Five landed on the HUD."

"Challenge response is Blue Twister," Pigeon reminded him.

Krawdaddy snorted. "Someone has a sense of humor."

The underbrush grew thicker as they drew closer to the clearing where Bronze Raven Five had landed. His HUD flashed as a sentry from 5th Squad moved around a tree and challenged him. Tavi responded immediately with the correct counter.

"Welcome to the shitshow," Private Gomes muttered and slung his rifle over his shoulder as the rest of Team Two gathered around. He fist-bumped Krawdaddy. "My man. The faster these fucking civvies go away, the sooner we can get our sanity back."

"That bad, huh?" Pigeon asked.

"You have *no* idea, but... you're about to. On the one hand, I'm glad to get rid of them. On the other, I pity you poor bastards."

"Yep, it's gonna be bad," Vixen growled. "Damn it."

"Well, if you guys hadn't Morty'd Morty..."

"He had it coming!" Vixen protested. Gomes shrugged.

"Whatever, man. Hurry up. Duck is expecting you. And good luck."

"Duck?" Tavi asked.

"Sergeant Cox?"

"Oh."

Though only two hundred yards apart, the difference between the landing zones was shocking. Where Bronze Raven Four had a clear landing area with low grass, Five's was rock-strewn and covered with the strange black lichen he'd seen in the jungle on their way in. Or perhaps it was rock, since it tended to crunch with every step he took. There was no grass here, either. It was relatively flat, which meant the Rhino could land, but it had clearly taken some skill to bring the transport in.

All in all, the area looked like someone had started a fire and, once it reached a certain size and remained in a perfect circle, extinguished it. This was a stark contrast to the rest of the area Tavi had seen so far. If the rest of the planet was this weird dichotomy of life and death, it was going to be one of those he scratched off his list of potential homes after his term of enlistment.

He blinked at the sudden thought. His entire life *was* the Legion. What had caused him to drift and think about something that would probably never come to pass? Odd. Shaking his head, he refocused on the mission as the High Value Civilian walked into view.

According to the pre-mission brief, Dr. Charles William Joseph Schmoyer IV was a Chief Expediter in the Survey Corps and very well connected, with family in all branches of government service. To make their day even worse, his ancestors were among the Five Hundred, the original survivors during the colonization of Mars Primus.

Quite a few of the legionnaires in 4th Squad hadn't understood the familial importance, mostly because they weren't Martian by birth. However, those who'd joined and grown up in the Protectorate were quick to explain just how important the originals had been, for both colonizations and financing purposes of the Great Endeavor. It had been with their sweat and blood and money that the Protectorate of Mars flourished.

At least, according to the Five Hundred. Privately, a few native-born Martians had differing opinions and had shared them rather... *exuberantly*.

There'd been more to the briefing after, but none of it pertained to the Five Hundred, so Tavi refocused on the man who was quickly approaching Team Two.

"You took *forever* to reach us!" the man said without introduction, his eyes focusing on Tavi instantly. His face clouded in anger and confusion. "They sent a *child* to protect us against possible aggressive *Loricatus lacerta aurora*? The *armadons*, as the uneducated would call them. What sort of shell game is the Legion playing here? The Survey Corps paid good money for quality security, and they send us a child?"

"Sir," Pigeon said, stepping between Tavi and Dr. Schmoyer. His voice was decidedly calm. "I am Specialist Ryan Pridgeon, Team Leader of Fire Team Two, 4th Squad, Bravo Company. You and your assistants have been placed in my care for the duration of your field expeditions here on Aurora. While Private Tavi is small, rest assured that he is more than capable of protecting you or any of your assistants should the need arise."

"Sure he can. Miss Mingo!" Dr. Schmoyer turned and yelled over his shoulder toward the small cluster of civilians waiting near Bronze Raven Five. All four of them hurried over to their boss. "He can protect her, then. They're about the same size. Your biggest and strongest should guard my taller assistants."

"This should not be an issue, sir. Now, if you'll follow me—"

"What about our personal effects?" the doctor said, sneezing once and slapping his forearm where an insect had landed upon it. "You don't expect us to *carry* it to your vessel, do you?"

Tavi was beginning to realize why Gomes had wished them luck.

"Your personal effects will be flown back to the Aurora Research Outpost, sir, and you can collect them there. Your field effects are back at our Rhino," Pigeon explained. The man's face scrunched up with confusion.

"So we have to walk all the way to your vehicle... your Rhino, as you called it? Trusting that some legionnaire won't steal our personal items, then conduct our initial survey, then walk *back* here to fly back to the outpost?" Dr. Schmoyer asked incredulously.

"That sums it up nicely, sir."

"This is unacceptable!" The doctor turned and looked directly at his four assistants, his fury directed at them. "Miss Mingo! You coordinated with the Survey Corps and the Legion! Why wasn't I informed of this?"

"I informed you via message and verbally on two separate occasions, Doctor," she responded in a meek and quiet voice as she shifted a small satchel she carried over one shoulder. However, Tavi spotted a flash of frustration and anger in her eyes. "I also forwarded you the confirmation the Legion and Survey Corps sent about the necessity of using two Rhinos and not one due to the increased security concerns. I received multiple receipt confirmations for the messages signaling you opened and read the contents, and you verbally acknowledged my information three days ago when I reminded you of—"

"That's *quite* enough, Miss Mingo." The doctor sighed and drew himself up to his full height. He wasn't quite as tall as Jabber, but it allowed him to stare directly into Pigeon's face. Dr. Schmoyer schooled his expression carefully. His tone turned polite. "Very well then. Proceed, Specialist."

Pigeon held out his hand. "One second, Doctor. If you would, please place the palm of your hand in mine."

"Whatever for?" Dr. Schmoyer asked, confused.

"The DNA of your skin will be read by my hamatic suit and mark you as a member of my fire team on our internal systems," Pigeon explained patiently. "We'll do the same for everyone on your team. When we're out in the jungle, it will allow us to track you in case something happens. It will also issue an alert should you stumble into our firing line if we're under attack by wild animals."

"Wait... you're going to *spy* on us?" The doctor sounded offended.

"Not spy, no, sir. This is observing."

"What's the bloody difference?!"

"Consent given, sir. Yours, more specifically. With consent, it's not spying."

"Oh..." The doctor looked slightly confused as he mulled it over for a moment. "This only extends to our activities in the field, correct? Nothing inside the research outpost."

"Correct, sir," Pigeon lied smoothly. "We will be unable to track any of you or your assistants inside the outpost."

Tavi looked at the doctor's assistants to see if any of them had noticed the blatant lie. They seemed to buy it. Except Mitzi. She had a look on her face he'd seen before, outside of Gunrunner's. Instead of speaking up and correcting the legionnaire, as he'd expected, she remained silent. Her eyes drifted to Tavi, and he thought he saw a faint glimmer of amusement under the anger. Why she seemed amused, though, he didn't understand.

"Very well then." The doctor placed his hand in Pigeon's open palm, and a biometric scan began scrolling across Tavi's HUD. It immediately shrunk to the lower right corner as it became more detailed, then disappeared as the baseline metrics were fully read by the system. A small blue dot appeared on the minimap on his lower left screen, joining the green dots of his fellow Team Two members around him.

One by one the others were scanned and appeared on the map. As soon as everyone was scanned and properly identified on the hamatic suit HUDs, Pigeon began partnering each of the doctor's assistants with a legionnaire. The two male assistants went with Vixen and Krawdaddy, while the other woman was assigned to Jabber. Mitzi, as the doctor had previously demanded, was with Tavi.

"Doctors Albert Childs and Rodrigo Morales," Dr. Schmoyer began introductions, nodding. "Meteorologists for the Survey Corp. That's Doctor Huyan Xi-Smith. She's a geologist. And that"—he paused, scowling, as if he was struggling to say her name for a second—"is Doctor Mitzi Wingo, a xenobiologist."

Tavi blinked. *Doctor?*

"Call me Mitzi, please," she said as the others finished with their own personal introductions. It was interesting the way the others tended to act like Dr. Schmoyer, whereas Mitzi acted more like a regular person.

His thoughts drifted back to what Pigeon and the others had tried to explain previously about academics. The conversation suddenly made sense, and he smiled. Understanding inside jokes always made him feel better once he was in on them.

With everyone marked on the HUDs, their journey to back to Bronze Raven Four began. They moved rapidly through the jungle at a clip far faster than before. In spite of his misgivings, Tavi was surprised to find that the group of academics actually seemed to know how to make their way along the game trail back to where Bronze Raven Four and the rest of 4th Squad were. While the group didn't *quite* follow directions as well as he could hope, they were still making much better time than he'd thought.

Until, that is, they ran into a small reptile Tavi hadn't seen on their first trip.

It was perched atop a fallen log covered with green moss, idly watching the group. It was a dark green, similar to the moss growing on the log, which explained how he'd missed it on the way through the first time. There were three small horns protruding from its head and nose.

Upon closer inspection, Tavi realized the lizard featured a multicolored belly, almost a blood red in color. However, the throat of the creature was black, which caused no small amount of excitement to pass across Dr. Schmoyer's face.

"Oh!" he exclaimed, his tone high pitched and filled with childlike wonder. The change in attitude was almost startling. "Is that a new species? It is!"

"I don't know..." Mitzi's voice trailed off as Dr. Schmoyer and the other three hurried and gathered around the small, two-foot-long reptoid. It cocked its head and stared at the gathered group. There was no fear in the creature's eyes, or even really an awareness of the potential danger it was in. Tavi wondered how the lizard had survived without any apparent survival instincts. The book he'd finished about the lizards had suggested that most smaller reptiles responded to danger with a "fight or flight" response. This one seemed to be doing neither.

"*Schmoyer gemmata lacerta*," he declared, not even waiting as Mitzi moved closer. It cocked its head at her but didn't flee. Instead, it acted almost domesticated as she approached. "Schmoyer's jeweled lizard!"

"Doctor, I think this is just a regular Aurora ruby-bellied lizard," she said as she leaned closer. Motioning with a hand, she pointed at the lizard's throat. "A big one, but not overly so. The black throat appears to be some sort of fungal growth and not natural coloring. Interesting. One sec."

Deftly she reached into her satchel bag and pulled out a small vial. Seemingly like magic, a small pen knife appeared from her pocket. Mitzi glanced at Tavi before jerking her chin at the lizard.

"Hold him by the back of the neck, and the midsection just in front of his hind legs," she instructed. "Gently. Like you're holding a delicate piece of glass, but firmly enough that it can't get away. Don't squeeze, but apply steady pressure."

"How do you know it's a he?" Tavi asked as he followed instructions. The lizard still made no effort at escaping, merely watching them with a frighteningly intelligent look in its eyes. It allowed Tavi to hold him down, and didn't even offer a struggle as Mitzi approached.

Meanwhile, Schmoyer seemed rather put out by the change in his assistant's attitude. "Miss Mingo, I highly doubt this is a discovered—" he began to protest. She quickly cut him off.

"It's *Doctor* Mingo at the moment, sir." She began to gently remove some of the black fungus from the lizard's throat. Using the flat of the blade, she carefully scraped it into the vial. A few more quick motions and half the throat was exposed, revealing a brilliant ruby color. She'd been correct. Folding the blade, she pocketed the knife once more. "It's a male because of the crest, see? Okay, I've got enough for a quality sample. Let the lizard go, Tavi."

He complied and it was as though the lizard spotted them for the first time. It scampered away at high speed, disappearing into a hole in the log. A second later they could hear it running across the jungle floor, tiny rustles of foliage quickly fading away.

Mitzi, meanwhile, had capped the sample vial and jotted something down on it. From her bag came a small scanner. She raised it to the vial, angling it at the barcode. After the beep, she nodded, apparently satisfied. Both vial and scanner were returned to the satchel.

"There was no need for rudeness, Miss—*Doctor* Mingo," Schmoyer said as he pulled himself up to his full height. "I was simply excited at the prospect of naming a new species."

"As you say, sir."

"We should get moving," Pigeon interjected. "We need to get your stuff set up and decide where the main encampment will be here in the jungle."

"Here in... Are you *mad?*" Schmoyer looked at the team leader, horrified. "We're not staying out *here*! Did you not read my memo? There was nothing in my memo about sleeping in the jungle!"

"I didn't receive a memo, sir," Pigeon said with the most patient tone possible. Tavi was impressed. "When did you send it?"

"Back on board the *Perseverance*, of course," the professor proclaimed. "I sent it to the Navy with instructions... Wait. You brought all our gear out into the jungle and unloaded it, and expect us to stay out here? The memo I gave the Navy *clearly* states that we will only be bringing the necessary equipment every day, and we will be staying within the safety of the research outpost's walls! This is unacceptable! I *sent* a memo, as I was instructed! This sort of presumptive behavior on the Legion's part is completely unacceptable!"

Tavi watched Pigeon struggle with his self-control for a full ten seconds before speaking again.

"Yes, sir. My mistake, sir. We should get a move on, sir. It's getting dark in a few hours, sir."

"Does the Navy share stuff like that with the Legion?" Tavi asked over a private comms within the team. Jabber snorted.

"No way, *tasawa*. Not because they don't like us, but because we use totally different systems, *ke*? Like trying to cook a bird and get steak."

Tavi didn't get the reference exactly but understood the gist of it. "Got it. Thanks."

"You can talk to one another without letting us hear?" Mitzi asked in a low tone as she moved around to the other side, using Tavi as a shield between her and Dr. Schmoyer.

"How did you know?" Tavi looked at her, confused, before remembering the face shields of their helmets were transparent. She'd seen his mouth moving. "Oh. Never mind."

"I pay attention. Child prodigy, you know," she reminded him as Pigeon and Doctor Schmoyer renewed their trek, with the other assistants and legionnaires following along like ducks in a row. She waited a moment, then continued on after the others.

"Tavi, take rear guard," Pigeon said quietly. There was a deep frustration in his tone Tavi hadn't heard before. "This guy..."

"Copy rear guard," Tavi confirmed and set off after the group, the incident with the strange lizard already forgotten. The rest of the walk was quiet, with all of them making good time following the path the legionnaires had come through the first time. When they reached Bronze Raven Four and the rest of 4th Squad, however, things fell apart.

"Not only did you ignore my memo about only bringing necessary equipment along on the trip, you unpacked it all and set it on the ground, exposed to the elements?!" Dr. Schmoyer practically shrieked when he arrived at 4th Squad's clearing. Tavi watched, confused, as the doctor turned on Sergeant Ord and began to lay into him.

He had no idea how the sergeant remained calm as the civilian brought up a litany of issues he had with their supplies. They were in the clearing for only a few minutes before the civilian demanded that they return to Bronze Raven Five. Sergeant Ord nodded in acquiescence.

As Tavi followed quietly behind on their way back, he was amazed that despite the deteriorating situation, Sergeant Ord remained calm and professional. During the entire trek back to Bronze Raven Five, the only time Doctor Schmoyer wasn't complaining to the sergeant was when he was focusing on some indigenous lifeform.

Finally, they were at the rocky clearing once more. Tavi, who had started to develop a pulse-pounding migraine simply listening to the doctor complain, was glad to pass off responsibility of the civilians back into the hands of Bronze Raven Five's crew.

Tavi sighed as the Expediter and his assistants boarded Bronze Raven Five at long last. Doctor Schmoyer loudly complained about the uncomfortable seats as Sergeant Tinnesz checked his safety harness. His assistants took their own seats without fuss. Mitzi, meanwhile, was staring thoughtfully out at the jungle beyond.

Tavi wasn't an expert on her expressions just yet, but he recognized the one she wore. The best way he could describe it was "troubled," which made no sense to him. He could have sworn she'd been both disgusted and curious at the sample she'd removed from the ruby-bellied lizard. Samples which were currently in her carry bag safely tucked away beneath her seat.

There might be a day when Tavi would finally and fully understand the mind of a woman. Unfortunately, it did not look like it was going to happen anytime soon.

With the Survey Corps team safely back on board Bronze Raven Five, Fire Team Two were finally free to ditch Doctor High-and-Snooty and go be miserable elsewhere. They wouldn't have to deal with him until the following day, since once at the research outpost the doctor and his team were no longer their responsibility.

With another heavy sigh, Tavi tromped away from the Rhino and headed back into the jungle toward Bronze Raven Four once more.

Whatever Blue had expected from a facility on a non-Protectorate world, the Aurora Research Outpost far exceeded it. The white stone buildings stood out from the surrounding verdant jungles like a beacon of civilization, paved streets laid out in an orderly grid, and various vehicles parked in neat lines. Everything was clean and well maintained and so utterly out of place on *this* world that she did a double take.

"Fancy," Twister commented as they circled overhead waiting for their turn to land. By unspoken agreement they'd let Bronze Raven Five take the lead so Killi could finish her checkride that much sooner.

Unease twisted through Blue at just how fancy the "outpost" was, and her hands tightened on the controls. Twister had insisted she fly the second leg of their flight plan so she'd be as prepared as possible for her checkride, randomly tossing possible EPs her way and quizzing her on command-and-control decisions.

As she ran through the landing checklist, Blue kept stealing glances outside the cockpit, studying the facility. It looked as if it belonged on one of the more established colony worlds. Like Aries.

The Norwood family had clearly sunk considerable funds into Aurora, either directly or through grants and political lobbying. With that much capital tied up in the project, there would be a lot of pressure on Sir Percival Norwood III to succeed. They would all need to be on their best behavior down there, just like Voodoo had ordered. Blue had already warned Twister and Witch about Norwood during their briefing, but she resolved to have a word with the legionnaire sergeants to keep a short leash on their boys.

The only indication that this wasn't a small idyllic city transplanted from a Mars Protectorate world were the imposing walls surrounding the outpost. Those walls weren't the standard fortifications, either. They'd been reinforced, with rolls of fortified wire along the entire base of the perimeter walls and smaller rolls lining the top. Small gun emplacements had been jury-rigged in a staggered interval with floodlights pointed into the thick, vine-covered trees. There were even two relay towers near the heavily wired outer wall of the outpost, fully equipped with an IR scanner. One faced east, the other west.

Behind the rolls of fortified wire, the base of the walls had strange markings. Frowning, Blue zoomed in with her helmet's built-in HUD.

"Claw marks..." she murmured.

The fortifications must be a new addition after the trouble with the unusually aggressive armadons. Twister tilted her head, eyes narrowed in concentration as she stared down at the walls.

"You're right. Big beasties." She grinned, eyes twinkling in amusement, though there was caution there too. "I wonder if they're edible."

Blue snorted a laugh. "Since they're native to Aurora, I doubt it."

"Bet you our boys are already debating if they taste like chicken."

"No bet."

In short order, she'd set the Rhino down next to Bronze Raven Five on the small landing pad to the rear of the outpost. They shared the space with half a dozen skimmers—compact, agile atmospheric aircraft used locally for transportation—and an old, bulky shuttle that looked slower than a pig in mud.

The massive Rhinos dwarfed them all.

Under a small hangar to the right of the landing pad was an expensive personal shuttlecraft, not top of the line, but light-years ahead of anything else on the planet, including the Rhinos. No doubt either Norwood owned it outright, or it "belonged" to the supervisor position.

Flexing her shoulders to shed the tension, Blue quickly ran through the postflight checks in practiced tandem with Twister. The engines spooled down, and the subtle vibrations that made the ship feel like a living thing fell away. Carvalho dropped the ramp, and multiple sets of boots thumped hollowly on metal as everyone disembarked at a slightly more leisurely pace than a combat drop.

Within a few minutes, silence fell over the ship, though they could faintly hear Sergeant Ord barking at his legionnaires outside.

"Good job." Twister leaned back in her seat and pulled off her helmet. "Seriously, you've got nothing to worry about for your checkride."

"Thanks," Blue said with a quiet smile as she pulled off her own helmet.

With an exhausted sigh, she unbuckled her harness, shoved herself to her feet, and wearily followed her command pilot off the Rhino, securing the cockpit behind her. She passed HeyHey, both corporals scowling and working to clean the gunner compartment under Sergeant Carvalho's watchful eye and acid commentary. Unsurprisingly, the permanent marker was stubbornly refusing to be erased. Quite possibly because Carvalho had only given them wet rags to use without a hint of cleaning chemicals staining the air.

As she slipped past the legionnaire-turned-Crow, Carvalho didn't pause berating the gunners, but he winked and subtly pointed out the bottle of cleanser he'd stashed out of their line of sight. *I wonder how long he'll make them suffer before letting them use it?*

Smirking, she walked down the ramp, stretching the kinks out of her spine and vaguely hoping to pass out soon because her sleepless night had long ago caught up to her, trampled her, and left her in its figurative dust. Even her hair felt tired. She dug blunt fingernails into the blonde strands and massaged her scalp as much as possible with her tightly braided hair.

With a low sigh, Blue tilted her face up to the deep blue sky. Late afternoon sun bathed her skin in a pleasant heat. The warm, green scent of growing things rode the humid breeze, and she drew in a deep breath of her first taste of Auroran air. She smiled at the heavy floral scents with just a hint of something darker, a welcome change from the slightly metallic recycled air she'd become used to on the ship. Twister sneezed violently.

"Damn allergies." She sneezed a dozen more times before she

managed to pop an antihistamine. Her nose wrinkled as she tried to hold back yet another sneeze, eyes watering, but within seconds she breathed easier and her expression eased. "Remind me to hit up the flight doc next time we're on the *Perseverance* to restock. I only have so much with me, and this place is going to play merry hell with my sinuses."

"Copy flight doc," Blue said with a sympathetic grin that turned more than a little evil when she noted some of their legionnaires eyeing her warily. She gave them a flippant wave, not caring in that moment that it was slightly less than professional behavior. She was tired and she had blue lady balls, damn it. They deserved everything she'd dished out and more.

Sergeant Ord moseyed over, amusement glinting in his eyes but his expression a blank mask. "Ma'am, my boys would like me to convey their deepest apologies for last night—not that I have any idea what they could possibly be apologizing for—and have stated they are willing to do whatever it takes to not have a repeat of those particular drop conditions."

Blue fought back her grin and attempted to match Ordo's professionalism. Mostly because she'd also noted a few legionnaires glaring at Tavi, and she didn't want to take things so far that they'd Morty him.

"I can't promise we won't hit turbulence like that again, but I'll do my best to make the next flight...smoother."

"Copy smoother, ma'am," he said solemnly. "Much appreciated."

"Thank you for your understanding, Sergeant Ord," Twister said. Her shoulders shook with suppressed mirth, and she nudged Blue. "Let's go see how Killi did."

The two pilots skirted around the orderly lines of 4th Squad and past the knot of civvies pawing through the gear the legionnaires had unloaded onto the landing pad. Blue noted without shock that Mister High and Mighty supervised their efforts without bothering to lift a finger to actually help. They cleared the Rhino's wing in time to see Fischer march down Bronze Raven Five's ramp, spine straight and shoulders back. He walked off the landing pad and into the outpost without waiting for anyone else.

What a prick.

Apprehension shivered down Blue's spine when 5th Squad stormed off the Rhino, every last legionnaire looking as if they wanted to murder someone. Everything had sounded fine over the ops channel during the field op. So what—

Sergeant Travis "Duck" Cox stalked down the ramp, hard eyes focused squarely on the evaluator's back as if marking his next kill. Witch ghosted up to his side, her expression one of barely restrained fury. There was a pause, and then Killi marched outside with her head held high and her expression untroubled... but Blue knew her best friend. Something was wrong.

Blue pushed past the legionnaires and rushed up to Killi.

"What happened?" She meant for it to come out as a question, but it was more of a demand, razor edged with a growing protective rage.

"I passed."

Killi's voice was hoarse and her eyes were bloodshot as if she'd been crying. When it didn't look like she was going to say anything else—like what was *wrong*—Blue pinned Witch with a fierce stare. The older pilot had ridden jumpseat on the sortie, a passive observer to the checkride.

"Captain Fuckstick's idea of constructive criticism is less constructive and more criticism." Witch's lip curled into a snarl. "He also didn't shut up the entire sortie."

"He *also* transmitted some of that crap over the ops channel 'by mistake,'" Sergeant Cox added in an irritated growl. He glanced at Witch and lowered his voice, but not so much that his legionnaires couldn't hear him. "All due respect, ma'am, but he steps on our bird again, he might not make it back in one piece. Nobody treats our Ravens like that."

Oh, hells no.

Blue was torn between chasing after the evaluator and holding him down for the sergeant and comforting her friend. Killi swiped the back of one hand over her face in a jerky motion that wasn't quite fast enough to hide the moisture that had spilled down one cheek. That decided things for Blue. Before she could take more than a single step after Fischer, a hard hand came down on her shoulder, gripping tightly enough it would take effort to break free. She snarled, but Twister didn't let her go.

"Okay, I take back what I said about your checkride. Maybe you should worry a little." Twister frowned and gave Blue a small shake when she wouldn't stop struggling. "That's enough, Lieutenant Eliassen."

"Ma'am?" Blue stilled at the formal address.

"I taught you better than that," Twister said sternly before a slight smirk broke free. "We get your checkride done first, *then* we bury his ass. Figuratively speaking."

"Literally isn't off the table yet," Blue snapped, her gaze drifting to where Fischer had disappeared behind the hangar. But she didn't try to charge after him again, and Twister released her shoulder.

Killi snorted a watery laugh. "It's fine, really. The important thing is I passed, it's over, and he's never allowed back in our cockpit."

"Damn straight," Witch muttered, throwing a supportive arm around her copilot. "Let's go get our accommodations sorted out. I need a drink."

This time Killi's laugh was more genuine. "*You* need a drink?"

"Yes, I do," Witch declared grimly. "I deserve a medal for not tossing that fuckstick out of the cockpit midflight. Barring that, I'll take a drink."

A welcoming committee of sorts met them at the edge of the landing pad. Norwood was not among them, nor were any of his top staff members. However, one of the waiting civvies greeted Mister High and Mighty effusively and led the team into the outpost, leaving the legionnaires behind. The two remaining civvies said all the right things, smiled at all the right times, but they didn't bother to introduce themselves. They also made it very clear they would prefer if the legionnaires stuck to their designated lodging or the landing pad and didn't "accidentally wander into restricted areas."

They were led in a circuitous route down the street that ran along the compound wall, able to see deeper within the bustling community without actually getting to step foot within it. Marching just behind the civvies, Blue was the first to catch a glimpse of their accommodations.

"Now this is more like what I expected," she muttered under her breath.

The civvies grandly gestured to the pair of ramshackle buildings as if they'd done them a favor, promised to deliver food shortly, and left. The legionnaires immediately started bitching, but their sergeants kept them under control. Personally, Blue was happy Carvalho had left

HeyHey to work on the interior of her Rhino. It would've been asking too much to keep those two quiet.

Both buildings looked like they were original to the outpost, probably from before Norwood had positioned himself here. Cautiously, Sergeant Ord pulled open the door of the closest structure. The hinges squealed a harsh protest before one broke off entirely, leaving the door half hanging in Ordo's hand. Something rat-adjacent streaked out of the dark entrance and disappeared into the weeds hugging the side of the building with a whistle-pop of displeasure.

"Well... that's encouraging." Ordo ducked inside but was back out within seconds, shaking his head. "There's a hole in the roof, the interior walls are sagging, and the floor is more animal droppings than anything else. The whole thing should be set on fire. Pigeon, take your boys and see if the other building is habitable."

While Pigeon trotted off with his fire team, Ordo had a quick discussion with Sergeant Cox before facing the pilots.

"We'll bivouac outside. It'll be safer. If the other building isn't suitable, we can either set up a separate camp for you, or you can bed down in your Rhinos."

Carvalho glanced at Sergeant Tinnesz, his counterpart on Bronze Raven Five. When the younger loadmaster shrugged, Carvalho said, "The Crows will bed down in the Rhinos. Not a bad idea to have a little extra security on them anyways. I don't trust these civvies as far as HeyHey can throw them."

Pigeon trotted back over. "The second building is in slightly better shape. The roof is intact, the structure is sound enough, and the rats didn't get in. I think we can clean out the ground floor for our Ravens at least." He hesitated. "It's all one open area."

Twister nodded. "Works for me."

Witch grinned. "Sounds like it's sleepover time, ladies."

"With alcohol?" Killi asked plaintively.

"All the alcohol," Blue said firmly.

In short order, the legionnaires had the building cleaned out enough to be survivable and their tents set up outside so nothing could get to their pilots without first going through them. Eventually, the welcoming committee made good on their promise of food, delivering barely palatable survival food—and Mitzi.

The mousy little scientist's expression was dejected as she struggled to drag her personal gear behind her. Before anyone else could offer to help, Tavi was just *there*, materializing like a ghost. Blue blinked, startled because she hadn't even seen the young legionnaire move. With a gentle smile, he took her bag from her. They exchanged a few quiet words, and then he escorted her over to the pilots. His earnest gaze focused on Blue, possibly because she was the closest to him, or maybe she was just the one he was the least intimidated by.

"Excuse me, ma'am. Miss Mitzi needs a place to stay, and I thought she could bed down with you."

So that's the little mouse's actual name.

Mitzi rolled her eyes before she gifted Tavi with a fond smile. "I've told you before, it's just Mitzi."

"No, it's not," Blue said decisively, both because she wanted to mess with the girl, and to give Tavi a chance to catch his equanimity, because his shoulders were stiff with something other than embarrassment.

"Um, it's not?" Mitzi asked tentatively, as if uncertain about her own damn name. Blue grinned, careful to make sure there was nothing mean in her expression. She had a feeling the poor girl had seen enough of that lately, and she only meant to tease.

"Nope, it's Mouse. You dropped, you get a drop name."

Tavi smiled, but a spark of fire ignited in the young woman's eyes.

"And the best you could come up with was *Mouse*?" Mitzi demanded. "Can't I have something better, like, I don't know, Crypto?"

"Sorry, you can't pick your own name. It's in the rules." Blue frowned. "Wait, why do you need a place to stay?"

Mitzi's shoulders hunched, any trace of defiance melting away as she mumbled something too quiet to be intelligible. Tavi clearly heard her though. Something dark passed across his face as he shifted closer to the young woman.

"Apparently," he said with quiet anger, "there isn't room in the accommodations the rest of her team were given. Dr. *Schmoyer* needed extra space for his dressing room."

The young legionnaire clearly felt protective toward Mitzi. Not necessarily a bad thing, because she just as clearly needed the protection, and his fire team had been tasked with protecting the civilians while out in the field. Idly, Blue wondered what had happened to the girl's spine. She'd caught a glimpse of it that first day on the orbital naval shipyard, when Mitzi had stalked after her team carrying far too much gear, chin up and murder in her eyes.

Maybe I can help with that little problem.

A commotion carried over the general background noise of eating legionnaires and the evening jungle just outside the looming walls. Blue sighed at the indignant cries and snarled curses. More than one legionnaire looked as if he were taking notes as her gunners let *everyone* know what they thought of the outpost's generous accommodations.

Speaking of little problems...

Corporals Hekekia and Hayashi shoved their way past the legionnaires and stared up at the ramshackle building the Ravens were going to bed down in.

"You've got to be fucking shitting me," Hekekia said flatly.

"Why not just ask us to sleep in the freaking jungle? It might be cleaner," Hayashi added in disgust.

"HeyHey," Sergeant Carvalho snapped. "I understand you're only saying what we're all thinking, but please say it inside those empty little skulls of yours, not loudly enough for the entire outpost to hear. Or I'll have you cleaning the *other* building, which is more rat shit than actual wood. You copy?"

"Yes, Sergeant," they grumbled. Hayashi did her best to look repentant. Hekekia didn't bother.

"If you'd bothered to ask before you decided to rant loudly enough to disturb whatever monkey fuckers are out in those trees," he continued acidly, "you'd know that sleeping in the Rhino with your precious guns is an option."

Both corporals immediately brightened. "We can sleep with our babies?"

"I'm sure I'm going to regret this, but yes," Sergeant Carvalho muttered. The gunners cheered.

Mitzi tilted her head, looking as if she couldn't decide between intrigued and appalled. "Your *babies?*"

"Our Aries Miniguns," Hayashi said with a dreamy cast to her voice.

"Oh!" Understanding lit up Mitzi's eyes. "You mean the M268 GAU-18 Aries Miniguns. A six-barrel Gatling-style machine gun that fires 30mm depleted uranium rounds, high-explosive incendiary rounds, or anti-personnel rounds at a high rate of fire. They're particularly effective at close air support and clearing drop zones of..." She faltered and crossed her arms defensively as both gunners stared at her. "What? I read."

Hekekia and Hayashi exchanged a quick glance before they grinned broadly.

"Do you want to stay with us tonight?" they asked in perfect unison.

"Um..." Mitzi looked at Tavi, then Blue. "Do I?"

"Yes!" the gunners said in unison again.

Blue glanced at the other Ravens, but Killi was talking quietly with Witch—quite possibly plotting the eventual murder of Captain Fischer—while Twister just looked on in amusement.

"HeyHey, it might be better for Mouse to stay with us," Blue said when it became apparent that Twister was content to let her handle the situation.

"We have pillows," Hayashi said enticingly.

"Those are ammo bags," Carvalho said dryly.

"Same difference!" Hekekia danced in anticipation. "Stay with us!"

Sergeant Carvalho groaned. "Miss, if you do, I'll be sure to sleep on the other bird. I want no part in whatever sleepover bullshit HeyHey might talk you into."

"Um...that is...I..."

Blue sighed. It was painfully obvious that Mitzi did *not* want to sleep in the back of a Rhino using ammo bags as pillows, but the other woman shifted her weight, hunched her shoulders further—something Blue hadn't thought possible—and mumbled under her breath.

"Just tell them no if you don't want to." Exasperation sharpened Blue's tone more than she wanted, but honestly, it wasn't like HeyHey would bite if they were told no. She paused and reconsidered. Hekekia might. When Mitzi just stammered a few more times, her face reddening, Blue's patience finally snapped. "I'm way too tired for this shit. HeyHey, grab some chow and then head back to the Rhino for the night with the other Crows. Little Mouse, you're bedding down with us."

"I-I thought my drop name was Mouse?" she whispered.

"I've downgraded you to Little Mouse." Blue softened her exasperation with a grin. "Once we find wherever you misplaced your spine, we can revisit the topic."

CHAPTER NINE
A New Deal

PNV PERSEVERANCE, *AURORA SYSTEM*

Ensign Garrett Campbell was exhausted, in an annoying amount of discomfort, and entirely out of patience for idiots.

After an interesting breakfast with Blue and the other aircrew, he'd spent the duty day catching shit from his crewmates for getting his "pretty face" messed up during liberty call planetside. Even more so when he refused to divulge exactly what had happened when he'd taken the hottest little dropship pilot out for a night in Yortugan Bay.

More than a few rumors had spawned over the course of the day, but he'd ignored all but the ones that cast Blue in a poor light. Those he had squashed with a ruthlessness he was careful to keep hidden except when the situation called for it. Let people be fooled into thinking he was nothing more than a pretty face. He preferred to be underestimated. But he'd be damned before he let Blue's reputation suffer for his idiocy.

Campbell straightened his shoulders as the lift *dinged* just before the doors slid open. He'd thought about going to the mess deck after his shift ended, but he didn't have it in him to deal with his peers. His fellow officers were bad, but the enlisted were absolutely *brutal* when it came to scuttlebutt. Sacrifices must be made, and honor kept intact. A cold dinner of protein bars and water in his quarters would have to suffice. If he was lucky and he'd timed it right, his roommate, Ensign Adrian Grimes, would already be gone for his shift in Comms.

He stepped out into the sparsely populated corridor, held the lift for a hustling pair of ensigns possibly late for their shift judging by their panicked expressions, and then slowly walked toward his room. He shook his head in disgust—at himself—as the events of last night played out in his mind again.

Getting caught with his figurative pants down by a Legion private—practically a kid, of all things. The fact that he'd been able to hold his own long enough for Blue to call Tavi off was as much due to luck as skill, and he felt he deserved every bruise that kid had left on him. He knew better than to let his guard down like that in Yortugan, but he'd been distracted... which was no excuse at all.

In a way, he owed that kid a "thank you." Blue deserved better than a make-out session behind a *bar*.

Outside of Blue, nobody knew Tavi had been the one to beat his ass six ways to Sunday, and Campbell intended to keep it that way. There was no other way to keep the kid from catching the kind of charges that ended up on permanent record, and Campbell knew how to read people. Tavi had legitimately been trying to do the right thing.

Campbell smirked despite the way it pulled at his split lip. Besides, there were other, less damaging ways to get a little payback. Ways that wouldn't damage the kid's career. He just needed to wait for the opportune moment. He was still smirking when the door to his shared quarters slid open and Grimes strode out.

Damn it all.

Grimes tested his patience on the best of days, and judging by the shit-eating grin on his face, he intended to see just how far he could push him. Unfortunately for Grimes, today really wasn't the day to try his nonexistent patience.

"Hey, Campbell. You look like you had a little too much fun last night."

"Not now, Grimes," Campbell said quietly and tried to push past, but the other man had the audacity to actually block his way with one arm. Grimes' grin widened as his gaze traveled over his bruised face.

"I heard the Ravens were wild cats in the sack, but damn, man. Eliassen fucked you up but good." Grimes let out a low whistle. "Must be some piece of ass for you to tolerate that shit."

Campbell stilled. Grimes was not only oblivious to his sudden danger, he was stupid enough to keep digging his grave deeper.

"I mean, I would do a lot to get between those pretty thighs, but letting her mess up my face is a step too far." He let out a rough laugh and slapped Campbell's shoulder. "You get what I'm saying, brother?"

Campbell's expression flattened and he stared *through* the other man. Grimes' laughter trailed off and he took a nervous step back. Campbell prowled closer, and Grimes retreated until his back slammed against the door to their quarters.

"Say one more word about her, and your face will look worse than mine," Campbell said. Grimes scowled, and Campbell lashed out, slamming his hand on the hatch directly next to the other man's head. Grimes flinched at the loud *bang*. "You get what *I'm* saying?"

The *ping* of his comm was probably all that saved Campbell from doing something stupid that might end up on *his* permanent record. Firmly regaining his grip on his temper, he stepped back.

"What the hell, man? I thought she was just a . . ." Grimes finally caught a clue bird and trailed off at the murderous look on Campbell's face. He held up empty hands. "Right, not another word about her."

"Better get to your shift." Campbell smiled and straightened Grimes' collar. "Wouldn't want you to be late."

"Right," Grimes said again, sidling along the hatch to get clear of Campbell. With a jerky nod, he slipped past and quickly walked away, but his low mutter wasn't quite low enough. "Fucking psycho."

Campbell flexed his shoulders and shook out his hands to release the tension. He liked Blue well enough and had made his interest abundantly clear, but his reaction wasn't really about her. Grimes was mostly harmless, more talk than anything else, but every so often the immature idiot needed a reminder of how a Navy officer should treat women.

It was for his own good, really. If the XO ever heard him saying moronic things like that, she'd eviscerate him and string up his guts as party streamers, a visual aid and warning to anyone else on board who felt like being terminally stupid. And that was probably kinder than what the legionnaires would do if they ever heard Grimes disrespecting their Ravens.

Another *ping* reminded him of what had saved Grimes in the first place. He turned his wrist to look at the new messages on his comm. His eyes flicked from the screen to his quarters and back. Technically, he had time to grab one of those protein bars, but it wasn't a good idea to keep the captain of the ship waiting.

He had no idea why he'd been summoned to the Officers Wardroom when he was off duty, but it was best to get there ASAP.

It was a truism that if you were early to a meeting in the military, you were on time. If you were on time, you were late. If you were late, don't even bother showing up because there was no saving your ass. He trotted down the corridor, heading back to the lift he'd only just arrived on.

A snort of laughter escaped his control when he passed Grimes in the corridor. The other ensign cringed back against the bulkhead as if he thought Campbell had decided to chase him down. Without slowing in the slightest, Campbell slid to a stop in front of the lift and hit the call button. A few seconds later, the door slid open and he stepped inside.

Campbell held the lift open, a brow arched in silent invitation, but Grimes shook his head.

"I'll catch the next one."

Campbell let the door slide closed and smiled, satisfied that the lesson had sunk home.

The Officers Wardroom hadn't changed since the last time he'd been invited—as the junior Operations officer he wasn't invited often. If Captain Eric Esper needed to meet with his officers, the senior Operations officer, Lieutenant Darin Stahl, was the one who attended the meeting. Though with the possibility of moving up in the next promotion cycle, Stahl had mentioned a few times that he planned to start bringing Campbell more often. Maybe that's all this was. A learning opportunity.

Campbell settled into the seat next to his supervisor, suppressing a wince as his ribs protested, and looked around the understated but undeniably well-appointed wardroom. The *Perseverance* might be old, but her captains had taken care to maintain her appearance throughout the decades, and this room had fared better than most. The table was polished wood, the chairs were plush, and the bulkheads were concealed behind paneled walls. It wouldn't have looked out of place in a mid-level Mars Primus business.

The chairs were filled by exactly the command staff he'd expect, both Navy and Legion. The ship's XO, Commander Beth Lobdell, sat in the chair to the right of the head of the table, fingers flying over her slate as she worked. The hint of dark circles under her eyes said she was long past the end of her duty shift, but her spine might as well have been steel for all it bent. Next to her was their new Intel officer, Lieutenant Commander Liam Hart, a reassignment from their sister ship *Tenacity*, home to the Bronze Legion's Alpha Company.

Campbell hadn't interacted with him much, nor had he been able to find out *why* Hart had been transferred. Of course, he couldn't throw stones when he kept secrets of his own. Gingerly, he shifted in his plush seat, the discomfort in his ribs spiking into a sharp twinge of pain.

Sitting directly across from him, Major Nikki "Voodoo" Ellingwood exchanged a glance with her Director of Operations, Captain Stephanie "Ditch" Baxter, before her piercing green gaze came to rest squarely on his bruised face. Voodoo's lips twitched in what looked like suppressed mirth, while her DO dropped him a wink.

To round out the command staff, Captain Oren "Tripwire" Truitt, commander of Bravo Company, sat at the foot of the table.

The only person missing was the captain himself.

No sooner did he have that thought than Captain Esper strode inside. Everyone rose to their feet and remained standing until the captain seated himself at the head of the table and waved them back down.

An older man with more salt than pepper in his close-cropped hair and deep crow's feet around his dark eyes, Captain Eric Esper was a twenty-year veteran of the Mars Protectorate Navy and had commanded the *Perseverance* for eight years. In all the time Campbell had served under him, he'd never heard of anything more than the usual grumbling and complaints from his crewmates, usually about things not even a ship's captain could change, no matter how politically connected.

And Captain Esper's family was damn near as politically connected as Campbell's.

"My apologies for the last-second meeting, but we've got a developing situation down on Aurora."

Tripwire straightened up, visible alarm stamping his tanned features. "My legionnaires?"

"No, politics," Captain Esper said, some of his dry sense of humor coloring his tone. The captain leaned back in his chair, the informal pose signaling he didn't expect anyone to stand on ceremony for this particular meeting. "Not entirely unexpected, given that the Norwood family is involved."

Campbell barely held back a groan. He might avoid politics as much as possible in his career, but with two older brothers and his mother thoroughly entrenched, he couldn't escape it when he went home. While both his family and the Norwood family were part of the Five Hundred, they were about as far apart politically speaking as possible. They weren't enemies, per se, but they weren't allies either.

"I went to the Naval Academy with a Norwood," Esper said musingly. "A surprisingly decent fellow—probably because he was only a distant cousin to the main branch. The shit that poor man would tell me about his family when he got drunk enough..."

Disdain flashed across his face as he shook his head. Campbell had no doubt the captain had allowed them to see it, because Esper had the best poker face he'd ever seen, and had a well-deserved reputation as a cutthroat spades player on top of that.

"It was no surprise he went career Navy to escape them, but I digress. The reason for the staff meeting is that Sir Percival Norwood III, the supervisor of the Aurora Research Outpost, has invited us to..." Esper paused, drawing out the suspense with an almost playful twinkle in his eyes. "A formal dining event."

This time, Campbell wasn't the only one who clearly held back a groan. Voodoo visibly shuddered, Tripwire's shoulders slumped, and the XO curled her lip, as disgusted as if someone had just invited her to eat spiders for dinner.

"Apparently, while Norwood wants the Legion in and out as quickly as possible, he's sniffed out that we have some politically connected officers on board. He's positioned himself to take the Aurora governor position should the planet be accepted into the Protectorate in the upcoming budgetary cycle, and he can't let an opportunity to add to his alliances pass by." Esper's gaze slid toward Campbell. "Or ensure some not-so-friendly parties don't stand in his way. The invitation is for no more than a dozen Navy and Legion personnel. With that in mind, I want to stack the deck in our favor, as it were."

Voodoo snorted. "If you want politically connected, you need to make sure Lieutenant Eliassen is included in that invite, *keiche*?"

"Norwood already insisted on inviting all of your Ravens already down on Aurora. He finds the concept of an all-female dropship squadron fascinating—or a joke, I honestly can't tell which." Esper paused, leaning forward in interest and no little surprise. "Wait, why Eliassen specifically? Her file says she's from a middle-class Mars Primus family, with a grandfather who earned his citizenship by serving in the Legion. Nothing out of the ordinary there."

"That's because you didn't look at her maternal side." Voodoo smirked. "Lieutenant Astra 'Blue' Eliassen is the granddaughter of Shava Turnien."

Actual shock rocked Esper back in his seat, but Campbell nodded to himself in understanding. It explained her dream to join the Survey Corps. She wanted to follow in her legendary grandmother's footsteps in the Exploration branch. And even to those outside the Survey Corps, Shava had been a legendary figure.

An anticipatory smile replaced the shock on the captain's face. "That might come in handy. Thank you, Major Ellingwood."

"Not a problem, *bossjna*," Voodoo replied before she grimaced and corrected herself. "Sir."

Esper waved away her informality with a slight smile. He braced his elbows on the table and steepled his fingers together.

"I'll be leading the Navy contingent while my XO remains in command of the ship."

Lobdell's tight expression melted into a relieved smile. "Oh, no. Please convey my regrets to the supervisor for missing his little shindig."

Esper regarded her calmly. "If it means that much to you, I could always leave Stahl in charge and we could both go."

"Though it pains me to miss it," Lobdell said solemnly, "I must insist on placing duty above personal preferences and remain with the ship."

Her lips twitched, and Esper barked a laugh. "Very well. Lieutenant Commander Hart, you'll of course accompany me, Lieutenant Commander Logan will go, and for Ops, I'll take Ensign Campbell."

"Me, sir?" Campbell fought to keep his surprise off his face, but he didn't have near the experience Captain Esper did.

"Yes, you. I need one of my Ops officers down there, and you're better suited than anyone else."

"Your family's political connections will give you a buffer I'd lack," Stahl said, nodding in agreement. The senior Ops officer had few ties outside of the Navy and no political capital to speak of. Someone of

Norwood's standing would bulldoze right over him. "Bad enough we have to send Tripwire into the lion's den."

Rather than take offense, Tripwire grimaced. "Not my sort of thing, but I can play pretend. They do have a tea and crumpets class at Officer Candidate School for us legionnaires, you know."

"Plus, while they might look down on the Legion, they won't dare piss off the most popular branch in the military," Esper added, chuckling. "So myself, Ops, Comms, Intel, and the Ravens on the ground, plus Bravo Company CO. Am I missing anyone?"

"An adjutant or aide-de-camp for Tripwire, sir," Campbell said as the opportune moment for a little vengeance presented itself practically gift wrapped. The fact that it would satisfy the political junkies down on Aurora was just the shiny ribbon on top. "If Norwood or his allies see Tripwire without some lackey running errands and being his busybody, they won't take him or, by extension, the Legion, seriously. We need someone who can *shine* down there, but someone who also looks the part of earnest assistant. Most importantly, they need a rare decoration or merit ribbon, something that will make people want to ask questions."

"Nobody's earned anything for valor in battle in almost thirty years now," Tripwire muttered as he leaned back in his seat, a thoughtful expression on his face. "I've got some senior legionnaires who saw action at the Madrigal Insurrection, but they're old and not really suited to being my aide. Master Sergeant Briggs, for example, but he's missing half his face. I mean, we could score some serious points if we wanted to throw them off their game, but..."

The hook was ready. And he had the perfect bait. "What about Private Diego Tavi, sir? 4th Squad, Fire Team Two? He's already on the ground."

"Private Tavi?" Tripwire tapped the bridge of his nose in silent contemplation for a moment. "Hmm... Tavi... Not a bad choice. Distinguished Honor Graduate from ACS, hasn't picked up any bad habits from the other legionnaires yet. The Bronze hasn't had an Honor Grad in over a decade. They typically get snapped up by bigger legions." Tripwire hesitated. "He's a little young, though, isn't he?"

"He's also familiar with the Survey Corps team," Campbell pressed, sensing his opportunity slipping away. "If I recall correctly, 4th Squad is tasked with escorting them out in the jungles of Aurora while they're evaluating the planetary status. They're comfortable around him, and he's small enough to look harmless, more like someone's kid brother than a legionnaire, sir."

"Valid point," Tripwire conceded.

"I've seen his file." Esper snorted. "He'll look like a poster boy for the Legion without making any of them nervous. He's perfect."

"Yes, sir." Tripwire nodded. "He even has his dress uniform stowed away in his bunk up here. Probably pressed and vacuumed so it comes out of the bag unwrinkled. I'll take it by the storekeeper, though, just to be sure. I can take it down for him and give him a quick briefing on how to act. I don't expect to have too much issue with him. Both his team leader and squad leader already speak highly of him."

"He's the one who called in the CAS during the exercise on Sagetnam, wasn't he?" Voodoo interjected, eyes glinting as she looked over at Campbell. There was something in her face which made him slightly wary.

"It was his idea," Tripwire confirmed.

"Thought I recognized the name." Voodoo smiled with just a little too much teeth, her eyes still very much focused on Campbell. "Quick thinker without any political connections, junior enough that nobody should try to sucker him into their political games. I'm not sure I like the idea of him being on his own though."

Campbell grimaced, wondering if he'd overplayed his hand.

"Honestly, it wouldn't be a bad thing for Tripwire to have an NCO as an aide as well." Campbell looked between Captain Esper and Tripwire. "I'd recommend Sergeant Ord over Cox. Ord is more likely to keep his temper, and Tavi is familiar with him."

Voodoo held his gaze for a long moment before she nodded. "That should do nicely, *ke*."

Captain Esper was not an unobservant man. He glanced between the dropship squadron commander and his junior Ops officer, but apparently judged whatever was going on was below his paygrade. He was the kind of commander who was content to let his people work out their issues—so long as it didn't interfere with the smooth running of his ship.

"Any further suggestions?" he asked firmly.

"I'll get a full personnel briefing prepped for everyone going," Hart said, the Intel officer's head bent over his slate. "Profiles of the major players, known political affiliations, and any red flags or landmines to avoid. You'll have it by tomorrow morning."

"Excellent. A reminder for those going—tread these shores lightly, people," Esper warned, rapping a knuckle on the conference table. "You're on treacherous ground with these animals. Don't think for a moment they won't use you for even the narrowest of political points before casting you aside, or destroying you simply because it made one of their sycophants laugh. We'll make the command-wide announcement at the top of the hour, and a shuttle will transport everyone down tomorrow at 1400 Zulu. Thank you for your time. Dismissed."

Voodoo and Campbell were the last two to leave. As he reached the door, however, she stopped and turned to him, allowing the door to slide shut. It left them alone in the wardroom.

"So now I know who kicked your shit in," she said, a terrifyingly calm expression on her face. "If you're trying to ruin him or *fech* with his chances of citizenship because he beat your ass square in a fight, I will find a way to end you."

Campbell noted she said "you" and not "your career."

"Not my goal, ma'am," he replied, raising his palms carefully. "If I wanted to do that, I would've just reported him. I didn't, and I have no intention of doing so."

"Is that so?"

"My word on it." He placed one hand over his heart. "He's a good kid. Earnest, a protector, and lives by his Legion Oath. The altercation was a misunderstanding. More than that, he was trying to do the right thing—protect one of your Ravens. I don't blame him, I *admire* him."

"Then what's this about?" Voodoo demanded, her eyes still narrowed dangerously.

"This is . . . just a little friendly payback for something *else* he did."

She raised an eyebrow. "I hope so, for your sake."

Tension leaked out of his frame when the woman turned on one heel and sauntered out of the wardroom. The captain of the ship made Campbell nervous sometimes. The commander of the Ravens fucking *terrified* him.

Blowing out a short breath, Campbell checked the time. Not quite top of the hour yet. Which meant he had a little time to mess with an entirely different Raven.

✧✧✧

After a quick dinner that tasted far worse than anything the mess deck had ever served—Blue wasn't even certain what it was supposed to be other than soggy vegetable matter and a tasteless grain—the pilots headed inside to set up their bedding, dragging Mitzi along with them. Under Pigeon's supervision, the legionnaires had done a passable job of making the space survivable, if not pleasant. The door even fully closed so they wouldn't have to worry about accidentally giving the boys a free show when they changed into PT gear to sleep. Small victories.

By unspoken agreement, the women set up their bedding together in the back corner of the room, where the floor was just a little cleaner and the odd, musty odor clinging to the walls was slightly less prevalent.

"So about that alcohol," Killi said somewhat plaintively once they were all changed and lounging on their bed rolls.

"I got you, girl." Witch pulled out a flask and tossed it to her. Killi didn't hesitate to unscrew the cap and tilt it up, pouring whatever was inside straight into her mouth... only to choke, eyes watering.

Witch let out a slightly evil cackle. "Careful, this is the good shit."

"Now you tell me," Killi croaked, wiping her mouth with the back of her hand before passing it to Blue.

Cautiously, Blue sniffed it, immediately regretted that decision as her nose hairs shriveled, and belted back a shot without letting the booze linger on her tongue. As warmth burned down to her belly—and possibly took some of her esophagus with it—she tilted it toward Mitzi.

"Little Mouse?"

"Oh, n-no, no thank you," she said, shrinking back and holding her hands up like a barrier as if afraid Blue would force her to partake.

"A simple 'no' would've sufficed," she said dryly. "Spine, Little Mouse. Find one."

Mitzi stiffened, fire flashing in her eyes, before she dropped her gaze. Blue sighed, capped the flask, and tossed it to Twister, who took a slow pull as if she drank paint thinner on a regular basis. After she handed it back to Witch, she eyed them all with a sharp grin.

"Okay, ladies. We can't do booze and sleepovers without story time." She softened her grin for Mitzi. "Here are the rules. You can tell us whatever you want, you just need to start your story with 'So there

I was,' and it has to contain at least ten percent truth. I can go first if you want—"

"I've got one," Mitzi said unexpectedly. Her gaze flicked up and held Blue's. "So there I was, trying to enjoy a night out, when I saw a certain pilot one drink away from climbing a certain Navy officer like a tree..."

Blue grinned when Mitzi finished her highly improbable and not even remotely flattering story.

"Now *that*, Little Mouse, is more like it." She accepted the flask from Killi and saluted the girl. "Here's to finding a little of that spine."

The night deepened as they exchanged stories, but soon enough the flask was empty, and their voices had fallen silent. Somewhere along the way Twister had turned off their camp light, and darkness held them in a soft embrace. The exhaustion Blue had been holding at bay all day slammed into her, helped along by a fair share of whatever the hell Witch had put in that flask, and she curled up under her blanket, more than ready for sleep.

She nearly snarled when her wrist comm quietly *pinged* to alert her to a new message, shattering the silence that had fallen over the room. After a quick glance at the screen, her irritation fell away and a small grin pulled at her lips.

ENSIGN HOTNESS: I PROPOSE AN ADDENDUM TO OUR CURRENT DEAL.

A surge of excitement rippled through her, pushing back her exhaustion just enough for her to keep her eyes open.

BLUE: TERMS?

ENSIGN HOTNESS: AN EXTRA DRINK FOR EXTRA INFORMATION.

BLUE: HMM...LET ME THINK ABOUT THAT.

Blue bit her lip to contain her smile and let him sweat for a few heartbeats.

ENSIGN HOTNESS: COME ON, BLUE. YOU KNOW YOU WANT TO SAY YES.

BLUE: HOW DO I KNOW YOUR INFORMATION IS WORTH IT?

Blue expected him to point out his information had always been worth it, or maybe get defensive. He didn't. He teased her back.

ENSIGN HOTNESS: THAT'S JUST A RISK YOU'LL HAVE TO TAKE, DARLIN'.

BLUE: LUCKY FOR YOU I'M A GAMBLER. I SUPPOSE I CAN SUFFER THROUGH AN EXTRA DRINK WITH YOU IN THE HOPES YOU CAN TELL ME SOMETHING... WORTH MY WHILE.

"I am *so* proud of you," Killi whispered, dramatically wiping at her eyes. She had scooted over onto Blue's bedding while she'd been distracted and was reading her messages over her shoulder. "Look at you flirting like a boss. Knew my girl had it in her."

Blue shoved Killi back onto her own bedding. "Would you quit being such a nosy bitch?"

"Hell no! We're all living vicariously through you right now!"

"All?" Blue glanced up to see both Twister and Witch watching her, eyes gleaming. The faint light given off by her comm wasn't enough to lift the thick shadows draped over the dilapidated room, but it was enough for her to make out their smug expressions.

"This is the best sleepover I've been to in a long time that didn't involve sex," Witch said with a wicked little grin that shaved years off her face.

With a slight shock, Blue realized the other pilot was maybe five years her senior at most. Twister was the oldest of the four of them, but even she wasn't that much older. It was just that Blue had categorized them that way because they were higher ranked officers, more experienced pilots, and had been with the Bronze for years by the time she'd shown up, nothing more than a wet-behind-the-ears newbie.

Twister propped herself up on one elbow and snorted. "To hear you tell it, this is probably better than anything you've gotten lately."

"A sad truth." Witch winked at Blue. "Here's hoping Ensign Hotness lives up to his reputation. We expect details later."

"Much later," Killi interjected sternly. "Make him—"

"Chase, I know, I know," Blue muttered. "Quit acting like it's my first rodeo."

Twister snickered. "Yeehaw."

"Ride 'em, cowgirl," Witch added with a sleepy cackle, pulling her bedding up to her chin.

"No riding," Killi declared, stabbing one finger into the air dramatically.

"I need a new bestie." Blue rolled her eyes and looked back at her comm.

ENSIGN HOTNESS: YOU CAN PAY UP TOMORROW.

Blue's eyebrows shot for the ceiling. They weren't scheduled to go back up to the *Perseverance* until the mission was over, and as far as she knew, nobody from the *Perseverance* was supposed to come down to the outpost.

BLUE: TOMORROW?

This time, Campbell was the one to make her wait. Impatience thrummed through her, and after less than a minute she broke with an audible growl.

BLUE: NAVY BOY, DON'T THINK I WON'T STAB YOU.

HOTNESS: THAT'S MY LINE.

BLUE: CAMBELL!!!

ENSIGN HOTNESS: SOOO IMPATIENT.

She could almost hear him laughing at her. Probably because he sent an image of him laughing at her. And then he sent her the information she'd bartered for. Frowning, she read through it again, slower this time, but the message didn't change.

ENSIGN HOTNESS: WELL? DID YOUR GAMBLE PAY OFF?

A slow smile pulled at her lips.

BLUE: GUESS YOU'LL FIND OUT TOMORROW . . .

Without waiting to see if he'd respond, she turned off the screen and looked up at the other women waiting with varying levels of impatience.

"Better clean the mud off your boots, ladies. Looks like we're invited to a political shindig tomorrow." Her gaze drifted to Killi. "And we need to be on our best behavior."

"Don't worry, I'll keep my mouth shut around Norwood," Killi said with a tired yawn.

"All of us need to," Blue said with a grim note in her voice.

Silence fell over the room again, only broken by soft snores from Mitzi, who had apparently managed to sleep through all of it. Not even a minute later, Twister's comm *pinged*. Her eyes flicked back and forth as she read the message, and then she looked up at Blue with a smirk.

"Your ensign played you. He barely beat the official notification."

"He did warn me it was a risk." Blue grinned, shaking her head in admiration. "I mean, I'm not sad about it."

"I wouldn't be either," Witch said, both amusement and envy riding her words.

"Can all of you *please* stop talking," Mitzi suddenly mumbled, her bleary eyes cracked open. "Or I'll take HeyHey up on their offer and sleep with them tomorrow."

All four pilots burst out laughing.

"If you think that would be quieter," Twister snickered, "then by all means, go for it."

The girl grumbled and rolled over, giving them her back. Blue rolled over as well so Killi couldn't see her comm this time and checked to see if there were any new messages from Campbell. There was just one.

ENSIGN HOTNESS: CAN'T WAIT.

CHAPTER TEN
Tea and Crumpets and Booze . . . Lots of Booze

AURORA RESEARCH OUTPOST, AURORA

Blue's grandmother had been many things over the course of her long life. Brazen explorer, brash pilot, unlikely hero—though she'd always hated that label—and rarely a fool. By the time Blue came along, Shava had been a canny veteran of both the Survey Corps and the political minefields of Mars Primus. Once she'd realized Blue was serious about following in her footsteps, Shava had made it her mission to educate her granddaughter in everything she'd need to know to succeed.

That included formal dinners with the political elite.

Those dinners had become a bonding experience in shared misery for grandmother and granddaughter. Neither enjoyed the constant scheming and maneuvering that came hand in hand with the grandiose events, and they always made sure to have something fun and relaxing planned for afterward. Ice cream when Blue was younger, copious amounts of booze when she was older.

During that time, Shava taught Blue to see behind the sweet smiles, to hear what lay beneath the honeyed words, and to dance among the elite without getting bogged down in the muck.

Late that afternoon, Norwood sent a representative to collect the Ravens for the dinner. Blue would've much preferred to wait for the arrival of the party from the *Perseverance*, but his representative insisted. The woman had the decency to look ashamed at the state of the Legion's accommodations, but she didn't comment on it either. She'd simply collected the pilots, suggested that whoever was acting as the Bravo Company CO's aides wait for their commanding officer's arrival in a way that wasn't a suggestion at all, and hadn't objected when Mitzi trailed along after them.

The woman, who'd belatedly introduced herself as Quinn Warrow, personal assistant to the supervisor's office, glanced back once as they walked deeper into the outpost. Shame flickered across her face again.

Blue quietly snorted. *She should've seen what it looked like yesterday.*

The Legion didn't believe in idle legionnaires, and with the Survey team taking the day to get settled and review their findings from the initial outing, the sergeants had put the squads to work. Fortunately for all concerned, while the first, larger building wasn't suitable for habitation, the plumbing still worked so latrines hadn't been necessary. Instead, they'd focused on making improvements to their impromptu camp, reinforcing the second building with materials carefully scrounged from the first, and of course, more cleaning.

But it was obvious there were other places the outpost could have housed the Legion, and Warrow knew it.

For their part, the Ravens had spent the day prepping for the next field excursion, which had included reviewing updated weather reports. That tropical storm was still building in the southern oceans and promised to be something nasty. If the projections were accurate—and Blue had put her atmospheric degree to use and verified the weather forecast numbers—they were looking at a potential hurricane within the next few days. The outpost itself was far enough inland that it would merely mean the legionnaires were in for a wet camp, but it would be more of a concern on the coast, where the Survey team wanted to explore.

If nothing else, it would make for some interesting flying.

As they walked down one of the paved roads toward the center of the outpost, Warrow gave them all a critical once-over. More specifically, what they were wearing. Only Mitzi seemed to pass muster.

"Problem?" Twister asked mildly enough, but Blue knew her well enough to catch the hidden irritation.

Compared to the flowing lines and bright colors of the civilian woman's outfit, their standard black duty uniforms were functional at best. But their bronze Raven patches stood out sharply from all the black, and their silver pilot wing badges had been polished until they shone in the sunlight. Even if the uniforms weren't pressed, they were clean, and a far better option than showing up to a formal dinner in dropship pilot armor.

"No, no problem. It's just..." Warrow wrinkled her nose. "I'm guessing you didn't bring any civilian clothes with you?"

"Sorry, I left my ball gown at home," Killi muttered.

"Behave." Blue sank her elbow in her best friend's side and offered Warrow a polite smile. "This was the best we could do."

The other woman's smile was strained. "Perhaps I could find you more suitable outfits—"

"What we have on will do just fine, *keiche*?" Witch said bitingly.

All of them had picked up random Passovan phrases from Voodoo, but for Witch to use one now was not a great sign for how the evening was going to go.

Blue bit back a groan and forced her polite smile to widen. "At the very least, we'll stand out from the crowd."

"You will, at that," Warrow replied and straightened her spine as if bracing for a reprimand. Since her eyes were squarely fixed on the elegant structure dominating the center of the compound, it was clear she didn't fear a reprimand from *them*. As they drew closer to the residence, she murmured, "I'm sure it will be fine."

It didn't look as if she believed her own words. Blue hoped the woman wouldn't actually get in trouble for their refusal to change, but at the same time she couldn't bring herself to care overmuch. Norwood had invited Ravens to his dinner. Let him see Ravens, not prim and proper civilian dolls.

The supervisor's residence had been thrown open for the dinner. Made of the same white stone as the majority of the *good* buildings, it had subtle touches that not so subtly emphasized its importance. At first, Blue eyed it with suppressed amusement, but a twist of apprehension quickly soured her mood. It so badly wanted to be a governor's residence, and if Norwood got his way, it soon would be.

Compared to the grand affairs of Mars Primus, the Aurora Outpost's event should have been laughable. But with a Norwood involved, Blue had a feeling it would be just as much a quagmire as the events she'd attended before joining the Legion. She just hoped Witch had another flask of the good stuff—they were all going to need a drink after this was over.

Warrow led them through the open double doors and down a white hallway with a high, arched ceiling. Their boots echoed off the polished stone floors, a distinct contrast to the quiet *click* of Warrow's heels and the nearly soundless footsteps of Mitzi, still trailing behind them like a forgotten shadow.

A faint hint of crisp citrus floated on the air with tropical floral overtones that grew heavier the closer they got to the end of the hallway. Shorter than Warrow even without taking those heels into account, Blue couldn't spot the source until the woman paused at the next set of open doors, turned sideways, and gestured for them to enter.

Now Blue understood why the construction had felt so familiar. It had been built in the style of the buildings popular in the tropical zones of Protectorate worlds, with wide corridors, thick stone, and an inner courtyard that varied in size and purpose depending on the owner. This particular courtyard had been transformed into a lush private garden, bursting with carefully cultivated flora native to Mars Primus—some of them quite delicate and difficult to grow. Blue immediately grasped the political undertones of such a space.

Not only was Norwood demonstrating that Aurora was a viable colony, deserving of joining the Protectorate, he was declaring his suitability for the role of planetary governor. One who would carefully cultivate the new world into a mirror of Mars Primus, following in the footsteps of Aries, the most successful of the Protectorate planets.

All without saying a word.

Artfully winding paths meandered through the garden, with an open central area and numerous smaller spots for conversation. Gracefully carved stone benches were scattered throughout, with small tables for holding the drinks the impeccably dressed waitstaff were carrying through the courtyard on trays. Opposite the door they had just walked through was a set of double doors leading to a legitimate, if small, ballroom. Twinkling lights had been strung across the courtyard in graceful lines, an amusing similarity to Gunrunner's outdoor patio.

The patrons, however, couldn't be more different.

Dozens of civilians filled the courtyard with dozens more in the ballroom. Politicians and government functionaries with soft hands and cunning eyes, veterans of an entirely different sort of battlefield than what the Legion trained for. All of them were dressed as if they were attending a state dinner at Mytikas, the capital city of Mars Primus, and every last one of them paused in their scheming to get a look at the new arrivals. Most gazes were simply curious, some were disdainful, but a few were blatantly interested.

A shudder of distaste rippled up Blue's spine. She would give up her next paycheck to be back at Gunrunner's, flirting with Campbell or watching 4th Squad teach some drunken locals respect instead of this snake pit disguised as a garden party.

"Smile, ladies," Twister murmured. "We're the stars of the dog-and-pony show."

"More like the exotic animals at the zoo," Witch muttered, but the other woman plastered a smile on her face and led the way into the courtyard. Sighing, Blue rolled her shoulders back and raised her chin, returning the looks with a polite expression as she followed.

The murmur of numerous voices washed over them as conversations resumed, more than one now centered around the Legion and the Navy and how their presence might impact the outpost's operations. Blue did her best to pretend she couldn't hear the less than flattering opinions, but Killi's expression slipped.

She gracefully blocked her friend's view of one cluster of civvies in particular and murmured in a singsong, "Your face is speaking for you again."

"Just pretend you're doing something you love," Mitzi said quietly. "That always works for me."

"Thanks, Little Mouse." Killi slowly exhaled and managed a smile that wasn't quite as murderous, though Blue didn't expect that to last long.

Witch guided them toward one of the small tables at the edge of the open central area. The pilots stood out from the finely dressed crowd like a murder of crows cutting through a flock of peacocks. Blue was grateful when one of the waitstaff intercepted them, drink tray in hand. Before any of them could accept, Twister gave a quick shake of her head.

"Water for all of us, if you don't mind." As the waiter nodded and slipped back to a side door that presumably led to the kitchen, Twister glanced at them. "We can switch to something stronger later in the evening, once Captain Esper is here to back us up. Even then, slow and steady, yeah?"

They all nodded, though Killi wasn't the only one to cast a wistful glance as another waiter slipped past with what looked like fine whiskey on his tray.

While they waited for their waiter to return, Blue gazed around the courtyard, attempting to get a feel for the currents. Shava had always insisted on observing for at least a few minutes before diving in, a lesson that had proved useful in all sorts of situations.

A slight smirk twisted her lips as she noted the various micro groups, the hangers on, and the power players. There were a surprising amount of the latter. She didn't recognize all of them, but the signs were unmistakable, especially when she picked out one or two younger scions of the political elite. Not the actual heads of their families or even the heirs, but still a strong sign of the support Norwood had gathered. He was making a power play, and he wasn't even being subtle about it.

And then there was the Survey team.

Mister High and Mighty held court at a table near the center of the open area. The other three members of his team were clustered around him like lapdogs, while members of Aurora Outpost's political elite circled like wolves paying homage to a bigger wolf. Blue's lip curled for an instant before she controlled her expression. Lapdog or wolf, one and all were looking at the man like they were hoping for scraps.

The one person Blue *didn't* see was Norwood.

She didn't know if that was because he was opting to be fashionably late—a valid if unsubtle tactic to establish higher standing—or because he was simply not visible from their current position. Out of the corner of her eye, she noted Mitzi twisting her hands, nervous gaze fixed on her boss, though she made no move toward him. Blue decided since nobody had gotten the balls to approach them yet, this was as good an opportunity as any to get some intel on the guy.

"What's the deal with Mister High and Mighty over there?" she asked softly, barely moving her lips. When Mitzi looked confused, Blue clarified. "That's what I've been calling your boss."

"Oh! You mean Dr. Charles William Joseph Schmoyer IV."

"What's up with all the long names?" Witch muttered, ducking her head to hide her eye roll. "We've got Dr. Charles William Joseph Schmoyer IV here, Sir Percival Norwood III there..."

"Long names to make up for short dicks," Killi said with the air of someone quoting a truism, devilish amusement dancing in her green eyes. Giving up on subtlety, Blue clapped a hand over her best friend's mouth.

"You promised to behave," she hissed.

Muffled laughter escaped Killi, hot puffs of air tickling Blue's hand, but it was Mitzi who laughed the loudest. The girl immediately slapped a hand over her own mouth, but it was too late. Schmoyer's annoyed gaze landed on the table of pilots and one mousy little assistant.

Mitzi was quickly summoned to Schmoyer's side with an impatient snap of his fingers, as if she was a dog who'd strayed when it was the man's own damn fault for not insisting she be housed with the rest of his team.

What a prick.

"He's an Expediter," Mitzi told Blue before she answered the summons. "The rest of us are just evaluators."

Blue's eyes widened. *That* information had most certainly been redacted from their official briefing. It was possible Campbell had known, but there were things he couldn't tell her. The Survey Corps sending an evaluator team headed by an Expediter—the branch charged with approving planets for admission into the Protectorate—definitely fell under "things he probably couldn't tell her."

She'd already known the Survey team had to be from the Evaluator branch. Exploration, the largest branch and the one Blue desperately wanted to join, was tasked with pushing the boundaries of known space and exploring new places never before seen by humanity. Evaluators, on the other hand, approved worlds for colonization, monitored terraforming stages, and issued hazard ratings.

Aurora already had preliminary approval to become a colony world but would need the appropriate hazard rating to qualify for Protectorate status.

Expediters were the smallest and most political branch, working directly with other Mars Protectorate government organizations, and they were only sent off world under very specific circumstances. Norwood must have gathered enough political support to trigger those circumstances. A somewhat alarming thought that was interrupted by Twister's elbow in her ribs.

"The crew from the *Perseverance* should've been here by now." Twister leaned closer to Blue, her words no louder than the memory of sound. "I can't get a message out on my comm. Try yours?"

Blue pulled up her message thread with Campbell and typed in a quick text.

BLUE: ETA?

The message bounced back.

NO SIGNAL

The hairs on the back of her neck stood up. Norwood had restricted comms. Her eyes darted around the courtyard, but there didn't seem to be any threats, not even visible guards. Hopefully this was nothing more than a paranoid politician taking precautions.

The murmur of voices swelled as the man himself stepped out of the ballroom and into the courtyard. He looked exactly as he'd appeared in the image on their briefing packet—a refined, smiling older gentleman with frozen eyes. A second man walked exactly one pace behind and slightly to the right. Taller, younger, far more attractive, and with a smile that rivaled Campbell's for charm. And trouble.

"*Hello* there," Killi murmured as they drew closer. "That's the Assistant Facility Supervisor, right?"

"John Delany, AKA the shiny distraction," Blue murmured back. "Don't be fooled by his pretty face. The Delanys are jackals."

Norwood stopped by the Survey team's table and exchanged what looked like pleasant words with Schmoyer. While he talked, his assistant supervisor turned that smile on the evaluators, brushing a kiss over Huyan Xi-Smith's knuckles in a courtly gesture that should have looked slimy but instead evoked old world charm.

"I mean, I wouldn't mind being fooled, just for a little bit," Killi said, her lips slightly parted as Delany turned his charm on Mitzi, who looked less than enthused.

"I volunteer as tribute," Witch added in a dazed tone. "As often as necessary."

Blue gave Delany bonus points for a well-practiced smolder, but really, he didn't hold a candle to Ensign Hotness.

Campbell meant it when he looked at a woman like that.

A few minutes later, Norwood ended his conversation with Schmoyer, a pleased expression on his face that didn't reach his eyes, and made a beeline for the Ravens. Again, Delany followed precisely one step behind.

"Ladies, I'm so pleased you could join us tonight," Norwood said as if they'd had a choice in the matter. "Please forgive my tardiness, I had to step away for an unscheduled meeting."

"Thank you for the invitation, Sir Norwood." Twister took a half step forward, placing herself firmly in the leadership position for the group. "Your residence is lovely, but we seem to be having an issue with our comms."

"Ah, please forgive the inconvenience," Norwood replied smoothly. "A simple security precaution for that pesky little meeting."

A casual motion of his hand toward his assistant supervisor and Delany pulled out a slate.

"My sincere apologies, ladies." As he tapped the screen, he glanced up with a sheepish grin. "I forgot to disable the comm restriction."

I just bet you did, Blue thought.

She also bet Delany practiced that expression in the mirror. Smile slightly crooked, warm green eyes crinkled just so, stray strand of brown hair falling across one eye. That boyish, earnest look didn't just ask for forgiveness, it made you *want* to offer it.

"There, all fixed," he said and tucked his slate away.

Twister's comm *pinged*, and she glanced at her wrist. The subtle tension in her shoulders eased but didn't vanish completely. Delany started an amusing story about the last time he'd forgotten to disable the comm restriction. He was everything a distraction should be—charming, witty, engaging. Despite their experience and Blue's warning, he quickly had the full attention of the other Ravens.

"Lieutenant Eliassen, if I might have a private word?" Norwood quietly asked. Blue hadn't even noticed when the man had moved, but he now stood at her side, one brow arched in polite query. And though he phrased it as a request, again, it wasn't as if Blue had a choice.

"Of course," she said, voice just a shade too loud. Twister shot her a sharp glance, but Blue gave her a subtle nod and allowed Norwood to draw her away from the other pilots.

With the skill of a seasoned politician, Norwood quickly isolated Blue from the rest of the party, guiding her with a polite hand under her elbow to the center of the courtyard. In pride of place was an elegant tiered fountain, the soothing rush of falling water just loud enough to prevent eavesdroppers.

"I hope I can count on your support for Aurora joining the

Protectorate as a full member during the upcoming budget cycle, Lieutenant Eliassen."

Blue blinked, the only outward sign of surprise she would allow herself. Norwood hadn't just dropped the small talk quicker than she'd expected—he'd dispensed with it altogether. Did he not think her trained enough to parse the political doublespeak, or was he being blunt because he didn't think he had the time for subtlety?

Fine. If we're going for blunt, I can be blunt.

"Sir Norwood, the last time I checked, I have no vote in the matter."

"Do you not?"

"No, sir. I'm just a Legion dropship pilot."

Norwood's gaze turned sharp, and a trickle of sweat worked its way down her spine. Where the *hell* was the crew from the *Perseverance*?

"While it is true you have no vote, you are not without a voice."

"I'm not sure what you mean, sir." She drew on her Legion training and held his gaze without trouble.

"Come now, let's not play pretend." Norwood gave her the kind of smile a grandfather might bestow on a particularly recalcitrant or stupid child. "No kin of Shava Turnien is without friends in the Survey Corps."

Somebody had done their homework.

Blue hesitated. Shava's passing hadn't diminished her legacy. In certain ways, it had cemented it. While what remained of her family wasn't a political powerhouse by any means—nor were they part of the Five Hundred—they were respected. More to the point, Blue still had access to all of her grandmother's vast network of friends and allies, and even a few friendly enemies.

Norwood pounced on that hesitation.

"I have the political support I need to secure the governor position of Aurora once it is accepted as a Protectorate world. But everything is riding on this evaluation. While I have a long-standing personal relationship with Dr. Schmoyer, the man is a stickler for the rules. Impeachable ethics, really, and I can't fault him for refusing to bend them."

So you want me to bend mine? Blue kept a snarl off her face by the thinnest of margins.

"My deepest apologies, sir," she began carefully, "but the Legion has very strict guidelines on participating in... extracurricular activities of any sort—"

On edge from the conversation, her head snapped around at a loud bang. Through the greenery and the milling guests, she watched a group of Navy and Legion officers march into the courtyard.

Relief whispered through Blue at the sight of Captain Esper at the head of the delegation. The older man was impeccably dressed in the full regalia of a Protectorate of Mars Navy officer, every gold button on his maroon blouse gleaming, black uniform trousers sharply creased, shoes shined to perfection, and service ribbons and medals on full display. Warrow, Norwood's personal assistant, stood to the side, one hand on the door she'd accidentally flung open with a bit too much force, or perhaps that had been Sergeant Ord, who stood just inside the courtyard wearing a savage expression.

Norwood drifted forward so he stood at her elbow again.

"Think on our little conversation. A word in the right ear from you could help me immensely. And a word in the wrong one from *me* could ensure you remain exactly what you are for the rest of your career." He leaned down and murmured in her ear. "*Just* a Legion dropship pilot."

Without another word to her, Norwood strode off with a welcoming smile.

"Ah, Captain Esper, so glad you could make it!" he called out in a hearty tone.

Blue stood frozen for a bare handful of seconds before she managed to unlock her spine and compartmentalize the threat.

Later. She could deal with it later.

For now, she focused on the official party from the *Perseverance*, because damn if Campbell wasn't one hell of a distraction. A far better one than Delany could ever hope to be. She allowed her gaze to drift over the man and felt a curl of warm anticipation supplant the cold dread in her belly. One thing the Navy absolutely got right—there was nothing better than a fine man in dress uniform.

Drawing in a deep breath, she forced herself to saunter back to the table the Ravens still occupied as if she hadn't a thought in her head outside of wanting to get Campbell alone and climb him like a tree. She didn't fool her best friend for a second, but Killi waited until Delany had gracefully excused himself to attend Norwood before she shot Blue a sharp glance.

"What's wrong?"

"Later." Blue smiled through her teeth. She downed the water that had arrived in her absence and smiled harder at Twister. "Everything's *great*. Can we have that alcohol now?"

The older woman stared at her. "I'm no longer sure that's the best idea."

A masculine throat cleared, drawing their attention. Captain Oren "Tripwire" Truitt, commander of Bravo Company, stood on the other side of the table. Sergeant Ord flanked him on his left, Private Tavi on his right. Tavi positively shone in his immaculate Legion dress uniform, even more than he had on that troop transport ship where Blue first met him.

"Any issues so far, Captain Latham?"

Twister arched a brow at Blue. "I don't know, you tell me."

"Nothing that can't wait until debrief," she replied quietly.

Blue rolled her shoulders in a desperate bid to shed the lingering tension. She wasn't so stupid as to think Captain Esper wouldn't want a full report from everyone attending tonight. He'd certainly be interested in Norwood angling for more support...even if his threat had been a little heavy-handed.

Tripwire nodded acceptance of her assessment and drew Twister and Witch aside for a quiet conversation. As Killi took advantage of their inattention to flag down a waiter, Blue raised her brows in amusement at Tavi.

"How the hell did you get roped into this mess?"

"*Apparently*," Sergeant Ord said, crossing his muscular arms, "somebody had the brilliant idea to include Tavi, the Bronze Legion's first Distinguished Honors Graduate in over a decade, as an aide to our CO." An amused gleam twinkled in his eyes. "I suspect this has something to do with the trouble he caused on shore leave."

Blue fought to keep her smirk off her face and felt she mostly succeeded. "Haven't you been punished enough yet, kid?"

"Apparently not, ma'am." Tavi somehow managed to sound completely miserable while still maintaining an impassive expression. It was impressive.

Sergeant Ord grinned broadly. "Isn't he shiny? That sort of professional bearing makes me proud."

Blue gave up on controlling her expression and matched his grin. "Very shiny."

Tavi's sigh was one of suffering, more befitting a man four times his age and experience.

A waiter swung by their table and dropped off a whole tray of beverages. Killi snatched a glass off the tray only a hair faster than Sergeant Ord. Tavi eyed the assortment with considerable interest, but his sergeant shook his head.

"Not here and now. Maybe later back at camp."

Blue hadn't thought it possible for Tavi to radiate more misery, but the young legionnaire managed. Sergeant Ord tilted his head toward Tripwire, who showed signs of finishing up his conversation with Twister and Witch.

"Break time's over. Back to acting as the captain's aides."

"Yes, Sergeant."

The two legionnaires left them alone with a table full of alcohol. Spotting a whiskey glass with a deep amber liquid that promised only good things, Blue snatched it before Killi could appropriate a backup drink. The smooth burn of excellent whiskey slid down her throat, and she sighed in gratitude as some of the tension she hadn't been able to compartmentalize melted away. Her comm *pinged* before she could take a second sip.

ENSIGN HOTNESS: THAT DOESN'T COUNT.

Blue snapped her gaze up, but Campbell gave every indication of being completely engrossed in his conversation with Delany. And then he casually looked at her and winked. She arched a brow, held his gaze in challenge, and took a deliberately slow sip of whiskey. Campbell's charming grin flashed for half a heartbeat before he returned his focus to Delany.

Blue firmly reminded herself now wasn't the time for flirting. Desperate for a distraction from her distraction, her searching gaze landed on Mitzi. The young woman carefully clutched a drink in both hands as she earnestly cut her way through the central courtyard, her focus on Schmoyer. The other three evaluators had drifted off into the crowd, but Mitzi must have gotten trapped attending to her prick of a boss.

Schmoyer had abandoned his table to mingle with other guests and had stopped at a cluster of politicians and a handful of industry moguls at the table adjacent to the Ravens. Blue recognized one statuesque woman as the CEO of Ralwood Tech, one of Mars Primus' leading aerospace corporations. Her business suit was sharp, but with just enough elegance to not seem out of place among the flowing outfits of the political elite surrounding her.

Meek and effacing, Mitzi sidled up to the group and handed Schmoyer his drink. Blue narrowed her eyes. There were waitstaff for that sort of thing. There had been no need to utilize the girl in that manner.

Mitzi had taken a step back from the group when her expression brightened. "Oh! Are you talking about Shava Turnien?"

Conversation ground to a halt, and red bloomed on the girl's cheeks as the group stared at her.

"A good assistant is seen, not heard," the Ralwood Tech CEO said as if making an idle observation, but her eyes glittered with malice.

The Expediter stared down his long nose at Mitzi but addressed the CEO. "Indeed, but it is so hard to find a good assistant these days."

Mitzi's expression froze and her shoulders hunched slightly before she abruptly straightened her spine. "My apologies, sir. I was simply excited to hear about Miss Turnien. I've read so much about her missions in the Exploration branch."

Schmoyer's supercilious expression deepened. "And this is why you're in the Evaluator branch. All you do is *read*. If you paid more attention to people, you might learn something useful. For instance, our esteemed host, Sir Norwood, was a close comrade of Miss Turnien."

Close comrade, my ass.

Blue took a healthy swig of whiskey to restrain her amused snort. Schmoyer honestly didn't seem to know what he was doing in the political arena, though she had to admit to reluctant admiration for standing his ground with Norwood. It would've been easier for the man to bow to political pressure and automatically approve Aurora for entry into the Mars Protectorate... but he hadn't.

Killie followed the direction of her gaze.

"If he sticks his nose any higher in the air he'll drown if it rains," Killi snickered, though her eyes were narrowed. Blue shushed her as the Expediter continued to loudly pontificate.

Schmoyer placed a hand on his chest. "I myself enjoyed working with Miss Turnien. We were very close."

Blue froze as her amusement died. She knew all of her grandmother's close friends and colleagues. Schmoyer wasn't among their number. He'd *lied*. A flicker of anger followed on the heels of shock. *How dare you claim to know her! You were so far beneath her notice you weren't even worth sport bitching about, you smug, self-righteous, arrogant shit-weasel!*

"One day, you will realize that book learning is no substitute for real life experience, Miss Mingo," Schmoyer said severely. "Now, if you'll excuse us, we have more important things to talk about than your deficiencies."

Oh, hell *no*. She knew a bully when she saw one and wasn't going to stand for him bullying Mitzi a second longer *or* making false claims about Shava.

Before she'd taken more than a single step, Killi grabbed her arm. "You said we *all* need to behave."

"I also said I get to jump on any grenades." Blue tossed back the rest of her whiskey and slammed her empty glass onto the table. "Found one."

With a deft twist of her arm, she broke Killi's grip and honed in on Schmoyer like a shark scenting blood in the water. It was no accident that she stood at Mitzi's side, no accident she allowed her arm to brush up against the girl's, a gesture of silent support while she offered Schmoyer a razor-blade smile that was all teeth.

"Good evening, ladies, gentlemen." Blue deliberately paused. "Schmoyer."

Distantly, she heard Sergeant Ord mutter a succinct, "Aw, fuck my life..."

"It's funny that you mentioned being close with Shava. She never mentioned you." Blue held Schmoyer's furious gaze without an ounce of fear. "You know what else is funny? When she passed away, all of her close friends and coworkers attended her funeral."

She tilted her head, smile turning positively poisonous.

"I didn't see *you* there."

Schmoyer looked askance at her utilitarian duty uniform and curled his lip. "And who are you to call her by her given name?"

"Her granddaughter," Blue said brightly.

Tavi watched as Mitzi went rigid. Not from fear, though. This was something far different, something he'd never really seen on the young doctor's face before. It took him a moment to recognize it but, once he had, his confusion only grew deeper.

"*Ohmygod, ohmygod, ohmygod!*"

"Are you okay?" he asked her quietly as Lieutenant Eliassen precisely pivoted and marched away, leaving Schmoyer slack-jawed and with a slow-building fury in his eyes. Tavi looked back at Mitzi. She was on the verge of hysterics. The raging furnace deep inside began to burn bright. "Did someone hurt you?"

"Oh. My. *God!*" Mitzi not-quite squeaked. "No, no. Nobody hurt me. But you...you know Shava Turnien's *granddaughter?!*"

"Who?" The name meant nothing to him. "Shava? Who's that?"

"Shava Turnien! Wait...don't they teach you anything on Myrkyma?" she asked, exasperated.

"No. I lived on the streets."

"Really?" She paused then continued without waiting for a response. "Dame Shava Turnien was only one of the most decorated Survey Corps officers in the past century!" Mitzi started ticking off points on her fingers, the normally reserved girl practically wiggling in her enthusiasm. "She led a Survey team in the Exploration branch for decades, discovered not one but *five* colony-class planets, solved the mystery of the vanished Ateri outpost, identified *so many* new species—some of them on the same level of sentience as Earth's whales, dolphins, and elephants—kept her team alive on Verlassen IV when pirates hijacked their survey ship and left them for dead, literally expanded our star maps in the Serenella Nebula region..." Mitzi sucked in a huge breath because she'd verbal-vomited all of that at him without bothering to stop for air. Her eyes sparkled. "She's a *legend*. Best of all, she facilitated the creation of the Evaluator branch in the Survey Corps! Her work and efforts made me want to do what she did! She was my role model growing up!"

"Oh. Interesting." Tavi still didn't get the fascination, but it sounded as if this Shava person was pretty important to other Martians. In Mitzi's case, a childhood idol. In his pilot's case, family. While he didn't necessarily understand it, he could respect it.

"And you get to fly with her granddaughter, Blue! You know, Lieutenant Eliassen?"

Tavi nodded. He thought back to their last drop and shuddered.

He wasn't sure that flying with her was such a good thing. Jabber and the others were *still* pissed off at him for that.

"I know there's a museum in here somewhere. I heard someone talking about it. But you know what else? Some of the really cool features of any official governor or supervisor's residence like this is that it has unique defensive capabilities..." she babbled excitedly. Tavi nodded as he slowly tuned her out, only part of his brain listening as he continued to watch their surroundings. The ebb and flow of people moving around was dizzying, so he tried instead to simply watch the walls. Unfortunately, those were as entertaining as midwatch while at Basic.

"Tavi?" Sergeant Ord appeared as though by magic next to him, a half-finished tumbler of whiskey in hand. He passed a second tumbler to Tavi. "Go check on Captain Oren Truitt, if you please. Offer him this drink. He has the face of a man who is in dire need of rescue by his young junior aide. I'll be right behind you."

Tavi stiffened. During the briefing, Ordo had given him multiple signs and words to remember should the need ever arise. They all depended on which title he used when describing the CO of Bravo Company. His team nickname? A simple brush by, check in with the captain and see if his drink needed topping off, which would then provide the captain with an easy excuse to speak with his aide and leave a potentially compromising position. "Captain Truitt" was slightly more serious, which meant Tavi would have to tread carefully when approaching, but again, it was all about deflecting and redirecting the inquisitive individual haranguing the Legion officer. However, using the captain's full name and rank suggested he was in dire need of assistance, and political niceties went out the door when it came to saving the old man from something gone horribly awry.

"On it," Tavi said as he squared his shoulders, drink in hand.

"Is he going to be okay?" Tavi heard Mitzi ask Ordo as he moved toward Captain Truitt.

"He'll be fine. That guy harassing the captain, on the other hand? Hard to say."

That "guy," Tavi realized as he homed in on Captain Truitt, was none other than Sir Percival Norwood III and a cluster of what could only be described as lackeys. He'd seen their type before on the dangerous streets of Overdark. The local big guy would have four to six others around him, those seeking to win his approval by enforcing his will.

"You do understand that a captain in the Legion is a *much* lower rank than a Navy captain, you see," Norwood was explaining to his small group of lackeys as they encircled Captain Truitt. Tavi slid in close to Captain Truitt's elbow, making sure that he was seen by all without actually interrupting their dressing down of the legionnaire. "And they are given their drop names because they screw up. Can you imagine? Being labeled a screw-up the rest of your career?"

"Ah, I see that your young lackey has elected to join us," one of the senior officials guffawed and took a small sip of his beverage. Tavi passed the glass to his CO with barely a nod of his head. Undeterred, or perhaps misreading the situation entirely, the official continued. "I heard that the worse an officer is, the lower rank assistant they give you. I only see a single chevron. Does that make you a recruit?"

"Private, actually, sir." Tavi offered him a cold smile.

"A private? Wow. The Legion must really be scraping the bottom of the barrel to allow someone your size in."

"I'll grow, sir," Tavi replied with a shrug. "And I'll learn more. Experience is an excellent teacher."

"Are you old enough to be in the Legion?"

"Old enough. *Sir*."

The man scoffed. "Desperate times..."

"I'm unaware of anything being desperate at this time, sir. The Legion only accepts the best, and the best of those end up under Captain Truitt." Tavi paused, considering his next words before deciding that the captain needed his full support here. "It makes me wonder, though, how a man hiding behind his boss can toss around insults without worrying about consequences. I've been meaning to ask how someone can be rude like you are without fear of being punched in the face. On my world, talk like that would earn a knife in the throat, at least. Maybe you can tell me?"

The laughter around them stopped abruptly. "Are you threatening me?"

"Threatening? No, sir. Curious? Definitely. You're insulting an officer in the Legion, a man who would willingly sacrifice his life to protect yours, and you have the nerve to insult him. I would like to know why."

"Is this a hill you're willing to die on, kid?" Another of the lickspittles sneered at him, his own empty glass in hand. It was clear by the tone and slight slur of speech that the man had had too much to drink.

"It's a hill I'm willing to kill you on." Tavi shrugged his shoulders and stared through the man. It was an old trick he'd picked up while living in Overdark and the Legion had refined to great effect. The hardest part was keeping a bored expression on his face. "Question remains, sirs. Is this your hill, or mine?"

Conversation around them completely stopped. Sergeant Ordo coughed gently, once.

"*Fuck, kid...*" barely even registered in Tavi's ear.

"Drop names are meant to be insulting, *Supervisor*," Tripwire explained calmly. He took a small sip of the whisky Tavi had delivered and continued. "Cocky legionnaires are more dangerous to themselves and their teams if they think they're the greatest. We care more about our actual combat drops and how many times we've brought everyone home safely. Why, I'm sure you can agree with that, *Supervisor*, since that's your job here. It's almost like a planetary governor only without the power, prestige, or responsibility. Huh. You'd think they would consider a supervisor position equally as important, but you know how it is back on Mars Primus. Sir."

"I understand completely," Norwood managed to spit out through his teeth.

"Let's see...I've had fifteen combat drops during my time in the Legion." Tripwire casually swirled the amber liquid in his nearly full glass, eyes distant and cold. "Quite an achievement, really. I've been given six feathers in my time with Bravo Company, two from Bronze Raven Six. Do you know how hard it is to earn a feather from any Raven, much less their commander? Oh, my apologies. The Ravens are our dropship pilots. We military folks just have a simpler but efficient method of communication sometimes, and I forget that some civilians aren't up to speed on most of our verbiage. Anyway, where was I...oh, right. I turned down a promotion opportunity last year because it would've taken me out of a combat slot. Being XO of a Legion is an honor, one very few people are given the opportunity to fulfill. However, my place is with my men, shoulder to shoulder with them. Hard to do that in a supervisor slot, wouldn't you agree?"

"Sir?" Tavi said in the purest and most innocent voice he could manage. He was still staring hard at Lickspittle Number Four, and had yet to blink. "What's a feather and just how hard is it to earn one?"

"Terribly hard, Private. But I have faith you will earn yours in the future."

It hadn't escaped Tavi's notice that the captain had dodged the first half of his question. Something to investigate later.

Tripwire raised his nearly empty glass. "*Supervisor*. Gentlemen. My drink needs refreshing. Private? Show me where Sergeant Ord found that delectable whisky, please."

"Yes, sir!" Tavi grinned and separated from the group, nearly running into Sergeant Ord and Mitzi, who were standing nearby. Ordo's smile could have melted butter but Mitzi stared at him, mouth agape. His grin widened.

"Hey, beautiful," a husky male voice murmured in Blue's ear. "Come here often?"

On edge from everything that had happened that endless night, Blue barely stopped herself from striking out.

It hadn't taken long for the news that Shava Turnien's granddaughter was in attendance to spread, or for the political animals to start seeking her out. Norwood might have known exactly who she was, but he'd kept that knowledge to himself for his own purposes. It also hadn't taken long for her to regret her rash decision to expose her familial relationship, though she didn't regret defending the little mouse. Needing a break from the unwanted attention, she'd retreated to one of the smaller conversational nooks within the gardens. She hadn't even had a chance to sit on the carved stone bench before someone had found her again.

Fortunately for both of them, she recognized that husky voice and welcomed the intrusion.

As tension of a different sort than what she'd dealt with all night curled through her belly, the rest of her body relaxed. "Is that going to be our thing now, Navy boy? Cheesy pickup lines?"

"Only when we're someplace we'd rather not be," Campbell replied with a self-deprecating shrug. "Medical, because I got my ass kicked by a kid. Stuffy political events... at least I'm not the only one suffering."

At first, Blue thought he meant her, but then she caught him smirking at Tavi on the far side of the courtyard. She bit back a grin.

"You wouldn't happen to be the someone that suggested him for Tripwire's aide, would you?"

He paused. One eyebrow crept up.

"Would you believe me if I proclaimed my innocence?"

"No."

"Then yes, it was me." His playful smirk widened for a heartbeat before he winced and brushed a finger against his split lip. "Just a harmless bit of payback for the unintentional cockblocking. Do you think we've paid him back enough?"

Blue's own grin broke free. "Trust me, between this and what I did to 4th Squad on our drop, I think we're more than even now."

They tapped their whisky glasses together and drank. It was only Blue's second of the evening, but even so a pleasant fuzziness accompanied the smooth burn and allowed her to relax even further. Or maybe that was just Campbell's presence at her side. While not as intimidating as, say, Sergeant Ord, there was something in his manner that had already discouraged two hangers-on from approaching them.

Campbell's glare softened as he shifted his gaze from a third person he'd scared off to Blue. "Was it smart, letting them know who you are?"

"No," Blue said ruefully before she shrugged. "It'll bite me in the ass, no doubt, but it's not like the information was redacted. All anyone had to do was look."

"Fair." Campbell stared at his half-empty glass for a moment and shook his head. "Can't believe I wasted a drink on this."

Blue sat on the bench and smiled up at him. "You did say it was a risk."

Campbell sighed and sat next to her. Unlike Blue, he couldn't lounge in his dress uniform, but while his spine remained straight his shoulders relaxed. They were silent for a few moments until he nudged her side playfully.

"So, how much trouble do you think you're in with your commander for that little dustup with Schmoyer?"

"Maybe a little, but worth it to help Little Mouse." Blue nodded toward Mitzi, who had wandered over to Tavi. Her smile turned more than a little savage when she remembered Schmoyer's shock. "Honestly, I would've done it just for the look on that prick's face."

"You're hot when you're vicious."

"Compliments will get you nowhere," Blue said with a wink.

"I've noticed." His expression turned rueful. "You know, I don't usually have to work this hard."

He wasn't talking about the political event. Blue patted him on the chest and shifted just a little closer to him. Still professional enough to anyone watching from a distance, but close enough she could feel his body heat through her uniform.

"It's good for you."

Campbell's quiet laugh was just audible over the background murmur of the party. Understanding dawned. Was this what Killi had meant? Blue wasn't playing games with him though, she was just... playing. And from the amusement dancing in Campbell's eyes, he was enjoying himself too. *Huh.*

"You're not really going to count this miserable experience, are you?" Campbell asked with calculated mournfulness, the amusement in his eyes not diminished in the least.

"You shouldn't, ma'am."

Campbell's gaze snapped up in surprise, but Blue startled so badly only Campbell's quick reaction kept her from tumbling backward off the bench. A pained hiss escaped him, and he clutched at his battered ribs—but only after ensuring she wouldn't fall.

Sergeant Ord casually stood next to them, whisky glass in hand and body language loose, casual even. The fact that the legionnaire had managed to sneak up on both of them without apparently trying was damned annoying.

"Where the hell did you come from?" she demanded, embarrassment sharpening her tone far more than she would normally allow when speaking to the experienced NCO.

"My mother," he said blandly. "A fine woman and a verified saint for putting up with me and my brothers."

Blue straightened back up and tried not to regret the loss of warmth when Campbell removed his hand from her lower back. She exhaled slowly and arched a brow up at Ordo.

"I shouldn't what, Sergeant?" she asked as calmly as she could manage.

"I don't think this should count as one of the drinks you owe him, ma'am. Just an old legionnaire's opinion." He took a slow sip of whiskey, met Campbell's eyes, and dipped his chin in a slight nod. "Sir, have a good evening."

With that, Sergeant Ord strolled out of the garden and back to the central open area of the courtyard. Blue's jackrabbit heart rate finally slowed, and she let out a low laugh.

"Not sure how you got Ord on your side after your little revenge against Tavi, but who am I to argue with my sergeant?"

Campbell eyed her hopefully. "So, you're taking pity on this poor Navy boy?"

"I guess it wouldn't be in keeping with the spirit of our agreement if I counted this clusterfuck of a night as one of our drinks." She bumped against his side companionably. "Don't worry. I still owe you."

Campbell's charming grin came out in full force. "Good."

"Yeah—wait." Blue stared after Sergeant Ord, but he'd been swallowed up by the crowd. Slowly, she shifted her wide-eyed stare to Campbell. "How the *hell* did he know about our deal?"

CHAPTER ELEVEN
All the Pressure of Being the Best

AURORA RESEARCH OUTPOST, AURORA

Blue was bored out of her skull, yet at the same time she was so tense with a competing mix of horrible anticipation she was barely sleeping. The decrepit building situation certainly wasn't helping—though after a strongly worded protest from Captain Esper, the outpost had provided actual cots and bedding for them—but that wasn't what was keeping her on edge.

It was the lack of retaliation or fallout from the political mixer.

While Blue had gotten a verbal slap on the wrist during the debrief with Captain Esper and an extra maintenance detail on the Rhinos for her little altercation with Schmoyer, she was still anticipating some sort of payback from Schmoyer himself. As Captain Esper had grimly pointed out, Blue hadn't exactly been circumspect in her verbal flaying, and the man had lost considerable face in front of some very important people.

Bullies didn't forget that sort of thing, but Blue judged Schmoyer a coward at heart. He wouldn't come at her directly. He couldn't even threaten her acceptance into the Survey Corps since that was protected by her Legion commissioning program. What he could and probably *would* do was wait until she'd been accepted into the Exploration branch and then use his Expediter status to mess with her assignments. That would be when those old connections her grandmother had made would come in handy, though she hated the thought of having to lean on anyone for protection.

She'd much rather solve the problem with a judicious fist to the face if it came to that.

She was also waiting for the other boot to drop with Norwood. Some sort of follow-up to his heavy-handed threat or another pointed reminder that her "voice" would be of great assistance to him. Her best advantage there was that so long as she was on active deployment status, she literally had no way to get in touch with her contacts, and Norwood was savvy enough to know that. Probably why he'd left her in peace. For now.

And then there was Captain Marx Fischer, the evaluator qualified *asshole*.

Blue and the other Ravens had been assiduously avoiding him since Killi's disastrous checkride. Mostly because they needed to stay on his good side until after Blue's upgrade sortie, but also because punching a Legion captain, even a reactivated one, would be bad for their careers.

But the days crawled past—no retaliation, no drama, no fun, just the same monotonous routine. Preflight, load up their human cargo, hop to the same boring spot of jungle real estate, kick their heels all day waiting at the LZ while the Survey team surveyed and the legionnaires slowly went insane from boredom, and then head back to the outpost.

Sleep, rise, repeat.

Today was different. The Survey team had filed an official request to go all the way down to one of the southern sea islands. That meant a suborbital hop. That meant today was Blue's checkride.

She'd spent the past few days dreading that event more than anything else. Witch had had *plenty* of time to give them the gory details on Killi's checkride. Killi still choked on rage whenever she tried to talk about it, but she'd given Blue a key piece of gouge—be ready to explain every action and decision she made in the cockpit.

That morning, flight planning and weather updates went far too quickly for Blue's comfort, and then there was no time left.

Ready or not, it was time to armor up and head out.

It was the first time they'd bothered with their armor since they'd made planetfall, but regulations dictated their use for void operations. While their flight plan didn't have them in the black for long, any length of time was enough.

As she walked with the other Ravens to the landing pad to start preflighting, she cast an apprehensive glance up at the flawless deep-blue morning sky. Not a cloud to be seen, and only a gentle breeze stirred the endless sea of green jungle surrounding the outpost.

It should've been raining.

If the tropical storm projections had held true, they would have been in for a wet few days, and a little excitement when flying near the coast. The storm had other ideas. It had stalled out over the warm southern sea. At first, the legionnaires had been happy. No wet camp conditions for them. That only lasted long enough for the word to spread that the tropical storm hadn't dissipated. It was growing, feeding off all that warm water and shaping up into a true monster.

It was no longer a question of whether it would make the jump to hurricane status. It was how bad was it going to be, and how long before it started moving north again.

In fact, that storm had prompted today's excursion. The Survey team wanted to get a good look at a southern group of armadons before the hurricane disturbed their typical behavior patterns. According to Mitzi, who was the team's xenobiologist—*not* just Schmoyer's assistant, regardless of what the man seemed to believe—the aggressive behavior of the northern armadons fell outside of previously observed patterns and they needed to see if it was a localized effect. After some discussion and a consultation with the Survey team's meteorologists, the Ravens had agreed they could get them in and out before the storm hit.

Because that was exactly what Blue needed—a real-world issue on top of her checkride stress.

Killi paused at the tail of Bronze Raven Four, bronze-accented black dropship armor gleaming in the brilliant sunlight, helmet tucked under one arm, and wild curls barely tamed by tight braids. The two women watched as Fischer approached from the far side of the landing pad, outdated armor scuffed but serviceable and slate already in hand. With a disgruntled huff, Killi turned away from him and tilted her head at Blue.

"You ready to kick your checkride's ass, girl?" she asked flippantly enough, but worry lurked deep in her green eyes. Blue grinned, pulling on every bit of training she'd had to mentally armor herself, and bumped her fist against Killi's.

"Let's rage."

A scrape of armored boots on pavement jerked their gazes up. Fischer was faster than he looked.

"Good afternoon, ladies. I was hoping to catch you before you began preflighting." He tapped a finger on his slate, where he had the sortie details pulled up. "There's been a slight change of plan. The beginning of Lieutenant Eliassen's checkride will be under simulated combat conditions. That includes takeoff."

Blue and Killi exchanged a concerned glance. That wasn't a slight change at *all*. Combat conditions meant a simultaneous takeoff. From a relatively small landing pad within striking distance of numerous civilian structures... and civilians. The dimensions and distances were within operating limitations and safety regulations. Technically.

"I've already cleared this with Captain Sanderson," he added when they took too long in answering.

"Yes, sir," Blue finally said.

If Witch had already agreed, there was no fighting the change. Blue kept her shoulders straight by an effort of sheer will. She was already dealing with a *hurricane* on her checkride. Might as well add an unplanned vertical formation takeoff just for funsies.

An annoyed, very quiet growl rumbled in Killi's throat, but she managed to keep her expression blank. "Copy simulated combat takeoff ops, sir."

"Good. That will be all, Lieutenant Killowen," Fischer said, flapping one hand in abrupt dismissal. "Lieutenant Eliassen, if you're ready to begin?"

"Yes, sir."

"Let's get started then." Fischer tapped his slate, frowned at the screen for a moment, then looked up. "Take me through preflight and we'll go from there."

Blue nodded and began going down the checklist, just as she did every time. But somebody had pissed off Murphy, that fickle saint, because everything that could go wrong, did go wrong.

First, her slate died. Working one second, as useless as a paperweight the next. Fischer didn't comment as she trotted into the Rhino to get the backup slate that was stored in the cockpit for just these situations, but his expression wasn't favorable. Next, the flight controls didn't pass the built-in pass/fail test on startup. Powering up the Rhino didn't just mean the main systems came online—a whole slew of secondary systems were tied into the startup process.

The Rhinos were old, and finicky at times, but they were finicky in predictable ways. The flight control computer failure indicator was something Blue had seen so many times, both in training and in the operational environment, that she didn't even have to think about what to do. She simply pulled the K14 circuit breaker to force the individual system to power cycle and slotted it back into place. A few seconds for the built-in test to do the pass/fail checks again, and the failure indicator cleared.

Satisfied, Blue moved on to the next step in her preflight checklist, but Fischer cleared his throat.

"Per the regulations, are you allowed to pull that circuit breaker?"

Blue froze as the blood drained out of her face, leaving her feeling lightheaded and halfway to a panic attack. *Oh fuck, did I fail before we even managed to get into the air?*

"No, sir," she said hoarsely.

Technically, he was correct. Per the regulations, only maintainers were allowed to pull circuit breakers under normal conditions. Fischer just stared at her with a blank expression and gave no indication if she should continue with the checkride or not. Her breath caught as she realized what answer he was looking for. Under *normal* conditions.

"However," she said as calmly as she could, "since we're operating under simulated combat conditions, pulling the circuit breaker is within acceptable risk margins."

Fischer's expression didn't so much as twitch. Blue's gut tightened as the silence stretched. And then he nodded.

"Continue."

The rest of preflight went without incident. As the last legionnaire strapped in and Sergeant Carvalho closed the ramp, Blue allowed herself a small sigh of relief before she locked it back down. Now wasn't the time to relax or get complacent.

They were just getting started.

Blue increased power to the engines in preparation for vertical lift. The *thrum* of the engines vibrated through her boots, and she couldn't quite keep her lips from curving upward as the ship came to life beneath her hands, metal and circuits and a thousand moving parts transforming into something real, something *alive*.

She activated the aircrew channel on her comms. "Aircrew, confirm ready to fly."

Sergeant Carvalho's cheerful voice answered immediately. *"Ready to fly, confirmed."*

Blue's hands tightened on the controls in anticipation. She drew in a steadying breath, and with a practiced flick of her eyes, used her HUD to switch channels. Fischer would make the majority of the comm calls during the flight, just like he would if he were actually her copilot, but as the lead pilot for the formation takeoff, it was Blue's responsibility to make the initial calls.

"Bronze Raven Five, Bronze Raven Four, ready for takeoff. Confirm status?"

"Bronze Raven Four, Bronze Raven Five, ready for takeoff, coordinated lift on your mark."

Killi's bright voice echoed over the comms, a timely reminder that her best friend would be flying on her wing. Some of the tension riding her shoulders faded, and Blue was able to loosen her grip on the flight controls.

"Takeoff status confirmed. Lift on my mark in five, four, three..." Blue checked her instruments one final time and pushed up the throttles. "Two, one, *mark!*"

Smoothly, she lifted in the air in tandem with Bronze Raven Five. Her gaze shifted in a practiced rhythm from her reference points outside the cockpit, to her instruments, to her port external camera feed on the main viewscreen. The viewscreen showed the other Rhino rising on their left wing at the precise distance required for a formation takeoff. The ground fell away beneath them as they achieved the minimum altitude to shift into forward flight.

"Min altitude reached, rotate engines."

Blue pulled back on the throttles to hold their current altitude, but Bronze Raven Five climbed for perhaps a second longer before Killi stabilized.

"Min altitude, confirmed. Rotating engines, confirmed."

Satisfaction washed through Blue as she reached for the switch to rotate the engines. That takeoff had been so textbook perfect not even an evaluator as picky as Fischer could find fault with it. Her fingers had just brushed the switch when he cleared his throat. She paused, her gaze shifting to his.

"You let Bronze Raven Five get approximately ten meters higher than us when you should be at the same altitude—"

The harsh blare of a proximity alert blasted through the cockpit. Blue snapped her gaze to the viewscreen. Killi had already begun the transition to forward flight, but her left engine had failed to rotate. The asymmetry introduced by the mismatched engines caused the Rhino to roll to the right—directly toward Blue's Rhino.

There was no time to warn anyone.

Blue wrenched back on the throttles, pulling the power just enough to kill their lift without putting the engines into idle. Without any forward momentum over the wings, they dropped like the rock they were.

For just an instant, weightlessness swooped through Blue's stomach. Bronze Raven Five spun past their cockpit, mottled gray metal missing them by inches. Heart racing, Blue couldn't spare them any further attention other than to be damn thankful they'd avoided a midair collision. The instant they were beneath the other Rhino, she slammed the throttles back up, praying there was enough time to at least cushion the impact.

They hit the landing pad *hard*.

Her breath exploded out of her and her bones groaned in protest. Heavy duty landing gear, meant to handle the harshest landing conditions, flexed beneath the Rhino's sudden reintroduction to the ground—and held. Shaking off the shock of impact, Blue quickly pulled back on the power and ran the emergency shutdown sequence in tandem with Fischer. Seconds later, the engines spooled down into silence, and the sport bitching of their legionnaires flooded the ops channel.

"What the hell was that?"

"I think my spine ended up in my skull."

"Tavi, what the HELL did you do to piss off our Raven this time?"

"I DON'T KNOW!"

"STOW IT!" Sergeant Ord roared. "*That was an emergency landing, you idiots. Stow your shit or I will stow it for you!*"

"LT, what the hell happened up there?" Sergeant Carvalho asked quietly over the aircrew channel.

"Engine rotation failure," Blue replied in a bare whisper, her horrified gaze locked outside the cockpit.

"*That didn't feel like a—*"

"It wasn't ours."

Boots thudded in an uneven rhythm on the deck. A second later, Carvalho barreled into the cockpit. He leaned between the pilots, one hand gripping the back of Blue's seat in a death grip. Muttered prayers spilled from his lips as the blood drained from his swarthy face.

Heart in her throat, Blue could only watch as Killi fought to stay in the air. Her Rhino slewed to the left and nearly clipped the tree line before rolling to the right again. Another correction to the left, another drunken roll to the right, this one costing them altitude they couldn't afford to lose. For a terrifying moment, Blue was certain they were going to crash into the jungle on the other side of the perimeter fence. But with a visible shudder, the stupid forward engine *finally* rotated back to vertical to match the broken one, and their desperate flight stabilized.

Blue slumped in her chair, boneless with relief as Killi safely set it down on the landing pad again—a much gentler landing than their own. Carvalho patted her shoulder. Even though she couldn't feel the comforting gesture through her armor, she still appreciated it.

"I'll go update Sergeant Ord and his boys," he said, his voice still absent its usual cheer. "And HeyHey."

"We heard," they said in muted chorus, pale faces peeking through from the gunner compartment.

Silence fell over the cockpit after Carvalho left, and Blue decided she'd stalled as long as she could. Reluctantly, she looked at Fischer.

The older pilot was calmly typing notes on his slate, expression cool and eyes focused on the screen. He didn't look up until he'd finished.

"Well, Lieutenant Eliassen, that wasn't the EP I'd planned for this sortie, but I suppose that will do to satisfy the checkride requirements."

Blue stared at him, but apparently that was all he was going to give her. No indication of how well she'd done or if she'd even passed that portion. Not even a good job, though she did note the lack of verbal criticism.

No, no. Don't thank me. Saving all our lives is just part of the job.

Oblivious to her internal sarcasm, he continued, still in that dry, inflectionless voice. "Obviously, the checkride is paused for now. I'll stay out of your way while you coordinate with your chain of command and sort out if we're still flying today."

Blue stared at him some more, but he simply went back to his slate without further comment.

"Yes, sir," she said belatedly. "I'll keep you updated."

A commotion in the cargo compartment alerted her to trouble seconds before it arrived in the form of one highly irate Dr. Charles William Joseph Schmoyer IV, Expediter-class Survey Corps officer, team leader, and incredibly annoying pain in her ass.

"Miss Eliassen, I *demand* to know the meaning of this!" His shrill voice grated unpleasantly on Blue's ears, even with the sound dampening provided by her helmet. "The unnecessary violence of that landing was totally uncalled for. You could have damaged some of our more sensitive equipment, not to mention you needlessly endangered our lives!"

Blue's gaze flicked over the red-faced Expediter's shoulder to Sergeant Carvalho looming just behind him. With a slight jerk of her chin, she dismissed the burly loadmaster. She could handle Schmoyer without any help.

"If this is the best the Legion has to offer, then maybe—"

"Stand by," Blue cut into his tirade with icy calm. When the man opened his mouth again, she twisted around in the seat and pinned him with a cold stare. "I said *stand the fuck by*. I will answer your questions in a few minutes. Until then, you will sit down and *shut up* until I am ready."

Schmoyer gaped at her as if he couldn't believe she'd dared speak to him in that manner. He frowned at Fischer, but the evaluator didn't even look up from his slate, wholly unconcerned with the unfolding drama in the cockpit. Huffing, he unfolded one of the jump seats and stiffly sat down, furious gaze never leaving Blue's face. That was fine, he could stare at the back of her helmet for all she cared. She had other things to worry about.

"Killi, Witch, status when able."

Blue was prepared to wait as long as it took, but Killi immediately responded, her voice rock steady.

"*Our status is fucked. No injuries, but our Rhino isn't going anywhere anytime soon. The rotator system on the left engine is completely fragged and it* shouldn't *be.*" Stress flickered through Killi's iron control but then she steadied again. "*Witch is on the line with Voodoo, let me patch you in.*"

A dry click, and Voodoo's grim voice rang out, her Passovan accent thick with frustration.

"... told you bad juju would follow. I warned you, didn't I, pojata? I guarantee you this is just the beginning."

"An asymmetric engine rotation failure followed by a near midair is plenty of bad luck," Witch's cool contralto replied. "I think we've hit our quota for the year."

"You would think, but it'll get worse before it gets better, keiche?" Voodoo huffed out a sharp breath and some of her accent fell away. "I've got Medusa and Ruby on their way down with a maintenance team. They can fly 5th Squad today while our maintainers get your Rhino back up and running."

"Copy all, ma'am."

Blue heard the reluctance in Witch's tone and winced in sympathy. No Raven liked letting another aircrew carry their boys, even on a milk run. An upgrade checkride sortie near a rapidly growing hurricane wasn't exactly a milk run.

Grimacing, Blue pulled up the latest weather report. The projections hadn't changed from a few hours ago. Her frown deepened as she verified Bronze Raven One's current ETA and ran the numbers. *If 5th Squad loaded onto Bronze Raven One as soon as they landed, and if they encountered no further delays, they should still be able to get the Survey team in and out before the storm got too close to the island.*

They'd just have less time on the ground than originally planned.

The entire time she worked she could feel eyes burning into the back of her skull, but the safety of her crew and her legionnaires was her priority. She'd be damned if she rushed anything on account of someone like Schmoyer.

Only after she relayed everything to the other Ravens and received confirmation from Medusa that they'd be ready to turn and burn did she finally spin around to deal with the fuming Survey team leader. When he opened his mouth, words of hate and vitriol no doubt ready to spill from his tongue, Blue held up a hand.

"This is the part where you listen, and I explain exactly how I just saved our damn lives."

Schmoyer's mouth snapped shut with an audible click. After providing a succinct summary of events, Blue pulled up the cockpit recording to *show* the bastard exactly what had transpired. Slowly, the blood drained from his face.

Blue watched as well, analyzing the situation from every angle. At the time, it had felt like a short eternity, but in reality everything had happened within a span of seconds.

Cold seeped through her gut.

The flight control system failing the built-in startup test was a fairly common problem in the Rhinos. An operational failure in the rotation system on the engines? Almost never. Not without external damage, and Blue knew Killi had preflighted them assiduously, just as they all did. Worse, the central flight computer should have immediately corrected for the asymmetric imbalance, but it hadn't. Killi had fought like a demon to keep the Rhino in the air until Witch could manually override.

Belated fear rocked through her as the playback ended. If she'd been just an instant slower, or if Killi's altitude had been just a little lower, there would've been no avoiding that collision.

"My god . . . if you hadn't . . ." Schmoyer blinked a few times and slowly stood. And then he did something that shocked Blue—he dipped his head in a respectful bow. "Well done, Lieutenant. Let me know when we're ready to depart. Please."

It wasn't an overabundance of gratitude, but it was heartfelt, and far more than she'd expected from him. Good enough.

Blue ran through the recording one more time, and noticed something she'd missed the first time around—Fischer hadn't even made an aborted grab for the flight controls. His hands hadn't so much as twitched. He'd barely even paid attention to what was happening outside their cockpit until they were safely on the ground. Instead, his focus had remained on Blue, expression dead calm, analyzing everything she did without giving anything away. They'd nearly suffered a *midair collision* and Fischer hadn't even looked vaguely concerned.

The man must have ice in his veins.

Blue shook her head in reluctant admiration before she unstrapped. "I'm going to go take a look at the landing gear. I'll have the maintenance team do a full inspection as well before we leave. That landing was within limits, but we've had gear issues recently."

Fischer nodded absently and didn't look up from his slate, where he was once again taking notes. Odd man.

By the time Blue was done inspecting the landing gear, Bronze Raven One had landed on the far side of Five. Controlled chaos ruled the landing pad for the next few minutes as a maintenance team boiled out of the back of the new Rhino, while 5th Squad trotted down Five's ramp, several legionnaires carrying additional Survey team equipment. The majority of the maintainers went straight for Killi's Rhino, but a pair split off to do a more in-depth inspection of Blue's landing gear system. She smiled when she noted it was the same duo who'd repaired her landing gear after Sagetnam and promptly got out of their way.

Killi drifted over while Blue waited for their assessment. Her helmet was off and sweat dampened her face. Wild curls escaped her braids in the humid breeze, but Killi just tipped her face up to the noon sun and breathed deeply before she tucked her hair behind her ears.

"You were amazing," Blue told her best friend sincerely. "How's your Rhino looking?"

"Like I said, fucked." While her expression was calm, Blue caught the signs of strain in the lines around her eyes and the tightness in her jaw. Killi shook her head. "Rodriguez is baffled. He said he's never seen the system fail precisely like that before."

Master Sergeant Carlos Rodriguez was their chief maintainer. He'd spent his whole career maintaining the aging fleet of Rhinos. If he hadn't seen it before, it was because it was impossible—and even then he'd probably seen it.

Her gaze shifted to Fischer, just visible through the front of the cockpit. Maybe there was something to Voodoo's superstitions after all.

A shuffle of boots on pavement drew her focus back to her maintainers, who reported her landing gear had survived the harsh landing without detriment or degradation. Seconds later, Medusa reported 5th Squad was secured and Bronze Raven One was ready to fly. Her Rhino's engines were already ramping back up. Killi clapped her on the shoulder hard enough she felt it through her armor.

"Keep it locked in, girl. You've got this." A genuine smile spread across her face as some of her normal cheer resurfaced. "We'll celebrate not dying when you get back from kicking your checkride's ass."

"Deal." Blue rolled her shoulders back and marched up the ramp. Apparently, Carvalho had spread the word on what happened, because her legionnaires cheered when she strode through the cargo compartment. Heat washed across her face, but she flashed them all a grin before taking her place back in the cockpit.

Startup went without issue, and they were soon ready to depart. Again. Fischer didn't insist on simulated combat conditions, so Blue took lead and lifted off from the landing pad. This time, their departure was without incident. Tension slowly faded from her shoulders, and Blue relaxed as they climbed through the atmosphere.

Any sense of relaxation quickly disappeared though, because Fischer kept up a constant stream of criticism. Everything she did could be just a little bit better. Her climb vector, her speed, her transition from atmospheric engines to void thrusters, her reentry angle, even her crew management techniques.

Personally, Blue thought she deserved a gold star in crew management since she hadn't thrown her "copilot" out of one of the gunner hatches. Not yet, anyway. Just when she was thoroughly questioning all the life choices that had led her to becoming a pilot—because apparently she was *shit* at it—his dry voice fell silent.

As they dropped through the upper atmosphere, she felt his sharp gaze on her, analyzing every move she made. Determination tightened her jaw, but she kept her hands gentle on the flight controls.

She wasn't going to fail.

Patches of clear turbulence buffeted the sturdy Rhino, vibrations that traveled through her hands, though her bones. She corrected for each one, easily riding out the bumps, wings level and staying within the acceptable margins of their flight path. Still high enough for the planetary curve to be visible, the tropical cyclonic storm was also within visual range. It was a monstrous black and gray beast of a storm, towering stacked bands of clouds churning and twisting and turning, an unstoppable force of nature. A jagged burst of lightning sliced across those bands, searing her retinas before her HUD automatically dimmed down to compensate.

Blue tore her gaze off the storm with a pained wince, and Fischer cleared his throat in that dry rattle that made her want to scream.

"I'd like to propose an alternate flight plan." His tone had shifted slightly to the one Blue thought of as his fake voice, the one he used when he was simulating her copilot. "I think it would be more efficient and give our Survey team more time to investigate the island fauna, which is the objective of this sortie."

No, the objective of this sortie is to crush my soul.

"I'll take a look," she said as pleasantly as she was capable of in that moment.

Gritting her teeth, she pulled the new flight plan into her HUD, dropping it in as an overlay on the current route. With practiced ease, she divided her attention between flying her dropship and studying his proposed changes.

Their planned route, the one they'd briefed that morning, steered well clear of the storm. While it would take longer to reach the island, it was safer. The new route was more direct and would shave a decent amount of time off their flight, but it cut through an outer band of the hurricane. That particular band extended like a puffy white tendril over the greenish-blue tropical waters, deceptively soft and undoubtedly concealing gusting winds and lashing rain.

"It's well within the Rhino's operational safety regulations," Fischer added, his tone earnest but his gaze still sharp and assessing.

Blue thought furiously. While this was obviously a test, he'd picked an excellent scenario. At first glance, neither choice was necessarily wrong.

He was absolutely correct in that it was well within their limitations, even outside of combat conditions, and it would get the Survey team more time on the ground. After the near disaster this morning, their window to conduct their investigation was vanishingly small and could disappear altogether if the storm did something unexpected.

Despite her distaste for Schmoyer's pushy arrogance and Norwood's political ambitions, the acceptance of a new Protectorate world was no small thing and would benefit *so* many people. Anything she could do to assist the process would be good PR for the Legion... it also wouldn't hurt her own ambitions in the Survey Corps.

Temptation's siren song was interrupted by a sharp *ping* and a flashing alert in her HUD. Fischer had waited until the last possible moment to propose the new flight plan. She didn't have time to further debate the options. She had to decide now.

Which path should she choose? Safe and possibly too slow? Or riskier but with greater reward? Another crackle of lightning drew her gaze back to that monstrous storm. Her gut tightened and she made her choice.

"We'll stick with the original flight plan."

"Are you certain?"

"The safety of our passengers, our legionnaires, and our aircrew comes first," Blue said, firmly shutting down any lingering temptation. "This isn't a combat situation, and I won't put lives at risk just to buy a few more hours on that island. Our operational window on the ground is narrow, but it'll have to be enough."

Silence descended over the cockpit, broken only by the hum of the engines and the rattle of metal as they slipped through another pocket of turbulence. The point of no return flashed by under mottled gray wings. With a practiced flick of her eyes, she dismissed the alternate flight plan from her HUD and held their course steady.

Fischer regarded her for a long moment, his expression flat. Finally, he nodded. "Very well."

Out of the corner of her eye, Blue could see him typing out more notes. Doubt twisted through her, settling deep in her belly like cold sludge. This wasn't just a Legion operation, it was a Survey Corps directed mission. It was entirely possible the choice she'd just made had not only cost her a passing score on her checkride, but could have a negative impact on her future with the Survey Corps, depending on what Fischer decided to do.

Embarrassing Schmoyer at a party was one thing. Interfering with the effectiveness of an Expediter-led Survey team in the field was another thing entirely.

With a slow exhale, she compartmentalized the doubt. She'd made her decision, and she'd stand by it. More, she knew her leadership would support her. That would have to be enough.

The steady *click* of the evaluator's fingertips on his slate stopped, and Blue's shoulders tightened in anticipation.

"Your rate of descent is a little on the fast side for this part of the flight profile."

Blue almost belted out a laugh at his unexpected return to "constructive" criticism. Her gaze flicked to the timer in the upper right corner of her HUD and any urge to laugh died a swift death.

Only five thousand years to go before this checkride from hell is over.

Soon enough though, the island was within range. A ring of black sand beaches and stunted, twisted vegetation lined the perimeter, hinting at strong winds and regular tropical storms. The center of the island was entirely covered by a thick jungle, with towering trees, vines, and an impenetrable canopy that prevented a visual inspection.

She flexed her shoulders to shed the tension and dropped into a low pass with Bronze Raven One flying off her left wing. The scanners picked up a number of large heat signatures. They could only be armadons, and in far greater numbers than the Survey team had led them to believe would be present.

She shot Fischer a quick glance. "Push the scanner data packet to One and have them confirm the findings."

"Bronze Raven One, Bronze Raven Four, confirm scanner data?" he asked calmly.

"*Four, One, scanner data confirmed. That's a lot of native wildlife down there.*" Medusa's tone was level, but Blue knew the other woman well enough to catch the concern underlying the steady calm.

Blue's eyes widened in alarm as they flew over the western end of the island. Even more armadons were on the beaches, sunning themselves on the rocks, sprawled out in the black sands, and even swimming in the shallow surf. Those beaches were also the only clear place to land short of creating their own LZ with liberal application of the Aries Miniguns, something she was sure HeyHey would definitely be in favor of. However, she had a feeling Schmoyer wouldn't approve, as that much destruction would absolutely disturb the armadons.

Blue circled the island again, searching for a clear landing zone that wasn't already inhabited by the local population of eight-foot-long armored murder lizards.

There wasn't one.

"The entire reason we're on Aurora is because of aggressive armadons. I'm not sure landing in the middle of a herd of them is the smartest idea," she said uneasily and glanced at Fischer. "What are your thoughts, co?"

"You're the pilot in command," Fischer said pointedly. "It's your call."

The implication being that if she *didn't* make the call, she wasn't ready for the left seat. Apprehension twisted through her gut. *How many ways can I fail this checkride?*

Dropping the right wing low to begin another circle over the island, Blue shook her head in frustration. Any other eval pilot would've paused the checkride to act as her actual copilot, not swept a real-world situation and a genuine safety concern into the evaluation. As she rolled out of her turn, Blue caught a glimpse of the second Rhino off her wing, mottled gray metal shining in the warm sunlight.

On a normal sortie, Medusa, who held the higher rank, would make the final call on whether it was safe to land—but Fischer hadn't paused the checkride, leaving Blue in the position of flight lead. A small grin twisted her lips. Just because she was in nominal command didn't mean she couldn't utilize crew resources to ensure she made the correct choice. If Fischer failed her for that, so be it.

Decision made, she danced her fingers across her console, pulling Schmoyer into the command channel with Medusa, Ruby, Fischer, and Sergeants Cox and Ord.

"We have a bit of a situation," Blue said grimly as she added a live feed of the island to everyone's HUDs and Schmoyer's slate. She also pushed the scanner data to the Survey team leader. "Is this what you were expecting, Dr. Schmoyer?"

"Not... precisely." Excitement overtook his typical arrogance. "*Look at them all! There's so many more than I expected.*"

"That's my concern," Blue said dryly. "Sergeant Ord, Sergeant Cox, assessment?"

"*That's a lot of critters, ma'am,*" Sergeant Cox said. "*We can establish a perimeter to keep them clear of the Survey team and the Rhinos, and we can handle them if they get uppity, but that's not the question, is it?*"

"No," Sergeant Ord agreed. "*It's whether the risk to our civvies and our boys is worth it. Not to mention the Rhinos. If those beasts swarm, they could damage our ride out.*"

"*But look how calm they are! How peaceful!*" Schmoyer practically crowed in enthusiasm. "*Do they look like they're going to swarm? This is precisely the behavior we need to investigate. We must determine if the northern armadon aggression is the aberration, and if the southern armadon behavior—the very behavior previously seen in the northern population—is the norm.*"

Fischer remained silent, listening but not participating in the debate.

"*If the Survey team needs to get boots on the ground, we can make it happen, ma'am,*" Sergeant Ord said firmly.

Once they were on the ground, the safety of the Survey team was in the legionnaires' hands. Until then, that responsibility rested squarely with the Ravens.

"Medusa, thoughts?" Blue asked.

"*Bronze Raven One will follow Four's lead,*" she said with quiet confidence.

Gee, thanks for the help, Medusa.

Blue drew in a deep breath. "Okay, we'll do this in stages. Bronze Raven One will set down first while Four provides top cover. Next, 5th Squad will establish a secure perimeter. One will then take off and provide top cover while Four lands. Per standard procedure, 4th Squad will provide security for the Survey team. Any sign of aggression from the armadons at any point in this process, and we pull out. Clear?"

She got an affirmative from everyone including Fischer and a vague protest from Schmoyer about her "excessive caution" and a need for haste. Blue ignored him and issued her gunners stern instructions over the aircrew channel. With Hekekia and Hayashi, it was best to be specific. The last thing she needed was her trigger-happy gunners stirring up the murder lizards by accident.

"*We'll behave,*" Hekekia promised.

"*Yes, you will,*" Sergeant Carvalho said firmly.

"*Spoilsport,*" Hayashi muttered.

Suppressing a grin, Blue marked her chosen LZ for Medusa. The black sand beach on the western side of the island quickly gave way to a wide swath of open, rocky ground with minimal vegetation. Short of creating their own LZ, this was the best possible location, though the ground was more uneven than she liked.

"Gunners ready?" she asked over the aircrew channel.

As she dropped the Rhino's right wing low and circled the LZ, she felt the slight drag of the gunner hatches opening. After a quick check to verify they'd locked into position, she glanced over her shoulder.

"*Ready on the guns,*" HeyHey responded with identical grins and a double thumbs up.

A high-pitched *whir* sang out over the background roar of the engines as Fischer rotated the chin-mounted railgun.

"Railgun ready," he quietly confirmed. For this part of the sortie at least, he was truly acting as her copilot.

Praying she was making the right call—and that the lizards

haphazardly lying across the rocky ground would scatter—Blue gave the order.

"Bronze Raven One, Bronze Raven Four, go for landing."

"*Four, One, confirmed landing, switching to VTOL ops.*"

Blue found herself holding her breath as Medusa shifted from forward flight to vertical, but the engines rotated smoothly and they landed without incident. The armadons did scatter, though they didn't go very far, nor did they seem all that bothered by the massive dropship. Exhaling slowly, she divided her attention between flying and monitoring the ground situation as 5th Squad trotted down the ramp, rifles up and ready.

Again, the armadons didn't react aggressively. In fact, Blue was almost certain one of them yawned. The ones in the surf continued to hunt, the ones who were sunning on the rocks or sand continued to be lazy, and the ones who had been displaced by the bulky Rhino and the cautious legionnaires soon found new places to stretch out.

"*You see? I told you your caution was excessive,*" Schmoyer said snidely over the command channel. Blue gritted her teeth. She'd forgotten to kick him off the channel and cut the external feed to his slate.

"Better safe than eaten," she said firmly. "They'll go for the squishy unarmored humans first."

The man let out an indignant squawk, but Blue rectified her oversight, cutting him out of the channel with a smug grin. As soon as 5th Squad had secured the perimeter, Medusa's Rhino smoothly lifted into the air and took up an overwatch position, Aries Minigun barrels extending out of the open gunner hatches.

"*Bronze Raven Four, Bronze Raven One in position.*"

"Four copies."

Well aware of the narrow window—despite what Schmoyer seemed to think—Blue quickly set the Rhino down. The armadons remained unbothered by their presence. That didn't change when 4th Squad escorted the Survey team down the ramp, or even when Schmoyer managed to drag his bodyguards over to one of the sunbathing murder lizards.

Once the legionnaires were satisfied the threat was minimal, Bronze Raven One set down next to Four, and both Rhinos shut down to conserve fuel. Blue finished her postflight checklist in aching silence.

Her checkride was over.

Tension tightened her shoulders and the base of her skull to the point of pain as she impatiently waited for Fischer to finish typing up his notes. Finally, he looked up from his slate, his expression blank, professional, and *no help whatsoever* in telling Blue if she'd passed or not.

And then he nodded.

"Well done, Lieutenant Eliassen," he said quietly. "You handled the EP flawlessly, made an excellent decision on the proper flight path, and utilized your crew resources to make an informed decision on whether to proceed with the mission or not. Being the command pilot means being able to make the tough decisions quickly, regardless of what external variables are thrown your way."

Fischer tapped a final time on his slate and tilted it so she could see the screen. Elation spiraled through her soul and brought a wide grin to her face.

He smiled. "Congratulations on passing your checkride."

With the stress of her checkride over, Blue was more than happy to spend a few hours on a tropical beach, even if the sand was black and the locals were scary. Her only regret was that Killi wasn't there to enjoy it with her, but she had fun with Medusa and Ruby. She lounged on Bronze Raven One's ramp with the other Ravens, hands braced behind her back on the warm metal as she kept a cautious eye on the armadons.

The Auroran lizards continued to display a complete lack of aggression, and more than once Schmoyer's strident voice echoed off the rocks. The man was increasingly convinced that the "so-called" aggression of the northern armadons was some kind of funding or publicity stunt. Blue silently disagreed. Bad publicity would be the last thing Norwood would want when the colony was up for review.

Warily, she eyed the nearest armadon as it pulled itself to its feet. The closest legionnaire jerked his rifle up, but the oversized lizard merely lumbered over to a large rock and rubbed its armored side against the jagged surface. A pleased groan tumbled from open jaws and echoed off the rocks. Another rolled onto its back at the shore and wiggled back and forth, tail curving lazy S patterns into the wet sand while all four legs waved in the air. Its tongue lolled out and its eyes closed in apparent pleasure.

Blue relaxed, and so did the legionnaire.

"They're *so* cute," Ruby cooed, a wide smile on her face. Medusa grimaced as an extra chonky armadon erupted from the shallow surf, some kind of aquatic creature with scales and far too many waving tentacles clenched in its massive jaws.

"Yeah, real cute murder lizards." The redhead shook her head at her young copilot's bouncy enthusiasm.

"Aw, they're just big ol' puppies!" Ruby's dark eyes shone with excitement.

She was the youngest of the Ravens, fresh out of pilot training and on her first deployment. Everything was exciting to her. Blue wondered if she'd be quite so excited once she saw where she'd be sleeping at the outpost that night. Then again, sleepovers were always fun. Especially since Medusa had brought more booze down with her.

The warm sea breeze gusted, and Blue tucked a wayward curl behind one ear as she cast her gaze out over the ocean. They'd kept their armor on but had taken their helmets and gloves off to enjoy the sun while it lasted. Even though Fischer had elected to remain in the cockpit to deal with the paperwork and had promised to keep an eye on the weather, she'd linked the weather radar to her comm. The more eyes on that storm, the better.

At another gust, she stood up, shading her eyes against the sharp sting of wind-borne sand. The first hints of darkness broken only by the faint flickers of lighting lay on the horizon, and the rolling waves out in the deep carried the first hints of whitecaps. Right on cue, her comm *pinged* with a weather alert. Fischer's dry voice came over the command channel an instant later.

"The outer bands of the storm just hit our warning marker. Time to pack it in."

As Sergeant Ord and his legionnaires began herding their charges back toward the Rhinos, the wind picked up into a steady breeze, heavy with moisture and the tang of salt. It blew straight in from the ocean, rustling the fronds and tossing the flexible trees lining the edge of the jungle. Armadon heads raised high, reptilian gazes focused on the distant horizon. As one, they all twisted around and retreated into the thick trees in a burst of unbelievable speed, leaving the beach empty but for the Survey team and the legionnaires.

"Holy shit." Belated fear sent an electric shock through Blue. The armadons had seemed so slow—right up until they weren't.

"Fast puppies," Ruby breathed out.

"Still think the murder lizards are cute?" Medusa asked dryly.

"Both things can be true," the youngest Raven shot back with an impish grin. Blue shook her head at the girl.

"Looks like our beach vacation is over." A hard gust whipped across the beach, hard enough to rattle the Rhino, and a savage grin creased Blue's face. "Time to earn our pay, ladies."

CHAPTER TWELVE
A Phreatomagmatic Event? What's That?

WESTERN COAST, AURORA

The next morning Tavi found himself on another black sandy beach on the western coast of the mainland, well away from the Southern Isles and the brewing storm. The Survey team, led by Dr. Schmoyer, was tromping around the area searching for armadons. Unfortunately, unlike their southern brethren, armadons in the north seemed more reluctant to appear for the scientists to study and were staying out of sight.

Not that Tavi minded, really. The fewer armadons around, the better the security situation.

There was very little wind today, which was a small blessing. Lifting from the Southern Isles the previous day had been an adventure as the high winds had buffeted the Rhinos about, making the ride back a bit of a roller coaster. They'd made it back without too much issue, but it'd been far more exciting than some of the others preferred.

The beach here was also wider, with the black sand staying comfortably warm thanks to the midmorning sun. The aircrew had decided to relax and play a game while the legionnaires continued to provide site security. Tavi hadn't ever seen anything like it before and would have loved to join in... except Dr. Schmoyer and the Survey team were still hell-bent on discovering the secret of the armadons.

"We must push further inland," Schmoyer said to Fire Team Two as they stopped for a quick bite to eat. Their supply packs were good for a few days' worth of rations, but every experienced legionnaire knew the eventual cost. Notably, when it was time for bowel movements to occur. "I thought I saw an armadon nesting area nearby on the satellite imagery, and I want to go check it out. It's only a few hours of walking, and the area is perfectly safe! Let's boogie!"

Tavi blinked at the doctor's excitement. He hadn't seen the man this happy since their first hike through the jungles when he had believed he'd discovered a new lizard species. Clearly something had happened to change his mood. Beside him, he heard Mitzi sigh.

"Everything okay?" Tavi asked her. She shouldered her satchel bag.

"It's fine."

"Good." He looked over at Pigeon for guidance. The team leader shook his head, clearly amused.

"One, Three, this is Two. We're going on a nature hike. Form up a perimeter at..." He paused for a moment before continuing, "Grid One-One-Three-Three-Four-One. Team Two, you heard the man. Let's move out."

Mount St. Nicholas had earned its name due to an errant delivery payload, but kept it due to a paperwork snafu, someone's idea of a bad joke, and bureaucratic laziness.

One thing Shava Turnien and her Explorer team had noted during the initial survey stage was that the westernmost point of the largest continent bumped against a geologically active zone. More accurately, three separate continental and oceanic plates were pushing against one another along this coast, creating a river of fire between the largest two of the tectonic plates on the planet and a smaller oceanic subduction plate. Nicholas Island was actually part of a larger chain of islands stretching for over 1,500 miles north to south, extending perfectly in line with the tectonic plates. However, since most of the island chain was underwater, the only marker placed on it by the survey team was "geologically active" and then, promptly forgotten as the research station was finally built over 500 miles away.

If they'd paid very close attention to it, they would have noticed something... unusual. More accurately, they might have seen that the dome on Mount St. Nicholas was growing a few inches every year.

Earthquakes were common at their location. The initial surveys had shown the geological activity, which was why the research outpost was placed hundreds of miles away from the ocean. It wasn't the earthquakes they were afraid of, no. It was the resulting tsunamis which could occur should an earthquake powerful enough rattle the coast. While they always suspected it could happen, in the forty years since the terraforming project began on the Class-II world, there had never been anything over a magnitude-three earthquake. Most of the initial worries of the Survey Corps were put to rest as "overly cautious."

They'd built their station far away, just to be sure. Outside of some world-ending scenario, they were perfectly safe.

In theory.

Beneath Mount St. Nicholas, roughly five miles down, lay a magma chamber almost fifty miles wide and twice as long. Due to the slow and gradual building of pressure, the chamber lay relatively stable for thousands of years, with only a few relatively minor eruptions long before humanity had ever begun reaching for the stars. It would have caused some concern for scientists had they known of its existence.

They didn't. Yet.

A gentle 3.1-magnitude earthquake rolled across the island at roughly 0822 Zulu time. It was nothing major, a simple tremor to wake up the local wildlife. Deeper beneath the surface, roughly seventy-five miles down, the earthquake was an order of magnitude stronger. The smallest of the three tectonic plates slipped a little further beneath the largest, which would have told any geologist studying the region specifically that the smaller tectonic plate was a subduction zone between the others. The movement and subsequent earthquake was powerful enough to cause a small fissure to appear above the magma chamber beneath Mount St. Nicholas.

It wasn't much, only two hundred feet by forty, but it was enough.

Suddenly, thousands upon thousands of gallons of seawater rushed into the massive magma chamber. With the sudden pressure of steam created by the icy waters colliding with the molten magma, there was no way to go but up. The dome of the mountain expanded rapidly as steam was forced up the main shaft and into the cone, where it stuck. Multiple other shafts began branching off as the steam sought to find a release. Another earthquake, this one shallower than the first but significantly stronger, ripped the small fissure open further. Millions of gallons poured into the magma chamber, creating more steam which had only one escape route.

At 1131 Zulu, roughly three hours after the initial earthquake struck Mount St. Nicholas, a much larger and powerful one slammed the entire island chain. Beneath the ocean's surface, more magma chambers became exposed to the saltwater. Explosions ripped across the seabed as the gaseous magma chambers reacted violently with the saltwater. Smoke began pouring from the peak of Mount St. Nicholas as the dome began to collapse in on itself, the widening magma chamber below unable to support it. This pushed the steam toward the eastern side of the mountain as a new shaft was forcefully created within. The entire side of the mountain expanded, then contracted, creating a small landslide as the face of the mountainside fell away.

With a final rumble, dozens of steam vents exploded simultaneously across the island, and the formerly dormant volcano cataclysmically erupted.

"Sir? I'm getting some strange readings from the western coast of the primary continent. Satellite imagery coming in now."

Campbell looked up from his seemingly endless amount of paperwork and frowned. In his admittedly short time in the Martian Navy, never had the words "strange" meant anything other than trouble. The distraction from his Pile of Responsibility was welcome, though, so he set the requisition forms aside for the time being.

"Relay me those images when you get them, PO," he said, leaning forward in his chair. Like other sections on the command deck, Operations had its own private area where the officer on duty could sit and read reports or, more often than not, fill out and respond to said reports. Most of it was automated, which saved him and every other division on the ship a lot of make-work, but there were still some which needed his attention.

Which meant more time in the duty chair. Not that he minded, actually. It kept him out of his shared quarters and away from Grimes.

"Aye sir, relaying now."

As the numbers began scrolling across the screen, Campbell felt a faint flutter of confusion ripple over him. The numbers *looked* fine to him at a glance, but the strange increase in gaseous readings over the western coast didn't track with anything which had been previously recorded on the planet.

"Confirm these readings yet, PO?" Campbell asked.

"Confirmed, sir. Ground readings in the area report seismic activity as well."

"Seismic... wait, earthquakes?" Campbell stared at the screen before he recalled something from the original mission brief about the planet. He'd mostly focused on the Operations aspect of things, but meteorological events impacted Ops, so he'd paid attention. One of the possibilities presented during the briefing had been a volcanic eruption at sea, along an island chain off the western coast—the same island chain in question now. "Confirm seismic activities, Petty Officer. We have sat imagery yet?"

"Coming in now... holy *shit*!"

Campbell's eyes widened as the gaseous readings began making more sense. The imagery on his screen showed a massive heat and debris plume, almost fifty miles wide and expanding rapidly, growing out of the island chain off the west coast. The plume had climbed into the troposphere already and was still going. He estimated it would be another ten minutes before it breached the stratosphere.

He looked across the command deck. "Comms, Ops. Lieutenant Commander Logan, are you getting this, sir?"

"Confirmed, Ops. Getting some interference in the area of the eruption now. Signal intercepts are spotty due to the upper atmosphere interference from the ash clouds of the eruption. Relays with the research outpost are still nominal. This shouldn't affect the base for a day or two, depending on the meteorological track of that southern storm. Jetstream might push the ashfall south of the base, too. I'll confirm with the aerographer planetside."

"It's not the base I'm worried about, sir," Campbell muttered as he brought up the day's itinerary and weather reports.

After a quick search he found what he'd recalled from the morning's briefing. Both 4th and 5th Squad were out in the field with a scheduled excursion along the coast nearby, with Bronze Ravens One and Four in support. A cold little ball of fear formed in his stomach as he recognized Blue's Rhino.

"Comms, get on the horn with the research outpost. Let them know about the eruption—assuming they haven't seen it yet, sir. Also, notify the Duty Watch Officer that we might have a potential red-zone situation, and let the XO know as well. And someone get with Captain Truitt. He's going to need to know what's going on down there, sir."

"I'm on it, Ensign. Wait...what do you mean, seen it?"

"They're over five hundred miles away, sir, but judging by the size of the cloud and the fact that they're near the coast, they'll definitely see something," Campbell explained, rapidly doing the math in his head. The air density was different on Aurora when compared to Mars Primus, but it was close enough for the math to work. "Probably hear it, too. Might sound like a gunshot or something similar, hard to say. It won't sound normal is all. It's been fifteen minutes since the eruption began, so they should hear it in about five minutes."

"Copy that. Relaying information now. Good work, Ensign."

"Haven't done anything yet, sir," he replied and focused back on his monitor as more satellite feeds began coming in across different frequencies. Most were dull, showing only the areas around the eruption site and the coastline. Only one showed any activity at all, and it was this one that drew his immediate attention.

The IR scanner was finicky on the best of days. On a planet such as Aurora, though, it worked well. Too well, which suggested the natural warmth of the planet was distorting the readings. Campbell scratched his chin, thoughtful, and waited for a firmer picture to appear.

Within minutes his thoughtful expression turned to one of confusion.

There was no glitch or reflection here, though. Nor was it a mistake. The signal was too diffuse, scattered, to be refraction of the lens. Not enough of them were flying through the air—the trajectories were off for that, which ruled out volcanic ejecta. Whatever it was, most of it was on the planet surface below.

"That's not lava or anything...not that soon." Campbell frowned. There weren't a few hundred heat signatures, but thousands, and their numbers were growing by the moment. Worst of all, they were heading away from the volcanic eruption—and directly toward the Aurora Research Outpost at high speed. Campbell swore as more appeared on the screen. "Not the pyroclastic cloud from the volcano, either. Some is probably debris from the volcano, but...looks like the local wildlife is fleeing the volcano."

"I'll let the research outpost know they've got incoming," Logan said.

Campbell nodded and looked back at the monitor as the ash cloud began to slowly cover the entire western coast—and the last known location of the Survey team, the legionnaires... and their pilots.

Slowly, his hands curled into fists. *Get the hell out of there, Blue.*

Blue was having a fantastically lazy day. She'd reached an uneasy truce with Schmoyer, Norwood had continued to leave her alone, and the paperwork for her successful upgrade checkride had gone through the system. She was now qualified to sit in the left seat, though she'd continue to fly as Twister's copilot for now.

Best of all, thanks to *Schmoyer* of all people, the Ravens got another beach day. He wanted to see if the aggressive behavior of the northern armadons extended to the herds on the coast.

Killi had nearly sweet-talked Ruby into giving up her copilot seat on Bronze Raven One on this run, but Witch had vetoed at the last moment. Bronze Raven Five was still down for maintenance, but the maintainers thought they might be ready to test the engines today, which meant Killi had to stay at the outpost again.

Her best friend had been less than pleased.

Hours had passed since Schmoyer had gotten a wild hair up his ass and led his Survey team and 4th Squad on an epic hike deep into the coastal jungle. Normally, the Ravens wouldn't be quite so far from their legionnaires, but the trees were younger here, thicker on the ground, and there weren't any good LZs where Schmoyer wanted to investigate. Instead, they'd checked the sat images, verified that the area was safe enough for 4th Squad to handle alone, and had left 5th Squad to establish a perimeter around the Rhinos.

A steady breeze kept the day from getting too hot, and the sun was a pleasant warmth on her bare arms and shoulders. They were close enough to the outpost that they'd flown direct. No void ops meant flightsuits instead of armor, and it hadn't taken long for both aircrews to strip down. Blue had unzipped her flightsuit halfway and tied the sleeves around her waist, leaving her torso clad in the black tank top typically worn beneath the uniform.

Once again, she'd chosen to recline on the Rhino's open ramp with the other Ravens and sunbathe, much like the handful of armadons scattered along the shore. For a time, the Ravens had played a brutally competitive game of ultimate frisbee with their Crows, but the enlisted aircrew had an unfair advantage in Sergeant Morrison, Medusa's loadmaster. The man was a beast on the field. Combined with Sergeant Carvalho's trickiness and the gunners' collective enthusiasm, and the pilots had gotten their asses kicked.

Bronze Raven One's gunners, Tyson and Jacobi, were still tossing the frisbee around with the loadmasters, but Hekekia and Hayashi had abandoned the game some time ago to hunt for treasures along the black-sand shore. They'd moseyed so far down the beach that Blue honestly couldn't tell which one was dancing around like a lunatic with some choice find clutched high overhead in her hand. Blue just hoped they didn't try to bring too many shinies back with them on the Rhino.

While 5th Squad hadn't participated in the game, Sergeant Cox had allowed two of his fire teams to relax and spread out down the beach. The third fire team had been sent into the coastal jungle about an hour ago to pick up samples left behind by Schmoyer's group as they'd continued along their hike.

Ruby, who had been cooing over the nearby armadons hunting in the wave-tossed ocean, AKA the "big ol' puppies," shifted her attention to Blue. Specifically to Blue's bare shoulders.

"I can't believe you get your Raven wings after this deployment." She sighed in envy as she eyed the black-feathered wings tattooed across Twister and Medusa's upper back and shoulders. Twister's tattoos even curled down her arms, mostly black feathers but with a handful of white "ghost" feathers in the mix. "I can't wait to earn mine."

Blue brushed a hand across her bare skin and smiled, envisioning the graceful tattoos. "You'll only need to complete a dozen more missions to earn them."

"Because that won't take any time at all," the young woman said with a bright laugh.

"It really won't," Medusa said, tugging her copilot into a sideways hug.

"It goes by faster than you think," Twister added with a chuckle. She winked at Blue.

"Yeah it does." With a contented sigh, Blue tilted her face up to the sun and let the chatter of her friends and sisters-in-arms wash over her, as much a backdrop as the constant swish of the incoming tide.

BOOM!

Pain slammed into her eardrums, and a concussive blast reached out and punched her in the chest. As startled screams and shouts rang out along the shore, Blue scrambled to her feet almost before her eyes snapped open.

"What the hell was that?" she shouted over the ringing in her ears.

"Was that gunfire?" Ruby stumbled to her feet, eyes wide and her hands clamped over her ears. "Or did one of the legionnaires blow something up?"

"No," Sergeant Carvalho said with authority as he limped over to the Rhino, sharp gaze scanning for threats. "That was too big for anything the legionnaires were carrying."

Sergeant Cox bellowed orders at his legionnaires, who hastily reformed a perimeter around the Rhinos, rifles unslung and hard eyes focused outward. The armadons had already disappeared into the thick trees with blinding speed. Blue scanned the shore, noting with relief that Hekekia and Hayashi were already sprinting back to them. When a legionnaire shouted and pointed across the waves, Blue followed his gesture.

And froze.

A dark cloud had appeared on the western horizon, expanding with almost supernatural swiftness and shooting up to the heavens. Lightning flickered, tiny strikes that highlighted the roiling darkness rather than illuminated it.

"That can't be the hurricane." Twister stood up, one hand shading her eyes. "It's still too far south."

"Then what the hell is it?" Medusa eyed the horizon grimly as she pulled back her red curls into a tight braid and zipped up her flightsuit. "And should we be running for the hills, so to speak?"

"I'll check the weather radar," Ruby volunteered, bouncing to her feet and darting into the Rhino, her typical enthusiasm already recovered.

"It's not a storm front," Blue said uneasily. The churning cloud was building straight up into the stratosphere, but it was all upward momentum and hadn't spread out like a squall line. "And it's the wrong shape for a nuclear or kinetic bomb..."

A cold spike of fear shot through her core when she remembered the additional mission prep they'd done for their training drop on Sagetnam. Mission prep that they'd done specifically because of Aurora's terraforming quirk.

Volcanic ash ops.

"Oh my god." Blue clenched her fists to stop the shaking. "It's an eruption plume."

"A what?" HeyHey demanded in unison with a fine edge of controlled fear and a great deal of panting from their sprint along the obsidian shore.

Blue tore her gaze off the rising cloud of ash and ruin. Both aircrews had gathered at the base of Bronze Raven One's ramp, gunners and loadmasters all looking to their pilots for information. Before she could explain, their comms crackled to life.

"*Bronze Ravens One and Four, Aurora Research Outpost. Be advised of seismic and volcanic activity off the coast.*"

Blue's gaze snapped back out over the ocean again. *Gee, you think?*

"*Report is from the* Perseverance. *We're still waiting on secondary confirmation.*"

Slowly, Twister raised her wrist comm, her eyes fixed on the horizon. "This is Bronze Raven Four. Volcanic activity confirmed. I repeat, volcanic activity *confirmed.*"

"*Understood. Survey team has already been informed. Aurora Research Outpost, out.*"

Ruby thundered out of the cargo compartment, slate clenched in one hand and her complexion pale. The weather radar filled half the screen, with a sat image on the other half.

"Volcano off the coast exploded, and I do mean *exploded.*" She swallowed hard. "And that ash cloud is heading right for us."

The eruption plume was already visibly collapsing, the prevailing winds shoving the top of the column toward them like the leading edge of an anvil cloud. Already, the steady breeze carried something other than the clean tang of salt and ocean spray. Gray ash and the sour stench of sulfur rode the wind. As the ash cloud spread across the sky, the sun dimmed, casting the black-sand beach in an ominous light. The first flecks of ash fell across the beach and the Rhinos like dirty snowflakes.

Fast. It was moving *so* fast. That cold spike of fear twisted and spread through Blue's gut as she stared at the ash settling across the Rhino's wings—and the atmospheric engines currently locked in the vertical configuration. In high enough concentrations, ashfall was deadly to those engines.

"Prep for launch," Twister ordered their aircrew, and the Crows scattered to handle their duties.

"Give me that." Blue snatched the slate out of Ruby's hands and manipulated the radar. "I *knew* that hurricane was going to screw us over somehow. It's close enough to affect the air currents and it's pushing the eruption plume right for the coast."

Steadily swearing under her breath as she worked, she overlaid the ash cloud projected path over the latest sat image before she added a marker for their current location. Fingers dancing over the screen, she pinged Sergeant Ord's HCS, grabbed 4th Squad's location, and added it to the image. They were southeast, deep in the coastal jungle and directly in the path of the heaviest ashfall.

"Don't forget Sergeant Munoz and 5th Squad's Fire Team Three," Medusa said urgently. Nodding, Blue added their location to the image. They were nowhere near as far away as 4th Squad, but they were still several klicks inland.

"*Bronze Ravens One and Four*, Perseverance, *ash cloud and tsunami rolling in to coast. Recommend recalling all personnel and evacuating current location ASAP.*"

"Yeah, no shit, skippy," Twister muttered before she raised her comm again. "*Perseverance*, Bronze Raven One, wilco."

Medusa shared a heavy look with Twister before she spun around. Her eyes skipped across the faces of the legionnaires spread out around the Rhinos until her hard gaze locked onto Sergeant Cox.

"Duck, recall your boys, we need to get gone *now*," she bellowed. "Ruby, get those engines running. Alert launch!"

The veteran sergeant immediately sprang into action, ordering the two fire teams onto Bronze Raven One and getting on the comm with his absent fire team.

"Alert launch?" Ruby stood frozen on the ramp, eyes wide and uncomprehending. Medusa grabbed her by the arms and shook her.

"That means you get your ass in the cockpit and skip everything that isn't fucking essential. You copy?"

"Copy." Determination flaring bright in her eyes, Ruby nodded sharply and sprinted inside the Rhino. The remaining three pilots jumped off the ramp, clearing the way for the running legionnaires.

"Get on the comms with Ordo, tell him we're coming for them," Twister said grimly before she pulled Medusa aside and spoke in a low voice. Blue studied 4th Squad's current location on the sat image before she made the call.

"Command net, 4th Squad, Bronze Raven Four."

"*Bronze Raven Four, 4th Squad, Ordo, go.*"

"Bronze Raven Four will be in the air in five mikes or less. Sat image doesn't show a clear LZ anywhere near your current location. We might have to make our own." Blue shook ash off her flightsuit and eyed her Rhino in concern. The ashfall was getting heavier. "Be aware, ash in atmo is already impacting flight ops. Sit tight, we'll be there as fast as we can."

"*Ordo copies all.*"

Blue glanced up to gauge the progress of the ash cloud and immediately regretted it. Cursing, she blinked stinging ash out of her watering eyes. Bitterness flooded her tongue as ash got into her mouth, and she leaned over and spat onto the black sand.

"Ordo's updated," she said as Twister and Medusa rejoined her.

"Good," Twister said absently, her gaze resting on Medusa. "See you back at the outpost, sister."

Blue pushed the sat image and radar overlay to all of the Ravens before she handed the slate back to Medusa. "Fly safe."

"Screw safe." The fiery redhead gave them both a fierce grin. "Let's go get our boys."

Medusa tangled her fingers with Twister's and gripped her hand tight for a half a heartbeat before she clapped Blue on the shoulder. And then there was no more time. Blue outpaced Twister to their Rhino and charged up the ramp without slowing, sprinting past Sergeant Carvalho buttoning up the cargo compartment, past HeyHey completing a rapid check of their guns, and straight into the cockpit.

The windshield was already covered in a fine layer of ash.

Practically throwing herself into the seat, she pulled up the alert launch checklist and ran through the abbreviated steps with shaking breaths and steady hands. Twister reached the cockpit seconds later, talking in a rapid fire with the *Perseverance* comm officer. The hum of the ramp closing echoed through the Rhino as she raced through the last steps and pulled on her helmet.

"Come on, come on," Blue snarled as she monitored the start-up sequence. "Faster, faster, faster."

A reassuring hum filled the cockpit as all the subsystems came online and the engines rumbled to life. Her HUD synced up with the central flight computer, and data scrolled past in a reassuring flow. They were green across the board. With a silent prayer that the old dropship wouldn't mind the rough handling, Blue pushed the throttles up before the engines were properly warmed in preparation for lift off. The engines ramped up with a roar, vibrating throughout the whole damn ship in an off-key pitch that set her teeth on edge before they settled, stabilized, *purred*.

"That's a good girl," Twister crooned.

Blue shot her command pilot a startled glance, but the older woman patted the console, making it clear she'd been talking to the Rhino.

"Get us in the air," Twister added sharply. "I'll take comms and coordinate with Ordo."

Nodding sharply, Blue firmly gripped the controls and activated the aircrew channel. "Confirm ready to fly."

Sergeant Carvalho responded immediately, but there was a distinct lack of good cheer in his voice. *"Ready to fly, confirmed."*

In the short time it had taken them to prep, visibility had fallen to less than a klick and was growing worse by the second. Blue's HUD automatically shifted to a multi-spectrum blend that cut through the haze.

To their left, Bronze Raven One was already taking off. Medusa must be flying, because they shifted to forward flight at the bare minimum altitude with a smooth competence Ruby didn't yet have the experience to imitate. She immediately tucked the nose low and hugged the terrain, flying due east into the coastal jungle to pick up their last fire team. Even with the HUD spectrum, the Rhino was very quickly out of visual range, the mottled gray metal blending with the falling gray ash.

More ash flew off the engines as they reached liftoff speed, and that off-key note briefly sang out before the normal pitch resumed. Gritting her teeth, Blue checked her sat image. As close to real-time as the relays could provide and with her weather radar overlay still in place, the updated image painted a grim picture.

"The ashfall's already ahead of our flightpath," she told Twister grimly. "Medusa's too."

"I see it. Get us into the air."

With no time or patience for Medusa's finesse, Blue jammed the throttles all the way up and launched. Black sand billowed up in great clouds as they lifted into the air, a harmless parallel to the roiling ash cloud raining down on the beach where they'd parked the Rhinos several hours and a small lifetime ago.

Within seconds, they'd achieved minimum altitude, and Blue rotated the engines into the forward position. As soon as the landing gear safely retracted, she pushed their speed up. They had further to go than Bronze Raven One and less time to do it in.

Gray-coated green trees flashed by under their wings, the steady breeze tossing the branches, keeping the wide fronds from getting too weighed down with ash. For now. Flight conditions continued to deteriorate. Lightning flickered in the rear external cameras, and a harsh gust rattled the Rhino. Blue adjusted, keeping them on course, but not before her tail end skewed to the left in a rapid jerk. Once again, Blue was grateful she never got airsick.

Over the aircrew channel, Hekekia groaned and muttered, *"This is what happens when you let balls in the cockpit."*

"And don't let us finish the good juju symbols," Hayashi added rebelliously.

"Not the time, HeyHey," Carvalho growled. *"And you can't seriously believe Captain Fischer flying with the Ravens caused a whole-ass volcano to erupt!"*

A short pause.

"We don't not believe it."

Blue wasn't sure which gunner spoke that time, and she couldn't devote the attention to figuring it out. The winds were growing worse, and rain splattered across the windscreen. There must be enough ash in the atmosphere combined with the already humid air to generate a thunderstorm. Right on cue, lightning cut across the sky. Not the tiny flickers from the eruption plume, but a massive bolt capable of frying a Rhino's secondary systems if they were unlucky enough to get hit. On its heels, thunder rumbled through the thickening clouds, a deep rolling boom Blue felt in her bones.

It was no longer possible to tell ash cloud from normal clouds with the naked eye. Everything was gray and churning and violent. The skies were angry and more than happy to take it out on her poor

Rhino. Blue's shoulders tightened as the ship groaned and bucked beneath her hands, and apprehension swirled low in her gut.

"You've got this, and I'm here to back you up if you need it," Twister said with quiet confidence. "But you're not going to need it."

Blue didn't dare shift her gaze, but she flashed her command pilot a quick grin. Exhaling sharply, she relaxed her death grip on the controls and rode the storm.

As the klicks raced by, Twister pushed the updated sat image to the main viewscreen, eyes sharp on the building weather system and the ashfall dispersion pattern. Bronze Raven One's icon had stopped moving. They'd set down in the coastal jungle, near but not directly on top of Fire Team Three's icon. Their heat signature remained hot, a telltale sign they'd kept their engines spooled up for a quick departure.

"Bronze Raven One, Four," Twister said over the comms. "Ashfall worsening in your location. You need to get airborne again ASAP."

"*Four, One, wilco,*" Ruby replied tightly. "*We'll be back up in the air in less than three mikes.*"

Worry strained Twister's voice. "You wait too long and that ash is going to frag your engines."

"*I know,*" Medusa said brusquely, taking over the comms. "*We landed as close to Fire Team Three as we could short of having our gunners mow down half the jungle. They're almost here.*"

"Medusa—"

"*We're not leaving them.*"

"Four copies all." Twister heaved a defeated sigh and got off the comm. "Stubborn bitch. Push our speed a little more, Blue."

Blue bumped the throttles up as high as she dared and pushed the nose low, flying barely one hundred meters above the tossing trees. They raced away from the coast, south and east, always east, pushing the engines as fast as possible but unable to outpace the ashfall. As they flew, the engines sucked in the ash. At first, the robust turbines chewed it up and spat it back out, but as they heated up the ash began to melt before it was expelled... coating the interior in a thin layer of glass.

The first warning alert flashed in Blue's HUD before they were halfway to their legionnaires. Between one controlled breath and the next, the engine pitch changed, climbing higher even though Blue hadn't touched the throttles this time.

"Shit," Twister muttered. "I'm going to try to redistribute the power load. Left engine is getting cranky."

Twister cursed and praised the Rhino by turns, but she managed to redistribute the power enough to settle the left engine and clear the alert. As the high-pitched whine settled into a more or less steady *thrum*, their comms crackled to life, full of static but still clear enough.

"*Bronze Raven Four, One, Fire Team Three recovered,*" Ruby said brightly. "*Be advised tsunami passing beneath our current location.*"

On the main viewscreen, Bronze Raven One's icon was on the move again, and Fire Team Three's icon traveled in sync with the Rhino's. Twister adjusted the sat image to dismiss the legionnaire's icon to simplify the image. She smiled as Bronze Raven One slowly gained altitude and speed.

"One, Four, nice to see you're finally moving your fat ass."

Medusa took over the comms from Ruby with a wicked laugh.

"*Please, there's nothing fat about* my *ass—*" The deafening blare of an alarm shrieked through the comms. "*Ruby, engine restart!*"

"*I'm trying, but they're not responding!*"

"*Try again,*" Medusa snarled. "*Fuck, brace for impact—*"

A horrible roar sounded over the comms, tangled with screams and shouts of pain, followed by the dead silence of a lost comm transmission. An instant later, an emergency beacon activated, quiet and steady as a heartbeat.

Terror sank icy tendrils through Blue's soul.

Bronze Raven One was down.

CHAPTER THIRTEEN
Oh, There's the Earth-Shattering Kaboom.

137 MILES WEST OF AURORA RESEARCH OUTPOST, AURORA

The concussive blast sent Mitzi and the scientists diving for cover, their hands covering their ears as they cried out in pain. Tavi's head snapped toward the west as he immediately detected the source of the noise. Around them, Aurora's bird analogues suddenly exploded from the trees and took to the sky, their leathery wings beating furiously as they all headed east. Far off in the distance, a steady rumbling could be heard.

"*4th Squad, Aurora Research Outpost. Be advised of seismic and volcanic activity to your west,*" Tavi's comms crackled to life unexpectedly. There was some interference, but not enough to interrupt the transmission. Something told him that "yet" hung in the air after the thought. "*Report is from the* Perseverance. *Waiting on secondary confirmation now.*"

"Copy that, ARO," Ordo confirmed in a low, flat tone. "Any danger to the civilians at this time?"

"*Unknown, 4th Squad.*"

"Copy that, ARO. Will advise if situation becomes untenable, over."

"Oh, *pokerro*," Jabber muttered as the communique ended. "They gonna throw us that sort of info and give us nothing else? *Fech*. What a bunch of shit, Ordo."

"Stow it," Ordo cut off Jabber before he could get going. "Check your civvies, all of you. Duck, this is Ordo. You copy that mess?"

"*Copy that. We're with the Rhinos. Nothing exciting here, but we're starting to see some ashfall. We're also seeing lots of fauna running to* the east," came the response from Duck. "*Nothing dangerous so far. Check one... Bronze Raven One is signaling that we're packing up.*"

"Keep an eye out," Ordo added. "We just saw an entire flock of those lizard bird things take off and head east. Didn't even see 'em in the trees. 4th, move in on Team Two's position."

"*Copy. Duck out.*"

The next comm came from their ride.

"*Fourth Squad, Bronze Raven Four.*"

"Bronze Raven Four, this is Ordo, go."

"*Bronze Raven Four will be in the air in five mikes or less. Sat image doesn't show a clear LZ anywhere near your current location. We might have to make our own.*" There was a brief hesitation, or maybe the comms had momentarily cut out. "*Be aware, ash in atmo is already impacting flight ops. Sit tight, we'll be there as fast as we can.*"

Tavi recognized Blue on the comms. While her tone was rock steady, there was a definite undercurrent of strain in the pilot's voice.

"Ordo copies all."

"That sounded pretty bad," Mitzi muttered as Tavi helped her to her feet.

She slung the satchel safely into place before her eyes moved off to the distance. Tavi quickly checked her over for any sign of injury. Not finding anything obvious, he started to ask her if she was okay but stopped. She stood frozen, staring at the darkening western sky.

Tavi could see the massive cloud rising high into the sky as well, but didn't know what to make of it. He'd never seen anything like it before. Mitzi shivered and then moved closer to him, dropping her voice low as she continued.

"I know the Ivanova and Garibaldi continental plates meet the Sinclair oceanic plate at a juncture somewhere off the west coast, but everything I'd read suggested they were tectonically stable and the risk of a volcanic eruption of this magnitude was low, almost negligible."

"Yeah," Tavi agreed, not knowing what else to say. There were many things covered at ACS. Talking to women outside his chain of command had not been one of them. Tectonic plates were another. "That's bad, right?"

"It can be," she said before jerking her chin toward Doctor Huyan, the only other female present. "*That's* the geologist of the group.

There's only so much you can learn from books. After that, you need field experience."

"Doctor Xi-Smith!" Schmoyer huffed as he picked himself off the ground. The front of his outfit was covered in mud and leaves. He brushed off as much as he could before continuing. "Nowhere in the notes or surveys of this planet did I read anything about volcanic activity!"

"I'm so sorry, Doctor," the geologist apologized profusely, dipping her head every few seconds. "According to the available reports, the tectonic plates were nowhere near the research facility. Because of this, I didn't prioritize them. I did plan to look at them soon, though!"

"Well." Schmoyer exhaled and tried again to wipe some of the mud off. "Not soon enough, apparently."

The anger which had come so easily to him had vanished just as quickly. Tavi found it a little odd, but brushed the thought aside. He'd learned that almost all Martians had strange quirks he would need to get used to.

"What's a little volcanic eruption, anyway?" Schmoyer chuckled weakly at his joke. "Any idea where that came from?"

"I'd guess Mount St. Nicholas," Mitzi offered as she squinted and peered at the growing cloud. "I think I read somewhere that they classified it as a dormant volcano."

"I asked Doctor Huyan Xi-Smith, our *geological* expert," Schomyer said coldly. "Not my xenobiologist."

"She's right though, Doctor Schmoyer," Xi-Smith answered quietly, dark eyes flitting out to the west and the rising ash cloud darkening the skies. "There's only one volcanic mountain to the west that's both big enough and close enough to cause that sort of ash cloud. I mean, in theory one could rapidly form and explode, but the satellites would've picked up anything beforehand. No, it would have to be some sort of preexisting volcano. Unless it was an even bigger one far out to sea that we don't know about, but ... no, Mount St. Nicholas was the likely culprit, Doctor."

"If that was the mountain, then there's going to be a tsunami," Mitzi said, her gaze shifting eastward. It was flat jungle for as far as the eye can see. "I don't think there are any hills high enough to deflect any wave over ten feet for miles."

"Tsunami?" Doctor Schmoyer frowned. "I hadn't considered this. Flooding will be bad, and debris will wipe everything out for miles inland, if not further. Depends on how much water was displaced during the eruption. We need to get in the air and back to the research outpost as soon as possible!"

"Not to interrupt this fine discussion of tectonic science and impending doom, but Bronze Raven Four is somewhere to the northwest of our position," Ordo said, stepping into the group. His face seemingly undisturbed by the idea of a giant wave coming to kill them all. "I've checked every possible LZ within two hours walk. As much as HeyHey would *love* to clear themselves an LZ, we should see if we have something a little better and more workable. Sat relay indicates there *is* a high probability of a tsunami pushing towards the entire west coast. Everything I've read about the oceans here on Aurora suggests the higher salinity makes the saltwater react differently to seismic events and anomalies. A paper by Doctor Roosevelt Jackson theorizes that a tsunami in waters like here on Aurora would actually travel faster due to the differing density of salt water, but his findings have been challenged by professors at—"

"I'm familiar with Doctor Jackson's theory!" Schmoyer interrupted with an irritated growl. "His theories challenge hundreds of years of proven science!"

"On Mars Primus, yes sir," Mitzi joined in. She bestowed a small smile on Ordo. "I read that paper as well. His findings are solid, but... well, looks like we're going to see if his theory is correct."

"You can read, *bossjna*?" Jabber asked, genuinely surprised. Ordo rolled his eyes.

"How are we going to see?" Tavi asked Mitzi, genuinely curious.

"Well, the tsunami is either going to hit the beach within the hour, or in ten minutes," she replied. "There's going to be no outrunning it. The shallower seas mean we're going to get a bigger crest, but there might not be as much behind it as there would be on Mars Primus." She shrugged. "It's an even bet, truth be told. I'm hoping for a bigger crest at the shoreline."

"Why?" Tavi asked.

"Means that there'll be a singular break of the water, then low-levels up to our knees until we reach an elevation change... about fifty miles east of here. Maybe more."

"Which means every single LZ west of us for our ride is out of the question," Ordo stated matter-of-factly. There was no fear in his tone, only acceptance. "Any of these trees thick and tall enough to keep us dry?"

"Hard to say," Mitzi responded before Schmoyer could really work himself up into an indignant fury. Surprisingly, he merely nodded as she continued. "There's going to be a lot of debris from further towards the coast. All those trees there with shallow roots are going to create a maelstrom when the water pushes inland. Without scientific equipment to study the effects of the volcano, I'm only guessing at this point."

"The issue is with how much water was displaced, and if it's a subduction earthquake that occurred when the volcano went," Xi-Smith added. Her brow furrowed in concentration. "We could be looking at a tsunami roughly sixty to one hundred feet high before it hits the shallower waters along the coast. It's both a blessing and a curse that the continental shelf is shallow and extends out pretty far."

"How?" Ordo asked.

"The shallower waters will slow a tsunami down, typically," she replied. "But like Dr. Wingo said, the wave usually crests higher as a result. Again, I'm sorry, but I'm guessing here. Ocean temperatures and even salinity affect this."

"Better than nothing, Doctor," Pigeon told her, patting her arm comfortingly. She flinched but didn't pull away. Tavi shifted uncomfortably and looked back westward. While not afraid of dying, he really didn't relish the idea of drowning. Dying in the toxic water was one of those terrifying tales kids on Myrkyma told to scare each other. The thought of black waters swirling around him, unknown objects in the water, battering his body and forcing him under, trapped inside his suit and sinking to the bottom of a newborn sea, alone... it sent chills down his spine.

No, he didn't want to drown. Not today, not ever.

"Ordo, check out Point Six-Three-Bravo," Vixen interrupted, bringing up the overlay map for all to see in their HUDs. "It shows flat, but look at the satellite imagery."

"Are those... rocks?" Ordo asked.

"Sure as shit looks like it, *bossjna*," Jabber said. Ordo turned and looked at Doctor Xi-Smith.

"We believe there's a rock formation roughly one mile southeast of here. They look like they're forty feet high, and large enough to keep everyone dry. Hell, might work as an LZ. We're approximately twenty miles from the coastline. Do you think they'll be enough to keep us all alive until our Ravens swoop down from on high to rescue us?"

Xi-Smith shrugged. "I'm sorry, I don't know. But I can tell you that it would be better than climbing some of the trees around here. I can't say with any certainty the tree roots would anchor and hold."

"There isn't much wind," Doctor Morales added, speaking for the first time since they departed the beach hours before. "But there is some. Wind means that the trees have deeper roots for stability. The leaves are broad and flat as well on the taller trees, so I'd say the roots are sturdy."

"But if the ground is soft from rain, then the flooding water might rip the roots clear out," Mitzi countered. "No, I don't think scaling trees is going to save us."

"The rocks look big enough for three squads of legionnaires, Sergeant," Tavi said as he eyed the satellite image on his HUD. "If the tsunami is as fast as Miss Mitzi says it is, then we can still get there in a maximum of twenty minutes. Fifteen if we push."

"Rocks it is. Sorry, Doctors, but this sounds like a better plan," Ordo said, cutting off any potential protests from Schmoyer. "Klau! Take Team One and haul ass. Blaze us a path for the civvies. Two, stick with your assigned civilians. Three, rear guard. The *Perseverance* said that there might be wildlife heading away from the sea and towards ARO. Let's make sure they don't eat us while we're all running for their lives. Doctor Schmoyer? We need to hustle."

"Yes, I agree." For the first time since they'd arrived on Aurora, the doctor did not argue.

As they moved quickly to the designated marker on their HUDs, Tavi focused primarily on Mitzi as she marched with purpose along the path blazed by Team One. He stayed practically on her heels, keeping an eye out for any signs of danger as they moved. According to the book he'd finished reading, it was probable the volcanic activity had amped up the armadon's aggressive nature and he wanted to be ready in case they appeared. Or worse, a herd of some sort of prey animal stampeding blindly through the jungle.

"Ashfall," Xi-Smith announced with a hint of fatalism in her voice.

Tavi looked up, surprised. For some reason he hadn't thought about ash falling on his head. He wondered how it would affect his suit before recalling the hamatic suits were put through the rigors of any and all environments. Undoubtedly volcanic ash had been included.

Right?

CHAPTER FOURTEEN
The Hardest Thing

150 MILES WEST OF AURORA RESEARCH OUTPOST, AURORA

Not turning back for Bronze Raven One was the hardest thing Blue had ever done.

Listening to Twister's increasingly desperate and unanswered comm calls to the downed Rhino was its own kind of torture, but she couldn't take her focus away from flying to offer her command pilot any comfort. She was too busy fighting her way through the storm and the ash, steadily cutting the distance to 4th Squad.

The volcanic eruption hadn't slowed in the slightest and was pumping an ungodly amount of ash into the atmosphere at a frightening rate. Redistributing the power across the linked atmospheric engines had helped a little, but they were struggling.

Blue could hear it, could *feel* it.

If it were possible to fly faster, to escape the ash quicker, she'd do it, but they were already maxed out for speed. The Rhinos were beasts in the air, but they weren't particularly fast. All she could do was baby the engines as much as possible while moving as fast as possible.

The entire time, that emergency beacon pinged. Steady, remorseless, and *entirely* unhelpful in providing any useful information. Like if the crash was as bad as it had sounded before they'd lost comms, if anyone was hurt... if anyone was still alive.

Ruby's bright smile flashed in Blue's mind in vivid detail. She'd been so damn excited about her first deployment, her first time "roughing it" in the decaying building the Ravens had been stuck in at the outpost, her first real sorties ferrying legionnaires around, even if they weren't "her" boys. Medusa's wicked laugh echoed in her memory, the fiery woman always ready with a quip or advice. As inseparable from Witch and Twister as if they really were sisters. Blue shot Twister a quick glance and flinched at the tightly controlled anguish hidden beneath the professional mask.

They had to be alive. There was no other acceptable outcome.

Twister fell silent, her knuckles white on the edge of the flight console and her dead stare fixed outside the cockpit. Blue didn't think she saw the storm-tossed coastal jungle or the churning gray skies. Rain lashed across the windscreen with a sharp rattle, but the older woman didn't even flinch... until their comms crackled to life.

Blue's heart leaped, but it wasn't Bronze Raven One. It was the comms officer on the *Perseverance*.

"*Bronze Raven Four, Perseverance, Bronze Raven One is down but intact. Be aware, atmospheric disturbance is starting to interfe... with comms.*" As if to emphasize his point, a burst of static briefly drowned out part of the transmission. "*... biometric data still coming through on our end. Bronze Raven One has zero fatalities, but definite injuries... medic team has been alerted and is on standby to receive them whenever they're evacuated.*"

Relief shot through Blue, but Twister didn't relax. Not even a little bit.

"*Perseverance*, Bronze Raven Four. Why isn't a Rhino already en route to evac them?"

Silence. Another burst of static. Then, "*Remaining Rhinos are needed elsewhere. Your orders are to extract the Survey team to the Perseverance. Once all other taskers have been satisfied and if conditions permit, you may be tasked with evac'ing them.*"

Twister snarled. "That could be too late to get to them. The ash cloud might be too thick by then."

Blue darted a sharp glance at the updated sat image. Twister was right. The volcano was as much of a monster as the tropical cyclonic storm, an enormous blight on the shallow ocean spewing ash and stirring up the atmospheric conditions into something truly hellish. By the time they picked up 4th Squad and their civvies, got up to the ship, kicked everyone off, and dropped again... conditions might have deteriorated past what even a Rhino could handle. She winced as their engines warbled alarmingly. For a heart-stopping instant, their power dipped before abruptly recovering.

It was nearly past what their Rhino could handle *now*.

"And that's assuming none of those injuries are critical," Twister added with a stubborn set to her jaw.

"*I'm sorry, Bronze Raven Four, but the civilians at the Aurora Research Outpost have priority over legionnaires.*" There was real regret in the comms officer's voice, but not even a hint of flexibility. "*Supervisor Norwood has ordered an evacuation, and we are required by law to comply.*"

Urgency thrummed through Blue as she verified the growing distance between their Rhino and Bronze Raven One's crash site. She muted their comms.

"We could get them. We could get them right fucking now. We've got the extra jump seats, and there's room in the gunner compartment for the Crows."

"And what about their legionnaires?" Twister snapped in frustration. "How are you going to fit 5th *and* 4th Squad on our Rhino? Are you going to strap some of those boys to the wings? Maybe hang a couple off the guns? And what about the Survey team?"

Blue's jaw tightened. "They *need* us—"

"*Bronze Raven Four, acknowledge orders.*"

Blue snarled soundlessly. *Fucking Grimes.*

Twister's face contorted in something like agony but she shook her head.

"Even if we could stack them like cordwood in the back, our weight and balance would be shot, and that's with healthy engines." Twister stabbed a finger out the cockpit. "Do those sound like healthy engines?"

Blue flinched at the scorn radiating off the older pilot. Helpless rage lit Twister's eyes, but she didn't think it was directed at her so much as the situation.

"We're already closer to 4th Squad than the crash site. If we turn back..." Twister's hands curled into fists, as if she were fighting to keep them off the flight controls. "We might not make it out of the ash cloud. You heard the comm transmission. They lost their engines, and it doesn't sound like we're all that far from losing ours."

"*Bronze Raven Four, acknowledge—*"

With a snarl, Twister unmuted comms. "Bronze Raven Four, wilco."

Blue let out a harsh breath but she held the Rhino's course steady—and then Medusa's voice crackled over the comms.

"*Four, One. If you haven't made it out of the ash cloud yet, recommend you hurry. Crashing is less than fun.*"

Shuddering breaths sounded in the background, and poorly smothered hiccupping sobs competed with distant groans of pain.

"*Breathe, Ruby, just breathe. You're okay, you're okay.*"

So much relief flashed over Twister's face it was painful to witness. She let out a shuddering breath of her own and keyed up the comm.

"One, Four, good to hear your voice. What's your status?"

Medusa didn't respond. Not right away.

"*Four, One, do you copy?*" A slight pause, and then Medusa switched channels. "Perseverance, *Bronze Raven One.*"

The comms officer immediately responded. "*Bronze Raven One,* Perseverance, *go.*"

Again, Medusa didn't respond right away. There was a longer pause before she transmitted again. This time, the stress and pain beneath her voice came through clearer.

"Perseverance, *Bronze Raven One is down with multiple injured personnel on board. Request immediate evac. Acknowledge transmission.*"

The comms officer responded, but Medusa actually stepped on his transmission, requesting an acknowledgment of her first message.

"I don't think they can hear us," Blue whispered, her hands locked around the flight controls so tightly her knuckles ached with it. A sharp gust of wind buffeted their Rhino, and they slung sideways before she recovered.

"I don't think they can either," Twister growled, more of that helpless rage breaking through her iron control.

"Medusa..." Ruby's tear-soaked voice trembled over the comm. "*I think... I think we're transmit-only right now.*"

Medusa snarled a steady stream of choice swear words that would do any legionnaire proud before her voice faltered. She let out a slow, heavy breath.

"That's fine, everything is fine." A slight pause and then her voice rang out strong. "*This is Bronze Raven One, transmitting in the blind on all flight channels. If anyone is listening, our Rhino is down and hard-*

broke. Multiple injuries on board. Requesting immediate evac. Trekking back to the outpost overland is an option—"

"Overland evac is not *an option*," Ruby broke in, an uncharacteristically harsh edge to her young voice. "*We are not capable of leaving the Rhino at this time.*"

"*Overland travel is an option for* some. *Several legionnaires are too injured to make the hike, and my gunners are in bad shape. I'm not going anywhere, either.*" Medusa barked a pain-soaked laugh. "*My leg is very much broken and very much trapped beneath what used to be our console. Our location is marked by our emergency beacon. That at least appears to be working correctly. Does anybody copy?*"

"I copy. Do you hear me, you stubborn bitch? I *copy*," Twister snarled over the comm. Medusa sighed.

"*I'm going to assume Bronze Raven Four at least heard us through this shit. It might be the ash screwing with long-range comms as much as our poor, fucked-up Rhino. Twister, if you can hear me, get your boys and get out of this mess. We'll be* fine *until the ash cloud thins.*"

"*Some of us will be more fine than others—*" Ruby's fierce voice broke into a startled gasp. "*What was that?*"

"*Relax, it's just one of your adorable murder lizard puppies running from the volcano and bumping into us.*" A metallic groan filtered over the comms, and Medusa cursed with more than a little pain in her voice. "*If they could bump into us less hard, that would be great. To anyone listening, we'll work on our comms and continue to monitor for any incoming transmissions. Bronze Raven One, out.*"

"Hang in there. We'll get to you as soon as we can," Twister replied, even though it was obvious by now that they couldn't hear anyone. Her jaw flexed when only silence answered, and she stared straight out of the cockpit. "Fly faster, Blue."

"Copy faster, ma'am," she said quietly.

"*4th Squad, this is the* Perseverance," the call came in shortly after. It was clearer than before, which made Tavi a little uneasy. With all the ash and electromagnetic interference in the sky, there should have been some sort of interference, however minute. Their comms were good, but not *that* good. "*Be advised tsunami is inbound, ETA roughly thirty minutes.*"

"Copy that, *Perseverance*," Ordo replied, the frustration easily discernible in his tone. "That gives us a five-minute window. Haul ass, people."

Tavi picked up the pace, as did the rest of Team Two. The legionnaires could make it, no problem. He glanced at Mitzi, whose face was uncharacteristically pale. She knew as well as he did that their chances of survival dramatically decreased if they slowed for the civilians.

Shockingly, Doctor Schmoyer didn't just keep the pace, he encouraged his fellow scientists to keep up as well. Their speed increased, the civilians struggled to keep up with the armored legionnaires. They could move quicker, true, but the members of the Survey Corps were clearly used to marking their own paths and not relying on a visually enhanced legionnaire to lead them. This unfamiliarity in team movements hampered them, and Tavi found himself grabbing Mitzi's arm more often than he felt comfortable with to ensure she didn't take a wrong turn in the winding, twisting jungle path.

Ten minutes later, Tavi could hear a faint rumbling somewhere to the northwest. It was an ominous sound. Mitzi heard it, too, and ran faster. They had already started to leave the slower civilians behind a little, catching up quickly with Fire Team One. Specialist Franklin "Stickboy" Simms was in the rear of that group.

"Slow down!" Stickboy yelled at them.

"Tell her that!" Tavi countered as he struggled to keep up with Mitzi.

Stickboy shook his head and chased after her. Risking a quick look over his shoulder, Tavi was shocked to see just how far the rest of Team Two had fallen behind. The worst was Jabber, who was struggling to haul Dr. Xi-Smith through the undergrowth. It looked as though every single branch or vine in the jungle was trying to trip her or cause her harm. Her arms and face were covered in multiple cuts and scratches.

"Ordo, Claw. We've reached the rockpile. Roughly fifty feet high and over one hundred feet around at the top. It's a plateau-like thing. We should be able to get everyone up."

"Copy. Get up and prep the middle of the peak for the civilians," Ordo told them. "Team Two, move your fucking asses!"

Tavi reached the rockpile at the same time as Stickboy did, well ahead of the rest of Team Two. He quickly tried to help Mitzi climb the rocks, but the young scientist easily scampered up past him, faster than anyone else, and only allowed minor assistance when she neared the flattened top of the pile. Upon closer inspection, Tavi realized the "rock pile" was more of a singular piece of stone than anything else. He checked his internal clock and saw they barely had two minutes to spare until the satellite said the tsunami would reach their location.

We're cutting it way too close, Tavi thought.

"Oh!" Mitzi exclaimed as she finally reached the top. She knelt down and began touching the rock with her fingertips, the urgency she'd shown racing through the jungle seemingly wiped away. "How interesting! It's an igneous rock, like a butte. Look, see how the columnar jointings are almost fused together as one? Look at the erosion patterns! This entire area was probably a giant caldera once upon a time, probably millions of years ago! Huyan is going to love this!"

"You are a very strange woman," Tavi observed as he turned to help Doctor Schmoyer up the rock as he and his escort Pigeon arrived next. The older man was in reasonably good shape, all things considered.

"She is very strange," Schmoyer agreed, gasping as one hand clutched at his ribs. "Brilliant, but strange."

"I know I am," Mitzi confirmed, taking some of the bite out of the doctor's statement. She looked up and smiled at Tavi. "Child prodigy, remember?"

"They shouldn't have given you your doctorates at such a young age," Schmoyer snarled as he moved to the center of the small butte. He sat down hard on the rock's flat surface. "Fifteen was too young. No eighteen-year-old girl should be an evaluator in the Survey Corps. You need seasoning!"

"You're only eighteen?" Tavi asked, shocked.

"Yeah, why?"

"I just thought..." Tavi's voice trailed off. "I thought you were older."

"What? How?"

"We can discuss the age differences later," Ordo cut them off as the two meteorologists arrived with Krawdaddy and Vixen. Team One was also on the large rock already. "Figure out a way to anchor into the rocks. Doctor Wingo! I recall you had some pitons and rope in that wonderful bag of yours."

"Oh, yes. I didn't know if we would get any rock climbing in while on planet, but I brought it along just in case. I'm an avid climber..." Mitzi's voice trailed off as she began searching through her bag.

"Hammer those fuckers into the rock and create a safety line for everyone, ma'am," Ordo told her as she pulled out a small hammer, some metal spikes, and cord.

"Jabber, where you at?" Vixen called as he helped his wheezing, gasping Survey Corps scientist to the top of the rock formation.

Tavi turned and scanned the forest. An instant later Jabber appeared on his HUD. They were still fifty yards from the rockpile and were not moving.

"Jabber? That wave is inbound *now!* Move it!" Ordo roared. "Thirty seconds!"

"I'm trying, *bossjna*! But the little *pojata* is stuck!"

"Tavi! Get down there and get that civvie up on this rock!"

"Yes, Sergeant!" Tavi barked and leapt from the rock pile without hesitation.

For a terrifying second he was over twenty feet off the ground and wondering if the suit was as good as he thought it was before he landed. The suit absorbed almost all of the impact and saved his legs and knees from being broken. Using his momentum to carry him into a forward shoulder roll, he was able to bleed off the rest of the landing's energy. On his feet, he began sprinting to where Jabber and Doctor Xi-Smith were stuck.

The path was narrow and winding, different from the one he'd brought Mitzi through. There were far more exposed tree roots here, and between the ash cloud overhead obscuring the light and the thick canopy blocking out the rest, it was easy to trip or become stuck. As he approached where Jabber and the geologist appeared on his HUD, he began having issues with the roots and vines himself. It took him almost half the allotted time he had to finally reach them.

"Help, *tasawa*!" Jabber called out the moment Tavi was near. The doctor had somehow managed to get her boot tangled up in a vine root near one of the many trees and Jabber was unsuccessfully trying to pry her free.

Tavi immediately began pulling at the root with his gloved hands, silently thanking HeyHey while he worked. The root had tiny, razor-sharp barbs on it which were almost invisible in the darkness. Even in daylight he doubted anyone would have spotted them. It took some twisting, but within moments he was able to pry her foot free.

"We're not going to make it," Jabber said with a heavy sigh as the doctor stumbled a few feet and fell a second time. She began to sob.

"Yes we can. Now *move!*" Tavi yelled as he pulled Doctor Xi-Smith to her feet. He gave her a shove in the right direction. She stumbled forward and began to jog. "We need to run! Follow me along the path straight ahead!"

Tavi sprinted off, trusting the doctor and Jabber to stay on his tail as he moved. The rumbling, faint before, was now a cascading roar as the wave drew nearer. He had no idea how big it was, only that it sounded as though a million Rhino engines were flying close by. The uncertainty propelled him, and he suddenly burst through a clump of trees to see the rock formation directly ahead.

Doctor Xi-Smith cried out in relief as she ran past him toward the rocks. Jabber, stumbling a bit right behind her, managed to keep his balance and sped after her. Tavi paused at the base of the rockpile and looked back to see if the wave was visible.

This was a mistake.

There were no trees, only a wall of water roughly fifteen feet high and barreling down on him at an impossible speed. Instinct threw him into a leap as the water slammed into the front of the rockpile, fallen and broken trees smashing into the rocks in a cacophony of destruction. Grabbing a small outcrop in the stone, he managed to get just enough of a grip to avoid being ripped away by the initial tide. Pulling himself up, he snagged a toehold on another chunk of rock as something large and heavy slammed into his left shoulder.

Grunting in pain, he refused to let go of the rock, even though the water was pulling at him with more force than anything he'd ever felt before. A branch smashed into his dangling leg, another struck his shoulder. Grimacing, all he could do was hold on. A strong pair of hands grabbed him, and then he was being hauled up and out of the water.

Looking up, he saw Jabber's eyes narrow as he continued to pull him up. Though tall and lanky, the Passovan was stronger than Tavi would have believed. Somebody else landed next to Jabber and helped pull, and suddenly Tavi was on the smoother surface of the rockpile and away from the torrent below, his knees aching, his HUD showing multiple yellow spots on his suit where he'd been struck. He remained on his knees for a moment, gasping in pain, before he remembered the civilian.

"Doctor Xi-Smith!" Tavi shouted, turning, scrambling to his feet. Sure enough, the evaluator was behind him, hanging on for dear life. Her eyes were wide with fear and Tavi could see her grip on the rock was slipping. "Hold on!"

"I'm trying!" she screamed. Tavi jumped over a small gap in the rocks and reached down to grab her. Seeing him coming to help, she tried shifting her feet to push up and toward him. It was a desperation move, one born of terror and fear.

Her footing slipped.

"No!" Tavi shouted as another wave slammed into her. He dove on the rocks and stretched out as far as he could. His fingertips just brushed her sleeve and, for the barest of moments, he had her.

It wasn't enough.

Tavi simply did not have a good enough grip to reel her in—but Jabber did. The Passovan managed to snag her other hand and together they hauled her up out of the water and to safety. Below, the waters continued to rage, and would do so for a long while yet.

Gritting her teeth, Blue pushed the throttles to the max, but almost immediately pulled them back slightly. The engines had *not* liked that. The off-key note was back and no matter how she adjusted the throttles or the power distribution, it wouldn't go away. The left engine shuddered, and an alert shrieked as the output dropped below acceptable levels.

"Shit, shit, shit... *Twister*."

"I'm working on it," she said tightly. Her fingers flew over the console. A second later, she had the power output stabilized, and the alert fell silent. "That's a good girl."

Blue blew out a shaky breath and exchanged a relieved smile with Twister. And then the left engine stuttered once, twice... and failed.

The strident alarm blared throughout the cockpit as the left wing abruptly dipped toward the ground. Blue fought to level them out, but the trees leaped closer as they lost altitude.

"Restart," Twister muttered as she rapidly ran the checklist. "Come on, you bitch, restart." She slammed one fist on the console, as if that would help. "You are *not* a good girl!"

The left engine didn't seem impressed at the name calling. A harried glance out the cockpit showed the turbines were still lazily spinning. It hadn't seized. Thank all the stars, it hadn't seized.

"Rerouting power from the right engine," Twister snapped when the third restart attempt failed.

Tension knotted Blue's shoulders as she fought to keep the unbalanced Rhino in the air while Twister worked. If they were flying anything but a low level, it wouldn't be as difficult, but they were barely fifty meters above the thick coastal jungle now, swerving and jerking like a drunken legionnaire after shore leave at Yortugan Bay. No matter what she did, she couldn't regain their lost altitude. Worse, the right engine had developed an alarming whine that set her teeth on edge, and she couldn't pull back the throttles any more than she already had—or they'd be getting a much better look at those trees flashing by beneath their wings.

As she wrestled with the Rhino, lightning struck barely thirty meters off their right wing, setting a tree on fire and searing her retinas. She hissed out a pained gasp. With the HUD set to a multi-spectrum blend, it hadn't dimmed down in time. She could still see the afterimage, no matter how many times she blinked watering eyes clear. Rain splattered across the windscreen, gray and choked with ash, leaving streaks behind that didn't help her vision issues in the least.

"Almost there..." Twister huffed out an unamused breath. "That's what she said. And done!"

The right turbine slowed slightly, but the left turbine spun up again, though only at half speed.

"Thank fuck," Blue breathed out as she adjusted the throttles. Their flight smoothed out again, but they were slower now. So much slower, and the high-pitched whine in the right engine actually grew worse.

"*Perseverance*, be aware Bronze Raven Four is single-engine ops," Twister reported grimly.

"Perseverance *copies single-engine ops. Say intentions.*"

"Stand by, *Perseverance*."

"Perseverance *standing by.*"

"Stand by?" Blue darted a sharp glance at Twister. "What the hell do you mean '*stand by*'? Our intentions haven't changed. We're going to pick up our boys and get back to the outpost. Right?"

Twister hesitated.

"Right?"

"Maybe." Twister ran a quick diagnostic on the right engine and pushed the results up to a secondary viewscreen. Blue couldn't take her focus off flying in the harrowing conditions long enough to read the data scrolling down the side of the screen, but the yellow and orange colors marking the various engine parts when it should all be green was not a great sign. "I'm not sure we can make it that far."

"We're less than ten mikes out from their position." Blue peeled one hand off the flight controls long enough to stab a finger at the updated sat image on the main viewscreen. 4th Squad's icon hadn't moved since that initial relocation, and they were closing in. Maybe not as fast as before, but steadily. "We can make it. You know we can make it!"

"This isn't like the thunderstorm on Sagetnam, or even that damn hurricane to the south. Ashfall is deadly and we've been flying in it this whole time." Slowly, Twister's expression hardened. "The Rhino can't handle this."

Blue's heart pounded in her chest and her breath turned choppy. All she could see was Tavi's young face, so like her brother's that her heart ached. Other legionnaires flashed in her mind's eye, all of them familiar after a year supporting them on missions. Jabber with his Passovan accent. Vixen with his colorful sport bitching, always entertaining even—or maybe especially—when his squadmates wanted to murder him. Sergeant Ord, gruff and experienced, Carvalho's brother-in-arms and fellow gossipmonger. Krawdaddy, Pigeon, Claw...everyone in 4th Squad.

She knew them all.

"We can make it." Blue bumped the throttles up, pushing the Rhino harder, but their speed barely increased...and a red warning flashed on the right engine diagnostic.

Twister gripped her shoulder. "Either we get clear and come back for them later, or we crash like Bronze Raven One."

Blue swallowed hard as that high-pitched whine in the right engine climbed higher, but she didn't immediately deviate from their course.

Twister's grip tightened. "Lieutenant Eliassen!"

"Why not the outpost?" she demanded with desperation she couldn't hide.

"Because the only way we're getting these engines repaired is up on the *Perseverance*." Twister rested her hands on her flight controls and looked at her with cold, clear eyes. "Now are you flying, or am I?"

Blue closed her eyes. Breathed out slowly.

"I am," she said grimly, snapping her eyes open again.

With only one operational atmospheric engine, they wouldn't have the necessary thrust to make orbit. They'd have to switch to void thrusters well below the recommended altitude and hope there was enough oxidizer to get the job done. With no time to run the numbers, she pushed the throttles up as much as she dared and pointed the Rhino's nose skyward to climb out of the ash cloud, out of Aurora's atmosphere. Out of reach of their boys. She tracked their altitude, delaying until the last moment to make the switch to maximize their chances of being able to reach the *Perseverance* without having to call for a pickup.

"Initiating emergency void engine burn." Blue's hands darted over the console. "Comm Sergeant Ord and break the news that we're abandoning them."

Rather than the anger or reprimand she expected, Twister regarded her with compassion and understanding, though her jaw was still tight. It helped that she didn't like what they were doing any more than Blue did.

"We're not abandoning them. We're making sure we don't add to the problems. Another downed Rhino isn't going to help anyone." She got on the comms. "*Perseverance*, Bronze Raven Four is RTB. Request maintenance team on standby for our arrival."

"*Perseverance copies all, maintainters will be on standby.*"

Twister closed her eyes briefly. "4th Squad, Bronze Raven Four."

"*Bronze Raven Four, Ordo, go.*"

Blue listened to Twister explain the situation as they climbed up through the turbulent atmosphere, their fuel levels dropping the whole way. Her gut churned and twisted with guilt.

She'd been wrong before. So very wrong. Leaving Bronze Raven One to their fate had been hard.

Leaving 4th Squad behind was so much harder.

CHAPTER FIFTEEN
To Tread Dark Waters Midst Turmoil and Tribulations

PNV PERSEVERANCE, *AURORA SYSTEM*

The flight up into orbit was the longest flight of Blue's life. Not only did they have to baby the damaged Rhino every step of the way to escape the grip of Aurora's turbulent atmosphere, but every minute put more distance between them and 4th Squad. Worse, they had to listen to Medusa's comm calls, with no way to respond.

"*Bronze Raven One, transmitting in the dark. Heh, literally. Between the storm and the ash, it's limited visibility out there. That tsunami passed through pretty quickly, but it flooded this whole coastal region. We're currently twenty degrees nose low in a newly formed, armadon infested lake.*"

A splash sounded over the comm along with a huffed laugh.

"*Rocks tore open the cockpit when we crashed, just enough for the water to come inside and say hello. Ruby kept complaining about the cold, so I sent her back to the gunners to try to make them comfortable. Pretty sure she's in shock, possibly with cracked or broken ribs. I'm fairly certain she's not the only one going into shock.*" There was a long pause, and then she softly added, "*The water doesn't feel cold to me.*"

Alarm shot through Blue, and she snapped a concerned glance at Twister. The other woman's face spasmed in fear before she locked it down and distracted herself by alternating between cussing the Rhino out and praising her, while Blue devoted every bit of her focus and skill to getting them clear.

Finally, the last wisps of Aurora's atmosphere fell away, and they broke free. Relief shot through Blue as the star-speckled black welcomed them home. A glance at their fuel levels proved they had just enough left for a min fuel burn to rejoin with the ship. With shaking hands, she set a course for the *Perseverance* and slumped back in her seat. Just for a moment, that relief was all she could feel. Relief that they'd made it out. Relief that she hadn't let down her aircrew, that her skill had been enough, and that Twister had been smart enough, *brave* enough, to make the call she couldn't.

Guilt swiftly followed on its heels, an anchor to the weightlessness. She should've been the one to make that call. But she'd let emotion get in the way, and a command pilot *could not* allow that to happen. A command pilot had to know how far past the operational limits they could safely—or not so safely—push their ship. Blue had ignored the signs. If she'd been in command, she would've made the wrong call and possibly gotten them all killed.

"I'm not ready to be in the left seat," Blue said quietly as they coasted through the void. "Am I?"

Twister regarded her silently for a long moment. "You fucked up, Eliassen. Learn from it."

Blue nodded tightly and returned her attention to the flight controls. The *Perseverance* was coming up quickly, a familiar gray behemoth nearly as old and battered as their dropships.

Home.

Habit took over, shoved back the guilt and the doubts. Comm calls and rejoining and docking procedures, along with the normal back and forth between command pilot and copilot, filled the next few minutes, leaving no room for anything else. Soon enough, they were back in the repressurized dropship bay, running the shutdown procedures and postflight checklists while a maintenance team waited impatiently for them to finish. Before they shut down, another transmission from Medusa came in.

"*Bronze Raven One, transmitting in the dark. Water's still rising, about knee height in the cockpit, and I'm still very much trapped.*" Pain and exhaustion threaded through Medusa's voice, though her words were still clear. "*There's more armadons out there than before. Gotta admit all those eyes in the dark are creepy as hell. I know they're not really staring at us, but it feels like they are every time lightning strikes. Green reflective eyes everywhere.*"

Medusa let out a shuddering breath that sounded of equal parts disquiet and exasperation before she continued.

"*Sergeant Cox sent some armed legionnaires outside with the murder lizard puppies to see if they can either patch the hole or do something to get the nose up. I wish them the best of luck. Even smashed, my Rhino's a big girl. Be nice not to drown though.*"

Another voice spoke up in the background. Judging by the deep baritone, it could only be Sergeant Morrison, Bronze Raven One's loadmaster.

"*You're not going to drown on my watch. Now hold still so Private Streicher and I can work on freeing you from this damned flight console.*"

Metal squealed, and Medusa *screamed*.

Instantly, the squealing metal sound cut off, but it took long seconds for her screams to die. Quiet panting breaths filled the comm, full of barely suppressed agony.

"*Sorry, sorry!*" a young male cried out, voice thick with panic. He blew out a sharp breath. "*We'll try something else.*"

"*That ... would be ... good,*" Medusa croaked. "*This wouldn't be an issue if we'd been in armor.*"

"*Maybe, maybe not,*" Morrison said after a heavy pause. "*Your leg's jammed in there pretty good. Don't worry. Like Streicher said, we'll try something else.*"

"*Maybe you should just cut the damn thing off,*" she said with a weak laugh. "*Then we wouldn't be stuck in a drowning ship.*"

Blue's breath caught, and Twister tightened one hand into a fist.

"*Now isn't the time for dark humor, ma'am,*" Morrison said in heavy disapproval.

"*If not now, then when?*" she shot back facetiously. "*Oh, oops. Was transmitting on our primary channel this whole time. Screw it, I'll leave this one open. If we ever manage to fix our comms, we'll hear them on the secondary channel. Transferring primary to the flight console so they can hear all of us.*"

A beat of silence and then the sound quality changed as Medusa switched the broadcast from her helmet's built in comms to the Rhino itself.

"*This is Bronze Raven One to anyone listening, we'll keep sending updates.*" In a bare whisper Blue didn't think they were meant to hear, Medusa added, "*That way they know we're still alive.*"

With a harsh breath, Blue completed her portion of the shutdown procedures and postflight checks as quickly as possible. The sooner the maintainers could work on their engines, the sooner they could get back down to Aurora. Back to 4th Squad, back to Bronze Raven One.

"Go coordinate with the maintainers," Twister said with controlled calm. "I'll finish up in here."

Misery twisted through Blue's guts at the cool look in her command pilot's eyes, but she drew in a deep breath and nodded.

"And Eliassen?" Twister waited until Blue met her gaze. "You *are* ready to be in the left seat, but you can't let emotion get in the way of making the right calls. You're also going to fuck up again. Just make sure you learn from the mistakes so you don't repeat them. You copy?"

Blue lifted her chin. "I copy."

"Good." Twister tossed her a quick smile. "Move your ass, Blue."

"Yes, ma'am!" Impatience thrummed through her soul as she threw off her straps and ducked back into the gunner compartment. Carvalho had already dismissed Hekekia and Hayashi, but the loadmaster waited in the cargo compartment for his Ravens.

"Go get cleaned up, rest, eat. Whatever you need to do to be ready to fly again," Blue said hurriedly as she strode toward the open ramp. "I'll update you the second our engines are repaired."

"What the hell did you do to my engines?" an incredibly irritated maintainer bellowed from outside the Rhino. Blue hesitated mid-stride and winced.

"Or, you know, replaced." Wearily, she scrubbed her face and forced a smile for her loadmaster. "I do not have enough caffeine in my system for today."

"Your Crows will be ready to fly," Carvalho replied solemnly. His eyes were grim, without a hint of his typical cheerfulness. They'd left two of his closest friends down on Aurora—Sergeant Morrison on Bronze Raven One, and Sergeant Ord with 4th Squad. His fist banged lightly against his prosthetic leg, and a muscle in his jaw spasmed before he nodded sharply. "We'll be ready."

He spun on his heel but paused and glanced back in sharp appraisal.

"Make sure you at least get something to eat to go with that extra caffeine, LT. You look like hammered shit."

"Gee, thanks." Blue flexed her shoulders in a futile attempt to shed the tension from ... *everything*, and followed Sergeant Carvalho down the ramp—where she was immediately intercepted by Master Sergeant Carlos Rodriguez. After the initial assessment of Killi's very broken Rhino, the chief maintainer had left a team down on Aurora to work the issue and returned to the *Perseverance*. Blue met the maintainer's gaze and winced again. If the man scowled any harder, he'd have permanent wrinkles, and his dark eyes were both exasperated and enraged.

Rodriguez already had a team pulling apart the Rhino's left engine, with a second team examining the right. Judging by the creative and constant cussing from both teams—some of which were new words that Blue added to her growing vocabulary specifically because her mother would hate them—they were in worse shape than even Twister had thought.

"I repeat, LT—and with all due respect—what the hell did you do to my engines?" he growled.

"Sorry, Master Sergeant. We were in the ash cloud too long, but we ..." Blue exhaled slowly as that tension traveled from her shoulders and wrapped around her spine. "We were trying to get 4th Squad out."

"Commendable, LT, but stupid." Rodriguez's gaze darted to Bronze Raven One's empty spot in the bay, and his jaw tightened. "Lot of that going around today."

"How soon until you can get us back in the air?" she asked. She refused to consider that he might not be able to do it at all.

Blue held her breath as Rodriguez pulled out his slate and tapped the screen in thought. She glanced around the half-empty bay. They'd arrived in Aurora with only seven Rhinos functional after the Sagetnam exercise. Bronze Raven One was down, Five was inoperative and still at the outpost, and thanks to Blue hesitating so long down in the ash cloud, Four was in bad shape. They were down to just four operable Rhinos for the outpost evacuation, and they'd only be able to carry twenty-five civilians each per trip.

"I know we're down to less than half strength right now, but if you can get our Rhino back in the fight, we can help with the civilian evacuation. The sooner we complete the evacuation, the sooner *somebody* can try to get Medusa, Ruby, and everyone else on Bronze Raven One." Blue let out a slow breath, trying and mostly failing to keep her voice level. "Not to mention 4th Squad and the Survey team."

Rodriguez scowled harder. "You'd have me repair her only to send her back into the shit that broke her in the first place."

"*Yes.*" Blue held his gaze. "Our only other option is to leave them until the ash cloud clears, and that could take days. We have injured down there. We have to try."

"Lieutenant, you think I don't know that?"

Blue winced at the senior NCO's use of her full rank, and forced herself to wait as patiently as she was capable of in that moment. Rodriguez's fingers tapped the edge of his slate faster, eyes unfocused.

Finally, he sighed and turned to the team working the left engine. "Walker, status report!"

A sharp-looking corporal who couldn't be much older than Blue broke away from his team and trotted over. His expression wasn't encouraging.

"Internal systems need to be cleaned out and both engines need to be replaced," he said without preamble, his Passovan accent thick with stress. "It's a miracle you made it back up here with her engines that badly fragged."

"*Replaced?*" Blue choked out. Her heart hit her toes. "How long will that take?"

"It's not the time that's the issue, *keiche*?" Walker grimaced and turned his slate so they could see the inventory he'd pulled up. "We've only got one replacement in the parts depot. The other three we're supposed to have by the regs have been on backorder for months. And if you haven't heard yet, two of the *tollejo* Rhinos coming up from the outpost are also reporting engine issues."

Blue's eyes widened. The hurricane must have really messed with the weather patterns if the ash cloud had reached the outpost that quickly. Corporal Walker raised his brows and looked to his chief maintainer.

"What do you want us to do?"

Fix my damn Rhino, that's what you need to do!

Desperation had Blue digging her nails into her palms, but she bit back the orders she had no right to give. The maintainers were outside her chain of command. If Rodriguez decided to save the engine for a less damaged Rhino, then short of going up the chain through Voodoo and over to the Maintenance CO, there was little she could do.

Rodriguez buried his nose in his slate for a handful of heartbeats that pushed Blue to the edge of her control. Then he nodded sharply.

"Get Gibson and his team in here. We'll scavenge one of the engines from Seven. Swapping out the engines on Four will take less time than trying to fix any of the other Rhinos, and if we can get one more back in the air, that'll be worth the effort."

"You got it, *bossjna*."

As the corporal strode back to his team, comm already raised and his accent thicker than ever, Rodriguez's gaze drifted back to where Bronze Raven One should be. His hands tightened on his slate until the case creaked in protest. The chief maintainer was just as worried about their downed aircrew as she was. When he looked back at her, his eyes burned with determination.

"We'll have her ready to fly within the hour."

Blue stared. "Seriously?"

"Seriously." Rodriguez clapped her on the shoulder. "The engines are designed to be an easy swap when you're replacing the entire unit."

"Thank you," she breathed fervently.

Rodriguez arched a brow. "Just do me a favor and try to keep the new ones from fragging out."

"We'll do our best," Blue said, but she made no promises. She couldn't, not with the volcano still spewing metric tons of ash into the atmosphere, not with the ash cloud already affecting the airspace around the outpost.

As the chief maintainer hustled off to help, Blue heaved a sigh of relief and sent her Crows a quick update. She spun around at the rapid thunder of boots on the ramp, intending to ask how Twister still had so much energy—and if she had a secret stash of caffeine in the cockpit—but her smile died at the fear on Twister's face.

"What is it?"

"Bronze Raven One is under attack."

Blue stared blankly. "Under attack? By *who*?"

"Armadons," Twister shouted over her shoulder, not slowing her pace in the slightest. "I've got to go report in to CIC."

"*What?*" Blue's exhaustion fell away in a heartbeat, and she dashed after her command pilot. "Armadons? Seriously? So much for Schmoyer's theory about the aggressive behavior being nothing more than a publicity stunt or a hoax."

Twister just shook her head tightly, her face bone white under the harsh lights as they sprinted past the maintainer team already removing Bronze Raven Seven's left engine. Blue followed the other woman out of the bay and down the corridor, barely dodging around another maintainer team running in the opposite direction. Even though Twister was older, her legs were longer, and she outpaced Blue to the lift.

Panic and alarm twisted through Blue's belly. Twister had said *she* was ordered to report, not *they*.

"Wait! Take me with you! I want—I *need* to know what's happening."

Twister met her gaze, eyes hard. The lift door started to slide closed.

"*Please*, I left them—"

Twister's hand snapped out, and she held the door open, impatience in every line of her body. Panting for breath, Blue gracelessly skidded onto the lift as the door shut on her heels.

"*We* left them." Twister's hard gaze pinned her in place. "We'll find out what's happening together, but you will keep your mouth shut in this meeting unless directly called upon. Do you get me, Eliassen?"

"Copy silent, ma'am."

As the lift smoothly rose through the decks, Blue practically vibrated with the need for more information, but Twister didn't seem eager to volunteer anything else. A single glance at her command pilot's face was enough to convince her to keep her mouth shut. Twister tapped her fingers against her leg in a ceaseless rhythm, jaw tense and eyes tight. She was afraid, and an answering fear spiraled up within Blue.

What the hell did you hear over the comms?

As soon as the lift opened, both women sprinted down the corridor to the command deck.

Even before the door opened, they could hear the fierce debate raging within. They exchanged a quick glance and ducked inside. A number of Navy and Legion officers, including Voodoo, were huddled around the central console. A 3D sat image, as close to real-time as possible, was projected above the console. Shock rippled through Blue when she realized it was an updated and expanded version of the sat image and weather overlay she'd cobbled together on the beach, complete with location markers for Bronze Raven One, 4th Squad, and even the outpost. The erupting volcano dominated the far west, a red-and-black open wound in the planet bleeding magma and spewing ash. A secondary screen on the console itself listed biometric data, though it was only for the legionnaires in 4th and 5th Squad. Bronze Raven One's aircrew hadn't been in armor.

Twister didn't hesitate to take the DO's typical position at Voodoo's shoulder, leaving Blue standing adrift in the small, crowded room. She shifted her weight, uncertain where to even stand, when a familiar voice quietly called her name. She glanced left and locked eyes with Campbell. He tilted his head to the open space next to him at the far side of the table, and she gratefully squeezed her way in next to him before she took a look at the rest of the room's occupants.

Lieutenant Stahl, the senior Ops officer, stood on Campbell's other side. The junior Comm officer, Ensign Grimes—who had hit on just about every Raven in the squadron—was across the table. Next to him was Voodoo, Twister, then Tripwire. Their new Intel officer was present at the head of the table, but neither the *Perseverance*'s captain or XO were in the room. If Blue remembered the schedule correctly, the XO was on shift on the bridge.

"Where's Captain Esper?" she whispered to Campbell without taking her eyes off Bronze Raven One's icon on the sat image.

"Tied up with Norwood and the outpost evacuation," he whispered back, subtly pointing to a secondary screen focused on the outpost. "Along with the rest of the operational Rhinos. Voodoo tasked your DO to handle the evac the second Bronze Raven One went down."

Blue's gut tightened as she scanned the sat image data. The ash cloud was so thick over the coast now that the downed Rhino was relaying both comms and the legionnaires' biometric data through the outpost's comm station, where the ash was still relatively light. 4th Squad's biometrics and comms were also being relayed through the outpost and up to the *Perseverance*. That comm relay was the only reason they hadn't lost contact with everyone down there.

"Ditch can definitely handle a simple evac," Blue mumbled, but at a quelling look from Stahl, both junior officers fell silent. The senior officers had resumed their debate, and she listened intently.

"What about utilizing one of *Perseverance*'s shuttles?" Voodoo asked, her Passovan accent so tightly controlled it was barely noticeable.

Stahl stared at her. "Are you kidding? They're nowhere near as robust as the Rhinos. We can't even use them to evac the outpost."

"Then what about a HALO drop?" Twister asked with quiet desperation. "We've got most of Bravo Company twiddling their thumbs up here."

Tripwire immediately shook his head.

"HALO drop from where? Orbit? That ash cloud is up to the stratosphere, that's sixty-five thousand feet AGL in that region. We don't have the gear to drop from higher, and the shuttle can't fly lower." Tripwire ran a hand over his short hair, frustration evident in the sharp, almost violent motion. "The closest we can drop anyone is no closer overland than the outpost itself, and there's no point dropping when they could just ride down in a Rhino. But even if they commandeer the outpost's ground vehicles, there's no direct roads to that area of the coast. At best estimate, it would take two days for my men to get there."

"Then load your men up on the Rhinos on their next trip down to the outpost so they can get started!" Twister leaned forward, barely restrained by Voodoo's hand on her shoulder, eyes more than a little wild. Again, Blue wondered what the hell Twister had heard over the comms.

"That won't work."

"Why the hell not?" Twister snarled.

Tripwire clenched his jaw, his eyes staring into the middle distance before his gaze snapped to the Comms officer. "Turn the comms back up."

Grimes hesitated for the barest fraction of an instant before he tapped the console. Disciplined gunfire shattered the tense silence, muted somewhat since it was being filtered through the open comm channel in the Rhino's cockpit. It was punctuated by the staccato *brrrt* of the Aries Miniguns, but the rate of fire was erratic. A hoarse scream rose above the noise before it descended into a horrifying gurgle—and one of the legionnaire's biometric data flatlined. Blue pressed a hand over her mouth to stifle her horrified gasp.

"I don't think they have two days," Tripwire said grimly. "Do you?"

Twister looked a breath away from lashing out at the legionnaire with her fist, but finally, she ground out, "No."

For the first time since Blue walked into the room, Lieutenant

Commander Hart spoke up. "The outpost evacuation is going well enough, but we can't spare a Rhino from that effort if we're going to beat the ashfall projections and get everyone out on time. If Bronze Raven Four can be repaired as quickly as maintenance estimates, we might be able to send you down to evac them. *If* it can be done at all."

His thoughtful gaze came to rest squarely on Blue. For a heart-stopping moment, she was certain he was about to kick her out. And then he gave her a little nod.

"Lieutenant Eliassen, you were the one who actually flew through the ash cloud and the storm. What are your thoughts? Can your Rhino get through the ash cloud *and* get back out again?"

Blue opened her mouth to respond in the affirmative—and hesitated. She'd been wrong before. She'd pushed the Rhino past what it could handle because she'd allowed emotion to cloud her judgment. She couldn't let that happen again. Not with the lives of her aircrew hanging in the balance. She felt Twister's gaze on her, desperation and doubt heavy in her eyes, a far cry from her previously cool composure. Understanding slammed into Blue.

Hart didn't trust Twister to make the call.

Another burst of gunfire rattled through the room, this time accompanied by the distant voice of Sergeant Cox bellowing commands, though only one came through clear enough to be understandable.

"*Hold the ramp!*"

More gunfire and what sounded like a grenade rang out, quickly followed by shouting and a heavy metallic groan. Medusa cursed viciously. Blue jerked forward, eyes slightly unfocused and her hands curling into fists.

"*Try not to blow us up along with the murder lizards! Balara legionnaires, isn't my ship already in enough pieces?*" Medusa's voice was hazy with pain, and it quickly dropped into an unintelligible mutter before it abruptly sharpened. "*Status update for our listeners. Good news—the water's about waist high in the cockpit now, but it stopped rising. I'm still trapped, but at least I won't drown. Bad news—everything's gone to hell and we're all going to die. Those damn lizards were one hundred percent staring at us before, and they've decided we're on the menu. So instead of drowning, I'm going to be eaten.*"

"*What did I tell you about dark humor, ma'am?*" Sergeant Morrison muttered in the background, barely audible over the *clang* of metal as he presumably worked on freeing her from the console.

"*That now is the perfect time for it,*" Medusa shot back with a harsh cackle, but it shifted into a pained gasp. "*How's it looking down there, Streicher?*"

A pause. Then Morrison carefully said, "*He's gone, remember? It's just me.*"

"*Right, right,*" she slurred. "*He left to go fight with the others. I forgot.*"

"*Yeah, he's... fighting.*"

Blue glanced at the biometric data on one of the secondary screens. Private Streicher's was red.

"*Now hold still, I'm going to try something else.*"

"*Is it a hacksaw?*" she asked in strained amusement. "*Because it might be time for the hacksaw. Either that, or it's time to leave me and get the hell out of this deathtrap.*"

Another gasp, this one from a painfully young voice. Ruby. "*We are not cutting off your leg or leaving you to die, you crazy bitch.*"

"*You might have to.*"

"*Not happening,*" Morrison said firmly. "*Besides, we're pretty well surrounded. Maybe a few of the legionnaires could break free, but they won't leave their wounded, and neither will we. If this is our time, we'll face it together.*"

"*Damn straight—*" Ruby's fierce declaration was interrupted by a terrifying *hiss*. Blue flinched hard at the younger pilot's hysterical scream. In the next instant, gunfire erupted in the cockpit, and the hissing stopped.

Ruby didn't stop screaming.

"Lieutenant Eliassen?" Lieutenant Commander Hart gently prompted. Then, sharper, "*Eliassen.*"

Her wide eyes snapped to him, and he raised his brows. "Assessment?"

Now she understood why the comms had been muted before. Listening to them fight made it so much harder to keep a clear head. But she wasn't going to do them, or her Crows, any good if she didn't use her head instead of her heart.

Determination burned through her like a wildfire.

"I need the latest data from the aerographer."

Before she'd even finished speaking, Campbell held out his slate, no trace of his typical smirk pulling at his lips or warm amusement dancing in his eyes. This wasn't the Ensign Hotness she was used to. This was the junior Ops officer, and there was nothing but focused professionalism on his face.

Wordlessly, she accepted the slate and swiftly reviewed the atmospheric data. Her gut tightened at the current density of the ash cloud and the volcano's estimated hourly output. To further complicate matters, the volcanic thunderstorm was still raging over the coast, and the southern hurricane was steadily moving north, increasing the winds and turbulence as the two weather systems began to clash.

Over the comms, the erratic bursts of fire from the Aries Miniguns fell silent. No matter how Blue strained her ears, they didn't resume. No more staccato *brrrt*, no more trash-talking from the gunners.

Plenty of shouting legionnaires and hissing armadons though.

No, no, no...

Moving faster, she yanked out her own slate and plotted the flight path that would give them the least amount of time within the ash cloud, along with the power output required from the Rhino to actually make it happen. She held her breath as she brought up Bronze Raven Four's flight data, calculated the time they'd been in the air before they'd developed engine issues, and compared it to the estimated flight time for her plotted flight path. A tremor ran through her at how close it was going to be, but it fell on the right side of feasible. Barely.

She lifted her chin and held Hart's gaze. "Challenging but doable, sir, especially if we egress from the pickup zone to the outpost for evac, rather than trying to burn for orbit."

So long as Bronze Raven Seven's engine doesn't have any underlying issues.

The Intel officer tilted his head toward the other Ravens. "Confirm her data."

Voodoo and Twister hustled around the console before Blue could so much as twitch in their direction. She placed both slates on the edge of the console so they could review the data and sidestepped to give them room. It put her even closer to Campbell's side. Warmth seeped through her flightsuit as he subtly pressed against her in silent support, but she refused to lean on him. She couldn't, not if she was going to keep it together. She flinched at the sound of more gunfire and 5th Squad's desperate shouts, but she just tightened her jaw.

She had to keep it together. For them.

"Confirmed," Voodoo said firmly after an endless minute. She checked her comm and grimaced. "Latest update from Master Sergeant Rodriguez estimates Bronze Raven Four operational in just over an hour. They ran into a snag."

Hart considered the Ravens for a long moment before he nodded.

"Permission for combat evac granted, so long as conditions don't deteriorate further between now and when the Rhino is ready to fly." His gaze flicked between Twister and Blue before settling on Voodoo. "The last question is whether we sub in another aircrew. One who hasn't been through the shit today."

Twister tensed, and Blue jerked forward, barely keeping all the words that wanted to spill out contained. But Voodoo was already shaking her head.

"All due respect sir, but that's exactly why I want these two in the cockpit. They've already flown through the ash, and they know what to expect." She glanced at Blue, her next words leaving no doubt that the squadron commander already knew exactly what had happened down on Aurora. "And how far to push it. I have every confidence in them. They can handle it."

"I'll take your word for it," Hart said gravely. His expression didn't change in the slightest at another burst of gunfire, another flatlined legionnaire. Blue would have thought him completely unaffected if it weren't for the white knuckles around the edges of his slate. "If you'll excuse me, Captain Esper needs to be briefed. I'll leave Bronze Raven One's recovery op in your capable hands. Stahl, with me."

After a quick murmured conversation with Campbell, the senior Ops officer followed the Intel officer out of the room, leaving just the two junior Navy officers, the three Ravens, and Tripwire standing around the console. Listening as 5th Squad fought for their lives... and for their Ravens' lives. Ruby's screams had long since descended into desperate, gasping sobs, but it sounded as if Sergeant Morrison had patched up whatever the armadons had done to her as best he could before going back to trying to free Medusa's leg.

A few minutes later, Sergeant Cox's voice rang out, louder this time, as if he were closer to the cockpit and the open comms.

"*Jordan, Heim, try and get those damn miniguns off the mounts. They're doing fuck all good where they're at, and those poor bastards don't need them anymore.*"

Blue closed her eyes briefly as grief tore through her. She'd desperately hoped the miniguns had fallen silent because they were out of ammo, not because the gunners were dead. She didn't know 5th Squad as well as 4th, but she knew Tyson and Jacobi, had worked and played and sport bitched with them for the past year. They had been good men and solid gunners, and now they were *gone*.

"*Morrison, try to get that hatch operational,*" Cox continued, no room for grief in his hard tone. "*There's so few of us left we can shelter in the cockpit until help comes.*"

"*Working on it, Duck!*" Morrison called back. "*Sorry, Medusa. Sit tight for me, okay?*"

"*Where else would I go?*" she said sarcastically. "*It's fine. The flight console and I are married now, never to be parted.*"

"*Your sense of humor sucks, ma'am.*"

"*That's not the only thing that sucks,*" she shot back with a wild cackle that quickly shifted into a hacking cough riddled with pain.

More gunfire, more hisses and cries from reptilian throats... and one very human shriek of pure agony that seemed to go on and on.

"*Miniguns are fucked, Sarge,*" someone shouted over the death cries of one of their own. "*Feeder belts are jammed.*"

Twister paced around the console, endless circles as her composure cracked around the edges. She kept checking her comm and shooting impatient looks at Voodoo.

"Any update from Rodriguez?" she finally demanded, as if Voodoo wouldn't have kicked them back to the dropship bay the instant it was time to preflight and drop.

Voodoo shook her head. Other than that slight head shake, the older woman stood still as stone, her expression unflinching and impassive, but her eyes terrible. Patience shattering with a nearly audible snap, Blue sent a message to Rodriguez, begging the chief maintainer for a status update. He shot back an irate message that it would go faster if every Raven on the *Perseverance* would stop messaging him and *let him do his job*.

Hissing out a slow breath, she returned her attention to the comm transmission and the legionnaires' biometric data. More than half of 5th Squad had already fallen.

The minutes ticked past, and another legionnaire flatlined. Sampson. Blue knew him as a small guy with a big mouth and a bigger laugh. Her nails dug into the soft skin of her palms as she stared straight ahead, vision unfocused and blurry. She wasn't the only one with tears running down her face.

Our friends are dying and we can't do a damn thing to save them.

And then a new voice rang out over the comms.

"Bronze Raven One, Five is en route," Witch called out with fierce determination. "*I know you can't hear me, but we're coming. Hold on just a little longer!*"

Hope kindled in Blue's soul, and she wiped her eyes clear with a shaking hand as she stared at the updated sat image. A new icon had been added—Bronze Raven Five. The newly repaired Rhino had departed the outpost and was heading straight into the depths of the ash cloud.

Together, the whole room watched in tense silence as it tracked ever closer to the crash site. Blue felt Campbell's gaze on the side of her face an instant before he nudged her side.

"Breathe," he murmured.

Blue snapped a glance up at him, sucking in a sharp breath as she did so. Oxygen flavored with the faint metallic tang of recycled air flooded her lungs. She hadn't realized she'd been holding her breath. He held her gaze for a moment, hope blazing bright in his own eyes, before they both turned back to the projected sat image.

The minutes stretched out, the occasional updates from Witch punctuated by the hissing cries of armadons, the harsh shouts of 5th Squad, and the constant gunfire, though the disciplined rate of fire seemed to have slowed. Silently, Blue urged Witch and Killi on, unconsciously leaning closer to the sat image as they crossed the halfway mark and began their descent. Campbell's hand clamping down on her shoulder was the only reason she didn't fall onto the console when she overbalanced. She shot him a grateful smile, relief burning through the fear and awful anticipation, but his expression froze. She snapped her gaze back to the sat image.

The icon's progress had slowed.

"No," Twister muttered. "Come on, Witch, *come on.*"

But the icon stopped moving. It held its position for an endless moment and a short eternity—and then it abruptly reversed course.

"*Bronze Raven Five . . . RTB to outpost,*" Killi said over the comm in a strangled whisper. "*There's too much ash in the engines. They're already failing. Power output is too low to make it into orbit. The outpost is our only option.*"

In the background, Witch snarled out an endless stream of curses, her voice thick with rage. They hadn't gotten anywhere near the crash site. They hadn't even made it as far as 4th Squad's position.

"Damn it!" Twister slammed one fist on the console in frustration, and Ensign Grimes, who Blue had almost forgotten about, sharply protested the mistreatment of his equipment. Twister glared at him. She didn't say a word, just held his gaze. He looked away first.

"Captain Latham," Tripwire said quietly.

That was all he said, but Twister dialed down the hostility. The larger concussive blast of a grenade transmitted over the comm seconds before another legionnaire's biometrics flashed an alert. Injured but not dead. Not yet. Bravo Company's commander somehow held his motionless position at the foot of the table, his shoulders bunched with tension and pent-up aggression, the need to act, to *do something* for his legionnaires writ large on his weathered face.

Sweat trickled down Blue's spine as she split her focus between listening to the battle and watching Bronze Raven Five's progress back to the outpost. They were only five miles out when the Rhino's telemetry data flashed an alert. Blue tensed, her core tightening with dread as the altitude data abruptly dipped several hundred feet . . . and falling. They were already below eight thousand feet AGL. She grabbed her slate from the console where Voodoo had left it and connected to Bronze Raven Five, her eyes darting back and forth as she scanned the data.

She froze. "Oh *fuck*—"

"*Perseverance, Bronze Raven Five, declaring an emergency,*" Killi said with admirable calm over the alarm blaring through her cockpit. "*Single engine ops, attempting restart.*"

Twister darted over and ripped the slate out of Blue's hands. She rapidly scanned the data and her face paled.

"No, no, no." She jerked her eyes up to the sat image, stark fear stamped onto her features. "I can't lose them both."

"Perseverance, *Five, engine restart failed*," Witch said, taking over the comms again as the icon bobbed like a drunken legionnaire. "*Rerouting power to rebalance, attempting second restart.*"

The alarm didn't stop blaring.

"*Damn it. We've lost both engines. Diving for max speed, attempting full restart.*"

Grimes jerked forward and hunched over the console, fingers darting over the screens as he worked the comms, muttering about relaying through the outpost and enhancing the signal and picking up the internal cockpit speakers. With a triumphant grunt, he lowered the volume on Bronze Raven One's open comm transmission and added Bronze Raven Five as a separate feed. Now they could hear Witch and Killi's back and forth as they fought to keep their Rhino in the air.

"*Come on, you bitch, restart.*" Witch growled low in her throat. "*Killi, keep us pointed at the outpost. Your angle of descent's good, just keep our airspeed up.*"

"*Copy all,*" Killi snapped. "*Holy hell, it's like flying a brick.*"

"*Restart failed. Trying again.*"

"*Come on, baby, you know you want to fly for us,*" Killi crooned.

"*And again. Come on, restart.*" There was a solid *thump* as if Witch had slammed a fist onto the console. "*Fucking whore, restart!*"

Blue now understood *exactly* how Tripwire felt and wished to every god in the Protectorate that she didn't. Because there was nothing they could do to help them. It was down to Killi's skill behind the flight controls and Witch's experience with EPs. She stared unblinking at the telemetry data and calculated their altitude and distance to the outpost.

Close. It was going to be so close.

Witch swore and slammed her fist on the console again before she let out a harsh laugh.

"*Killi, how'd you do on your engine failure landing EP sim?*"

A pause, a harsh breath, and then Blue heard the savage grin in her best friend's voice.

"*Better than you.*"

"That's my girl," Blue murmured as she watched their altitude dip below a thousand feet. "Come on Killi, you've got this."

"*Think we can make the landing pad?*" Killi asked.

"*I think we can make it... no. Shit. We're going to be short. Aim for the flat outside the fence.*"

Blue jerked forward, one hand outstretched toward the sat image as if she could keep them in the air by sheer will alone. Alerts blared over the comm as the Rhino's altitude rapidly dropped toward zero.

"*Flare, flare, flare! Get that nose up!*"

"*I'm trying—*"

Their comms cut out.

Terror spiraled through Blue's soul, and her nails cut into her palms, tiny pinpricks of pain barely anchoring her sanity. Campbell gripped her shoulder again, but all of her focus was devoted to that tiny little flashing icon. Witch and Killi had crashed hard enough to set off the Rhino's emergency beacon, and it quietly pinged in a steady rhythm.

The sat image rippled as it updated.

Bronze Raven Five's icon was barely fifty meters from the landing pad and squarely intersected the outpost's perimeter fence. Twister tried to raise them on their primary channel as well as the aircrew channel.

There was no response.

Grimes turned away, already talking rapidly over his comm. "Aurora Research Outpost, *Perseverance*, I need a team out to that downed Rhino *now*."

"*We're down to min personnel,*" an unfamiliar voice replied. "*They're already loading up the next round of transports. We need to get out of here before we're trapped by the ash.*"

"Give me that," Voodoo growled as she stalked around the console. She didn't give Grimes a chance to argue, she just took over. "This is Major Ellingwood, Raven Squadron Commander. You either get a team over to my aircrew, or no more Ravens will fly, *keiche?*"

"*You can't do that! Supervisor Norwood won't let you abandon us down here!*"

"Watch me, you *tollejo* prick," Voodoo said coldly. "Atmospheric and weather conditions have already deteriorated below published safety minimums. Whether we continue to fly or not is *entirely* my call. So what call am I making, *balara?*"

A frustrated silence, then, "*I'll send a team.*"

"Good," she purred with barely restrained menace before releasing the comm back to Grimes. The Navy ensign grimaced, but Tripwire nodded in distracted approval at Voodoo's bluff before returning his full attention to his legionnaires' battle.

Blue couldn't tear her gaze from the sat image, could barely breathe past the terror constricting her throat. *Not Killi, please not Killi.*

Campbell still hadn't let her go, his hand a warm weight on her shoulder, an offer of comfort and support that she could *not* afford. Not when she was seconds away from shattering. She pulled away from him and stood on her own. It was either that or break, and she couldn't do that, not until she knew for sure—

The comms crackled.

"Perseverance, *Bronze Raven Five, we're down but still kicking,*" Witch said, fierce triumph riding her tone. "*Minor injuries only.*"

"*Feels like my spine tried to climb into my skull, and my tailbone isn't speaking to me,*" Killi laughed, giddy with the high of survival.

Blue braced one hand on the console, a shuddering breath full of relief escaping her control. *Alive, they're alive.*

"*Maintainers and some outpost personnel are working to unjam the ramp. We'll wait for the next round of Rhinos to evac us out of here.*" Despair tangled with triumph as Witch added, "*Our girl isn't flying anywhere anytime soon.*"

"*Or ever,*" Killi muttered.

"*None of that,*" Witch said sharply. "*I couldn't have kept us in one piece. You did. I'm just...*" She faltered, so much pain in her voice that Blue wondered if she'd lied about the injuries being minor. "*I'm just sorry we couldn't get to them. So damn sorry. We failed.*"

Again, Voodoo took over the comms. "*You tried. Now take care of your crew and standby for evac. We're pulling everyone out of that outpost.*"

"*Wilco,*" Witch said after a long moment. "*We'll pull out on the last Rhino. Civvies first, as always.*"

Silence fell again, broken only by the open comm in Bronze Raven One's cockpit. Voodoo dropped her eyes to the console, a distant expression on her face. Her fists clenched, and then she looked up at Blue and Twister. Dread barely had time to form in her belly before Voodoo spoke, her Passovan accent once again tightly restrained.

"You're not going."

"*What?*" Twister lunged forward, hands balled into fists. Blue stood at her command pilot's side in support. Even Tripwire finally moved, his grim gaze focused on Voodoo, though he remained silent. Blue couldn't keep the frantic words from spilling off her tongue.

"We have to go get them! My flight plan will keep us in the ash for less time than Bronze Raven Five. We can still make it work. We *have* to make it work." She jabbed a finger at the sat image and the legionnaires' biometric data. So few of them were left. "They're running out of time."

"No." Their squadron commander slashed her hand sideways. Her stoic expression spasmed before she regained control. "I'm not losing another Rhino or aircrew on this deployment. The ash cloud is too thick. Your flight plan was a good one, but it's comparable to what Witch just tried. You'll fail too, and we'll lose even more people."

Voodoo turned to the legionnaires' commander, standing so very still once more. Her expression softened without losing an inch of her resolve.

"I'm sorry, Trip. We can't get to them."

"No!" Twister didn't even seem aware of the tears rolling down her face. "We have to at least try. Witch tried. Let us try!"

Blue snatched her slate back, fingers flying over the screen as she compared the data—and briefly closed her eyes.

"She's right. We can't make it. Not anymore."

Twister shot her a look of betrayal, but Blue tilted the screen so she could see the results for herself. The clashing weather systems had accelerated the ash cloud disbursement beyond their worst projections. Her command pilot breathed a silent, terrible cry of loss before she spun around, turning her face to the wall, all the privacy she could get in that small room short of leaving it altogether. Blue knew she wouldn't leave unless forcibly removed. She returned her gaze to the sat image, giving Twister time to pull herself together, and her eyes snagged on a different icon. Tavi's face, so much like her little brother's, flashed in her mind.

"What about 4th Squad?" Blue pinned Voodoo with a fierce gaze. "They're not quite as deep as Bronze Raven One."

"They're deep enough." Tripwire shook his head before Voodoo could answer, the hoarseness of his voice the only indication he was struggling. "They'll have to get themselves clear. Trust them to put their heads down and do the work."

"But—"

"Ordo's one of my best," he said simply. "If anyone can get them clear, it's him."

Blue's shoulders slumped, and she nodded once in reluctant compliance. At the sharp rattle of gunfire, she jerked in surprise. She'd been so focused on everything else that the muted sounds of battle had nearly become background noise. Remorse rippled through her as she checked the biometrics. Another legionnaire had died and she hadn't even noticed.

The concussive blast of a grenade overwhelmed the rattle of gunfire, and a legionnaire bellowed loudly enough to be heard from the cockpit.

"*I'm out! Does anyone*"—static momentarily eclipsed the transmission—"*any ammo?*"

Nobody answered him, and the volume of gunfire became just a little quieter.

"Grimes, see if you can boost the signal," Campbell said quietly as the static worsened.

Grimes stretched out a hand for the console. He hesitated as a terrible scream rang out, as Ruby's sobs grew just a little louder. Twister spun back toward the console, her eyes wild with grief and despair. Grimes stared at her for a long moment, hand frozen in midair, compassion and hesitation tangled in his conflicted gaze.

"No." He turned back to Campbell and rolled his shoulders back. "I'm turning it off. There's no point in torturing anyone with this."

Blue snapped an incredulous glare at the junior comms officer, a protest rising to her lips as he reached for the console once more. Campbell reacted faster, slapping the other ensign's arm away.

"Belay that!" Campbell roared.

"There's nothing we can do for them," Grimes shouted back.

"We can listen," Campbell said grimly. "Those people down there deserve better than dying alone in the dark, unheard. We're here, and we'll listen as long as they need us to."

"They don't even *know* we're listening." Grimes shook his head, shoulders slumping as if he took the comms failure personally, despite the issue being on the damaged Rhino's end.

"*We* know." Campbell held his gaze, unflinching even as the ferocious hiss of an armadon filtered through the comm. "That'll have to be enough."

Grimes stared at him for a long moment before he dipped his chin in a nod. "I'll see what I can do to boost it."

At first, his fingers stabbed at the console in barely restrained aggression, but he quickly grew absorbed in his work. His fingers danced in a graceful rhythm across the screen, and utter focus claimed his features. Finally, he shook his hands out and glanced up at everyone.

"This won't last forever. Eventually, the ash and atmospheric disturbance will overwhelm even the outpost's relay point. But for now, it'll hold. Probably..." He sighed. "Probably long enough for us to keep the watch. Until the last legionnaire falls."

"Thank you," Tripwire said quietly.

"For what it's worth, I'm sorry I couldn't do more," Grimes said softly before he entered a final command on the console and turned up the comms. The static was gone.

Bronze Raven One's last stand came through loud and clear.

The next few minutes were a confusing blend of shouts, screams, and increasingly frantic gunfire. First one legionnaire flatlined, then another, then two more. Sergeant Cox roared out orders and encouragement and curses in equal measure over the cacophony of battle, never faltering, never failing—and then his biometrics flashed an alert before showing signs of extreme distress. There was a harsh scream of searingly bright agony, but he didn't flatline, and after a long moment his voice rose up again, rougher than before but still strong.

Angry voices rose up to counter his orders. Sergeant Cox roared a denial. His remaining legionnaires ignored him.

"*Take him!*" an unfamiliar voice barked. "*We'll hold as long as we can.*"

"*I've got him,*" Sergeant Morrison's deep voice replied.

"No!" Sergeant Cox snarled. "*Put me down, damn it. There's enough room in the cockpit for all of us. We can hold the hatch.*"

"Yes! Maybe we can still get to them when the ash cloud thins," Twister cried out with a harsh edge of desperation and denial. "So long as the cockpit is sealed, they'll be okay."

As if he'd heard her frantic words, Sergeant Morrison let out a bitter laugh.

"*It won't lock. Frame warped in the crash.*" Morrison grunted as if hauling a heavy weight. Water splashed, punctuated by snarls of agony as Sergeant Cox cussed out his legionnaires, the loadmaster, and every last armadon on the planet. Morrison cut him off. "*We'll hold the gunner compartment. You shut that hatch behind me best you can and take care of my Ravens. You hear me, legionnaire?*"

"Fuck," Sergeant Cox ground out. "*I hear you. Go!*"

A moment later, metal clanged, and the sounds of battle became muted. Blue's nails cut into her palms, the pain less effective at grounding her this time. Voodoo murmured something into her personal comm before striding over to have a hurried conversation with Grimes.

He frowned. "Are you sure?"

"The Ravens and Crows will bear witness," Voodoo said firmly. Tripwire's head snapped up, his eyes burning with intensity.

"Bravo Company will bear witness." The legionnaire sent out a quick message and nodded. "Route it to the Raven's briefing room and Bravo Company's viewscreens in their berthing spaces."

The comms officer stared at them for a beat before he sighed and tapped a few times at the console.

"Done."

The room fell silent again as they did the only thing they could do for their brothers- and sisters-in-arms. They listened.

Campbell stood at her shoulder, close but not touching. He didn't say anything, didn't give her false hope or try to comfort her. He just stood next to her as they kept the death watch. She looked up at him and saw that same helpless anger in his eyes, which was oddly more comforting than any empty words could ever have been.

Time stretched.

One by one, the remnants of 5th Squad fell, until Sergeant Cox was the only legionnaire remaining. Until the only sounds were Ruby's quiet sobs, Medusa's slurred curses, and the faint splash of water in the flooded cockpit.

"*Shhh*," Sergeant Cox whispered, his voice more the memory of sound than anything else. "*If they don't realize we're in here, they might leave.*"

Ruby's sobs faded to muffled whimpers, and Medusa let out a shuddering breath. Tense silence fell. Hope tried to rise again in Blue's heart—and then heavy thuds and metallic groans echoed through the cockpit as armadons slammed into the hatch.

"*So much for that plan,*" Sergeant Cox snarled.

Splashes followed as he moved through the waist-deep water, closer to the console that trapped Medusa. Ruby sobbed louder, fear as much as agony in her terrible cries.

"*My Crows are all dead, aren't they?*" Medusa asked, her slurred words barely audible over the frenzy outside the cockpit.

"Yeah."

"Ruby?"

"*Here, Medusa. I'm here,*" a small voice said, wobbly with pain and shock.

"*Take Ruby and get out of here. I can blow the windscreen...*" Medusa panted harshly, each inhale ragged as if she were fighting for every breath. "*I can... buy you time.*"

"*To hells with that,*" he snarled.

"*Gods damn it, Duck! Just fucking go!*"

Sergeant Cox let out a harsh laugh. "*Medusa, between the two of us we have one working set of legs. I'm not getting far with the one I have left. And Ruby... she's not getting far either. We're staying.*"

Metal groaned and warped. The hissing cries of the armadons grew louder, more rabid. Ruby wept, and Medusa cursed, but Sergeant Cox grew oddly silent.

And then the legionnaire raised his voice into a ringing battle cry.

"*I can hear the reaper calling our name, ladies! How do you want to answer him?*"

Ruby's sobs slowed, stuttered, died. A final sniffle, then her voice rang out strong and clear. "*Give me your sidearm.*"

"*Atta girl,*" Sergeant Cox said with grim approval.

The hatch gave way. Armadons swarmed into the flooded cockpit. Gunfire exploded, deafening, so loud Blue could almost feel it in her chest. A shout of agony cut off almost as quickly as it had arisen.

"*Duck!*" Medusa cried.

Sergeant Cox's biometrics flatlined, and the gunfire grew quieter. Seconds later, Ruby screamed, a shrill cry of agony that seemed to go on and on. At last her cries ceased, but the steady *crack* of a sidearm didn't falter even as Medusa shrieked in rage and pain. Above it all was the hissing of a single armadon.

Finally, the last gun fell silent, and Medusa's savage laughter filled the cockpit.

"Took you with me, you scaly bastard." Her fierce voice faded into a quiet whisper. *"Took you... with me."*

An aching silence spilled from the comm, blanketing the room.

The only thing to break it was the steady *ping* of Bronze Raven One's emergency beacon.

CHAPTER SIXTEEN
Do Not Cry for the Dead, Tasawa.
Cry for the Balara *Living.*

137 MILES WEST OF AURORA RESEARCH OUTPOST, AURORA

"You did nothing wrong, *tasawa*," Jabber told Tavi for the umpteenth time.

Once more Tavi didn't answer, instead he simply stared out into the distance as the waters continued to slowly recede. He wasn't quite sitting at attention, but it definitely was not the pose of a calm, relaxed legionnaire. His inner turmoil was making him sick.

They'd been on the rockpile for almost four hours, and the evening was casting a shadowy pale as the volcanic ash filled the sky above. A fine layer of black ash fell from the sky, settling on everything not disturbed by the waters. The civilians were miserable but alive... only just so. His slip, his loss of grip, had almost meant the end of Doctor Xi-Smith. She and the others were off to the side, taking stock of their belongings to see what supplies they had which would be useful over the coming hours and marveling at the fact they had survived a tsunami.

"C'mon *tasawa*, you did nothing wrong. We saved her. Blaming yourself for something that didn't happen is gonna eat you up, *ke*? It's not good. She screwed up but she alive. You think you're the first legionnaire to not be able to save someone? Tavi... it's okay. Nobody is mad for you losing your grip. You saved her *and* me, *tasawa*."

Silence.

Instead of responding, his eyes watched the west, patiently waiting.

His heart beat almost perfectly in time with the clock, steady, consistent. The HUD said that sunset would start soon and a tiny part of him wondered if he would be able to see it through the ashfall. Most of his mind, however, was replaying Doctor Xi-Smith's terrified face as he lost his grip over and over again.

The desperation in her eyes screamed for him to help. Her hand, just out of reach. Worst of all, the absolute silence when Jabber had managed to pull her out. She hadn't yelled at him for almost failing, hadn't begged Sergeant Ord to punish him. He was waiting for that moment to come, though.

That was worse than condemnation for the young man. Blame he could handle. He'd fully expected someone, anyone, to ream him out, his failure at keeping his grip when he'd had her. They should have. It would have been proper, after all. He deserved it.

Yet nobody had. Instead, Jabber and the others in Team Two had tried talking to him at random intervals, telling him he'd done well, that there was no shame for his bravery. But Tavi didn't believe them. It *was* his fault. If he had only been slightly bigger, or maybe a little faster, he could have reached her, and Jabber wouldn't have had to make the save. Better still, if he had been quicker moving through the jungle to help Jabber pull the doctor free in the first place, he would never have been in a position to fail.

"Private Tavi." Ordo's voice cut off his silent misery. "A moment?"

Tavi popped to his feet and rotated immediately, potential sunset forgotten. Ordo was standing there, his eyes on the distant horizon.

"Jabber, could you find somewhere else to be?" Ordo asked.

"*Bossjna*, not like there's really anywhere else to go on this rock..." the Passovan muttered but moved further away from the duo. Ordo waited until they had some breathing space.

"You're from Myrkyma, aren't you?" Ordo asked. Tavi looked at the sergeant, confused.

"Yes, Sergeant."

"Knew a guy from there once. Real piece of work," Ordo said and sat down on the edge of the rock. He pointed at the space next to him. "Sit, Private. Take a load off for a moment. We're not going anywhere in a hurry, you understand?"

Tavi nodded. "Yes, Sergeant."

"Drop names, Tavi," Ordo said and smacked the rock next to him. "Sit."

Tavi carefully sat down on the rock next to Ordo as ordered and waited. After a minute of silence, Ordo continued to speak.

"So the kid was from Myrkyma, like I said. Had a vicious temper and a tendency to slice and dice with a blade. Got so good at it they called him Cutter. Hell, it wasn't all that long ago. Ten years, about. Maybe you heard of him?"

Tavi shook his head. Ordo chuckled.

"Would have been surprised if you had. One of the things about the Overdark... the Shadows are quickly forgotten."

Tavi started at that. "That's what they called me sometimes when I was a kid. All the alley orphans. *Shadow*."

"No kidding? Huh. Never would have pictured someone with your genetics ending up on the streets. Half-breeds usually end up in the Reina. At least, as far as Cutter knew."

"Cutter... oh. Was that his name?"

"That was his name indeed," Ordo said, then sighed. He leaned back and stared off into the distance. "Cutter walked into the recruiting station one day, right smack dab in the middle of one of those nasty acid rains that happen when it's flooding up on the surface, and said that he was tired of being someone else's hired hitter, that he wanted off Myrkyma, away from everything, off that stinking hole of a planet. But you know how the Legion is. Can't have any actual murder warrants out against a person. He was pretty earnest, though, so a few quiet inquiries said that while he was suspected of about twelve murders, there wasn't enough evidence to bring charges. Hell, nobody even wanted to try. Killers killing killers doesn't make for a high priority when it comes down to local law enforcement. Myrkyma is a strange sort of world, you know. The Legion was reluctant, but... quotas, you get me? But since he was offering to sign a twenty-year contract right out the gate instead of the usual ten, he was accepted and shipped off to Mars Primus. Joined the Legion under his new name."

"Okay..." Tavi's voice trailed off. He wasn't really sure where the sergeant was going with this, but then, other than his in-processing meeting with the 4th Squad leader, he really hadn't had a lot of one-on-one interaction with him yet.

"He made mistakes, Tavi. But he made even poorer choices. Even later, he made mistakes. But he learned from them, and moved on. You didn't make a mistake. No, don't shake your head at me. I'm serious. Jabber made a mistake, maybe, but even he isn't really to blame. You're looking at an act of nature as your fault. That's arrogance, and I hate arrogance with a passion. You, young man, accomplished your mission. You got your civilian here first, and then you went back and freed Doctor Xi-Smith. You then led her and Jabber both here faster than anyone has ever moved before—I know, I was tracking your suit on my HUD." Ordo paused and turned to look over at Jabber for a moment. "It's killing him, too, you know. Jabber? He blames himself for letting her lead him through the jungle. Rightfully so, but the fact that you're taking all the blame and not even letting him accept his role in this is eating him up inside. You fought like a demon against the jungle to get to them, again when you barely were back and safe. Instead of taking a breath, you immediately leapt into action once more, without hesitation. You *did* save her. You just didn't do it alone.

"But Tavi...you expect the impossible of yourself. There's absolutely no way you should have saved her at any point. You didn't see the tree that hit her when she was on the rocks. You missed another branch that probably weighed as much as she did snagging her pants, trying to pull her beneath the water. Jabber is bigger, stronger. You saved her when the water hit. He finished the job. You worked as a team.

"We are legionnaires, Tavi. The Protectorate expects a lot of us. But they don't demand we perform the impossible, only that we don't quit while trying to do the mission. You, Jabber, everyone in 4th Squad... nobody quit today, and functioned perfectly *as a team*. Everyone made it. Nobody stopped in the middle of our mad dash to lay down and wait for the inevitable. That tells me more about my legionnaires *and* our civilians than anything else could. We're not quitters. Not this fucking team. So don't you start now. Unless you've somehow learned to control volcanoes with magic or something, there was no way any of this was your fault."

It was a lot to take in. Deep down, though, Tavi's gut told him that Ordo was probably correct. It really wasn't his fault, and beating himself up over something completely outside his control was not what he'd been taught. Guilt had a time and place, and this was not it.

He needed to be Private Diego Tavi, Distinguished Honor Graduate, and not little Diego, guttersnipe of the Overdark.

"So... what happened to him?" Tavi asked, shaking his head. Ordo *was* right. There was no point in trying to deny it. The sergeant had far more experience in this than he ever would. People weren't perfect. His promise he'd made, all those months before, had been to be the best legionnaire possible.

Not a perfect legionnaire.

"Who?" Ordo asked.

"Your friend Cutter."

"Oh. Heh. Yeah, wouldn't call him my friend, exactly. But Cutter? He died. Nobody mourned him at all," Ordo said before shrugging. "Which was fine. Cutter was just a person, another parasite in the underbelly of a society which didn't want him in the first place. But the person he became after taking his vows... Emmett Ord, legionnaire? That man has worth, meaning. He has drive. And like the Legion asks, he never quits, be it the mission or on one of his legionnaires."

"Wait... *you're* Cutter? You're from Myrkyma?" Tavi's eyes widened in shock.

"The Overdark, to be specific. Same as you, though I think a different street." Ordo grinned. "What, you think you were the only kid who wanted to escape? Honestly? You were probably the bravest. No kid your age risks everything to get out... even when a bunch of zealots are trying to dismember them piece by piece."

"So, you know... I'm half Tyrant?"

"Well, I did call you a half-breed, yeah," Ordo reminded him. "It's on your file. Something like that is easy to hide when you're young, not so easy when you get older. But look... do you know why the Legion is so special? Why us legionnaires fight so hard, and train the way we do? Why we do the insane stuff they ask us to, like protecting civilians on some backwater world trying to gain admission as a colony world in the Protectorate?"

Tavi shrugged. "I just thought it was because it was what we were told to do."

"That's part of it, yeah. But another part of it is giving us something to believe in, to defend, and something to earn." Ordo tapped Tavi's chest armor right above his heart. "You give a man his freedom, his rights, and he might use them and cherish them, or he might ignore them and not recognize their worth. It depends on a lot of different things, like upbringing, family, stuff like that. But... you ask a man to *earn* it? Well, our species has always cherished what we've earned through hard work and toil. The reward for a job well done is greater than something handed to you for minimal effort. You believe in what you protect because you *want* to earn that right. That's what makes you, me, guys like Jabber, and even Voodoo, a little different. We weren't born in the Protectorate. We're trying to earn our right to be a part of it. *That's* what makes us fantastic legionnaires—and why our Ravens are so damn good. We weren't given anything. We're earning it because we truly, deeply, *want* it.

"The Tyrants didn't earn what they had. They were bred into it, inheriting it through nothing but who their genetic progenitor was. It made them arrogant, and caused them to lose their way. They were horrible people when I was there, and I can only imagine how much worse it became after. But imagine if Tyrants had to earn their status, their place as rulers? You think things would have been different? I don't know about you, but maybe... yes. Things just might have ended up differently, and hundreds of heads wouldn't have ended up being mounted atop spikes around a city just because of their genetics.

"So when you earn this—and I don't think there's a force in this universe that is going to stop you—what do you want to do with it?" Ordo slowly pulled himself to his feet. Tavi began to follow but Ordo waved him off. "Don't answer me now. Just sit, keep an eye on the west. No sunset tonight, though. Ash clouds are too thick. But maybe tomorrow, or the next. That should give you enough time to think about what you want, what you'll cherish. In the meantime, I have a Passovan to go yell at to boost his morale for needing a cherry private to save his ass."

"Thank you, Ordo." Tavi meant it, too. The sergeant looked back down at him and nodded.

"Anytime, kid. That's what sergeants are for, after all. Motivational speeches, liberty passes, and berthing inspections." He paused, and frowned. "I would kill for a steak right now. Jabber! Get your butt over here, you mouthy little... explain to me why I found a package of crackers open in your berthing space two days ago. Do you want insects in your tent? This is how we get insects in our tents..."

Tavi chuckled. He doubted he would ever be as good a leader as Ordo, but at least he could try. Silently, Tavi continued to watch the west, hoping against hope that some word would come, that Bronze Raven One and 5th Squad were all right, and that SAR from the *Perseverance* was on their way down to pull the entire team out.

And maybe, just maybe, catch another sunset.

He blinked as realization washed over him. "Wait... how did he know I like watching sunsets?"

Blue wasn't sure how long they all stood around that console, listening to the steady *ping* of the emergency beacon, but between one heartbeat and the next, her knees gave way. She leaned on the console, the hard edge biting into her white-knuckled hands as she gripped it with all her strength.

"Breathe," Campbell had told her earlier, so that's what she did. She breathed, and she bowed her head, and she wept silent tears for her friends.

At a quiet *bzzz*, Voodoo glanced down at her wrist. She froze for a moment before she swore a rapid litany entirely in Passovan, ripped her comm off, and threw it across the room. It bounced off the bulkhead and rolled across the deck, the sturdy case leaving it undamaged. Their squadron commander breathed deeply for long seconds before she spoke.

"Bronze Raven Four is ready." Her piercing gaze landed on Twister and Blue, utterly without mercy. "Can you both fly? Every Raven was listening to that transmission. Every Raven is just as fucked up as you two. And I've only got two operational Rhinos after this last run. I need Four back in the air to finish the evac, and you've both flown in this shit. Am I sending you down to help or not?"

Twister lifted her chin, eyes solid chips of blue ice. "We've got this. Right, Blue?"

Blue shoved herself upright. She didn't bother to wipe her face. Let them see her tears. She wasn't ashamed. How could she be, when a legionnaire like Tripwire had shed tears for his men? She couldn't help Bronze Raven One, and she couldn't help 4th Squad. But this? This she could do.

"Let's go."

It felt like decades had passed since Blue followed Twister up from the dropship bay, but it took a blink for them to race back down. The bay was utter chaos. A wave of sound hit them the instant they ran through the hatch. The normal sounds of the bay had been overtaken by the uproar caused by a large number of civilians pouring down the open ramps of four Rhinos. They milled around, uncertain where to go and somehow managing to get in everyone's way, despite a pair of Navy personnel trying to corral them and usher them to wherever they were *actually* supposed to wait out the ashfall over their outpost.

Maintainers fought against the tide of shouting civilians to get to the Rhinos. A familiar Passovan corporal was already throwing up his hands over the state of the atmospheric engines, and one of the Rhinos was parked more than a little crooked, as if the pilots had difficulty with the landing.

A cold chill swept through Blue as she dove into the chaos. If the ash had managed to invade the systems that regulated the maneuvering thrusters, that could make their return flight challenging. A heavyset civilian rammed into her shoulder, his wide gaze darting everywhere except in the direction he was moving. Blue grunted but didn't stop to listen to his distracted apology. There was no time, not with the latest weather update that had popped up on their way down to the bay, not with the estimated number of civilians left at the outpost, not with only three operational Rhinos to airlift them out.

Blue gritted her teeth and ran faster. If the estimates were accurate, they'd have to do another drop after this one to pick up Killi, Witch, their Crows, and the maintainer team.

Carvalho met her at the base of the ramp. His eyes were red rimmed, but his voice was steady as always.

"Walker said the engines tested good, external preflight is already done." A faint smile creased his face. "Fair warning, HeyHey is pissed they don't get to ride down. They want payback, but we need the extra weight allowance to carry the max passengers."

"Not to mention there's no fucking armadons at the outpost," Blue growled as she charged up the ramp, through the cargo compartment, and all the way into the cockpit. Twister was already in the left seat, running the remaining preflight checks at a rapid pace. The whine of the ramp retracting hit a moment later. Blue strapped in, pulled on her helmet, and threw herself into the work.

"All checks complete, green across the board," she said a few minutes later. Outside the Rhino, the bay had emptied out in preparation for their departure. Blue wished whoever had been saddled with the civilians the best of luck.

"I'll fly this time," Twister said grimly. "Get on the comms and let them know we're ready."

"Bronze Raven Four, ready for drop." As soon as Blue got an acknowledgment, she switched to the aircrew channel. "Drop in three mikes. Confirm ready to fly."

"*Ready to fly, confirmed.*"

Blue let out a shaky breath, the memories of the last time they'd flown, all the mistakes she'd made, everything she could have, *should have*, done differently, flashing through her mind in one terrible instant. As Twister gripped the controls, she flicked a sharp glance at Blue.

"Let's get it done and get our girls back. Then we'll deal with... everything else."

Red lights flashed and a blaring siren echoed through the cavernous bay, a warning for anyone foolish enough to remain within. Blue compartmentalized, leaning hard on the lessons she'd learned from the Legion, from flight training... and from her grandmother.

"*Bronze Ravens Three, Four, and Twelve, drop is a go. In five, four, three, two...*"

"Let's rage," Blue whispered.

They dropped.

Despite the monstrous hurricane slowly creeping north and the thunderstorms raging around the newly exploded volcano, most of the flight down to Aurora went smoothly. While their window of opportunity to complete the evacuation of the outpost before the falling ash grew too thick for the Rhinos to fly through was shrinking, it hadn't closed yet. Twister took over as flight lead and led the small formation along a more cautious northern route through the upper atmosphere where the skies were still clear of everything but a few innocuous bands of cloud cover.

As they closed in on the outpost, the light began to dim, and not just because it was nearing sunset. Ash fell from the sky, light flurries that mimicked snow, though not nearly as pretty. Or safe. Blue's gut tightened as they flew into the cloud, worried eyes constantly flicking toward the engine readouts.

"So far, so good," she breathed out. As they flew over the outpost, a red sun sat on the horizon, one last gasp of daylight burning through the ash. Her breath caught when they flew over the western side. "Holy shit..."

Twister whistled low under her breath and circled over Bronze Raven Five's crash site. Somehow, Killi had managed to keep the dropship in one piece. It helped that the Rhinos were tough and designed to handle the harshest of landings. The outpost perimeter fence, on the other hand, had never been designed to handle a Rhino crashing into it.

A good portion of that section had been flattened beneath the bulky dropship, and more had sagged on either side of the outstretched wings. One of the atmospheric engines had completely torn free and tumbled across the landing pad and into a collection of ground vehicles, while the other was half rotated into the vertical position. It seemed as if the maintainers and outpost team had given up on fixing the mangled ramp and evac'd everyone through one of the gunner hatches.

Twister kept them in the air until Three and Twelve had landed and loaded up their civilians. As soon as the pair of Rhinos had cleared the pad, she set them down, and Carvalho got the last huddle of personnel onboard and strapped in. Just as Blue had feared, there wasn't enough room for anyone else.

Across the ash-covered landing pad, Bronze Raven Five's crew and the maintainer team sheltered beneath the small hangar. Blue met Killi's gaze as she lifted her personal comm.

"We'll be back for you."

"*I know you will.*" Killi smiled, though even at a distance Blue could tell it was forced. "*Hurry up, will you? I heard the chow hall is serving tacos again tonight.*"

"But no tacos for Ensign Hotness, right?"

"*I mean... maybe? You've done a pretty good job making him chase so far. At some point you need to let that boy catch you.*"

Blue snorted a watery laugh even as she ran through a quick crosscheck for Twister. "Copy catch. We'll see you soon."

Twister wasted no time in launching them back into the air, pushing the engines to the limit to get them out of the ash cloud, flying back north as fast as the lumbering Rhino could go. The other Ravens hadn't waited, which was good, but it left them climbing for the stars alone once more.

Back on the *Perseverance*, Carvalho kicked out the civilians as quickly as even Blue could have wished. Anticipation tightened her belly—Twister had received permission from Voodoo for them to make the last run down to Aurora.

The older pilot glanced at Blue as they prepared to drop again. "You ready to fly?"

Blue practically lunged for the flight controls. Normally she wouldn't be so eager to fly, not addicted to the rush like some of her fellow Ravens, but this was for *Killi*.

"Ready."

Soon enough, they were back in the black, boosting for the green world below their mottled gray wings. Blue followed Twister's previous flightpath, but nervous sweat coated her palms and trickled down her spine as they cut through the increasingly turbulent atmosphere.

The ash cloud had reached the northern route.

Pushing the old Rhino to the limit, they dropped onto the outpost's landing pad but kept the engines running hot. Unlike the civilians, nobody had to tell the Legion to move quickly. Bronze Raven Five's aircrew and the maintainer team sprinted up the ramp the instant Carvalho lowered it, every last one collecting a fine layer of ash across their shoulders and heads. Within seconds, the ramp retracted and they were back in the air.

"How are the engines looking?" Blue demanded as she rotated them into the forward position and pushed up the throttles.

"In the green," Twister said with a fine thread of relief weaving through her tone. "But we'll need to have the maintainers thoroughly go over them before we come back down for 4th Squad in a few days."

Blue nodded and used every trick Twister had taught her over the past year to get every last bit of speed possible out of the old dropship. Neither engine had developed that off-key pitch yet, but she couldn't help but listen for it the entire way back into orbit. After one nasty patch of turbulence, the engine they'd inherited from Bronze Raven Seven developed a slight rattle, but it was possible it was unrelated to the ash. Fortunately, the rattle didn't stop them from breaking atmo, and it disappeared the instant Blue switched to the void thrusters.

Relief slammed into her so hard the walls she'd built within her mind to compartmentalize the loss of Bronze Raven One trembled. Gritting her teeth, she shored them up and lost herself in the familiar routines of returning to the *Perseverance*. She didn't think about their losses, didn't think about Killi strapped in the back or how every so often Twister's breath hitched. None of it mattered until they were safely back in the dropship bay.

Quickly, they ran through the postflight checks. For just a moment, Blue slumped in her seat. Flying was tough on the body during good conditions. An endless day fighting a volcanic eruption, storms, an engine loss, and ashfall was so far from normal it was laughable.

And they'd started the day out on the *beach*.

A strangled laugh escaped before she managed to lock it down. Blue had a feeling that if she started laughing, she'd probably break down in the middle of the bay, and Killi needed her. She forced weary fingers to cooperate and unbuckled her harness before standing and following Twister out of the cockpit. The maintainers were already busy working on their Rhino, but Bronze Raven Five's crew had all waited for them to finish up, and they walked down the ramp together. The Crows were dismissed to find their own rest and whatever brand of release worked best for them. Twister and Witch quickly followed, leaving just Blue and Killi.

Her best friend's eyes were red from crying, and her expression was haggard. Voodoo must have had Grimes relay Bronze Raven One's transmission down to the outpost too. Not only had Killi lost Medusa and Ruby, she'd also lost her legionnaires.

Inexorably, her thoughts were drawn back to her own legionnaires, and she fired off a quick message to Campbell.

BLUE: STATUS ON 4TH SQUAD?

Blue expected a wait, but Campbell responded almost immediately.

ENSIGN HOTNESS: STILL STATIONARY. LATEST UPDATE FROM ORDO PUTS THE OUTPOST WITHIN 4 DAYS AT THE WORST. GO GET SOME REST!

Despite everything, Blue smiled.

BLUE: BOSSY.

ENSIGN HOTNESS: DARLIN', YOU HAVE NO IDEA. NOW GO TAKE CARE OF YOURSELF—AND YOUR FRIEND. WE'VE GOT THEM ON COMMS, AND WE'RE TRACKING THEIR PROGRESS. THEY'RE FINE. I'LL KEEP YOU UPDATED IF ANYTHING CHANGES.

BLUE: PROMISE?

ENSIGN HOTNESS: PROMISE.

Killi shoved her sideways, a hint of her typical smirk playing on her lips. "Flirt later, food now."

Corporal Walker stalked over, catching them before they could make their escape. "Any issues?"

"The engine scavenged from Seven started to rattle on the last ascent," Blue said as her stomach grumbled at the reminder that food was a thing it desperately needed. "Both need a good scrub before we fly again."

"Tell me something I don't know, *pojata*," he said with a tired grin. "Don't worry, we'll take care of your girl."

"Thanks, Walker."

CHAPTER SEVENTEEN
Armadons Don't Surf, Tasawa

137 MILES WEST OF AURORA OUTPOST STATION, AURORA

"*Perseverance*, this is 4th Squad. Come in, over."

It was almost midnight before the waters receded enough for them to leave. However, Ordo made the command decision to stay on the rocks overnight. It was safer than being down in the debris fields of the flooded plains between them and the research outpost. Doctor Schmoyer agreed that their best course of action would be to stay put.

"*This is* Perseverance," the response came back a moment later. "*Good to hear your voice again, Sergeant. Be advised, extraction unavailable at this time. Ash cover is too thick and hazardous. Recommend overland route to Aurora Research Outpost. Copy last, over.*"

"Copy extraction unavailable at this time," Ordo repeated tonelessly.

Tavi looked over at him, then turned to see if Mitzi or any of the other members of the Survey Corps had heard. None of them were paying attention. Instead, they were huddled together in the center of the rock pile, discussing the volatile nature of the tsunami thanks to the strange salinity and water density levels of the planet. The rope Mitzi had tied on earlier remained, a stark reminder of just how close it had truly been.

The falling ash from the volcano had continued unabated for hours after the tsunami passed. According to Mitzi, it would continue until the volcano quit erupting. The ash, thick and black, blanketed everything around them. The suits of the legionnaires weren't spared, either. While the thick, black ash didn't seem to hinder their hamatic suits so far, Tavi couldn't help but wonder if the plate armor would be affected the longer the ash rubbed along it. The suits were designed to stop impacts, not deal with constant wear.

The Survey Corps members were worse off. Their rugged outdoor wear was designed to deal with harsh weather climes and their boots, made with long sojourns into the wilderness in the mind of the manufacturers, typically held up well under most circumstances. Unfortunately for them, most circumstances did not include the abrasive dust from a volcano.

Breathing was also quickly becoming a problem. The air was thick with smoke and ash. None of them had packed respirators in their daybags—there was no reason to, so not even Doctor Schmoyer could fault any of his aides for this. Mitzi, however, had brought multiple changes of shirts and blouses. With a knife, she was able to quickly fashion covers for their noses and mouths.

"Always stay prepared for any preventable incident," she had told Tavi after finishing with the final protective covering, this one for Schmoyer. "It's not the best, but it should help us breathe until extraction gets here."

Extraction which isn't coming, Tavi thought once more as he listened in to Ordo's conversation with the *Perseverance*.

"*Perseverance,* be advised we have had zero fatalities," Ordo continued. "All civilians are safe and mostly unharmed. 4th Squad reporting only minor injuries at this time."

"*Confirm civvies are safe,*" came the quick reply. "*Do Doctor Schmoyer and the other members of the Survey Corps understand that the only safe course of action would be to traverse overland to the outpost, over?*"

Tavi frowned. Could they? He had no idea. Legionnaires were trained for longer distances under harsh circumstances, but other than the brief workup they'd done at Sagetnam during pre-deployment, they really hadn't prepared for something like this.

"They do, *Perseverance,*" Ordo replied instantly.

"*Downloading a new route now for your map overlays,*" the voice up on the *Perseverance* announced. Tavi brought up his map in his HUD and recognized points of interest which had been previously marked by the initial Explorer of the planet, as well as other landmarks later by researchers at the outpost.

Tavi looked at the various overland routes proposed by the *Perseverance*. They weren't exactly a straight shot to the research outpost, but close enough. There was one point where they would have to dogleg around a creek, but the map indicated it was shallow enough to ford.

Four days at the most to make it to the outpost. It would be a rough march under the best conditions, and after a volcanic eruption of this magnitude, the march was at the complete opposite end of "best conditions." Five scientists, unknown quantities really, though Tavi suspected that Mitzi was tougher than she appeared. The journey would be rough on them all.

Can we do this? he wondered as the reports from the *Perseverance* continued to roll in unabated.

They could do it. 4th Squad had one task, and that was keep their civilians alive. Everything else was secondary at the moment.

He mulled it over as sleep continued to elude him.

A few hours after Bronze Raven One's final transmission, Blue and Killi had dragged themselves back to their quarters and changed into off-duty clothes. Blue carried her blanket over to Killi's bunk, sat next to her best friend, and waited. It didn't take long.

Killi let out a ragged exhale and leaned against Blue's side.

"Voodoo told us to take care of our boys, and I failed mine. I wasn't there, and they're gone, and I can't make that right."

Blue's throat tightened. "It wasn't your fault. It wasn't anybody's fault."

"If I'd... if I'd just managed to convince Ruby to switch with me, I could've been there. I could've done something. Ruby would still be alive."

"And you'd be dead!"

Blue blinked back the burn of tears at how close she'd come to losing Killi. If the maintainers hadn't been nearly finished with the repairs to Bronze Raven Five, if Killi hadn't been so amazing at engine failure landings... Blue let out a shuddering breath.

"You weren't there," she said quietly. "As bad as the ash was where you flew, it was worse on the coast. You would've died with them."

Killi curled her hands into fists.

"Yes! I would've died with them... or maybe I might have been just a little better than Medusa and Ruby and I could've saved them all. And I'll never fucking know." Tears rolled down her face and her breath hitched in a sob. "Oh gods, Ruby was a *baby*. And Medusa... she might as well have been attached at the hip to Witch and Twister. And their Crows... Morrison and Tyson and Jacobi. I might have been able to save them all."

Tears ran down Blue's face, but she shook her head fiercely. "You quit that! You quit it right now. You can't take on that guilt or it'll eat you alive. It's not your fault." She swallowed hard and blinked away the tears. "Any more than it was my fault that I couldn't get to them. It's not our fault."

If Blue said it enough times, eventually her heart would believe it.

Killi sighed, and the tense set to her shoulders relaxed, but it was a long time before she stopped crying, and longer before either woman was ready to move. Finally, Blue stirred herself enough to check her comm and winced.

"It's past midnight. We should get some sleep."

Blue snapped her head up at a sharp rap on the hatch. With a gentle pat on Killi's shoulder, she extricated herself from the blanket nest and slowly walked to the door. Exhaustion weighed down her shoulders, but she couldn't help her smile when she found Campbell standing in the corridor outside.

"They finally let you off shift?" Blue glanced over her shoulder, but Killi had burrowed so far beneath the blankets that only her face was visible under her thick hoodie. Even so, her best friend mouthed "catch" at her. She rolled her eyes as she stepped out into the corridor and mostly shut the hatch. "As much as I'd love to get those drinks, now isn't the best..."

Blue trailed off as the man just stood there, staring at her with an expression she couldn't quite interpret. As if he were trying to hold onto his professional bearing but the mask was cracking around the edges.

"Campbell?" She stepped closer and stared up at him, barely keeping her voice level. "What's wrong?"

"We..." Campbell ran a hand through his short hair, dark eyes turbulent. "We lost contact with 4th Squad."

Dread sank through Blue's gut like a cold stone, but she shook her head, desperately holding onto hope.

"It's just the ash cloud, right?" Despite her best efforts, her voice rose in pitch. "Grimes said it would interfere with comms."

"It's not just comms. Their biometrics... all of them flatlined." Campbell slowly shook his head. "They're gone. I'm so fucking sorry, Blue."

There was no stopping her tears this time.

"Be advised. Weather conditions are be—" the voice abruptly cut off. Tavi's head snapped up instinctively to look into the night sky before he caught himself. There was no way anyone could see through the ash cloud.

"*Perseverance*, repeat your last, over." Ordo waited a moment, but only the faint hiss of static could be heard. "*Perseverance*, this is 4th Squad, come in."

Nothing.

Tavi swallowed. He'd suspected that the ash cloud above might interfere with the relay between the *Perseverance* and their comms, but the research station should have been able to continuously transmit and relay the signal. The only way they would have lost comms with their ship was if something happened to the outpost.

"4th Squad, gather round," Ordo said. Everyone came closer and Ordo, after confirming with Pigeon that all the civilians in their care were occupied but secure, broke it down for them. "Team leaders, check supplies. If everyone loaded out like they were supposed to, there should be enough food for a few days. You're going to be using the hell out of your water purifiers, though. Keep an eye on the filter cleanliness. The ash is going to clog them something fierce. Comms with the *Perseverance* are out. We have a recommended overland route to extraction, so we're going to take it."

"*Pokerro*," Jabber growled.

"Overland?" a small, timid voice asked. Tavi started. Somehow, Mitzi had slid into the middle of the huddle of legionnaires and was listening in. "How far of a walk is it?"

"It's going to be a hike, ma'am," Ordo replied instantly. "But it's the only way to get you and the others out. Give us a minute, please."

"Oh. Okay." Mitzi wandered back to Schmoyer and the shell-shocked scientists.

"It's 137 miles to the outpost, Ordo," Pigeon said in a quiet voice, switching back to private comms between the legionnaires once she was far enough away. "I don't know if any of the civvies can make it. We've got a topographical layout and recommended route from the *Perseverance*, okay, great. But flooding from that tsunami has probably changed all that. Ponds could be lakes now, rivers might be all sorts of screwed. Plus, how much food and water is it going to take? We've got three days' supplies, four if we stretch it out. That's including what we have for the civilians. I think only Doctor Wingo came prepared with more than a day's worth of rations."

"Not to mention we have no idea what's *in* the water down there," Claw added. The armorer's frown was deep. "We all heard what happened to Bronze Raven One, Ordo. You might have killed the comms, but we *know*. We know there are armadons out there. The aggressive ones, I mean."

As if on cue, raspy barks echoed loudly nearby. Everyone flinched at the sounds, and lumens were activated on rifles. Beams of light speared though the ash-filled darkness, but whatever was making the sound couldn't be seen.

"Hunting cry of the armadon," Mitzi helpfully provided. She sounded nervous. "They're close, and working as a pack. Coordinating. This...is not good."

"We need to get the hell off this rock and to a safe location," Ordo said tiredly. He pointed toward the west. "SAR standard operating procedure is to remain in place. But if we stay here, those rocks can be climbed. The armadons will be up them easily. Plus, that volcano out there is spewing enough ash to blanket the northern hemisphere. There's no way any Rhino is getting down here in one piece unless there's some damned miracle. As much as I love staying up on this rock, we need to get somewhere safer, like the outpost. If we can make it there, we can hole up and wait for extraction. There's enough food and resources in storage there to last a full company for a year. We're only a squad. How long do you think it'll feed us?"

"Plus, if those armadons remain aggressive, the walls at the outpost can easily hold them off for months, if not longer," Pigeon muttered, nodding his head. "If it were just us, Ordo, I wouldn't be complaining."

"But it's not just us," Ordo confirmed. He turned and met Tavi's eyes for a brief instant before continuing. "Doesn't matter if we think they can or can't make it. Our job is to ensure that they do."

"Dawn?" Pigeon asked. Ordo nodded in agreement. Pigeon chuckled. "Or at least, what's going to pass for dawn. I'm not a volcano expert, but I don't think we're going to see blue skies for a long time."

"Sun's scheduled to rise at 0714," Claw pointed out. "Pigeon, you think you can get them up and moving by then?"

"They'll probably complain, but yeah, I think so. If not, I'll sic Tavi on them," Pigeon responded. This elicited a laugh from everyone nearby. The story of what he'd said at the fancy dinner had spread like wildfire amongst the legionnaires of Bravo Company.

"Eh, blue skies are overrated," Ordo said before he ran a finger along his suit. The trail left a deep furrow, courtesy of the constantly falling ash. "Damn. No matter where I seem to go, I always find the place with poisonous water and toxic air. Remind you of home yet, Tavi?"

Tavi shrugged. "At least out here I'm not worried about anyone shoving a knife in my back."

"Spoken like a true Shadow of the Overdark," Ordo said. "Well, water shouldn't be a problem so long as the filters hold. I saw the little survivalist doctor with a water filter that looked like it could work on anything, so they'll have water. Our suits will keep us up and running for a week. Food we'll ration so we can make it five days if needed. We're going to be burning calories, though, so keep an eye out. There are supposed to be fruits on this planet we might be able to eat. Check with Doctor Wingo and see if she knows what's what.

"Pigeon, Claw, get your teams rested. I don't want anyone on more than a two-hour watch at one time. We've got a long way to go and a short time to do it in. First waypoint is twenty-four miles out. At three miles an hour—if we're lucky—it's going to take us almost the entire day of walking to make it if we want to sleep on dry land. Otherwise it's the soggy marshes because I'm not sleeping in some tree. Orders are to escort the civilians back to the research outpost. You heard Doctor Schmoyer. The safety of the Survey Corps members is paramount.

"Make sure everyone focuses on the objective, not on what happened to 5th Squad. You get me?" They all nodded. "Good. Tavi? Front and center."

"Sergeant?" Tavi asked, a little confused as he moved to stand in front of the senior NCO.

"Your little civvie friend..." Ordo began, his eyes flickering behind Tavi for a brief instance. "She's the biologist of the group, right?"

"The xenobiologist."

"Perfect. Pick her brain. I have a very bad feeling about what's coming." Ordo let out a deep, weary sigh. "Ask her about everything we might run into that can eat us. I know armadons are a danger, but is there anything else here we weren't briefed on? Pigeon, get with that Schmoyer asshole and see if he has any information either. The two meteorologists are going to be helpful, but right now they're in shock and practically worthless. We can quiz them tomorrow after they've had some time to process."

"What for?" Claw asked, confused.

"Always have a backup option, just in case," Ordo reminded him. Claw nodded and grunted in agreement. "All right, enough jabbering. Get your boys up at 0630. I want to be on the way as soon as possible tomorrow morning. Get to it."

Tavi sighed. He was simply too keyed up to sleep, or rest, or anything other than worry. Glancing over at Mitzi, he was unsurprised to see she was passed out, curled into a small ball, her head on a makeshift pillow. He smiled. *At least someone will sleep tonight.*

CHAPTER EIGHTEEN
*It's Not About the Destination
but the Carnage Left Along the Way*

124 MILES WEST OF AURORA RESEARCH OUTPOST, AURORA

It was just after noon when Tavi began to think that twenty-four miles in a day was profoundly optimistic. Surprisingly, it wasn't even any of the civilians' fault, but nature's.

While the water from the tsunami had receded, it hadn't gone entirely. The ground, thanks in large part to the thick mossy undergrowth of the jungle without end, had turned what had been soft dirt into a muck-filled swamp. The water level was just below his knees, which created many tripping hazards for any obstructions hidden by the black waters. Every step caused the mud to pull at his boots, though he didn't have it the worst by far. Being smaller and lighter than the normal legionnaire here was a benefit.

Unlike Fire Team Two, Team One was filled with bigger, burly legionnaires primarily from Mars Primus. Constantly bogged down by the unseen hazards beneath the black waters, they were starting to fall behind the lighter legionnaires like Tavi, Pigeon, and even Jabber. By the time the clock on Tavi's HUD said it was noon, the entire squad was spread out across over two hundred yards as they moved single file through the warm waters.

Combined, this made for slow going. More than once Ordo had called a halt to the hike to give everyone a little extra rest time. During these breaks Tavi would first ensure that Mitzi was doing well—Ordo had insisted that Team Two remain responsible for the civilians instead of sharing the load—before ranging around to scout.

It was absolute ruin everywhere they went. Trees from the coast were found wrapped around larger trees which had withstood the tsunami, and dead animals were dangling in some of the branches like discarded party favors. It was horrifying, and Tavi could only imagine how much worse it would become as the bodies began to rot in the unforgiving heat.

It would get hot, too, Mitzi had assured him, after which the temperatures would drastically decline for a few years. The meteorologists offered a few points of discussion involving a debate between scientists regarding whether or not the volcanic ash produced on some worlds differed from others, but otherwise they let Mitzi answer all the questions Tavi could think to throw at her.

Despite everything, Mitzi remained upbeat throughout. Tavi was impressed by her attitude but also by Schmoyer's motivational tactics. More than once the two meteorologists of the Survey Corps appeared on the verge of giving up only to be prodded and encouraged by Schmoyer. None of the others could get them to move as quickly as he managed.

"Jabber? You think this world is feral enough for you to live on?" Tavi asked as the lanky Passovan passed by. Jabber slowed down, looked at Tavi, then fell in step on the other side. Mitzi walked slightly ahead of the two, giving them a little space as she followed the path being laid out by Claw and Fire Team One.

"I don't know, *tasawa*," Jabber admitted after a moment's contemplation. "No plants trying to kill us."

"But a volcano is," Tavi pointed out. Jabber pursed his lips before nodding.

"*Ke*, you're right. Volcano is feral ground, *keiche?*"

"What does *tasawa* mean, anyway?" Tavi asked. "Is it good?"

"Just means, ah, something like a term for small friend," Jabber explained. "Like a little buddy, but better."

"Passovan dialect is so rich in diversity," Mitzi added from ahead. "It borrows from seven or eight distinct languages to merge its own identity. Much the same how Martian deviated from Anglish when the Exodus occurred."

Tavi checked his comms and realized he'd left the channel open. "Oops. Sorry, miss. I forgot to close the comms."

"It's fine. I enjoy talking to people. When I get left out it's...well, it's frustrating," she admitted as she slowed her pace, allowing Tavi and Jabber to catch up and walk on either side. "I earned my doctorate, but nobody appreciates it. I know more about the wildlife on this world than just about anybody, and I'm probably smarter than everyone else! Uh, no offense."

"None taken," Tavi said. Jabber, though, clicked his tongue and grinned.

"I think I understand things now."

"You do?" Mitzi asked, suspicion coloring her tone. Jabber nodded.

"Yeah. These big doctors, they've been doing this for a long time, *ke*? I hear the big doctor say he's been Expeditor for ten years. Morales and Childs? Survey Corps for eight years each, and a dozen expeditions between them." Jabber nodded. "I get it. Makes sense when you see it like that."

"What makes sense?" Mitzi asked. She was clearly frustrated. "What don't I see?"

"It's not that they don't trust your mind, *pojata*. It's that they are much more experienced in the field. This your first expedition in the Survey Corps?"

"Well, yes, but I don't see—" Mitzi began, but Jabber cut her off.

"They been on many. Even Huyan has been on five expeditions, and she's only a few years older than you. Do you understand? They trust your mind, but not your *experience*, because you don't have any...yet."

"Still doesn't justify their treatment of me," she said.

"No, it doesn't," Jabber agreed. "Those *buckos* are mean for no reason. Not even real hazing, *ke*? Just being dicks. But next time you go out as a team, they'll trust your experience because they will remember what you did during this field trip from Hell, *keiche*? It's that simple."

"You...are a surprisingly knowledgeable man for someone who grew up on a world where the plants eat you," Mitzi said, though it was with a smile.

"He tried, but he'll never be a child prodigy," Tavi reminded her. Mitzi's eyes widened before she laughed. It was soft, but it was there.

"Yeah, I guess you right, *tasawa*. Just gonna try harder, *ke*?"

"That's all we can do, Jabber. Try harder, be smarter, and have a plan to kill everyone in the room," Ordo said as he seemingly appeared out of thin air. He raised his voice. "Hey, Doctor Schmoyer! Careful over there. This is supposed to be a creek but it looks funny. I think there's a pond there under all that ash. Tread carefully!"

Tavi turned to see what Ordo was talking about. Sure enough, there was a cluster of downed trees at one end of a shallow ravine, creating a pond of sorts. While it didn't look too deep, Tavi had more than one lifetime's experience in dealing with poisoned water and decided he was going to walk the long way around to avoid it, unlike some of the others. Team One, unsurprisingly to Tavi, had followed Pigeon and Doctor Schmoyer into the little pond.

"Hey, something moved in here!" Stickboy called out and began to take purposeful steps back toward the shore. "Nope. Not having it. Nope nope nope."

"I'll go first," Doctor Schmoyer said as he picked up a long, broken branch and began testing the waters. "It's only a few feet deep here. Once I clear it, the next person goes. I don't believe that there has been enough time for this to form and for wildlife to establish itself here."

He slowly moved into the pond, each step a cautious one. The Expeditor looked back, nodded triumphantly, then abruptly gave a shrill scream and disappeared beneath the black waters of the makeshift pond.

"Shit!" Pigeon shouted and dove into the waters after him. A moment later he came back up, his helmet turning back and forth, ash and water running down his shielded face. Tavi, recognizing immediately what he was doing, also began looking for the bio signature of the doctor. After a few seconds of frantic searching he found him over forty yards away and moving quickly.

"There!" Tavi yelled, pointing. "Forty yards and outbound fast!"

"No shot!" Stickboy shouted from the opposite shore, water dripping from his hamatic suit. "Eyes!"

"Moving left," Pigeon said and began tromping through the dark waters as quickly as he could. "He's moving too fast!"

"I told you there was something in there!" Stickboy screamed.

"Yeah, we get it, you were right," Krawdaddy called out as he pulled Doctor Morales away from the water. "Moving north!"

The blue blip on Tavi's HUD had accelerated. He quickly realized that as long as whatever had grabbed Schmoyer remained underwater, they wouldn't be able to rescue the man. Looking back where the trees had created the impromptu dam, he dug into his combat ruck and found two of the small concussive grenades he'd been issued when they first dropped on Aurora.

"Grenade! Grenade! Grenade!" he called out as trained before pulling the pin on both explosive devices and tossing them toward the downed trees blocking the creek. They sank beneath the water quickly, then two seconds later exploded with muffled *whoomps*, geysers fountaining into the air. The dam remained, however. He swore and was prepared to grab another one when a cry of alarm stopped him.

It was Mitzi. Her face was pale and her eyes wide as she stared across the pond at the opposing bank. Tavi turned, followed her gaze, and saw with his own eyes the monster which had taken Schmoyer beneath the waters.

The armadons down on the southern islands had been chubby, lazy, and placid, content to eat fruit and fish in the waves along the coast. This brutish and muscled reptilian looked like an entirely different species as it opened its mouth to adjust its grip on something—an arm, Tavi realized.

The rest of the doctor was nowhere to be seen.

This armadon wasn't just ugly, aggressive, and *mean*. Its crest was larger, more pronounced than the ones they'd seen previously lounging on the beaches, and its coloring was darker, almost black in many places. This feature allowed it to blend in perfectly with the black ash and dark waters around them. Intelligent eyes seemed to size up the legionnaires before it dropped Schmoyer's arm.

Tavi raised his rifle and squeezed off three shots. One struck the armored shoulder of the armadon, while the other two kicked up the dirt just beneath its belly. It hissed at him, almost mockingly, then slithered into the underbrush and disappeared, leaving the severed arm behind. Where the rest of the Expeditor's remains lay, Tavi could only guess.

"*Pokerro!*" Jabber screamed in frustration. "Did you see that thing move, *ke?*"

"Who cares how it moved! Did you see how it *looked* at us?" Mitzi shouted, her eyes locked on the dismembered arm of Doctor Schmoyer. "It was smart, not just animal cunning! There was intelligence in those eyes! Too much intelligence!"

Tavi scanned the water but there was no other sign of the Expeditor or the armadon. He let out a slow breath and eyed the pond suspiciously. "There could be more than one armadon in that pond."

"Map says this was a small stream not too long ago, easily passable," Pigeon pointed out. His voice was shrill as he scanned the dark waters. "Where'd the pond come from?"

"Then the map's outdated," Ordo calmly stated. "We already knew that was possible... hell, probable. Shit. All teams, head count. Check in with your buddies. Two, check your civvies. And get the *fuck* away from the water."

But the waters remained still. After ten painfully long minutes it became abundantly clear there was nothing left in the dirty pond. Ordo, along with Team Three, began strategically tossing grenades into the far end of the pond, where the trees were blocking the creek's runoff point. It took five explosions before the downed trees shook. Satisfied, Ordo ordered everyone else who hadn't thrown one yet to aim for a certain spot.

Tavi, already down two grenades, simply watched as more grenades were tossed. As expected, within five seconds another series of muffled *thumps* rippled across the pond. The branches and downed trees which formed the dam were broken by the concussive blasts underwater, and a small whirlpool formed. It quickly grew to five feet across in moments. Ten guns were aimed at the pond as the impromptu dam was ruptured by the grenades. Nothing moved beneath the surface, or even appeared. There were no other signs of armadons as the water levels dropped. The makeshift pond drained swiftly but, in the end, they never found the remainder of Dr. Charles William Joseph Schmoyer IV's corpse.

Later that night, Tavi pulled himself awake and reported for watch as the rest of 4th Squad tried to get some rest. Opposite him on duty was Specialist Oscar "Banger" Kolbinger from Team Three, someone Tavi really hadn't associated with too much since joining the Bronze Legion. Banger wasn't the talkative sort, so Tavi had time in the pitch black of night to think.

Doctor Schmoyer's death had hit Mitzi harder than Tavi thought it would have, and the xenobiologist had retreated back into an emotional shell, all the confidence she'd built up completely shattered. Doctors Xi-Smith and Morales were silent but Doctor Childs had started talking to himself in low, confused tones. Vixen, concerned for the man who was supposed to be in his care, had tried talking to the meteorologist, to no avail.

With the armadons now a confirmed threat, Ordo had decided they needed some sort of early warning system. No electronic sensors of any kind had come along with them. Everything of that sort was back at their original coastal base camp on the obsidian shore, and now drowned beneath the ashy waters.

But legionnaires are an ingenious bunch, and soon enough Mitzi's rope encircled their position with metal spikes attached in a way to make them hit one another should anything hit the rope. With a bit of testing Tavi figured a way to make the spikes hit one another louder, and suddenly they had a tripwire alarm.

"Captain Truitt would be so proud of you," Ordo had said before crashing out for the night.

That had been four hours ago. Tavi had napped, checked on Mitzi quickly, then reported for watch duty.

"Quiet night so far," Private Alec "Loosey" Luta from Fire Team One informed him in a quiet voice. It was clear to Tavi that the private, barely older than he, was exhausted. "That crazy doc is muttering still. Not sleeping. Just going on and on about electromagnetic storm clouds interfering with telepathy or something. Weird shit, man."

"Okay, you're relieved. Get some rest," Tavi said and Loosey nodded gratefully. Tavi waited for him to go lie down on the soggy ground near one of the larger trees before he made his first rounds.

The campsite, while not quite silent, was still for the moment. Tavi did a quick headcount of all those sleeping, himself and Banger, and came up with eighteen. He blinked and counted a second time, and again he reached eighteen. There should have been nineteen. He reached for his comms to sound the alert, then paused.

"Banger," Tavi quietly murmured. "I'm short a body. Anybody get up to go to the head?"

"Naw, I didn't... wait. I saw one of the civilians get up a few minutes ago. He's probably out pissing or something," Banger responded before yawning. "This shit is killing me."

"Which civilian was it?" Tavi asked.

"I don't know. One of the dudes?"

Tavi inwardly sighed. Team One hadn't worked with the civilians much, and it showed. Turning, he let his HUD find the missing scientist. It didn't take long for the suit to find the man's biometrics. The problem was the man was outside the tripwire.

"You're not supposed to be outside the line," he muttered. Not wanting to wake everyone up by yelling at the doctor, he quietly headed toward the man, careful to step over the makeshift tripwire along the way. It didn't take him long to catch up to the doctor. He gently laid a hand on the bigger man's shoulder, recognizing Doctor Childs from his height and build. There was almost no response or movement, save for the man scratching his arm. Tavi gave him a shake. "Sir? Doctor Childs?"

"...eyes burning bright, so bright, should never have come here..." the doctor whispered, his voice haunted as he stared into the dark jungle.

"Sir? You're outside the line," Tavi said, moving around. The man's face was haggard and drawn, a far cry from how he'd been a mere two days before. "If you're done relieving yourself, we should get back inside."

"...so bright, like candles, flickering flames dancing in the depths of the dark, promising death..."

"Sir? Are you okay?"

"Don't you *see* them?" Doctor Childs looked down at Tavi for the first time. He continued to scratch his arm nervously. "The flames in the dark? They're everywhere. Watching. Waiting. They *hunger*. More intelligent than we ever gave them credit for. Will o' wisps of the darkness, luring, calling. The hunger is too much..."

"I don't understand..." Tavi said, though deep down he thought he did. This worried him more than ignorance. If the man had gone insane, it would make getting him safely back to the research station difficult at best, impossible at the worst.

"One thousand eyes in the jungle, burning bright, filled with hatred and malice...they hate us, they want us gone, just like the others..."

Turning his head, Tavi looked out into the darkness, trying to see through the tangled undergrowth. At first there was nothing to see. The night was black and, with the constant ash cloud overhead, there was absolutely zero moonlight. For a brief instant, Tavi wondered if the man really had gone insane. There was no possible way he could see anything out there without assistance. Confused, he switched through his filters on his helmet, trying the different views to see what, if anything, the poor, confused doctor was looking at.

Exasperated, he killed all the enhanced lighting the helmet provided and waited as his eyes slowly adjusted to the absolute blackness of the jungle around them. Still nothing. Sighing, he pulled the doctor on the arm to guide the deluded man back to the safety inside the tripwire.

He started to turn away, but a brief flicker caught his eye. Turning, he saw something green in the forest, low to the ground. It was dull and faint, but there. Tavi blinked. Not one, but two identical glowing objects. Then four.

Six.

Twelve.

Dozens.

"Oh, that's not good," Tavi hissed and unslung his rifle and flicked on the light. He kept his voice as calm as he could while easing toward the campsite, his free hand gripping the back of Doctor Childs' shirt. The light swung back and forth, revealing glimpses of armadons in shadow. "Sound general alert. All teams, all teams. Alert ready one. Repeat, alert ready one."

Doctor Childs desperately scratched his arm as if he were trying to remove his skin. Whatever was going on with the scientist, it was obvious words weren't going to sway him. Before Tavi could force him to retreat to the safety of the camp, a pair of armadons charged. He shoved the doctor behind him and opened fire—but the 1mm hypervelocity rounds bounced off the upper back and spine of the lead armadon.

More rounds bounced off the armadons as the ammo counter ticked down. One of them gave a painful high-pitched scream as a round struck true. The smaller armadon flipped over onto its back and began frantically digging at where the round struck it. With the lighter-colored belly exposed, he pumped six straight shots into the vulnerable spot. The armadon mewled, then ceased struggling.

Unfortunately for him, this seemed to draw the attention of the remainder of the large, aggressive pack. The big brute from earlier, easily recognized compared to the smaller ones, ghosted out of the underbrush and feinted. While he was distracted by the *very large threat*, two more slipped out of the darkness and attacked. Tavi got lucky and put a round directly through the eye of the first one dropping it instantly, and the second backed off. The larger one roared and the others responded in kind as a dozen sets of eyes turned as a single entity to stare at Tavi.

"Fuck my life," he breathed. Those eyes watching them reminded him eerily of street thugs on the streets of Overdark, and the big one was a gang leader.

"The fuck did you do, Tavi?" Pigeon's voice echoed in his ear. "Looks like you pissed off a gaggle of monsters."

"It's not my fault!" He squeezed off another two shots as Banger grabbed the doc and hauled him back to the campsite. Tavi quickly ejected the spent magazine. It took him a moment of numb fingers digging into his hip pouch before he found a fresh one. He pulled the magazine out and reloaded quickly. "Stupid doctor decided to go for a midnight hike!"

"That's going to make for one excellent AAR read later," Ordo said in a calm tone as he and the rest of Team Three formed a firing line to Tavi's right. "All right, boys. Pick a target. Light 'em up."

Five CCR-95's opened up, sending the armadons scattering to avoid the gunfire. But the aggressive aliens quickly recovered when the gunfire proved ineffective.

"I thought they said these would penetrate," Vixen snarled.

"So to speak," Jabber coughed.

"Well, somebody didn't know what the hell they were talking about," Pigeon said calmly.

Every time they had an opening, the reptoids pushed again, acting as a coordinated pack. Only the strict, disciplined shooting of the methodical legionnaires kept the armadons backpedaling.

Between shots, a small part of his mind wondered if Mitzi would classify these as the same species of armadons that they'd seen lounging around on the southern isles, or if she'd proclaim them a subspecies.

He felt Jabber at his side, the lanky Passovan a steady presence as they fought to protect the camp. Steady shots plowed into the thick and scaly chests of the armadons. A formidable protective circle formed around surviving members of the Survey Corps team, with more concentrated fire from all the legionnaires pushing the armadons back from the campsite. While most of the gunfire was not fatal, they wounded enough of the aggressive reptilian aliens to force them to retreat into the darkened jungle once more.

"That was not how I wanted to end my night, *tasawa*," Jabber murmured as he slapped in a fresh magazine. "Those little *angstas* look ready to eat us all, *ke*?"

"I don't think that was the end of the night," Tavi replied. He frowned and considered just how aggressive the armadons had become once they'd been spotted. It was something he wanted to ask Mitzi about. "I think it's more of a beginning."

"Beginning...?" Vixen asked. There was an edge to his voice, one tinged with worry. "You think they'll be back."

Mitzi, meanwhile, was working on Doctor Childs with the other doctors. Tavi approached slowly, wondering how to ask her about the armadons and the one he'd tagged as their leader. He watched as Mitzi sat the confused doctor down and began to thoroughly inspect him. He was still desperately scratching his arm. Mitzi frowned and rolled up his sleeve.

A large black spot had formed just below his wrist. With practiced precision, Mitzi pulled out her pen knife and began to scrape the material off. It looked exactly like the fungus she'd removed from the small lizard on their first drop. Doctor Childs immediately calmed down, and she began to apply some sort of ointment from her bag to the affected area.

"Antifungal," she explained without looking up.

"What does that mean?"

"It means we have bigger problems than just angry armadons," Doctor Xi-Smith replied softly, a trace of fear in her shaky voice.

"It means all scientists need to inspect themselves for any sign of the black fungus daily," Ordo said, appearing out of nowhere. "Check each other as well."

"But—" Morales began to protest but Ordo cut him off.

"Two men, two women. I'm sure you can do the math, weather man."

CHAPTER NINETEEN
Just a Quiet Stroll Through an Armadon-Infested Jungle World

SOMEWHERE WEST OF AURORA RESEARCH OUTPOST, AURORA

For three straight days Tavi and the rest of 4th Squad, along with their surviving scientists, dredged through the cold, ash-covered muck on a world doing its absolute best to kill them all.

Sometimes the obsidian-colored mud swallowed them up to their ankles. Other times, it came all the way up to their knees. Ash always fell from the sky, and nobody had seen the sun since the volcano had erupted. The darkness, the mud, and the ash were ceaseless. A weariness which went beyond bone deep, almost an affliction of the soul, cast a pall over them.

Everyone except the scientists, that is.

During this time, Tavi also discovered that as much as legionnaires like to complain, it was nothing when compared to a scientific debate amongst academics. While he only caught bits and pieces of the scientific jargon they were tossing about, he found himself inadvertently agreeing with Mitzi all the time.

"No! Sentience is simply being able to taste, feel, smell, sense, and react to it accordingly," Mitzi argued hotly as Childs opened his mouth once more. He'd been slowly returning to normal after she had liberally doused his arm with antifungal cream, which unfortunately also meant he returned to his contradictory "normal" self. "By your own definition, Doctor Childs, you're suggesting that bacteria is a higher life form. No, these armadons are showing clear signs of *sapience*. They know where we're going, lie in wait to ambush, but back away if they recognize that we've spotted them. That is the ability to reason, to come to a conclusion, and take further actions."

"But—"

"No, the young doctor is right," Xi-Smith added. "If these creatures were merely sentient, I wouldn't be afraid."

"Hogwash," Morales stated. "If I poke a butterfly with a needle and it flies away, does that make it sapient? A butterfly, stabbed. Reacts. Behold, intelligence!"

"Your argument has no basis in scientific theory! You're just relying on a philosophical straw man to be the backbone of your argument!" Mitzi snapped.

The arguments between the four scientists were endless, but it kept them from complaining about the ceaseless muck they were trudging through.

It would have to end, he knew. The map, though not without fault, was guiding them to the Aurora Research Outpost. They were making slow but steady progress every day, taking brief rest stops lasting only thirty minutes at most. Every single one of them was sore, exhausted.

The armadons never let up their relentless pursuit. Mitzi repeated numerous times to Tavi they were like humans, persistent predators... which set everyone on edge. Every time Ordo would call a halt and allow the scientists to rest, within an hour they would hear the snarls and hisses of the armadons as they closed in. Some of the legionnaires—Vixen in particular—wanted to stand and fight, but Tavi understood why Ordo didn't want to. They were only fifteen, and with the scientists under their protection, it would mean almost certain death if they tried to take down the fast moving, aggressive armadons in the open like this. Not to mention that, to Tavi, the armadons almost seemed to *want* them to stand and fight.

No, Tavi agreed with Ordo's assessment that their best chance would be to get to the outpost, where the rest of the automated turrets and more assistance from the guards at the station would help fight off the growing horde of armadons. Then, once the volcano quit blowing its top, they could extract everyone to safety above and take stock of their situation. So long as the armadons didn't push through the walls of the outpost.

The pack of armadons was growing by the hour. There'd been dozens before. Now, it looked like their numbers were well into the hundreds. Every time he looked, there were more eyes staring at the group, fangs glinting in the dim light, dark shadows moving in the underbrush behind and around the legionnaires.

This is not going to end well for any of us, Tavi thought as he rotated toward the front of the patrol, leaving Mitzi under the watchful eyes of Pigeon. Krawdaddy and Vixen, meanwhile, protected their charges.

"Tavi, Ordo. You're on point, kid. *Be advised we should be seeing the relay tower from the outpost soon,*" Ordo's voice came over the comms, clear and steady. Four days of trudging through the jungle while fighting off random armadon attacks didn't seem to be affecting the sergeant at all. In fact, Tavi was beginning to wonder if the man even slept. "*Keep a look out, and try not to get eaten. We still don't have a drop name for you yet. You know the rules. Not allowed to get eaten by massive alien creatures before you get your drop name.*"

"Tavi copies. No getting eaten." Tavi shook his head and smiled.

Leave it to the sergeant to remind him that he hadn't earned his drop name yet.

Blue had lost enough people in her life to know grief was never consistent.

That would be too easy.

It could be suffocating one moment, razor sharp the next, with periods of dull exhaustion and bright levity and no way to predict which particular flavor would roll through next. Blue had experienced them all when her grandmother had passed, and she'd gone through the emotional roller coaster again after Campbell delivered the news of 4th Squad's loss.

After Captain Esper had issued a stand-down order to the Bronze Ravens, Blue and Killi had isolated themselves in their quarters that first day. Officially off-duty for the foreseeable future and free to let grief run its course. Eventually, they emerged from that safe cocoon and ventured into the Ravens' common area. Better to be around the others and give those moments of levity a chance to spread, to lighten the heavy pall of grief that hung over them all.

The small common area was at the heart of Raven country and central to their living quarters. The stark gray room had been softened with a motley assortment of couches and armchairs and was where they hung out when the Squadron Heritage Room—AKA their legally sanctioned bar—was closed. Blue loved both, but if the common area was the heart of the Ravens, the Heritage Room was their memory.

"I never want to leave this couch again," Killi mumbled as she dramatically let herself sink deeper into the thick, faded purple cushions. "It's mine now, I've claimed it."

"Please tell me you didn't lick it," Blue said dryly, wrinkling her nose and purposefully shifting her legs a little further from her best friend.

"That only happened once, and it wasn't a *couch* I licked."

"No, it was a Bronze Eagle pilot."

Lieutenant Tina "Tiny" Tragarz looked up from her slate. The tiny blonde was curled up in the corner of the couch opposite theirs and hadn't spoken much the last few days, preferring to lose herself in a book, but she smiled at them now.

"I've never seen a man more startled in my life," she said with a quiet chuckle.

"It worked, didn't it?" Killi purred, smug satisfaction curling her lips. She rolled her eyes at a scandalized glance from one of their baby copilots. "Get your mind out of the gutter, girl. I licked his *arm*. Besides, Tarian wasn't walking around Yortugan Bay shirtless on *accident*. That man has abs for days and gives Ensign Hotness a run for his—"

A fist banged on the open hatch.

"Ravens!"

Blue snapped her head up as their XO leaned inside. Ditch swept a sharp gaze around the room, her golden-brown hair neatly braided, black uniform pristine, and eyes red rimmed. The murmur of conversation cut out, the brief bubble of levity popped by harsh reality. Half a dozen or so pilots looked to their XO and waited.

"Roll Call in ten mikes," Ditch announced in the heavy silence. She smiled. "Don't be late."

Blue jerked her chin up in acknowledgment and bid farewell to the comfortable couch. She stood and took the time for a full, arms-over-her-head stretch, feeling her vertebrae snap back into alignment with a handful of *pops*.

Piloting a Rhino was hell on spines.

She turned to follow everyone else out but stopped when Killi didn't get up.

"I'm not..." Killi huffed an irritated sigh and tucked a wild black curl behind her ear. "I'm not ready."

"It's been four days," Blue said gently and held out her hand. "It's time to drink to our fallen and tell ridiculous, mostly true stories about them."

Green eyes glared up at her before they softened. Killi sighed again, but she slapped her palm into Blue's and allowed herself to be dragged to her feet.

"Fine, but maybe we just stay for the mandatory part and leave the fun to the others?" A slight smile pulled at her lips. "I hear the chow hall has tacos on the menu again."

"Tacos, huh?" Blue bumped Killi as they headed for the Squadron Heritage Room. "Is Campbell allowed to have any?"

"I said catch, didn't I?" Mischief slowly kindled in those green eyes. "Better hurry before someone else decides to claim him."

"If you lick him, I will slap you."

"You could try."

Belting out a laugh, Blue let the bubble of levity carry her above the heavy grief and slung an arm over her best friend's shoulders. "Do you think we should tell the story of how Ruby's first alert mission went?"

Killi grinned, the first real one Blue had seen on her face in days. "Nah. I'm thinking of her first time at Yortugan Bay."

"Oooh, spill."

"So there I was..."

As soon as he'd replaced Corporal Tom "Ratman" Coonradt on point, his entire mentality shifted. Before, he'd been aware as the others, waiting for the armadons to burst from the undergrowth of the jungle and attack. On point, things were different. Adrenaline pumped through his veins as his eyes watched every suspicious movement in the brush, his ears hearing the skittering movement of the unseen armadons in the dark. He couldn't see them, but knew they were close by.

Persistent predators, Mitzi had told him. *Just like us.*

The jungle began to thin as he moved along the path, then abruptly he was standing in a large clearing. Ahead, the immense relay tower of Aurora Research Outpost loomed above. The tower was almost six hundred feet tall and was capable of stretching comms signals all the way to the western coast. Tavi wasn't sure how far it reached to the east, but he guessed it was just as effective.

At least we aren't limited by the horizon anymore like back in the old days, he thought, remembering a lecture while at ACS on the limitations of line-of-sight comms. It'd been brief, only an hour in between trips to the range, but it'd stuck with him.

There was a gate around the comms tower which appeared undisturbed. Glancing up, he noticed the warning light at the top was not blinking.

"Ordo, got eyes on the communications relay tower," Tavi subvocalized, his eyes immediately darting around the open clearing. He was pretty sure he'd been there before, but not entirely. They'd done some preliminary recon work just outside the walls of the outpost during their first few days on planet, back before the eruption and the ashfall. Part of him was fairly certain this was where they had almost set up a firing range before their request had been shot down by Norwood. "Looks like it's up, but the warning light isn't working."

"*Ordo copies. I've got you at Clearing Sierra Two. Confirm location, over.*"

"Confirmed?" Tavi looked around, then compared it to his HUD. "HUD confirms. Visual confirmation... unsure."

"*Copy that. Tavi, get to the outpost and find out why the hell they shut down comms,*" the sergeant ordered him. "*Try not to shoot anyone, but if they resist, shoot them.*"

"Copy all." Tavi glanced around but the armadons were nowhere to be found. They were no longer skittering around in the jungle, either. It was unsettling. "Moving now."

The ground here was covered by two inches of ash, but wonder of all wonders, it was dry. Instead of a slog through the muck they'd been suffering through the past few days, he was on dry land. It almost caused him to rush forward, hurry to the base. It took a lot of willpower, but he kept his approach slow and measured as an old mantra from ACS ran through his mind: those who rush forward unprepared die first.

The tower loomed ominously overhead. For the life of him he couldn't figure out why he wasn't receiving *anything* from the tower. If it were on standby mode, it should have still been transmitting, even if it was nothing but white noise. If it had shorted out or faulted, it would have been transmitting an SOS code. There was no reason outside of deliberate sabotage that it wouldn't be transmitting.

Unless the base itself was attacked, Tavi rationalized as he passed the base of the tower and continued toward the outpost. With the thinning of the jungle closer to the station, the ash was thicker on the ground. Which made a certain amount of sense the more he thought about it. Keeping his eyes tracking left to right, he pushed onward. The station, according to his map overlay as well as his memory, was only half a mile away, though he was still unable to see any sign of the defensive wall.

"Oh, that's why," he murmured five minutes later as he finally laid eyes on the outer defensive wall—or what remained of it.

It was no longer as impressive as it'd once been, mostly in part due to the simple fact that a massive Rhino dropship had crash-landed into it. The nose of the Rhino was pointed toward the interior landing pad. The wings were a crumpled mess, with one of the VTOL engines twisted and the other completely gone. The ramp appeared jammed shut.

"That's going nowhere," he muttered as he checked the tail markings on the bird. He recognized them immediately. "Ordo, this is Tavi. I'm at the outpost. Uh...someone crashed into the wall. More specifically, Bronze Raven Five."

"*Repeat your last, Tavi. Did you say Bronze Raven Five crashed into the wall?*"

"Confirm Bronze Raven Five crashed into the wall," Tavi repeated as he moved around the wreckage. There didn't appear to be any sign of casualties, which made him sigh in relief.

"Looks like they all got out and sealed it up after."

"*Hold position. Do not enter the base alone, Tavi. Confirm last.*"

"Holding position, confirmed."

"*Ordo, out.*"

It took another thirty minutes for the rest of 4th Squad and their civilians to make it to the breach in the wall. All seemed duly impressed at the partially destroyed Rhino. When Ordo saw it, he whistled softly.

"Witch and Killi got damned lucky on that landing."

Tavi nodded. "Did you notice there weren't any comm signals at all when you passed the tower?"

"Didn't want to point it out, but yeah, I noticed," Ordo murmured as he eyeballed Claw and Pigeon. "Too smart for a private sometimes, Tavi. Team One, form a perimeter here. Nothing gets in past this Rhino. Three, on Banger. Get in there and look around. Check the guard station at Gate Four first, since that's closest, then report in. Two, stick with your civvies but get inside that wall. Tavi, get in that Rhino and see if you can dig out the miniguns."

"Got it," Tavi said and peeked into the right door gunner's hatch—*the starboard side*, he quickly corrected as he recalled Mitzi's lessons from their first day aboard the *Perseverance*. The gap between the ruined airframe of the Rhino and the self-sealing door of the gunner's position was small, but big enough for him to squeeze inside.

Do the Ravens call it port and starboard? he wondered as he pushed against the metal frame. The gap was barely wide enough for him to fit. Perhaps he'd gained some weight after all? Once inside, he was able to scour it a little more thoroughly. Whoever had landed the bird had managed to do so without any visible injuries. Sure, there'd probably been some bumps and bruises along the way, but nobody had died messily during the crash. His mind drifted back to the different pilots as he wondered who'd been flying the Rhino before he shook the thought away. He had a job to do.

Unfortunately, he quickly learned the job was next to impossible without heavy machinery. The so-called quick-release switch had been crushed on impact, and with the mechanism jammed, there appeared to be no easy way to get the ammunition out of the storage in the belly of the Rhino. Moving to the other side of the bird, it was the same thing. Bronze Raven Five's point of impact on the wall had perfectly severed the mechanisms controlling the gun doors and everything behind them.

Cursing under his breath, Tavi went back to the rear loading bay. The hatch was shut, but the force of the impact had jarred the ramp off kilter. A small gap was evident between the fuselage and the ramp, which was currently filled with Claw's face.

"Find anything good in there, Tavi?" the Team One leader asked.

"Just a bunch of broken stuff, Claw," he replied, looking around. "Thought I could strip out the gun mounts but the mechanism is broken for both of them."

"I could have told you that," the 4th Squad's armorer said.

"Underbelly's crushed. No way to procure ammo. Did you check the comms in the cockpit?"

"No," Tavi admitted, feeling sheepish. He returned to the front of the Rhino and crawled into the cockpit. His eyes scanned the console and he frowned. "You know what the comms buttons look like in this thing?"

"Hells no."

"Me neither."

"Well, that pretty much sums up my week right there. You see anything blinking?"

Tavi searched the console, but everything appeared to be dead. "No, nothing."

"Battery's shot," Claw decided. He didn't sound convincing to Tavi's ears, but he suspected the explanation was far more involved than they had time for.

"Come on out, Tavi," Ordo said from the other side of the Rhino. "I don't think we're going to get much out of this."

"On it," Tavi said. He made his way back to the gunner's hatch and slipped outside.

"All right, teams, listen up," Ordo's command voice brought everyone to a standstill as Tavi rejoined 4th Squad. "Inside the gate is the guard post. We need to secure that first. There's a keycoded armory inside it. There won't be much, but they might have extra weapons. Everyone still green on ammo?" There were confirmations all around. "Good. Team Two, you secure the guard post with Team One. Three, we're forming a perimeter. Let's roll."

Breaching the secured front gate was easy when one wasn't worried about the condition of the lock afterwards. Using a crowbar found inside the guard post, Claw and Private Adam "Toejam" Thompkins managed to break the lock without making any noticeable noise. Three quickly spread out to secure their immediate surroundings while One and Two slipped inside the guard post.

Mitzi climbed the stairs to the second floor of the guard post to get a better look at the compound, so Tavi followed her up. There was barely enough room for one person up there. Fortunately, both of them were small enough to fit. Not easily, though. Down below, Tavi heard Sergeant Ord and the rest of Team Three return a few minutes later.

"Well, that's not going to work," Ordo grumbled. "There's no power anywhere."

"The life of the legionnaire, Sergeant," Claw said. "Constant disappointment."

"Amen to that. We need to find a place to hole up, turn on the power, and then get the comms back up," Ordo said. "Claw, you think we can do that?"

"Comms'll be easy enough," the armorer said with a shrug. "Power could be a problem. Someone seems to have shut down the entire backup system. Hopefully by accident, but this is seriously against regs. Even if there's an evac order, emergency backup generators are in place and are supposed to run for six months to a year to provide data to any ship in orbit with the correct access codes. Somebody dropped the ball here."

Tavi, not sure what else to do while the two sergeants plotted and schemed, looked at the interior of the base . . . and blinked.

There were armadons *everywhere* in the northern part of the outpost. Hundreds of them roamed the lower streets, their long claws finding easy purchase on the pavement. They were sniffing the ground and moving along steadily, their thick heads swinging back and forth. Tavi wondered at their behavior. It wasn't like they were hunting. He'd become all-too familiar with that over the past three days.

If they were going to have any chance at keeping the scientists alive, Tavi knew they would have to find somewhere secure, a building with thick walls and food and water. The legionnaires as a whole were extremely vulnerable here.

There weren't many options in the compound that he knew of, but he did know one place. The problem was it was all the way across the outpost. With as many armadons as there were, it would be a fighting battle through the narrow streets the entire way. But it was better than staying in a guard post with flimsy walls and absolutely no way for all of 4th Squad to fit. Tavi took a deep breath and chimed in.

"Sergeant Ord? We got armadons inside the walls, but in the north. I might have a terrible idea about where to hole up . . ."

"I'm all ears," Ordo said. Tavi moved back to the lower level and rejoined the squad. Tavi told him his idea, slowly at first and hesitating at some points, but with growing confidence as the sergeant didn't immediately shoot the idea down. By the end of his pitch, Ordo was nodding along and smiling. "I like it. Only problem I see is getting there."

"Yeah, haven't come up with an idea how to do that," Tavi admitted. A small bubble of frustration sat in his gut. "Outside of just blowing everything up, I mean. And I can't do that."

"Blowing stuff up?" Jabber nudged Tavi's elbow and grinned. "*Tasawa*, we're legionnaires. We *live* to blow shit up."

"Well, hold on a sec." Krawdaddy held up a hand as Mitzi joined them. "Why can't we?"

"Why can't we what? Blow stuff up?" Vixen shook his head. "Because...uh..."

"The argument isn't whether or not we can blow stuff up, but what we blow up, and how," Pigeon interrupted before Jabber could gain a head of steam. He looked at Tavi. "What would you blow up, and why?"

"Well...there's only two ways to get to the building from here," Tavi said, staring at the map of the outpost on his HUD. His eyes flickered back and forth as he scanned to make sure he was seeing everything before continuing. "We blow things up over in the Blue District, the east area, and move to the location when the armadons are rushing over to check it out."

"I like it!" Vixen exclaimed.

"Think they'll take the bait?" Claw asked.

"They like to chase things, *keiche?* I think they'll chase this," Jabber decided.

"Only one problem—no explosives," Ordo reminded them. "Without power, we don't have access to the outpost armory. Our grenades are anti-personnel and don't pack enough of a punch. Even if we bundle them all together and activate them at once, it won't do much to a building. Much less get the attention of the armadons."

Everyone was silent for a moment, thinking, before Tavi spoke up in a timid voice.

"What about a biofuel reserve tank? Like the one Supervisor Norwood has at his storage facility for his personal vehicles?"

"Why me again?" Tavi asked in a whisper as he and Private Josh "Crusty" Kruschke from Team One methodically made their way through the narrow alley between Norwood's private residence and vehicular garage, doing their best to not draw the attention of the armadons. Both of them had rolled around in ash to coat their hamatic suits for extra camouflage before they'd set off, but Tavi privately wondered if it would actually work. He suspected the guys really just wanted to see if the two lowest-ranking privates were gullible enough to make ash angels on the ground, and wondered if bets had been made.

"Your idea, genius. Just don't know why I have to go, too," Crusty muttered as they pressed themselves against the wall as another small pack of armadons wandered by. Fortunately for them they passed by, unaware that a fresh meal was less than fifty feet away. "Fuck my life. I didn't sign up for this."

"Yeah, you kinda did," Tavi reminded him. "Remember? You took the Oath..."

"Nobody likes a smartass, Tavi."

"Plus, you know how to disable the safeties..."

"Yeah, yeah. I know. Sheesh. Shut up already."

It had taken them almost twenty minutes to get this far. The armadon packs wandering the outpost had been difficult to avoid. Both men were on the slighter side, however, which made it easier. Not too much so, but just enough for them to avoid drawing the unwanted attention of the armadons. Tavi noticed Crusty was almost as adept at moving through the shadows as he was. Almost.

"Just reminding you."

"Why is this fuel depot marked on the map, anyway?" Crusty asked as they slipped around a corner and found the back door to the parking garage of one Sir Percival Norwood III. The door was appallingly unlocked, which hurt his meticulous legionnaire soul, but Tavi whispered a belated "thanks" to the departed supervisor as he slipped inside. Crusty followed right behind him.

"Required by law to mark any flammable containers and their locations for anything larger than an initial settlement on a proposed colony world," Tavi recited from memory. "It also allows for fire crews to know potential locations where a fire might break out so first responders can get there quicker."

"How do you know all this shit?"

"Doctor Wingo told me once."

"Doctor... oh! Mitzi, the cute one. Yeah, she seems to know her shit," Crusty said quietly as he looked around the garage. He whistled, impressed by the collection. "Damn. It's good to be a planetary supervisor. You into vehicles, Tavi? Naw, probably not. I hear bad things about Myrkyma. My old man was into classics and restoring them, though. Damn, he'd have thought this was nirvana if he were here. That one right there? The orange one with black trim? That's a '32 Mars Special Edition Ranger right there. Over there you got a Borelli Nighthawk, classically restored '57 with the radial-electromagnetic engine. The two-wheeled one. It's called a motorcycle. Only two hundred were ever made. Bet that cost a pretty dinar. Oh, damn. No way... is that a '55 Phevelle? It is! It's even got the combustion engine intact! Holy shit. Man, I would give my right nut for one of those. Probably an arm, too."

Vehicles like this were nonexistent in the Overdark, but Tavi had seen some Martian vehicles while at Basic and ACS. They'd looked strange to him at first, with their sweeping lines and design which seemed to favor beauty over functionality, though he didn't truly understand the desire to have so many. If he ever needed a vehicle, he surmised one should be capable of doing everything he needed. A utilitarian vehicle for utility work.

Still, Tavi could appreciate the appearance of them. A shame he was about to blow them all up.

"There's the fuel tank," Tavi said, nudging Crusty and getting his focus back onto the mission at hand. "Bag."

"Hope the doc isn't gonna be mad we're ruining her satchel," Crusty said as he passed over Mitzi's bag. Inside was every last grenade 4th Squad had available. "I kinda want to ask her out when we get back to Mars Primus. Just for dinner, not anything serious. She seems way too wrapped up in work for anything else."

Tavi looked at Crusty oddly. "You mean, like a date?"

"Yeah, like a date, Tavi. What did you think I meant?"

"I don't know," Tavi admitted after a moment. "I don't understand some things."

"Like dating?"

"People."

"Oh." Crusty nodded. "Yeah, I get that. But yeah, a date. C'mon, let's hurry this shit up and get back to the squad."

"That pump looks motorized. Does that mean it needs electricity to do that we want?" Tavi asked, frowning.

"Nope. Look," the other legionnaire pointed at a small handle on the side. "This man spared no expense. That's a lever pump. Give it a few pumps and the fuel will flow. Damn, is that biofuel avtur? Even better. This is all gonna burn *nice*."

"Just need to draw the armadons over this way," Tavi reminded him. He was already beginning to regret this idiotic idea, and wished he'd thought things over more thoroughly before opening his mouth. "Timers are all set on the grenades. Ready to pump?"

"Yeah," Crusty said with a sigh. He looked fondly at the vehicle collection. "Damn shame. I almost feel guilty about this. My pops would be *pissed*."

"Norwood insulted Captain Truitt during the dinner party I was at. The Legion, too. He's a *balara*."

"Man, you've been hanging around Jabber too much. But yeah, fuck that Norwood asshole. Let's blow all his shit up."

Working quickly, Crusty removed all the primary safeties of the pump which were in place to ensure what they were about to do didn't happen by accident. Tavi, meanwhile, set up the grenades near the pump which fed the smaller tank from the larger underground fuel reservoir. If all went according to plan, they would blow a massive hole in this section of the outpost without damaging the surrounding buildings. If the armadons were truly sapient like Mitzi suggested, then the explosion would definitely cause the reptoid aliens to come and investigate, or flee. Either outcome was desirable.

"Can you believe back in the day they used to only have fused timers?" Tavi asked as he set the satchel bag of grenades next to the pump. Crusty stopped and looked at him oddly.

"That sounds dangerous as fuck," Crusty acknowledged as he finished and wiped grease from his gloves. "We'll remote start the timers once we're back at the door. You got it ready?"

"Ready and waiting," Tavi confirmed. A faint noise rustled behind them. He paused and tilted his head. "Did you close the door?"

Both men froze as a low rumble noise could be heard from the back entrance of the garage. The rumble turned into a growl, one which was all too familiar to them. Turning his head slowly, Tavi saw the telltale, low-slung form of an armadon sniffing around near the open door. It hadn't come in quite yet, but it was clearly interested in the garage.

"Aw, shit," Crusty muttered.

"Stay still," Tavi replied back softly.

"We gotta blow these grenades soon," Crusty reminded him. The armadon hissed and let out a loud sniff.

"We shoot at it, we might draw more of them. See anything sharp around here, like a knife?"

"On the workbench. Looks like a flathead screwdriver. You're closer."

"I see it," Tavi said as the armadon pushed the door wider and slipped inside. The elongated head swung back and forth as it walked across the tiled flooring, claws clicking ominously with every step. The tongue flickered in and out as it tasted the air, and the eyes glowed in the filtered view on Tavi's HUD. It moved behind one of the smaller classic vehicles and was out of sight.

Tavi ghosted across the open space, his eyes tracking the direction the armadon had disappeared to as he moved. Within seconds he was at the workbench. He quietly picked up the flathead screwdriver and checked the edge. It wasn't sharp by any measure, but the tip appeared just pointy enough to suit his needs.

From the opposite side of the garage the armadon hissed, and the clicking of its claws increased in pace and noise as it rushed around the corner, searching. Tavi froze as the armadon's gaze fell on him briefly. The creature's tongue flickered in and out and the head swung side to side.

"Tavi," Crusty warned. The armadon had frozen in place and was staring directly at him. Tavi swallowed as the armadon began to move toward Kruschke with deadly purpose.

There wasn't a lot of time. The decision needed to be made, but it wasn't a difficult one. He would need to keep the other legionnaire alive any way he could—even if it meant his own death. Crusty was only on this shit detail because of Tavi's bright idea.

"Hey!" Tavi shouted and waved his arms. The armadon skidded on the tiled floor for an instant, the bright luminescent eyes turning his way. He could almost see the thought process in the monster's little reptilian brain. "Come get me! Hey, ugly! Fresh meat! Come on!"

The head of the armadon snapped around. The eyes locked onto Tavi. Its maw opened wide and the creature let out a thunderous roar—one that was echoed by another outside the garage. And another.

And more beyond.

"Oh, shit," Crusty said, no longer worried about being quiet. He quickly moved on to dismantling the secondary set of safeties of the fuel pump. "Tavi! I need more time!"

The rifle was up and aimed before his consciousness caught up with muscle memory, screwdriver nearly forgotten in the moment until it brushed the trigger guard. Afraid of hitting Crusty, he let the weapon fall against his chest and flipped the screwdriver to his dominant hand. Not sure what else to do, he whipped the screwdriver at the armadon, hoping at best to distract it and force it to come after him.

Luck was more than on his side. Instead of bouncing off the armored skull of the armadon, the flat end of the screwdriver nicked the very edge of the luminescent right eye of the alien creature. It howled in rage and pain, and ran into one of the vehicles headfirst, denting the fender and then leaving a long, deep gouge in the paint.

Shocked by the result, it took Tavi a few moments to realize precisely what had happened. Fortunately for him, Crusty finished disabling the safety valves and set the satchel bag filled with grenades at the base of the pump. He began priming the pump with the lever, then abruptly stopped the biofuel midway. Outside, armadons began howling louder. They were drawing closer now.

"Got it!" he cried out triumphantly. He quickly moved over to Tavi. "Got a fifty-fifty mix of air and avtur in the line. This fucker'll blow as soon as the grenades go. Like a fuel-air explosive, but now bioengineered to be clean and energy efficient! Kill the damned thing, set the timer for one minute and let's scoot."

Tavi brought the CCR-95 up. Taking aim, he squeezed off five rounds, aiming low to avoid the thick armored shoulders of the wounded armadon. Three struck the chest, but two missed low and ricocheted off the tiled surface and plowed into the cherry red vehicle Crusty had fawned over previously. The armadon roared as more rounds struck, with two punching cleanly into the softened underbelly. The reptoid fell to the floor, screwdriver still sticking out of its eye as it struggled to get back up. Tavi squeezed off two more bursts of five rounds before he was finally satisfied the armadon was truly dying and no longer a threat.

"That hurts my soul so much," Crusty muttered as more bullet holes appeared in the lower part of the '55 Phevelle's body frame. The armadon quit twitching at last. "Ah well. Pop's dead anyways, so only his ghost can be pissed at me. Don't forget to set the timer."

Tavi did and the counter appeared on his HUD. Crusty turned to run toward the back entrance—

—only to run into another armadon which had found its way into the private garage, clearly drawn by the roars and the gunfire. The heavy creature leapt up and ripped long, sharp claws against the hamatic suit's armor before Crusty could even get his arms up to defend himself. Unable to stay upright due to the enormous weight of the alien beast, Crusty fell to the tiled floor, screaming, armadon jaws chewing nosily on his armor, the sharp teeth struggling to rip through.

Tavi hurried to where Crusty and the armadon were on the ground. He tried to pull the armadon off the other legionnaire but the reptoid was having none of it. Instead of fighting Tavi off, it latched harder onto Crusty's arm.

"Fuck! Fucking thing is trying to *eat* me!" Crusty screeched.

Tavi tried to grab the armadon's tail but it whipped it across his chest, hurtling him into one of the two wheeled vehicles Norwood kept in his garage. He tumbled over it and landed heavily on the ground. He picked himself up and came back for another go at it.

This time the armadon simply dug in. Over Crusty's panicked cries for help and the constant growling of the armadon, he remained acutely aware of the time on his HUD counting inexorably downwards.

"Shoot it! Shoot it!"

"I can't! Not without hitting you!"

The timer continued to tick down.

"Go! Get the hell out of here, Tavi!" Crusty screamed as a bone *snapped* in his arm. He let out a fresh shriek of pain. "*Go!*"

The timer was at eighteen seconds now. In a moment of near panic, Tavi tried one final time to pry the armadon off Crusty, jamming his thumbs into the beast's eyes. It simply would not let go. The scaled head began shaking Crusty's arm violently and, for a fleeting moment, Tavi wondered if the arm would be severed. At least then he might be able to drag Crusty out while the stupid monster chewed on the arm left behind, distracted.

Twelve seconds. Tavi hesitated for half a second longer before jamming his CCR-95 straight into the eye of the armadon and pulled the trigger.

The results were explosive. The round punched into the brain, through whatever passed for the medulla oblongata of the armadon, and out the spine at the base its neck. The armadon fell heavily on top of Crusty. Another bone snapped as the heavy weight pressed down upon the other legionnaire.

Eight seconds.

Tavi shouldered the armadon off Crusty and hauled him as best he could to his feet. With one arm around Crusty's waist, Tavi began half carrying, half dragging his fellow legionnaire out the partially open door of the garage.

The two of them made it outside and to the middle of the alley when the world exploded around them.

The last thing Tavi thought as his body was ragdolled by the blast was satisfaction that Crusty wasn't going to die alone.

The searing agony coursing through his head, neck, and torso was an unwelcome reminder that somehow he was still alive.

Tavi had woken up in pain many times in the past—life in Overdark was not for the weak—but never had it been this severe before. It felt as if he'd been bounced around inside a funhouse made of concrete and hate, then rolled by some gangers looking for money or scraps. Plus, there was a constant, throbbing pain on his left arm which simply would not go away.

As he slowly regained his bearings, the pain in his arm increased, and he became aware of just *why* his entire upper body hurt. He was partially buried, in tremendous pain, and *something* was gnawing on his unburied arm.

His HUD flickered but remained on. He could actually see out into the ruined street which had once housed the large garage for Norwood. Wiggling slightly, the pressure on his shoulders eased as debris fell away. The weight on the back of his head, while still present, wasn't as much as he'd originally thought. Turning his head, he spotted an armadon busily gnawing on his hamatic armor.

Resisting the urge to jerk his arm out of the creature's maw, he took stock of his situation. The rubble was heavy, but since he was able to breathe, then the concern of being crushed to death in spite of the armor's resistance wasn't really an issue. His right arm was trapped but fortunately enough his carbine was pressed against his elbow, the tactical sling working as intended. His ankle now hurt the most, oddly enough. Other than being chewed on, sore, and with random pain in places that he didn't know *could* hurt, he was in relatively good shape.

The same couldn't be said for Private Kruschke, though.

He wasn't too far away, out in the open but down at an odd angle. There wasn't any sign of movement. Tavi, who hadn't ever seen someone's suit show up as red before on an HUD, stared uncomprehendingly at it until he realized that Crusty was actually dead and not simply unconscious.

The chewing sensation continued unabated. Tavi shifted his trapped arm and some rubble fell away. His gloved fingers brushed the trigger guard of his CCR-95. Carefully turning his head, he saw the armadon either hadn't noticed the shifting rubble or simply did not care.

As smoothly as if he'd done it a million times in the past, Tavi grasped the grip on the gun, brought it up and put four rounds into the gaping mouth of the armadon.

Blood and gore exploded out the back of the alien creature's head and it slumped, twitching once as the nervous system struggled to figure out what had just happened before ceasing all movement. Using every ounce of energy he could muster, Tavi pushed up and managed to escape the pile of rubble.

The pressure on his upper back and neck disappeared the moment he was free. The soreness throughout the rest of his body, however, remained. Nor was the weight on his soul any easier as he looked at the still form of Private Kruschke. Both the HUD and his own eyes said there was nothing he could do.

Looking around, he saw dozens of armadons sniffing around the blazing bonfire, searching for signs of food. There wasn't any sign of the supervisor's garage, though. It took him a few more seconds to gather his bearings. The street was absolutely ruined, with zero chance of him going out the way they had come in. Glancing up, he realized that the ashfall had ceased slightly, seemingly driven away by the expanding heat from the flames of the massive fire. It would return, he knew. The past four days had shown him that the ash would never cease falling, not until they were off this world. Even then, it might never end.

"Ordo, this is Tavi. Objective complete. One casualty."

"*Confirmed.*"

"Do you want me to bring him?"

"A body is a body. We'll come back for the remains when it's safe. Stay alive, kid."

"Copy. En route to checkpoint now."

With one final look back at Private Kruschke, he quietly set off toward the other side of the outpost, the HUD showing him the way.

It took him the better part of an hour of sticking to the shadows and dodging roving packs of armadons before Tavi was able to rejoin 4th Squad. He found them in the supervisor's residence as planned, which looked much safer and stronger than the majority of the other houses he'd come across during his journey from Norwood's destroyed garage. If he hadn't had their location marked on the map, he wouldn't have ever suspected anyone was inside.

"*Tasawa!*" a familiar voice cried out as Tavi slipped through the door, with Ratman closing it behind him as soon as he was clear. Tavi barely had time to turn before Jabber had picked him up and gave him a bear hug. He groaned in pain as all the injuries he'd sort of forgotten about during his game of hide and flee from the armadons came flooding back. "We saw the big fireball and knew you two were behind it! All the little *angstas* went running off that way and haven't been back since, *ke*? It was *valkan* beautiful!"

"Where's Crusty?" Childs asked quietly. Tavi shook his head.

"Dead." He quickly relayed what had happened during their mission to sabotage the fuel depot beneath the private garage.

"Damn it," Pigeon swore. "Ordo told me to have you report in to him the moment you're back. Head up those stairs over there. We just got the power generators primed. Klaw and his boys should have them running soon, and we can call the *Perseverance* to come pick our asses up."

"Your civvie is fine, by the way," Vixen told him. He jerked a thumb toward the stairs. "Up, take a right, and fourth door down."

"Welcome to the official residence of Sir Percival Norwood the Third," Krawdaddy added. "Not to be confused with the location you just destroyed, from the looks of things. Ah, but you've been here before, right?"

"*Ke,* who needs a private storage facility for their vehicle collection, *keiche*?" Jabber added, sounding disgusted. "*Balara* needed to get his shit blown up."

"After the sarge is done, get back down here to get some food in you. Our dearly departed host left some high-end quality rations, enough for us to eat well for at least six months," Pigeon instructed.

Jabber gave Tavi a playful thump on the shoulder as he quickly made his way up the stairs, taking them two at a time. It caused his shoulders and neck to ache, but he did his best to ignore it.

The residence of the outpost supervisor was impressive, Tavi noted as he made his way down the long hallway. He'd been here before but hadn't had a chance to explore the inside, with almost all his time spent out in the courtyard or the main floor. Before he'd thought it was over the top and a bit too opulent for his tastes, but after seeing just how many people had come to the party, Tavi began to understand that for someone important like Norwood, a residence is both a workplace as well as somewhere to live. It just made sense to have such a larger than normal place.

He hoped he never had a job where something like that was required of him. Living in a place with so much space to fill gave him a sense of foreboding he did not like at all.

At the door he stopped and saw Ordo was in the room with two other legionnaires, Ratman and Banger. They nodded to him as he peeked inside, their faces inscrutable. Ordo half turned and motioned for him to come in.

"Give me a brief rundown of how it happened," Ordo ordered. Tavi swallowed, nodded, and replayed the events for the sergeant.

It took him longer than he thought it would. Between stopping at one point to take a drink of water—fresh from a carafe, and not the recycled stuff in his suit—and again while explaining why he disobeyed Private Kruschke's order for Tavi to leave, it took almost ten minutes. By the time he finished, Tavi was emotionally drained, no longer hungry, and wanted nothing more than to go take a very long nap.

"Well, I'd reprimand you for disobeying a direct order, but under the circumstances I'm not too concerned about it," Ordo said as he had Tavi sit down in one of the chairs in the room. The sergeant waved Ratman and Banger away. The duo stepped outside the room, leaving Ordo and Tavi alone for a moment. "Someone might try to use it as political leverage later, but I'm sure Captain Truitt will squash that in a hurry. Are you holding up?"

Tavi shrugged. "I think so, Sergeant. Just tired. How are the scientists holding up?"

"Mitzi's in good shape. You should go see her. She's asked about you a few times since you and Crusty headed out. Childs is back to normal. Still arguing with Mitzi about sapient armadons. The man won't let it go. Morales is doing okay. He's trying to get the meteorological sensors up and running with Xi-Smith, but some idiot killed the power and backup relays when they abandoned the station," Ordo groused as he leaned back in his seat. "It's what we're trying to fix now. Doctor Xi-Smith thinks we can get comms back up, but... did you notice the ashfall lightening up out there?"

"No," Tavi said immediately, then hesitated. Had the ashfall been lighter? "Well, maybe? I just thought it was from the fireball from the explosion..."

"Doctor Morales thinks that the hurricane is pushing the ashfall north, which... means something, I don't know," Ordo admitted. "He had a lot of science in there, low pressure changing wind directions, but what he thinks is that if we can get comms up and running, there might be a window in the next twenty-four hours that we can get a ride out of here and back home, to the *Perseverance*."

Home. It was a weird feeling for Tavi, thinking of a ship as his home. However, no other place filled that longing as the *Perseverance* did. Strange. During his early life on Myrkyma, he never considered the Overdark to be his home, merely a place he survived. The call of returning to the Legion ship, where he could lie down on *his* bed, was strong.

"Comms are up," Claw said, poking his head in the doorway, sans helmet. He spotted Tavi and gave him a respectful nod. "Good work drawing off those armadons, Tavi."

"I'm sorry about Private Kruschke," Tavi said.

"He was a good legionnaire. Quiet kid, didn't make my life as an armorer difficult. He completed the mission. We'll drink to him later when we're off this fucking mudball." Claw scratched the four-day-old stubble on his chin with his prosthetic. "Got the ship yet, Ordo?"

"Just about to transmit. Tavi, once I'm done here, I want you to shower, eat, and get some shuteye," Ordo said as he began keying in command codes. The Legion override codes, used only in times of emergency, superseded all lockouts for anyone below planetary governor status. Aurora Research Outpost's computers, run by only a supervisor-level position since it was not yet a full-fledged member of the Protectorate, were well within Ordo's Legion-authorized override command.

"*Perseverance*, this is Sergeant Emmett Ord, 4th Squad, Bronze Legion. We see you are receiving. We are broadcasting live and in the clear. 4th Squad is currently at Aurora Research Outpost with four surviving civilians in tow. Local wildlife is attacking the base with reckless abandon, situation noncritical but growing worse. With all due respect, sir or ma'am, where the *fuck* did everyone go?"

CHAPTER TWENTY
This Is the Special Hell...

PNV PERSEVERANCE, *AURORA*

Campbell hunched over his console in Operations, listlessly reviewing the volcanic data and the latest weather reports from the aerographer. Blue's expression when he'd told her 4th Squad was gone haunted him. He hadn't expected quite that level of devastation from someone who supposedly couldn't wait to sidestep out of the Legion to the Survey Corps. Then again, the Ravens typically formed strong working relationships with their assigned legionnaire squads. Add in the terrible loss of Bronze Raven One and the helpless agony of bearing witness to their deaths, and it was no wonder that 4th Squad's loss had been one blow too many.

When Captain Esper ordered the Bronze Ravens to stand down in full, Campbell understood the reasoning. Their mission was over. All evacuations completed, all civilians rescued but for the lost Survey team, and with Aurora currently impassable, there had been no reason to keep the aircrews on alert.

There were a few protests—notably from Norwood—but Esper had stood firm. A good commander gave his people time to grieve when the situation allowed for it. A lesson Campbell made note of for the day when he was in a command position.

Sighing, Campbell ran a hand over his face and struggled to pull his focus away from the memory of Blue's tear-streaked face and back where it belonged. It took more effort than expected. But he owed Lieutenant Stahl an update on when the civilians could safely return to the Aurora Outpost, so he went back to the first report and read through everything from the beginning.

Thanks to the volcanic eruption and resultant thunderstorms and atmospheric disturbance, the southern hurricane had tracked in a direction the original weather forecast hadn't predicted. Their aerographer, typically a quiet, reserved individual, had hardly been able to contain her excitement over the rare and violent confluence of atmospheric events. She'd spent the past days bouncing over her console, feverishly recording everything and babbling nonstop at anyone unfortunate enough to get too close to her workspace. She hadn't seemed to process the fact that men and women, that *legionnaires*, had died as a direct result of her precious weather data, or maybe her duties just kept her too isolated from the Legion for it to seem real to her.

Regardless, she'd been diligent in providing constant updates every time the weather patterns shifted yet again, as well as projections on volcanic activity and when the ash output should slow enough for the atmosphere to clear. Campbell winced as he reviewed that section of her report. Those projections were depressing and nowhere near soon enough for comfort.

Nobody wanted the civilians on the *Perseverance* any longer than necessary. And both the Raven and Bravo Company commanders were chomping at the bit to recover what was left of their fallen legionnaires.

Voodoo in particular scared him, but at least she'd left him in peace the past day or so. Thanks to the stand-down order, the pilots were busy honoring their fallen in the time-honored traditional manner.

Halfway through the stack of reports, Campbell leaned back in his chair and rubbed between his eyes, trying to massage away the sharp pinch of a building tension headache, with limited success.

"Only a few more hours on shift, then I can go see if the Ravens have any booze to spare a poor Navy boy," he promised himself, though he wouldn't let Blue count it as one of their drinks, any more than that charlie foxtrot of a political dinner had counted. Or their legionnaire-interrupted date at the bar. He was beginning to wonder if there was something to the Passovan obsession with superstition, because it was almost like they were cursed.

Bending his head over the current hurricane data, he scanned the aerographer's conclusions on how it would interact with the ash cloud and potentially affect the area around the outpost.

"Huh... that's interesting—"

He snapped his head up as somebody cleared their throat. Grimes stood a cautious distance away, his slate in hand. Campbell kept a scowl off his face by the thinnest of margins.

"What do you want, Grimes?" he asked coldly.

Campbell hadn't quite forgiven the other ensign for trying to shut off the comms and leave Bronze Raven One's crew to die alone in the dark. The only reason he was speaking to him at all was because he understood Grimes had been trying to spare everyone the agony of listening without being able to do anything to save them. Grimes hadn't understood—it had been their duty to bear witness.

"You need to listen to this," Grimes blurted, shifting his weight side to side before darting forward and slapping his slate on top of Campbell's stack of reports. "Now."

The junior Comms officer jabbed a finger on the screen and a recorded transmission played.

"*Perseverance, this is Sergeant Emmett Ord, 4th Squad, Bronze Legion. We see you are receiving. We are broadcasting live and in the clear. 4th Squad is currently at Aurora Research Outpost with four surviving civilians in tow. Local wildlife is attacking the base with reckless abandon, situation noncritical but growing worse. With all due respect, sir or ma'am, where the fuck did everyone go?*"

Campbell shot to his feet, heart pounding in his chest so hard he was amazed his bones didn't rattle to the heavy beat. He shook the slate in Grimes' face.

"Has anyone else heard this?" he demanded.

"No." Grimes ripped his slate out of Campbell's hands and held it against his chest protectively. "Everyone else is in that damn staff meeting with Norwood or on the bridge. You were the only one free."

The distaste on his face told Campbell his roommate wouldn't have come to him if he'd had any other available option.

"Besides, I'm not sure it matters." Grimes' shoulders slumped. "I'm glad they're still alive, but the ash is too thick over the outpost for any of the Rhinos to get down there. It's Bronze Raven One all over again. At least they've got better options for hunkering down until we can get to them in a few days... or weeks. Fuck."

Now Campbell understood why Grimes had come to him. He might be the only *Navy* officer available, but there was no reason he couldn't have gone to Tripwire to at least let the man know his legionnaires were still alive down there, if fighting a losing battle against local wildlife gone mad. No reason except he didn't want to be the bearer of more bad news.

Grimes was a coward.

Holding onto his temper by the skin of his teeth, Campbell stepped into the other ensign's personal space and pinned him with a hard stare.

"You listen to me, Grimes. Go straight to Captain Esper. I don't care if you have to break down the door, he needs to know this right the fuck now."

Grimes stepped back with a scowl. "Why?"

Anticipation and urgency sent a tremor through his hands as he snatched the report he'd been reading before Grimes had interrupted.

"Because we might have an opening."

Campbell barely waited for Grimes' nod of assent before he sent Lieutenant Stahl a priority message. His boss replied immediately.

STAHL: UPDATE TRIPWIRE AND VOODOO AND GET THEM TO THE WARDROOM. I'LL PAVE THE WAY WITH THE CAPTAIN.

Moving quickly, Campbell got Tripwire on the comm. The Bravo Company commander listened intently as Campbell spat out a rapid-fire update and a request for him to get to the Officers Wardroom, where Captain Esper was meeting with his top officers, Norwood, and the outpost staff. It sounded like Tripwire was already running before he got off the comm.

Voodoo didn't answer.

Swearing under his breath, Campbell tried the DO, Ditch. She didn't answer, and neither did Twister, who occasionally stepped up as the DO. Nobody even answered the squadron's duty desk line, which was *always* supposed to be manned—and then he remembered. Voodoo had gotten clearance for a Roll Call.

Feeling that window of opportunity shrinking with every second lost, Campbell didn't try to comm anyone else.

He ran.

It was a universal truth that if you put enough pilots together, they would inevitably find a bar or, lacking that option, build one. Legion rules would normally prohibit a bar like the Bronze Raven's Heritage

Room, but the 13th was different. They lived on their ships, and so special concessions had been made.

Campbell sprinted through the corridors and took a lift down to the level where the Ravens were located. His boots thundered down the corridor as he passed by their briefing rooms and common area, and he slid to a stop outside their bar. The little placard next to the door claimed it was a document storage room, which was accurate... to a certain extent.

Pilots were required to keep hard copies of their main regulations, an archaic rule going back longer than the Mars Protectorate had existed. Voodoo was a stickler for the rules, so when Campbell hauled open the hatch, he was greeted with a small space where all three walls were lined with metal shelves filled with binders. Rolling his eyes at pilot dramatics, he strode to the shelves at the rear of the room and pulled on the frame. The entire section of wall swung open, and noise and light spilled into the tiny storage room... which if you looked at the *Perseverance*'s blueprints, wasn't actually tiny at all.

Some long-ago Ravens had turned the bulk of the space into the squadron's Heritage Room, complete with a bar filled with alcohol, comfortable couches, and card tables. The walls had been covered with framed pictures and memorabilia, though his keen gaze spotted a new squadron picture hanging over the bar since he'd been here last.

One that prominently featured Medusa and Ruby.

Party lights had been strung along the low ceiling, and low music filled the room. Campbell stood in the entryway and searched for Voodoo, but the bar was *packed* with over a dozen Ravens in various states of inebriation and what looked like more than half their Crows. He found the DO, but Ditch was standing on the bar, telling a highly improbable story about Medusa and didn't so much as glance his way no matter how he waved his arms.

Before he could force his way through the crowd, Voodoo strode over to intercept him. Relief filled Campbell, because she gave every appearance of being stone-cold sober. Then he noted her bleary eyes and realized with growing despair that she was as drunk as her crazier companions. She was just quieter about it.

"What do you want, Ensign Hotness?" Voodoo asked, her Passovan accent so thick it took Campbell precious seconds to interpret her words.

"4th Squad is alive."

Now he had her attention, though her eyes still wouldn't quite focus.

"They've reached the outpost, but those damn lizards are everywhere. They need an immediate airlift out before there's nobody left to extract."

Voodoo shook her head almost before he'd finished speaking, grief tightening her features. "I'm not losing another aircrew to that damn volcano. They'll need to hole up until the ashfall thins, *keiche?*"

"Winds are going to shift in our favor and clear the atmosphere over the outpost, but it's a short window of opportunity."

Understanding flashed across her face. Even drunk, Voodoo was sharp.

"The hurricane?"

"Yes, but we don't have much time if we're going to make this work." Campbell glanced around the room desperately, but found only drunk and drunker pilots. "Aren't any of your fucking pilots *sober*?"

Unexpectedly, Voodoo grinned.

After the official Roll Call was over, all Blue had wanted to do was get drunk. It might not make her feel better but, if nothing else, it might give her a break from the nightmares. She just needed enough alcohol to drown the memories, and their bar had that in spades.

Unfortunately, Killi had zero interest in drinking, so outside of a single drink when they toasted the fallen, Blue had abstained in solidarity. They'd stuck around for the initial storytelling and each shared a story of their own—like all pilot stories, every last one contained a minimum of ten percent truth and began with "so there I was"—but had left the Heritage Room when things had devolved into drunken revelry and remembrance.

"You know what goes good with tacos?" Blue muttered to Killi as they left the chow hall and headed back to their quarters.

"I feel like this is a trick question," Killi said with a faint smile. "Because the obvious answer is margaritas."

"Yes, and we could be drinking some *right now*."

Killi snorted and turned down their corridor but froze midstride. She glanced over her shoulder, that faint smile widening into a wide grin.

"But I hear hot ensigns also go good with *tacos*."

Heat flooded Blue's face and she shoved Killi to get her moving again. Any embarrassment faded when she caught sight of Campbell's expression as he pounded a fist on the hatch to their quarters.

"That's his Ops officer face. This isn't a social call."

"Oh, so you know his different faces now, huh?" Despite her teasing, Killi raised her voice to a carrying shout. "Campbell, over here!"

Campbell spun around. His gaze paused on Killi before landing on Blue.

"Both of you, perfect. Come with me." He ran past them toward the lift, clearly expecting them to follow. "Why weren't you answering your comms?"

The pilots exchanged a quick glance and trotted after him.

"They're in our room," Killi snapped, waving her bare wrist in the air as if Campbell had eyes in the back of his head. "You know, the one we're currently running away from."

"What's the rush?" Blue called out, already regretting that third taco as her belly protested the unexpected physical activity. Campbell darted onto the lift and held the door open for them, his dark gaze resting squarely on her.

"4th Squad's alive."

Hope flared up so hard it hurt to breathe, along with a rising tide of disbelief... but there was nothing but sincerity and determination on Campbell's face. A dozen questions rose up within Blue's mind, but she squashed all of them in favor of running faster. She lengthened her stride into an all-out sprint and beat Killi onto the lift by half a second at most, and only because her best friend had lost a step to shock. The door slid shut on their heels.

"What are we doing about it?" Blue demanded over the background hum of the rising lift.

"You're going to go get them."

Campbell quickly filled them in on everything, including the window of opportunity he'd identified. He hesitated.

"The only clear path intersects the hurricane. You'll have to punch through to reach the outpost. Can the Rhino handle that?" He looked between Blue and Killi. "Can you?"

Blue wanted to say yes, the Rhino could handle it. She wanted to snarl in his face for questioning their skill.

Instead she drew in a deep breath and said, "Let me see the data."

Campbell smiled and handed her his slate. "Thought you might say that."

Blue angled the slate so Killi could review the atmospheric data with her. Slowly, Killi nodded and traced a potential path through the storm.

"It could work." A slight smile tugged at her lips. "So long as you're flying it."

"And so long as you're landing it. Flying through the hurricane is going to be the *easy* part—"

"Yeah, for you."

Blue ignored her and pointed at the forecasted crosswinds over the outpost. "It's the landing that'll be tricky as fuck, and you know you're better than me. Still think it can work?"

Killi was silent for a moment then nodded firmly. "Between the two of us, we've got it covered."

Blue handed the slate back to Campbell and frowned. "Why *us*? And where the hell is Voodoo?"

Exasperation stamped Campbell's handsome features. "You're currently the only sober and *experienced* pilots on the *Perseverance*."

Killi wrinkled her nose. "That ... checks out."

"Voodoo should be in the Wardroom by now," he added as the lift doors slid open again. "She just had to stop by Medical for a little something to sober her up." He waggled one hand side to side. "As much as it *can* sober her up. I swear, damn Passovans can drink anyone else under the table."

In the next instant, all traces of humor were wiped away clean as the Ops officer strode down the corridor and led them into the Wardroom. As a very junior Legion officer, Blue had never been invited inside before. She got a blurred impression of polished wood, plush chairs, and understated elegance, but the details quickly faded into the background as she took in the attendees, a mix of Navy, Legion, and outpost civilians. There were far too many people inside, and the room was stuffy and hot.

As packed as it was, Blue expected it to be as noisy as the Raven's bar, but tension crackled in the air, and the only people speaking were Captain Esper and Supervisor Norwood.

The last time she'd heard two men speak to each other in such icily polite tones, she'd been at a political event with her grandmother. She'd been young enough to mistake the interaction for civility, but Shava had been quick to point out the subtle signs in their body language that not even experienced politicians could quite disguise. Blue saw those signs in the tightness around Esper's eyes, the ticking of Norwood's jaw.

In any other place, with any other men, they would have already come to blows.

"Per Navy *and* Legion regulations, the outpost's emergency backup generators should have been left running," Captain Esper said with a precise delivery that was somehow more chilling than if the man had shouted.

"Per *Mars Protectorate* government regulations, the entire power grid—including the generators—should have been shut down to conserve fuel and ensure a smooth startup upon our return," Norwood said, his voice calm but his eyes narrowing slightly. Not a glare, nothing so obvious as that, but telling all the same. "Which is what occurred."

Blue bit back a smile. Norwood was on the defensive.

Blue and Killi sidled over to stand behind Voodoo, who stood tall in her perfectly pressed uniform next to Tripwire at the foot of the table. If it weren't for her bloodshot eyes and the faint smell of alcohol surrounding her, Blue would never have guessed her commander had been drunk less than twenty minutes prior.

Captain Esper leaned forward like a master fencer about to score a point. "Two problems. First, and most importantly, the moment you requested a full evacuation due to a catastrophic natural disaster, you placed your entire outpost under military regulations. There are very specific guidelines for placing a facility in temporary hibernation. Guidelines which include leaving the backup generators running for situations exactly like the one we currently find ourselves in." He paused before he gave Norwood a thin smile. "I'm sure you were too busy coordinating the evacuation from the *Perseverance* to have time to properly review the guidelines."

"And the *second* problem?" Norwood all but snarled.

"The private residences established below might fall under the jurisdiction of the Protectorate of Mars, but the Aurora Research Outpost—and Aurora as a whole—is not an official member of the Protectorate yet. Your premature decision has risked not only the lives of every legionnaire on the ground, but also the surviving Survey Corps members—who, I might add, are the very individuals determining if Aurora is deemed capable of becoming a full member of the Protectorate. Well, those poor four souls who are still alive, at least."

Blue barely held back a polite clap at the Navy captain's mastery. He'd made the regs clear but graciously given Norwood an out, all while subtly calling attention to the fact that Norwood had been the first to evacuate, rather than the last.

The cowardly civilian had ordered Fischer to fly him up to the *Perseverance* in his personal shuttlecraft long before the first ash flake had fallen over the outpost, taking only his favored staffers with him. He'd left his assistant facility supervisor, John Delany, on the ground to coordinate the remainder of the evacuation. Voodoo had been furious when Norwood refused to allow Fischer to assist in the evacuation efforts, claiming his fancy shuttlecraft wasn't as robust as the Rhinos, when in reality it was probably better suited to handle the ash than anything the Legion or Navy possessed.

Judging by Norwood's clenched jaw, he knew Captain Esper had scored a major point. The politician was no novice though, and he didn't remain on the defensive for longer than it took him to blink.

"It was a hectic time for all involved," he agreed with a matching smile. "Regardless of any minor inconsistencies in the evacuation process, the fact remains that we cannot afford to lose any more dropships to this unprecedented situation. They are simply too valuable and difficult to replace, and you've already lost two to incompetence."

For a moment, Blue thought they would have to restrain Voodoo, but her commander contented herself with staring a hole through the side of Norwood's head while muttering Passovan profanities under her breath. Or maybe it was a *curse*. Blue wasn't fluent enough to be sure. Voodoo subsided as Twister slipped into the room and took up the DO's position at her commander's side. Her uniform was just as perfectly pressed as Voodoo's, her eyes just as bloodshot. The steady tremor in her hands told Blue she'd also stopped by Medical on her way in. Asodephedrine wasn't kind to the system, but if nothing else it sobered a body up in a hurry.

"Volcanic ash and horrendous atmospheric conditions hardly

qualify as incompetence." Captain Esper's smile widened. "And I'm sure you don't mean to imply that equipment is more valuable than the lives of Captain Truitt's men." When Norwood opened his mouth, Captain Esper held up a hand. "And before we get into a useless debate on the value of a person's life, may I remind you that we're talking about a squad of highly trained legionnaires and Survey Corps personnel? We may not be able to quantify the value of a man's soul, but we can quantify the cost to train a single legionnaire. Should we run the numbers, Supervisor Norwood?"

"That won't be necessary," Norwood replied stiffly.

"Excellent. Now that that's settled"—Captain Esper turned toward the foot of the table—"Major Ellingwood, do you have an aircrew prepared to fly the extraction mission?"

"Yes, *bossjna*." Voodoo grimaced but didn't bother to correct her slip. "Lieutenants Killowen and Eliassen will fly Bronze Raven Four. Maintainers have already prepped the Rhino for launch."

"Excellent."

Captain Esper dipped his chin in a respectful nod to the Ravens, but Norwood's gaze landed on Blue. Dread swirled low in her belly as his expression subtly shifted. He wasn't done fighting yet.

"You're both dismissed to mission prep. Godspeed—"

"Pardon me, Captain Esper," Norwood cut in with a thin veneer of civility, "but while the evacuation fell under military regulations, the Aurora Research Outpost remains under government authority. In addition, the Legion was deployed under the Survey Corps authorization, which also leaves them under government authority. Your Legion sergeant reported the death of Dr. Schmoyer." He waved a hand to pull attention away from a flash of very real grief in his eyes. "As the ranking government representative on site, that authority falls to me."

"A technicality," Captain Esper said coldly.

"But real, all the same. Which means I have a very real say in the deployment of your personnel."

"Try to stop us from rescuing our boys," Voodoo snarled, the leash on her temper slipping. Twister gripped her shoulder, a precaution Blue felt was wise as their Passovan commander looked two seconds away from launching herself across the table. Norwood just held up a hand, his body relaxed and expression supremely unconcerned.

"My dear commander, I would never suggest such a thing," said the man who had very much suggested or at least implied exactly that not five minutes prior. "I would merely like to point out that sending the pilot who crashed into my outpost and the pilot who exercised poor judgment while flying in the initial ash cloud are perhaps poor choices for such a demanding mission."

A chill walked down Blue's spine. There was no way for Norwood to know how close she'd pushed the Rhino to the point of no return on that sortie, not without spies within the Legion itself.

"I'm prior Survey Corps myself, you know," Norwood continued, raising his brows high. "I do recall how to interpret atmospheric data, and this so-called window of opportunity of Ensign Campbell's will take exceptional skill to successfully navigate. Surely you have better qualified pilots."

Voodoo placed her hands on the table and leaned forward, though she waited for Captain Esper's nod before speaking. Barely.

"One, per *Legion* regulations, the selection of pilots falls squarely within *my* authority." Voodoo glared at Norwood through bloodshot eyes. "Two, both pilots are fully qualified for the mission. I have every confidence that they will succeed. Three, they are currently the *best* qualified pilots we have available."

"I see two perfectly qualified and *far* more experienced pilots standing right before me," Norwood pointed out with a jovial smile, as if Voodoo were being a particularly difficult child. "I see no reason why you wouldn't fly the mission."

Voodoo and Twister exchanged a quick glance before they held up hands that shook no matter how they tried to steady them.

"At the moment, almost every other qualified Raven is DNIF." Voodoo's smile was razor sharp. "For you civilian types, that means Duties Not to Include Flying. The only other two pilots are babies fresh out of training that I wouldn't trust to handle a rainstorm, let alone a drop this complicated."

"Then one of them can act as copilot to Lieutenant Killowen while she does the actual flying," Norwood said casually enough, but his cold, calculating gaze rested on Blue. "No need to send Lieutenant Eliassen as well."

Understanding slammed into Blue along with a healthy dose of rage. This wasn't about her poor decision making when Bronze Raven

One went down or even her qualifications. Norwood had said it himself—he was the highest government authority on site, which meant the ultimate responsibility for every loss, equipment and personnel, rested squarely on his shoulders.

And Norwood didn't want to face the political fallout if Shava Turnien's granddaughter was lost on his watch.

"Absolutely not," Voodoo snapped, a little more of her temper slipping the chain. "As you said, this mission will take exceptional skill to successfully navigate from *both* pilots. Skill that Lieutenants Killowen and Eliassen possess in spades."

Blue let out a slow breath and pushed the rage down where it wouldn't show. She'd *known* admitting to that personal connection would come back to bite her in the ass, but she'd let her temper get the best of her, and now they were paying the price for her indiscretion. More to the point, *4th Squad* was paying the price, because every second they wasted arguing was a second they weren't focused on extracting them from a deadly situation. She could almost see her grandmother watching with her patient smile, waiting to see how she'd handle the self-inflicted difficulty.

Nerves tightened Blue's belly, because she did see a way to fix things. She was also fairly confident it would make things worse in the long term—for her. The faces of her legionnaires flashed in her memory, starting with Ordo and ending with Tavi. And then she thought of Mitzi, a little mouse surrounded by monsters and protected by courageous men. Determination burned away everything else. *The short term is all that matters right now. I can deal with the fallout later.*

Remembering the slap on the wrist from antagonizing Schmoyer publicly, Blue narrowed her gaze. *I just need an opening...*

"If you feel your young pilots aren't up to the task, Major Ellingwood, you could even utilize Captain Fischer since I don't need him for other duties," Norwood said with a gleam of triumph in his eyes. "I'm sure he's capable of flying one of your Rhinos down to the outpost and back."

"I already checked with *Captain* Fischer. He declined, you—" Voodoo shifted into Passovan and snarled at him.

One of Norwood's flunkies was apparently fluent enough in the language to understand what Voodoo was saying and took offense. The resultant uproar gave Blue the opening she desperately needed, and she slipped through the crowded room. As she passed by Captain Esper at the head of the table, he caught her arm in a gentle grip.

"Lieutenant?" he murmured, his voice soft but his gaze iron.

"Sir, I need to speak with Supervisor Norwood for a moment," she whispered. "Please, it's important."

After a long moment, Captain Esper released her arm.

"Do what you can, quickly." He glanced over her shoulder. "If you see an opening, help her."

"Yes, sir," Campbell said quietly. Blue hadn't realized he'd followed her, but even though she was grateful, she still needed to try alone first. She scooted past the captain and came to a halt next to Norwood.

"Sir, if I might have a private word?" she asked politely. She was careful, so very careful, to keep the rage boiling within her concealed, using every last trick her grandmother had taught her.

Norwood raised his brows, and for a terrified heartbeat she was certain he'd refuse, but then he dipped his head in a nod and drifted away from the table to a corner of the room. It wasn't precisely quiet, but Campbell positioned himself between them and the table, granting them a modicum of privacy, a courtesy that seemed to set Norwood slightly at ease.

That wouldn't last long.

"Withdraw your objection to me flying that mission," she said without preamble or subtlety. 4th Squad had no time for either, and she couldn't, *wouldn't*, fail them.

"Or what?" Norwood asked snidely.

Blue drew in a deep, calming breath—and then she set aside the Raven she'd worked so hard to become and embraced the buried political savage her grandmother, Shava Turnien, had trained her to be.

"Or I will use every connection I have to burn your career to the ground."

Norwood stared at her. Blue wasn't done yet, though she had to work to keep her hands steady over the rapid pounding of her heart. *No turning back now.*

"You wanted my support for governor, but the best you will get out of me now is *neutrality*." She stepped closer and dropped her voice into an icy croon. "And you want my neutrality, Norwood. My grandmother might be gone, but her friends are *my* friends, her contacts are *my* contacts. That advantage might not have been enough to get me straight into the Survey Corps, but I promise you it's more than enough to set fire to everything you hold dear."

Rage burned in Norwood's eyes, but he managed to hold onto his polite, fairly disinterested expression. After several rapid-fire beats of Blue's heart, he conceded.

"Very well. Your neutrality is acceptable, but if you die, I will turn you into a martyr and use you to fuel my career." Norwood's smile dripped malice. "You have a younger brother, yes?"

Cold fear shot through her. "Leave Aeric out of this."

"I will. For now. I highly suggest you survive this little stunt." This time, Norwood was the one to lean close to her, to croon words of spite and hate in her ear. "Because I'm not done with Shava Turnien's descendants yet. Whether that means you or your brother is entirely up to you, Astra."

Goosebumps rose up on Blue's arms, but she refused to show him any further weakness. She lifted her chin and held his gaze.

"Withdraw. Your. Objection."

Norwood's smile deepened and he strode past Campbell, raising his voice over the raging argument.

"It seems the blood of heroes runs strong in Shava Turnien's line. Lieutenant Eliassen made such an impassioned appeal to rescue her legionnaires, how could I possibly tell her no?" Norwood bowed his head in a courtly gesture completely out of place in the Officers Wardroom. "Major Ellingwood, Captain Truitt, please proceed with the rescue of your brave legionnaires. All objections withdrawn."

Under the cover of relief and several cheers, Campbell leaned toward Blue and murmured, "Was that wise?"

"You're asking the wrong question," Blue murmured back.

"What's the right one?"

She met his dark gaze. "Was it worth it?"

Slowly, he smiled at her. She stilled, caught by the warm approval in his eyes, but shook it off at an impatient shout from Killi. He caught her arm before she could walk away.

"Blue, that window is narrow. If you miss it... what happened to Bronze Raven One will look like a picnic. I don't want that to be you."

For just a moment, deafening gunfire, hissing armadons, and those terrible screams of pain and rage filled her ears—along with the aching silence that followed that had somehow been louder than everything that had come before it. Terror iced down her spine. Campbell saw it, and his expression hardened.

"*Don't* let it be you."

Blue pushed aside her fear and gave him a wicked grin. "I didn't know you cared, Navy boy."

Campbell's lips curled up into a playful smirk, but worry shadowed his gaze. "You still owe me drinks, darlin'."

"I'll do my best to pay up soon," Blue promised before she pulled free of his grip and hustled over to her best friend and copilot. Voodoo was locked in a discussion with Tripwire, but Twister followed them out of the Wardroom and into the blessedly quiet corridor.

"Are you sure you're both up for this?" Twister asked, no room for mercy or softness in her tone.

"Yes, ma'am," Blue said without hesitation.

Killi nodded sharply in agreement, but there was doubt in Twister's bloodshot gaze. Blue stepped closer and lowered her voice.

"You said I was ready for the left seat. I know I fucked up before, but I won't make the same mistakes this time. I can do this. Let me save 4th Squad." She let out a sharp breath and lifted her chin. "Let me save *our* boys."

Twister's stare seemed to burn down into her soul. Blue let her command pilot see her determination, her fear, her desperation. She let her see everything. Several heartbeats passed before Twister gave her a fierce grin and clapped her on the shoulder.

"Go get our boys back."

Tavi didn't have time to shower or sleep, though he did manage to scarf down some of the quality rations before the armadons locked onto their new location. What had been a tense situation ratcheted up as more and more of the reptoids began swarming around the building, searching for an easy way inside.

"Barricade those doors! Move the heaviest shit you can find and block the outer doors!" Pigeon ordered as Tavi ran into the entry hall, joining the rest of Team Two as they worked to move an oversize silverware armoire in front of doors.

"Wait!" Mitzi shouted as she came running down the stairs. "Latches in the walls... they drop blast shutters down and block the entire entry!" Tavi scanned the door frame and found it almost immediately. Mitzi continued giving directions. "Silver switch, left side!"

"Got it!" Vixen replied and pulled the switch down. In the walls, clicking sounds could be heard by all as the mechanisms activated. In seconds every window and outside exit had a solid steel sheet protecting both interior and exterior. The snarls of rage from the armadons outside could still be heard, but they were impotent roars, nothing more. Tavi's relief was short-lived, however.

"They're segmented! Each wall and room has its own mechanism." Mitzi's command voice got the rest of the legionnaires moving. "There were four other entrances I saw around the first floor. Come on, I'll show you!"

For someone untrained as a legionnaire, the young doctor was in surprisingly good condition, especially considering nobody had really gotten any rest the past four days. Still, Tavi was not about to be left behind and followed Mitzi closely as she sprinted down the stairs. Within minutes she'd located all the remaining locking mechanisms and activated them. The supervisor's residence was now tightly locked and secured, and no one—or *thing*—was coming in unannounced.

"Clear!" Tavi called out over the comms. "Building secured."

"*Confirm secured. Team Two, stand down and get some rest. Team One, overwatch rooftop. Team Three, chow. No arguments,*" Ordo instructed.

"*Two copies,*" Pigeon replied. Tavi sighed and leaned against the wall as exhaustion hit him like a sledgehammer. He wasn't physically tired, though he was still in some pain from the explosion, but mentally he was absolutely drained. He also knew, though, that getting in a nap was very dangerous. ACS had taught him all about head injuries.

"Tavi? Why don't you go get some sleep?" Mitzi asked from behind him.

"Got knocked out when we blew up the garage," he answered. "Not a good idea for me to sleep yet."

"Oh, concussion. Smart. Well, you want to explore this place?" Mitzi asked before shrugging her shoulders. "I'm bored and already got in a good power nap earlier."

He wanted to say no, to politely decline so he could go lie down, but Mitzi was still under his protection. If she wandered around and got lost, it would be his head served on a platter to Ordo. He nodded, albeit slowly.

"Sure. Where do you want to go, miss?"

"Oh, so we're back to that again, are we?" she asked sternly. "I thought running for our lives across a flooded continent meant we were past that."

"I'm sorry, uh, Mitzi. Really."

"I'm teasing you, Tavi."

"Ah. Okay."

"Come on." She motioned for him to follow as she set off down one of the many hallways of the massive house. "Last time I was here, Doctor Schmoyer told me all about the trophy room Norwood has. I never got to see it, but I know it's in here somewhere."

Tavi couldn't even begin to understand her fascination with exploring when there were murderous lizards outside the building determined to eat them all, but he was a legionnaire, and he would do as he was told. No matter what. Holding in a defeated sigh, he slowly plodded after the doctor.

He was almost afraid to ask what a powerful man like Norwood's trophy room was filled with. He knew some of the more psychotic cutters in Overdark liked to collect trophies from their victims. His brief time with Martians suggested they didn't do this, but Aurora was a very long way away from Mars Primus, and everything he'd seen so far suggested that Norwood ruled here, which was very much like the Tyrants back on Myrkyma.

It took her checking a dozen rooms before she finally found what she was looking for. Before letting Tavi in, though, she barred the door and flashed him a quick smile.

"So, lots of powerful people use rooms like this to show off their wealth," she explained as Tavi tried to peek around her to see inside. It was too dark beyond the entrance to see much. "They like to collect weird things, so be prepared to see objects which might best be described as exotic. Do you understand?"

He didn't, but nodded anyway. There was some doubt in her eyes, but she accepted his answer. Stepping inside the darkened room, she flipped the switch and light flooded into the large, cluttered room.

"Oh!" Tavi exclaimed as his eyes drank in the sight. "This is a trophy room?"

"Uh-huh," Mitzi said with a smile.

It was a verifiable museum, filled with random bits of collectibles and antiquities. From a full samurai armor set to a knife collection which would have made any ganger from the Overdark green with envy—and invite regular burglary attempts—the vast wealth and influence of the Norwood family was on full display here. Tavi, filled with awe, entered the room and immediately moved from piece to piece, stopping every so often to inspect them. While not necessarily recognizing them for what they were, or being able to fully read the descriptions in the handwritten notes next to them, the displayed items were still fascinating.

When he came to a sword which was taller than he was, he had to stop and look it over. It was the most impressive thing he'd seen so far, and his eyes could pick out the intricate swirls in the blade where the metals were joined as one. He wasn't any sort of bladesmith, but he definitely liked this one. Next to it on a separate display stand were smaller versions of the sword, the smallest being the length of his forearm.

"It's the Norwood family *zhanmadou*," Mitzi explained as she moved beside him. She then looked closer at the display and smiled. "No, I was wrong. This is a copy, not the original."

"Okay...?" Tavi shrugged. There was still so much for him to learn about the Protectorate as a whole. He always felt like these were things he should know. Fortunately, Mitzi explained.

"The *zhanmadou* blades created by Forgemaster Aoki are considered to be some of the most prestigious historical relics from before the Exodus. Every family of the Five Hundred was gifted one upon successful settlement of Mars Primus by the First Progenitor. They've been passed down within every single family since."

Tavi frowned. "How'd you know it was a copy, though?"

"This is made from a combination of carbon and tungsten steel," Mitzi said, pointing out the wavy patterns in the blade. "Damascus patterning. The originals were silver and nickel, more decorative than anything else, no patterning. It's a symbol of the Norwood family power. I'm just surprised there's a copy here... well, actually, no I'm not. He's gunning for the governor position, probably thinks it's all sewn up but the actual affirmation. But it's not law yet, so he didn't want to seem too presumptuous. The original is probably back on Mars Primus with the rest of his family holdings."

"How do—oh, right." Tavi exhaled and offered her a small smile. "Child prodigy."

"You're catching on," she said.

Interestingly enough, there were a few sets of bulky, outdated armor in the collection as well. The armor should fit Morales and Childs, which was promising. Perhaps the antiquated armor could keep them alive if the armadons managed to breach the residence? However, none of them looked like they could fit Mitzi or Xi-Smith. The women were simply too small.

He was just beginning to give up hope before he saw them. Tucked into a small, dark corner, more sets of armor had been casually tossed aside, forgotten. They were very similar to the others on display, only they looked worn, having seen battles long forgotten. Two of them looked about the right size, though, and appeared like they just might be able to protect Mitzi and Xi-Smith. He smiled and moved back to the center display.

Tavi eyed the massive sword again as an idea began to form. It was almost as big as he was, and would be comical to wield, and yet... his mind drifted back to the garage and the screwdriver he'd managed to injure the armadon with. He'd admittedly gotten very lucky, but the idea of using some sort of blade to help kill armadons wasn't exactly a stupid one. His gaze then drifted to the smaller blade on the stand next to it. Rather than a Damascus pattern, the blade had a distinctive monomolecular edge. That shining silver edge called to him.

"You think anyone would complain if I borrowed that one?"

Four hours later, Tavi and the rest of Team Two were up on the rooftop, keeping an eye on the armadons swarming the streets below.

After the tour of the museum, he followed orders and got some rest while Mitzi headed back up to Ordo in the comms room. While sleeping long periods of time was out of the question, he did manage to give his aching body a chance to recover with a serious power nap. Fortunately, he'd always been quick when recovering from injuries as a child roaming the streets of Overdark—a benefit of his Tyrant genetics he was now enjoying as he looked down at the seething mass below.

The alien creatures, it turned out, could climb the walls a bit and teams were taking turns shooting any who made it up too far. Norwood's residence was tall, so the armadons were only able to make it halfway up at most. Still, some of the larger ones managed to get into the courtyard and were searching for a way inside the building. Thanks to Mitzi's quick thinking, they were growing more frustrated by the minute.

"No word on an ETA yet, Tavi?" Vixen asked as Tavi leaned over the edge to look. At the moment the armadons were simply milling around on the ground, with one occasionally looking up and hissing at them. He searched for the one Mitzi had tagged as the leader, but there was no sign of the brutish armadon.

"Not yet. Preflight stuff I guess," he answered. "Ordo said he'd give us a ready alert when our ride is descending from orbit."

"Hey, check it out. The ash isn't falling like it was yesterday," Krawdaddy said, his eyes skyward. It was still overcast but the clouds looked darker, more ominous. "Kinda reminds me of that storm that hit the southern isles last week."

"Doctor Morales said we might get some clear air with the storm," Pigeon stated. "*Perseverance* concurs. Which is why we might be getting a ride now, instead of two or three months from now. If you paid attention to a briefing every now and then, you'd know these things."

"Extra work? That's what we got you for," Krawdaddy muttered. He jerked his chin down to the streets below. "I don't think we'd be able to last more than a week here, not with that horde."

The armadon numbers were starting to swell to the point they couldn't easily see the streets below. The seething mass of reptoids were angling around the building steadily, with every single one of them intent on figuring a way into the residence.

"You call that an unending horde of murder lizards," Vixen said, spitting on the tarmac of the rooftop landing pad before donning his helmet. "I call that a target rich environment."

"Wiser words have never been spoken," Ordo said, shouldering his rifle. "Who are you, and where did Vixen go?"

This elicited a laugh from all the legionnaires on the rooftop.

"Help's on the way. Might as well kill some of these bastards," Pigeon added helpfully.

"I'd like to get a piece of Crusty back from them," Tavi said. He raised his weapon and took aim. "More than a piece. I feel like we owe them some serious payback for the past few days as well."

"Same here." With a savage grin, Ordo gave the command. "*Light 'em up!*"

While Blue and Killi armed and armored up, Sergeant Carvalho rounded up HeyHey. By the time Blue and Killi sprinted into the dropship bay, their Crows were ready to fly, just as he'd promised. Even better, he'd added a little something extra to the Rhino, something their gunners—and his Ravens—very much approved of. Briefing and preflight had been a hurried, hectic thing, with almost no time for either, and then they'd dropped through Aurora's turbulent atmosphere in the southern hemisphere, where a monstrous hurricane raged.

They were operating so far outside the ASL-71 Rhino's safety minimums it was laughable, but those regs went out the cockpit during combat drops—and with murderous armadons attacking 4th Squad in the outpost, there was no question this was a *combat* drop.

With the power restored to the outpost's relay, they'd connected with 4th Squad's ops channel. Blue and Killi flew with updates from Sergeant Ord in their ears, along with disciplined gunfire, hissing armadons, and cursing legionnaires. It was Bronze Raven One all over again, only 4th Squad wasn't trapped in a half-submerged Rhino, wasn't anchored by a pinned-down pilot, wasn't alone in a world gone dark.

4th Squad had slogged across a sunken land, doing all they could to keep themselves and the Survey Corps team alive.

Now it was Bronze Raven Four's turn.

Blue was *finally* in a position to act. No more listening to her people die while they were safe in orbit, no more helpless agony while they sat on their hands. Fighting a hurricane was infinitely preferable to that special hell, even if it was turning into the most challenging sortie Blue had ever flown.

Horrendously strong winds threatened to spin the Rhino on its tail, to twist and turn her from her flightpath. Lightning branched across the blackened skies, searing her retinas before her HUD dimmed down to compensate. Gusts in excess of 200 mph battered their old dropship, and metal groaned and rattled in response as sheets of rain lashed the cockpit. Outside was nothing but a dark morass of boiling clouds illuminated by periodic flashes of lightning and patches of lighter clouds. Never a hint of blue skies, and they hadn't seen the sun since they'd left orbit.

Blue's hands ached from how tightly she gripped the flight controls, and her shoulders burned with tension, every bit of her focus going to flying their planned route. A gust slammed into their belly, and she grunted as she fought to keep them from going completely inverted as the view outside skewed sideways. Before she leveled the wings out, another burst of lightning crackled through the clouds, so close minor branches skimmed off their mottled gray hull before harmlessly spilling off the wing tips. As she wrestled against the winds and pulled the Rhino wings-level again, she recalled Twister's question several days and a lifetime ago.

And if they were on the ground, operating in hostile conditions, and needed an immediate extraction?

A savage grin pulled at her lips. They were going to get her boys, and nothing, not even the worst storm Blue had ever flown through, was going to stop them.

Killi updated Sergeant Ord on their ETA before turning to Blue.

"I've got their new location from Ordo. They turned Norwood's supervisor residence into the freaking Alamo and are holding on the roof. Current crosswinds are shit, but I'll give the LZ a shot." She braced a hand on the console as the winds threatened to flip the Rhino again. "Tell you what, you get us through this storm, and Ensign Hotness can have *all* the tacos."

A slightly hysterical laugh burst out of Blue.

At her lapse of control, the Rhino bobbed like a drunken legionnaire. Nothing was going to stop them—except for possibly Killi's horrible sense of timing. Still laughing, she steadied the dropship ... and relaxed her death grip on the controls. She stopped fighting the winds and flowed with them instead.

Even a beast like the Rhino could dance if the pilot knew the song.

Blue lost all sense of time as she guided them through the storm. A flash in her HUD that wasn't lightning brought her out of her intense focus. The next phase of the flight profile was approaching quickly. Surprise and a touch of relief flashed through her as she realized the hurricane winds had lessened. Not by much, but enough to be noticeable. They had reached the outer bands, just now curling over the northern continent.

At another prompt from her HUD, she pushed the nose low, shedding altitude at a rapid rate. The Rhino shuddered around them, but she just rolled her shoulders to shed the tension and pushed up the throttles. Just because time had temporarily ceased to exist while she danced with the storm didn't mean it hadn't ticked past, and the skies over the outpost wouldn't remain clear for long.

They had to *move*.

Thick jungle passed beneath mottled gray wings in a green blur, but Blue grimaced at their airspeed.

"Not fast enough," Blue muttered and pushed the throttles to the max, still dropping altitude. The Rhino bucked and shuddered and groaned, but Killi just patted the console.

"Suck it up, you cranky bitch." Killi got on the comms. "Ordo, Bronze Raven Four, five mikes out."

"*Copy five mikes*," Sergeant Ord replied calmly over the rattle of gunfire.

The minutes sped past nearly as fast as the wind-tossed trees below. Blue leveled off their altitude and pushed the Rhino into a left bank, setting them up for a western approach. The skies overhead were overcast and the winds were rough, but ash wasn't falling and the hurricane hadn't yet reached this far inland.

Good enough.

Blue pulled back on the throttles as the outpost came into visual range. Shock stole her breath. The outpost was *crawling* with the reptilian armadons. Smoke billowed up from somewhere in the interior, black with angry red embers, and scorch marks marred many of the white buildings. The legionnaires had fought a hard battle. She dropped the right wing low and swept over the perimeter fence—and Killi's crashed Rhino. Bronze Raven Five was swarming with armadons, but the landing pad itself remained relatively clear.

With a practiced flick of her eyes, Blue marked it as a secondary LZ in her HUD before she reduced the power again. Her hands tightened on the flight controls as the moment to hand over the ship to Killi ticked ever closer. A completely irrational part of her wanted to be the one flying when they rescued her boys, and she was reluctant to disengage.

As she rolled out of the turn, the brutal crosswinds slammed into them again. Blue course corrected... and loosened her grip. She'd let emotion dictate her command decisions once before, and she'd be damned if she let it happen again.

Killi was the better pilot for this phase.

"Ready?" Blue asked. In her peripheral, she glimpsed Killi wrapping her hands around her flight controls. Her best friend flexed her shoulders once and nodded.

"My ship," she said crisply.

"Your ship," Blue responded and released the controls. Her hands threatened to cramp, but she shook them out and took a heartbeat to breathe. Then she threw herself back into the work.

"Ordo, LZ in less than one mike." Blue waited for his acknowledgment and switched to the aircrew channel. "Gunners ready?"

This time, she couldn't just look over her shoulder and see Corporals Hekekia and Hayashi strapped into their harnesses at their Aries Miniguns. A combat drop meant the cockpit hatch was sealed—that didn't mean she couldn't see their savage little faces on the internal camera feed she pulled into the upper left corner of her HUD. She felt as much as heard the gunner's hatches opening, the hum of the machinery competing with the slight drag on the Rhino.

"*Gunners ready and standing by,*" Corporal Hekekia reported.

As they neared the primary LZ marked on their HUDs, Killi reduced their airspeed further. Norwood's supervisor residence grew larger outside their cockpit, but Killi timed it perfectly.

"Rotating engines." She pulled the nose up and hit the switch to rotate the engines, smoothly shifting to VTOL operations.

"Engine rotation confirmed," Blue replied after a quick check on both engines. After the issues they'd had on this deployment, neither pilot was taking any shortcuts. Both engines were green across the board though, and had smoothly locked into the vertical position. "Loadmaster, ready on the ramp?"

"*Loadmaster, standing by,*" Sergeant Carvalho reported.

Blue pushed the cargo compartment camera feed to one of their secondary screens. The armored loadmaster was strapped into his harness and standing next to the ramp controls, one hand wrapped around a crew strap and his legs spread wide to ride out the turbulence. And there was turbulence. The outer bands of the hurricane might not be overhead yet, but it was clashing with the volcanic weather patterns with brutal results.

Killi's jaw tightened in concentration as she positioned the Rhino over the LZ. Dismay tightened Blue's gut when she got a good look at the legionnaires clustered on the rooftop. They looked like they'd been through hell, and the surviving scientists looked worse. Mitzi stood out from the armored figures, a tiny, battered little mouse wearing clunky, outdated armor, but one who was still alive.

"Good boys," she murmured.

Smoke rose up from the central courtyard and obscured part of the building. Norwood's precious imported Mars Primus garden was on fire. Judging by the charred armadon bodies scattered throughout, the courtyard was a victim of judicious application of grenades. Blue's smirk died when the winds shifted yet again and whisked the smoke away. The back half of the residence, where the roof was the widest and most likely to support the weight of the Rhino, was also on fire. The sides of the building were far too narrow, but the front wasn't much better, and it lacked the reinforcement of the rear.

"I don't think that'll hold us," she warned Killi.

"Plan B it is," she replied, eyes tight with concentration. Alarm spiked Blue's heart rate as they descended toward the front of the building.

"Killi, we can't land there."

"No shit." Killi tossed her a serrated smile. "That's why we're not *landing*."

Blue's eyes widened when she realized what Killi intended. While the Rhino was fully capable, even designed, to hover midair with the ramp dropped on a solid surface like a mountaintop or a roof, Blue wouldn't want to attempt it in these conditions. The winds weren't hurricane force yet, but they were heavy and gusting unpredictably.

The Rhino rocked side to side as they dropped lower. A sharp gust pushed the tail sideways, but Killi quickly recovered with a muttered curse.

While her copilot fought the winds to attempt a "nose up, ass down" hover at the edge of the rooftop, Blue used the external cameras to check the streets, but the outpost was built on narrow, if elegant, lines. None of the other buildings were big enough to land on, and the streets weren't wide enough.

They were also infested with murder lizards.

Blue glanced sideways at Killi, who had a white-knuckled grip on the flight controls, and silently urged her on. If she couldn't manage to safely hover—and if *Killi* couldn't do it, Blue wouldn't even bother to try—the nearest feasible LZ was the landing pad.

The next gust of wind to batter the Rhino carried gray flecks of ash. They were out of time.

"Killi," Blue said quietly.

"Almost had it," she whispered through gritted teeth as she centered the dropship over the LZ again. But the winds relentlessly buffeted the Rhino, and every time Killi got close to the roof, she couldn't hold it steady long enough for Carvalho to drop the ramp. Finally, she admitted defeat. "Fuck... I'm calling knock it off. Tell Ordo... tell him we have to go to the backup LZ."

Her shoulders slumped as she pushed the throttles up and nudged the Rhino higher into the air, clear of any potential obstructions as the winds continued to gust.

"Ordo, unable to safely land at current location. Transferring backup LZ now. Confirm receipt."

Silence.

Frowning, Blue checked the comm connection, but it was strong. Sergeant Ord had heard her, he just wasn't responding. She winced as the silence lengthened. And then Sergeant Ord roared over the comms.

"*What about unsafely? Could you do it unsafely, because we just trekked halfway across this motherfucking compound and unless my hearing has suddenly gone bad in the past thirty seconds, I believe I heard you say you want us to go* back?"

Blue glanced at Killi. "Think he's pissed?"

Over the aircrew channel, Hekekia and Hayashi laughed without humor.

"*Have you seen how many murder lizards are down there?*"

"*Sooo many murder lizards.*"

"You know, ladies, you're right," Blue purred.

"*We are?*" HeyHey chorused.

"*They are?*" Carvalho added incredulously.

"Yup, that's a lot of murder lizards. Killi, hold position for me." She switched to the ops channel. "Ordo, standby for route."

Down on the rooftop, her HUD identified the legionnaire glaring up at the Rhino as one Sergeant Ord, but Blue just hummed absently and began running one of her favorite checklists. Killi gave her a little side-eye as she did her best to hold against the winds.

"What's got you so cheerful?"

"Wait for it." Blue finished the checklist, activated the controls, and synched up the targeting software with her HUD. A targeting reticule floated in her vision. "Nose down a little for me, would you?"

Killi laughed in gleeful understanding. The disappointed slump to her shoulders disappeared in a heartbeat as she nudged the flight controls enough to give Blue a great view of the streets below. She focused on a particularly fat armadon, then shifted her gaze to one missing its tail tip on the other side of the road—and with a mechanical *whir*, the six-foot barrel of the chin-mounted railgun swiveled to follow her line of sight.

Grinning as savagely as her tiny gunners, Blue triggered the railgun, and the 20mm tungsten sabot round ripped through the murder lizard at 7,000 feet per second. Blood misted the air, and the armadon dropped. If her railgun did that kind of damage, she couldn't wait to see what the Aries Miniguns would do.

"Now that I know that'll work against those armored assholes..." Working quickly, Blue pulled up the outpost map on the main viewscreen and highlighted the shortest path to the landing pad before turning to Killi. "Think you can do a CAS run on that route? Or do you want me to fly it?"

"Low and slow with gusting crosswinds above and murderous lizards below?" Killi arched a brow. "Girl, you know I've got this."

"Good." Blue transmitted the route to Sergeant Ord. "Ordo, confirm receipt of LZ and route."

"*Confirmed*," he growled. A slow grin crossed Blue's face.

"Good. We'll clear you a path."

"*Be advised, anti-personnel rounds likely to be ineffective.*"

"*Duh, have you seen those things? What does he think we are, noobs?*" Hekekia demanded over the aircrew channel. Hayashi sniffed in affront.

"*Clearly. Anti-personnel rounds are for* unarmored *personnel. Those murder lizards are armored.*"

Even in the tiny feed in the upper left corner of her HUD, it was impossible to miss the gunners rolling their eyes at the Legion sergeant.

"*Which is why we switched the ammo load out to high-explosive incendiary/armor-piercing rounds,*" Hekekia concluded smugly.

"Pat yourselves on the back later, ladies," Blue ordered sternly, though she couldn't suppress her grin. "Cleared hot. Let's clear the road."

HeyHey cackled in savage delight and opened up with the Aries Miniguns in tight, one-second bursts. In a heartbeat, they'd cleared the entrance of the residence and the immediate area around it.

Brrrt! Brrrt! Brrrt!

Armadons exploded. The gutters of the narrow streets were flooded with ash-filled blood. It was *glorious*.

"Hey, Ordo!" Blue called out over the ops channel. "That good enough for you?"

"*That'll do.*" Sergeant Ord still didn't sound particularly enthused about trekking back across the outpost, but at least he no longer sounded pissed. "*4th Squad, moving. ETA fifteen.*"

Blue exchanged a fierce grin with Killi. "Let's rage."

CHAPTER TWENTY-ONE
This Will Not Be Our Alamo but Their Funeral Service

AURORA RESEARCH OUTPOST, AURORA

Tavi watched as Bronze Raven Four swept in and proceeded to deliver enough rage to level a city.

The armadons raised their heads and roared defiantly as the Rhino swung low overhead. They were the apex predators on this forsaken world, with very little which could threaten their mastery of the food chain. They did not know fear, nor were they accustomed to being pushed around by any other predators, known or otherwise. The Rhino roared back, and the armadons understood for the first time ever just what prey felt like as the high-velocity rounds blew them apart.

It was . . . *unwelcome*.

At an intellectual level, Tavi knew a Rhino could *theoretically* move low and slow as it rained hell and hate down upon the gathered armadons outside. Actually *seeing* it, though, was something else entirely. *Feeling* it was even better. It was almost a religious experience for the young man.

The steady *brrt brrt brrt* of the Aries Miniguns rattled his bones as the Rhino plowed forward, bits of armadon and street kicking into the air with every controlled burst. The chin-mounted railgun on the Rhino also was at play, destroying any armadon who didn't flee the destruction caused by the miniguns. Ash kicked up into the air with every round's impact, creating a low, hazy wall of ashy mist on the street. Some of the places where the hazy ash hung in the air were tinged the color of armadon blood.

"Just like we rehearsed, people," Ordo growled and clicked his tongue. Tavi swallowed nervously and checked Mitzi, but the young doctor seemed distracted by her borrowed armor. "One, lead the way."

Tavi waited as Claw and his team took the lead. It was slow going at first, with the legionnaires pushing through the piled-up bodies just outside the door.

"Two, Three. Move. Keep the scientists safe, no matter the cost," Ordo reminded them.

Needlessly, Tavi silently opined, but kept his mouth shut as they moved out.

Ash continued to fill the air, making their visibility poor. More than once Tavi would have been turned around if not for the path marked on his HUD, courtesy of the pilots in the Rhino above.

Their civilians were having issues with the dust, but the masks and armor they'd borrowed from the supervisor's museum gave them some protection from the elements.

The further out from Norwood's residence, the thinner the dead armadons became, until there weren't many to see anywhere. None of the creatures seemed interested in pushing the legionnaires at the moment, for which Tavi was immensely grateful. The alien creatures were nearby, watching, but wary.

Bronze Raven Four had definitely raged, and the reptoids had taken note.

Tavi's smile was mirthless. The armadons had been hunting them for days, and he only thought it fair that the shoe was on the other foot—or in this case, claw. The buildings practically flew past them as they trotted down the street, following the clear path of the dead created by their close air support. Familiar locations passed, and Tavi felt his hope rise as they drew closer to the landing pad and their old bunking area. His eyes caught sight of the ruined shape of the crashed Rhino on the outer wall.

"We're gonna make it, *tasawa!*" Jabber crowed.

"Hell yeah!" Stickboy added from point. He'd been the first one out of the supervisor's residence. "I see the LZ and the Rhino! Marking now!"

A glowing blue circle appeared on Tavi's HUD, as did a smaller square with an elevation indicator next to it. The Rhino was hovering a mere thirty feet off the ground. Tavi guessed they were waiting for the rest of 4th Squad to arrive before setting down. There was no reason to give up their air superiority too early, he reasoned.

They were just past the guardhouse when the armadons struck.

"*Ambush!*" Stickboy managed to scream before the first armadon latched onto his arm. Jerking sideways from the impact, Tavi had a bare instant to react as the barrel of Stickboy's rifle swept Team Two and their civilians. Tavi grabbed Mitzi's arm and pulled her down.

Just in time, it turned out. Flinching as the armadon struggled to rip his arm out, Stickboy squeezed the trigger and 1mm hypervelocity rounds sprayed the legionnaires behind him. The first two rounds struck Jabber's armor, which saved his life but caused him to double over with a grunt of pain. The third whistled harmlessly overhead, and the fourth barely missed Morales.

Crying out, Morales spun and ducked. Krawdaddy moved to help him. Pulling the terrified civilian to his feet, Krawdaddy turned around and put his own body between him and Stickboy.

"Trigger discipline, you *stupid fuck!*" Krawdaddy screamed.

More armadons emerged through the misty ash, like demons flitting through the shadows. Ratman, closest to Stickboy, tried to help his friend but was dragged into a nearby alley by a trio of armadons. Stickboy's cries of pain turned to shrieks as the armadons managed to rip his helmet off. Razor sharp teeth shredded his face. A strange *cracking* sound echoed across the streets. Stickboy and Ratman's icons turned red simultaneously.

Another shape moved between Tavi and Mitzi.

Whirling, Tavi pulled the borrowed blade from his belt and drove it into the snout of the armadon racing for Mitzi. He had a brief moment to wonder how the creatures knew who to attack before he wrenched his wrist and jerked the blade out of the armadon's thick hide. A spray of blood erupted and the creature flopped onto its side. Moving quickly, he pushed the tip of the sharpened blade into the exposed throat. The armadon gave a final gurgle and quit struggling.

"*Tavi!*" Mitzi screamed as an armadon broke through the line and grabbed her leg. The borrowed armor saved her life, but the pure strength of the alien jerked her off her feet. She landed heavily on the ground and the armadon began dragging her away.

Tavi raced over to her and grabbed her outstretched hand. Planting his feet, he raised the CCR with his off-hand. He looked down at her and saw her eyes wide with terror.

"I got you! Trust me!" he shouted, took careful aim, and put a round directly through the eye of the armadon. The round exited the back of the creature's head, black membranes and brain matter splashing across the armadon's ridged neck and back. It dropped like a sack of potatoes and Mitzi was able to extricate herself from the maw of the beast.

"Doctor! Vixen, grab him!" Ordo shouted. Tavi turned but couldn't see the doctor, or any members of Team Three. One, meanwhile, had their hands full dealing with more armadons.

Tavi raised his rifle as Mitzi scooted behind him. He targeted an armadon running across the street and put two rounds through its throat. It flopped on the ground, leaving a trough in the ankle-deep ash as it slid to a halt.

"Nice shot," she said shakily. "Where are the others?"

"On the way," he replied, looking around.

"Tavi! Get her to the landing pad!" Ordo called as more gunfire erupted.

Tavi had to tug on Mitzi's arm to get her moving. Together, they raced past Team One as they battled for their lives. Claw ripped out an armadon's throat with his prosthetic and was rewarded by being tackled by three more of the beasts. Loosey ran over to his team leader and shot one of the armadons on top in the back of the skull. The round ricocheted off the spines.

Without breaking stride, Tavi slammed his blade into the throat of the biggest of the three armadons on top of Claw. Black skin sloughed off as he ripped the throat open. Claw pushed the wounded armadon off him, shot it twice just to make sure, then kicked a smaller one away. Loosey finished off the third armadon by dumping half of his magazine into its face.

"Yeah! You like that, bitch!" Loosey's triumphant scream turned to panic as an armadon latched onto his leg and knocked him off balance. Claw reached down and yanked the creature off. Toejam took aim and shot the armadon in the belly.

"Fuck my life," Tavi hissed as an armadon jumped onto Toejam's back and dragged the legionnaire to the ground. His screams abruptly ceased as three of the large aliens cracked his helmet open like an egg.

Claw turned and shot one of the armadons, but he only succeeded in annoying the massive beast. Tavi raised his weapon to fire as well but hesitated. He looked back at the rest of Team Two.

More armadons were coming. Jabber was limping, struggling to keep up, while Krawdaddy and Pigeon were providing excess fire support. Other than Ordo and Banger, Tavi couldn't see any other survivors from Three.

Tavi shifted his aim and shot one of the armadons moving toward Jabber in its soft underbelly. It dropped to the ground. Two more replaced it. He shot those as well, but only one of them fell. The second roared, the noise nearly overcoming his helmet's auditory dampener. Dozens, hundreds of roars answered it. Further off, an even *louder* one echoed.

"*Thunder run! Go! Go! Go!*" Ordo screamed, and the survivor's steady march across Aurora Research Outpost became a disorganized sprint to the landing pad.

Bronze Raven Four circled over the landing pad, the disciplined *brrt* of the miniguns rattling through Blue's bones as HeyHey cleared straggling armadons off the new LZ. Both gunners were riding high on destruction, and even Blue was feeling the exhilaration. They'd left a trail of blood and death behind them, a safe path for the legionnaires to follow home.

As soon as the landing pad was clear, Killi shifted to VTOL ops. The instant the engines locked into the vertical position, she pivoted the Rhino so it was pointed directly at Bronze Raven Five where it lay across the damaged perimeter fencing a short distance away. The mottled gray hull was covered with ash—and armadons.

Unlike the sleepy armadons of Aurora's southern beaches, there was nothing lazy about this group. They were just as murderous as the rest of the armadons infesting the outpost, just as murderous as the ones who'd killed everyone on Bronze Raven One.

Just as easily shredded by railgun rounds.

Blue watched for a moment as the armadons scrabbled at the cockpit, at the warped ramp, at the hull itself, desperately trying to break in even though nobody was inside. One armadon had even managed to jam half its bulky body through the open gunner hatch.

"Do me a favor," Killi said grimly. "Get those fuckers off my girl."

Blue smiled and picked them off as fast as the railgun would fire. One round went through the black patch on an armadon's throat—Blue had quickly realized it was a soft spot on the otherwise well-armored beasts—and shattered the reinforced windscreen behind it.

"Really?" Killi demanded.

"Uh, oops?" Blue winced as her best friend glared.

"Hasn't she been through enough?"

"Hey, look. There's Sergeant Ord and 4th Squad," Blue said brightly as the legionnaires raced out of the blood-drenched street and onto the ash-covered landing pad.

The look on Killi's face said she wasn't going to forget that easily, and she grumbled Passovan curses under her breath as she set the Rhino down in the exact center of the pad. No sooner had Sergeant Carvalho dropped the ramp than a veritable swarm of armadons burst out of the same street, rapidly catching up to the sprinting legionnaires. The pair in the rear spun around and laid down covering fire, but their weapons were largely ineffective—and the Rhino wasn't positioned correctly for HeyHey to bring their guns to bear.

Fortunately, Bronze Raven Four had a loadmaster who used to run with the legionnaires—and had a creative mind toward destruction and mayhem.

"Hey, Carvalho," Blue roared over the aircrew channel. "Light 'em up."

"4th Squad! Drop and eat dirt NOW!" Carvalho screamed.

Tavi heard Carvalho's call, saw *precisely* what was being aimed behind them, grabbed Mitzi, and pulled her out of the way as the Crow shouldered the massive machine gun and opened fire.

He'd felt the deep *brrt* of the Aries Miniguns earlier due to the immense power of the large 30mm guns. Mounted within the confines of the Rhino, they were some of the most powerful weapons the Legion fielded during any drop. They were big, bad, and beloved by all legionnaires, whether they were the ones firing or those benefiting from the massive rounds during any combat drop. To have one provide covering fire was almost a religious experience for some.

The firearm Carvalho wielded, however, was much smaller. Up close and personal as Bronze Raven Four was, it didn't really matter. The 10-gauge solid-tungsten armor-piercing slug of the full automatic shotgun/machine gun bastardization took delivery of pain and hate to a whole new level.

Armadons simply *exploded* as the large slugs slammed into their chests. The chin-mounted railgun on the Rhino had done wonders, and the dual Aries Miniguns had plowed the road and killed hundreds, but the steady hammering of the fully automatic belt-fed weapon finally gave the armadons pause, made them reconsider attacking this flying machine of death. It wasn't much, merely a few seconds, but it was all Tavi needed to get Mitzi up the loading ramp and safely inside the bird.

With the other civilians already secured, he turned around and began providing more cover fire as the surviving legionnaires from 4th Squad slowly straggled into the rear, each one taking turns dumping a full magazine behind them at the armadons before making their way up the ramp. Tavi counted them off silently as they passed.

Jabber.

Vixen.

Pigeon and Krawdaddy.

Loosey.

Claw.

Banger.

"And Ordo," he whispered as the sergeant limped up the ramp. Ordo turned and eyeballed him.

"Good work, Tavi. Let's go."

"Where are the others?" he asked, confused. "What about everyone else?"

"Check your HUD, Tavi. We're it."

He blinked. They'd started this trek with fifteen legionnaires and five Survey Corps members. Now they were down to nine, though they had managed to keep four of the Survey Corps civilians safe. He swallowed against his suddenly dry throat and coughed.

"Get your ass in there so we can skedaddle," Ordo said sharply.

Nodding, he hurried up the ramp as Carvalho continued to lay waste to any armadon who dared come near the loading ramp. Most appeared to be avoiding it now. With all the survivors safely on board and ready to lift, Carvalho paused and slapped the ramp lift button. It rose quickly and sealed.

"*Ramp secured. Thirteen souls accounted for.*"

✧✧✧

Blue let out a shaking breath as the ramp sealed shut. The last legionnaire was on board. They were in the clear, they could get out of this stupid outpost, leave the murder lizards and the deadly ashfall behind. Regret and sorrow followed on the heels of relief as she checked the cargo compartment's camera feed. *So few...*

Shaking it off for later, she opened the aircrew channel to check with her Crows. "Confirm ready to fly."

"*Ready,*" HeyHey chorused over the erratic *brrt* of their miniguns.

The remaining armadons on the landing pad were mostly clustered around the rear of the Rhino, but enough were in their field of fire that they were able to take a few more out. Hekekia cackled like a maniac as one round hit her current target just right and the beast exploded. Blood misted the air and chunks of meat rained down. Blue curled her lip as a few pieces of armored reptilian actually bounced off the windscreen.

As Killi pushed up the throttles, Blue kept a careful eye on the latest engine diagnostic. They were still in the green, but the ashfall was growing thicker by the second. They needed to leave before they fragged another set of engines and got stuck down here. Her gaze snapped back to the cargo compartment camera feed when she didn't get a response from Sergeant Carvalho.

The loadmaster had paused before Mitzi, probably to make sure she was safely in, before he strode to the front of the compartment where he typically strapped in. He grasped his straps and tilted his face up to the camera, a slightly feral smile on his face. He'd obviously had fun cutting loose with his abomination of a gun.

"*Ready to fly, con—*"

"*Oh... FUCK!*" Hayashi yelped.

BOOM!

Something hit the Rhino hard enough to shake the massive dropship. Both pilots were flung sideways, only their harnesses keeping them in their seats. Carvalho didn't have that luxury, and he staggered hard into the bulkhead. Blue saw his head snap up, saw terror and rage twist his broad features—and then Hayashi *screamed.*

Blue still had the gunner compartment camera feed in the upper left corner of her HUD, and she could only watch in horror as the brutish, dark armadon that had forced its way through Hayashi's gunner hatch shook its head with her gunner's arm in its toothy jaws.

Hayashi screamed again as the armadon thrashed in the confined space. With a metallic groan, the harness release clip on her armor bent and snapped, and she was dragged free of her minigun. The brutish armadon flung its thick head sideways, and the tiny gunner slammed against the cockpit hatch. The thick metal *boomed* with the force of the impact. Hissing in agitation, the armadon clamped its jaws tighter around Hayashi's arm and snapped its head in the opposite direction, flinging her against the bulkhead. Terror choked the breath in Blue's lungs.

Blood spilled from its jaws, proof that its fangs had pierced the thinner armor around Hayashi's wrist. The armadon slammed her against the cockpit hatch again, and Hayashi went limp.

Blue snarled in helpless rage and gripped her sidearm, but she hesitated. She'd have to unseal the cockpit hatch to use it. Her agonized gaze landed on Killi, whose hands were white-knuckled on the flight controls, braced to take off and unable to without risking their gunner. Cold realization washed through her in an icy wave. She couldn't open the cockpit up to attack. They could lose a gunner and still make it back to the *Perseverance*. They couldn't if they lost the pilots.

Blue let her hand fall lax at her side. She couldn't help her.

But Carvalho could.

Roaring the battle cry of a legionnaire, the loadmaster threw himself into the fight. He moved like he was twenty years younger, like he didn't have a prosthetic leg. His armored fist repeatedly slammed into the side of the armadon's head and the corner of its jaws, trying to force it to release Hayashi. When that didn't work, he flipped open his utility knife and jammed it into the armadon's eye.

The brutish armadon stiffened, and for an instant, Blue thought it was over. But then it thrashed and slammed its bony head into Carvalho's armored side. The loadmaster tumbled into a shrieking Hekekia, who was doing her best to lay down covering fire while the battle for her best friend's life raged at her back.

Hissing in agony, the armadon scuttled backward out of the gunner hatch—dragging Hayashi with it.

No, no, no!

Blue flipped the external camera feed to the main viewscreen. Hayashi was struggling. She was still alive. And there was no way they were leaving her behind.

"Somebody get my fucking gunner back!" Blue roared over the ops channel.

Tavi wasn't even consciously aware that he was outside of the Rhino until he'd driven his blade through the fourth armadon standing between him and Hayashi.

His grip on the handle of the blade was like iron. The scales of the armadons were thick, normally difficult to penetrate. At the moment it didn't matter. The monomolecular edge on the blade was sharper than anything he'd ever dealt with before. His eyes were locked on the massive, dark armadon dragging Hayashi through the ash. It was the same one that Mitzi had called the leader before. He moved as fast as possible to cut off the monster's escape. Every single armadon who got between them met a singular, bloody fate.

The armadons swarmed him. Those who got too close died by the blade. Those which hung back, waiting to strike, died by gunfire from the dropship. Every dead armadon brought Tavi one step closer to the badly wounded Hayashi. The ash made the air around her thick, sometimes causing her to disappear.

Tavi's dance of death began to take its toll. He was half a heartbeat slow dodging a tail swipe of one armadon, the impact rattling his spine through the suit. Another claw lodged in the plate armor covering his chest, pulling him slightly off balance and nearly causing him to fall. A heavy weight crashed into his knee, causing it to pop. Panting inside his helmet, he ignored the searing pain and pushed on.

The added fire of the legionnaires from the rear of the Rhino helped push the armadons back further. No longer in a constant scrum against the murderous lizards, he was finally able to catch up to Hayashi. The brutish leader was nowhere in sight. Instead, a smaller armadon was attempting to savage her through her armor. Tavi drove the tip of his knife into its brainpan. It stumbled, let her go, and fell lifeless onto the thick, ash-covered pavement.

"Hayashi!" he shouted, lashing a kick into the snout of another armadon who'd gotten a little too close. Pain lanced up his shin but he ignored it. Gunfire kicked up more ash nearby, but he didn't hear the telltale sounds of a near miss, so he focused on the little injured gunner.

She was bleeding from her arm. Scooping her up carefully and ignoring the blazing pain in his ribs, back, and shoulder, he speed-walked back to the Rhino, doing his best not to jar Hayashi along the way.

Gunfire whistled past. Armadons lunged, hissed, roared, screamed, and died as his legionnaires provided withering cover fire. Tavi felt his strength fading with every step. Gritting his teeth, he focused on one step. Then another. And a third. Every step brought him closer to the Rhino, and to safety. It didn't matter if he survived, no. His only intent now was to bring little Hayashi back to her Ravens.

Walking up the ramp without jarring her was a challenge, but he managed. Kneeling down was worse. Pain didn't matter. She was alive still, and back where she belonged. As gently as he could manage, he set the wounded door gunner on the floor of the Rhino and began checking to make sure she was all right.

"You with me, Hayashi? HeyHey?"

"...Tavi?" Hayashi asked, her tone one of wonder. Her gaze was unfocused and her pupils dilated, but the bleeding on her arm had finally stopped, the built-in tourniquet doing a proper job for the time being. The wound began to clot immediately.

"I got you," he told her, breathing a sigh of relief. This passed quickly as he was shoved aside by Carvalho who, while looking worse for wear, was at least in better shape than he felt. The burly Crow immediately began checking the tourniquet while thoroughly inspecting her for any other injuries.

"...yeah you do...my..." Her head lolled back and her eyes partially closed. Tavi reached out for her, concerned, but Carvalho gave him a look and shook his head.

"Gave her a sedative." The loadmaster held up the small injector before pocketing it. His expression softened just a bit around his own pain and injuries. "Good work, legionnaire."

Tavi nodded and slumped down to the floor of the Rhino. Everything hurt. He knew he'd been beat to hell and back during his rampage through the armadons to rescue Hayashi. Which, he was surprised to find, he couldn't remember much of. Most of his memories were a haze of blood and ash. He lay down on the floor next to Hayashi and closed his eyes as the pilot accelerated to orbit, leaving Aurora and the raging armadons in its wake.

Just a quick nap, he promised himself before blacking out.

CHAPTER TWENTY-TWO
Why Do We Always Find Ourselves Here at This Hour?

PNV PERSEVERANCE, *AURORA SYSTEM*

Blue sat on a cot in Medical. Possibly the same one she'd shared with Campbell after their disastrous date. Not that it mattered. The cot was against the wall and out of the way, *she* was out of the way, and that was all that was important right now.

The room was packed with every remaining member of 4th Squad—none of them had escaped Aurora without injury—and her Crows. The only people in that room who weren't injured were Blue and the medics themselves, who bustled between the cots, treating wounds, setting broken bones, and providing pain relief.

By all rights, Blue should be down in the dropship bay, but Killi had taken one look at her face and sent her to Medical with everyone else while she handled postflight. Sometimes, Blue didn't feel like she deserved a friend like Killi. She leaned her head back against the wall and tried to control her breathing. Her hands shook as her adrenaline tanked, the memories of that desperate flight back to the *Perseverance* playing in a blurred loop in her mind.

Killi fighting the hurricane winds and the ashfall, pushing the Rhino to its limits to escape Aurora's grasp.

Blue requesting medical personnel on standby, only Killi realizing she'd been holding onto her professional tone by her fingernails.

The groan and rattle of their old dropship competing with the groans and screams of pain of its passengers.

And then the controlled chaos of the dropship bay as medics

swarmed Bronze Raven Four the instant Carvalho dropped the ramp. Broken ribs, and he'd still refused to let anyone else do his job.

Blue's gaze drifted over to the next cot and landed on her steadfast loadmaster gripping her poor gunner's hand. Carvalho had refused treatment until they took Hayashi back for surgery.

At least she wasn't screaming anymore.

They'd given her the good drugs before they'd even carried her off the Rhino, and the head surgeon had begun preparing the *Perseverance*'s surgical suite the instant he'd gotten word of the extent of her injuries. Hekekia sat on her other side, silent tears pouring down her face.

"This wouldn't have happened if you'd just let us finish our woowoo," Hayashi slurred, her eyes glazed over.

"Woowoo?" Carvalho asked absently. Hayashi pulled her remaining hand free of his grasp and wiggled her fingers.

"Magic, protection against bad juju, balls in the cockpit." She frowned vaguely at him before her gaze slipped past him and settled on Blue. "I'm too pretty to die."

"You're not going to die," Blue said immediately. She clenched her hands into fists to hide the shaking, the tiny bites of pain from her nails sinking into skin grounding her.

"That's right," Carvalho said firmly. "We're all too pretty to die."

"Tavi's pretty." A dreamy smile wavered across her face. "He can't die either."

"Tavi's fine," Carvalho said with a snort, then winced and rubbed his cracked ribs. "Ow."

"Yeah he is." Hayashi's eyes drifted shut, her lips still curved up in that little smile.

A harsh sob escaped Hekekia, but her hand was steady as she smoothed her palm over Hayashi's forehead, pushing sweaty strands of hair out of her face. A deep breath, and she regained control. A few minutes later, the surgical team wheeled Hayashi out, and Blue's Crows finally allowed themselves to be treated. Her gaze skipped across Tavi, who had collected an impressive number of injuries, and then on to the rest of her legionnaires, checking to make sure everyone was getting the care they needed.

All of the strength seemed to drain out of her, and she sagged back against the wall. She wasn't injured, and her people were being taken care of. *Her* people. That was all that mattered.

A warm body settled next to her on the cot.

"Hey, beautiful," Campbell murmured. "Come here often?"

Blue choked out a laugh but it quickly turned into a sob. Without even thinking about it, she leaned against him. He didn't hesitate to wrap his arm around her shoulders. Tears poured down her face and she shivered, desperately trying to hold herself together.

"You don't have to, sorry, I just..." Heat swept across her cheeks at her jumbled words, but she forced herself to hold his warm gaze and pulled in a deep, shuddering breath. "You don't have to be here."

Campbell's arm tightened around her when she would've pulled away.

"Got nowhere better to be, darlin.'"

With a low sigh, she leaned against him again and accepted the offered comfort. She couldn't before, but now...now she could. Time passed, and then footsteps drew to a stop in front of their cot.

"You two again?" an exasperated medic demanded. Slowly, Blue looked up as the man ran an assessing gaze over her. "Any injuries? No? Then both of you get out of my clinic so we can do our job."

While he wasn't unkind, there was a measure of steel in his voice that Blue didn't feel up to testing. But a thread of defiance and responsibility prompted her to check on each of her legionnaires before she could allow herself to leave. She gripped Sergeant Ord's hand in wordless respect before she stopped by Tavi's cot.

"Hey, kid." Blue forced a smile for the battered young man. "You look like you went to hell and back."

"I feel like it, ma'am," Tavi said before his glazed eyes narrowed. The pain meds were clearly kicking in. "And I'm not a kid."

"No," Blue said quietly. "You're a legionnaire."

Tavi nodded once and glanced up at Campbell. "Sir, could you do me a favor? Could you check on Mitzi for me? I promised...promised I'd look out for her, but she's not here and I..." His bruised hand clenched into a fist. "I can't leave."

Campbell frowned. "Should she be in Medical?"

"No, sir. She's already been cleared, but..." Tavi slowly blinked and forced his gaze to focus. "I don't think she's resting and she *needs* to rest. Please, sir?"

"Don't worry, I'll check on her. You get some rest." Campbell smiled. "Heard you earned your drop name. I like it. Shadow suits you."

"Thanks, sir." Tavi slowly slumped onto the cot, out cold. With his face relaxed in sleep, he looked more like her younger brother than ever before. The resemblance was uncanny, and she couldn't help but stare down at the young legionnaire who looked so much like family. Campbell nudged Blue.

"Come on, let's get you back to your quarters so *you* can rest." A glimmer of amusement shone in Campbell's dark eyes. "Or that medic kicks us out with his boot."

Blue was too tired to protest. And really, she didn't mind Campbell walking her back to her quarters. She wouldn't mind a lot of things right now. A distraction from the nightmares she was sure to have would be nice, and Ensign Hotness was one very nice distraction. She paused with her hand on her door and looked up at him. His eyes darkened at the blatant *want* in her gaze, and he took a step closer. One hand came up and caressed the side of her face, and she leaned into the touch.

"Blue!" Killi barreled down the corridor and shoved Campbell aside in her eagerness to get to her friend. "I stopped by Medical, but a grumpy asshole said he'd just kicked you out."

Killi threw her arms around Blue and wrapped her in a tight hug. A faint grin tugged at her lips as she met Campbell's rueful gaze over Killi's shoulder. *Cockblocked by my best friend. Figures.*

"Thanks for keeping me company, Campbell."

"Anytime, darlin'." He smiled at her. "I'll collect on those drinks later."

"Can't wait," she whispered as he walked away. And then she was hugging Killi back with the desperation she hadn't quite allowed herself with Campbell. "I can't believe you cockblocked me."

"What was it you said earlier?" Killi snorted. "Oops?"

Blue stiffened in her arms and pulled back to glare at her best friend. "You did that on purpose."

"My Rhino needed to be avenged." A sly grin crossed her face. "Besides, a little more chasing won't hurt anyone."

"You're lucky I love you, bitch." Blue gave her a slow grin. "Since there's no *tacos* for Ensign Hotness, then how about some margaritas?"

"Gods, yes."

✧✧✧

Campbell hadn't wanted to leave Blue. Walking away from her had taken a surprising amount of effort. There was so much devastation and trauma lurking in those pretty blue eyes... but duty came first, duty always came first.

At least he hadn't left her alone. That curvy little terror she called best friend would take care of her. He was actually grateful Killi had interrupted them. Blue was difficult enough to resist as it was, but when she'd looked up at him with so much heat in her eyes, he'd nearly given in. But whenever they did hook up, he wanted it to be because she wanted *him*, not a convenient warm body to chase away the shadows in her eyes. He could be that too just... preferably not the first time.

He paused midstep and shook his head at himself. Not that a second time was necessarily going to happen. They weren't a thing, would never be a thing. She was just a hot little distraction on what was supposed to have been a boring little deployment.

Several corridors and a lift ride later, Campbell strode down the corridor toward Operations. As boring as the deployment had started, it hadn't ended that way, and he still had a job to do. Starting with analyzing the composite data recovered from the legionnaires, aircrew, and Rhinos. He could get a few programs working on the data and then go track down Mitzi for Tavi. If nothing else, Campbell was a man of his word.

But when he walked into Ops, he found that he didn't have to track her down after all. Mitzi was hunched over the console, her filthy clothes and dirt-streaked face making it clear she'd come straight from Medical. The ash from the planet still caked her arms and she smelled like a proper legionnaire after being deployed for a month.

"You should be resting," Campbell said mildly, pitching his voice so as not to startle her.

Her head snapped up, eyes bloodshot but clear.

"Ensign Campbell!" The tense set to her shoulders relaxed, but urgency tightened her expression. "You need to see this."

"Okay?" Campbell said and moved around to the duty station. "What are you up to?"

"Reviewing recorded footage of the battle inside the research outpost," she said, her tired eyes staring into his. "You *really* need to see this."

"Why?"

"Because...I saw something while reviewing the footage," she stated with only a slight hesitation.

"No, I mean, why are you reviewing the footage?"

"Oh! I'm the xenobiologist of the Survey Corps team—"

"Okay...?"

"—and it's my responsibility to ensure that certain parameters are met," she continued, ignoring his interjection. She flexed her jaw and continued determinedly. "Which means I should review footage to confirm what I saw down there."

"And what did you see?" Campbell said as patiently as he could. The little scientist was brilliant, but sometimes it seemed as though the bookish types took forever to get to the point.

"Watch this replay. It's from the bodycam of Corporal Tom 'Ratman' Coonradt," Mitzi said quietly. "He was one of the ones who died."

The sadness in her tone killed any exasperation he might have felt. The legionnaires had sacrificed almost half their numbers to get their civilian charges off Aurora. He understood her need now. She felt an obligation to the dead to try and make sense of things, to justify their sacrifices. Without it, guilt would slowly eat her soul, consuming her.

With a nod, he pulled up a small stool and sat next to her. She rewound the vid and pressed play. Campbell suddenly was watching the last moments of Corporal Coonradt as he fought valiantly against the rampaging armadons.

It wasn't much, really. The armadons' reptilian scales blended perfectly with the dark, almost black ash from the volcano, and it was nearly impossible to see them until they drew closer. They were invisible for all practical purposes, though the longer he watched the better he became at tracking their movements. The trick, he learned, was to watch the trail they left in the ash behind them as they moved. Using this, he was able to—

"The *fuck*?" He hissed as his eyes caught something...*weird*. "Rewind and replay."

Mitzi said nothing, merely did as he said. He watched it a second time, his conscious mind waiting to catch up to the strange event his eyes had noticed. He stared hard until he glimpsed it. Confused, he looked at Mitzi. Her eyes were wide *for a reason*. Suddenly it clicked in Campbell's head what she was showing him.

"Rewind and replay," he told her again. She did, and he watched a third time. Now that he knew what to look for, it was painfully obvious as to how Corporal Coonradt had died—as well as the horrifying implications of what, precisely, killed him.

"What do we do?" she asked in a quiet voice. His eyes drank in the scene, his brain analyzing every frame.

"*Shit*. This... needs to be passed up the chain immediately."

"What if we're wrong?" Mitzi pressed. "What if it's a distortion or-or... what if we're *wrong*?"

"We're not. *You're* not," Campbell said, stabbing a finger at the screen.

The image of an armadon clearly wielding a firearm of some kind filled the screen. It was only four frames, but it was there, as clear as day. The device—some sort of large-bore projectile weapon—was pointed directly at Ratman and was the last thing his bodycam caught before he died in the alley.

"That right there tells us we're not wrong." Campbell took a deep breath as the implications raced through his mind.

Had they just made first contact with a sentient alien race and not even realized it? Had they lost any chance at diplomacy before it could even begin? Most importantly, had the Protectorate of Mars inadvertently started a war with the very first sentient species mankind had ever come across?

"You're right. We need to tell the captain," Mitzi whispered.

"Not just the captain," Campbell murmured quietly. "Forward it to Captain Truitt and his XO. The Legion's going to want to review this."

Campbell stood in the back of the Officers Wardroom. Nerves prickled along his spine and it was all he could do to maintain a professional bearing. Unlike the excited Survey Corps xenobiologist standing beside him, he fully grasped the implications of the priority call to Mars Primus—and the political power held by the man on the other end of the screen.

"What's the current status on the ground?" Budgetary Commissioner James McCoombs asked. The ranking civilian on Mars Primus, he worked close in hand with the planets seeking to join the Protectorate of Mars. He was, for lack of a better term, *the* person who needed to be convinced by any planet seeking admission.

"The ash cloud is obscuring visual and thermal at the moment, sir," Captain Esper responded. "But what we did see during the brief break the hurricane granted was—"

"It was a mass migration!" Mitzi blurted excitedly. Campbell nudged her subtly in an attempt for her to rein it in a bit. She barreled over it gracefully. "This is a behavior pattern never observed before. They are clearly a sapient species with some sort of hierarchical status for their leader!"

"Thank you, Doctor Wingo." McCoombs nodded his head. "You did include these observations into your notes for the next budgetary cycle meeting, yes?"

"Yes, I did."

"Good."

"This is merely a hiccup in the plan for colonizing Aurora," Norwood interjected, his voice higher pitched than what Campbell was used to hearing from the officious supervisor. Norwood even *looked* nervous to Campbell which, he was not at all ashamed to admit, he found absolutely hilarious after how he'd treated Blue. "The mass migration won't affect our plans at all."

Mitzi began to splutter, but this time when Campbell nudged her pointedly, she got the hint and snapped her mouth shut.

McCoombs remained silent for a quiet moment before nodding in agreement. "Are you sure this will not affect your plans?"

"We can set up some sort of zones to keep the armadons confined to areas well away from the outpost," Norwood continued. This was too much for Mitzi.

"Oh, sure. Discover a sapient species and *promptly throw them in camps!*" she spat disgustedly. "Like this has *always* worked out for humanity in the past!"

"These aren't humans, though," Norwood sneered. "You said it yourself. They are not subject to the same laws and treaties which we must abide by."

Campbell glanced at Captain Esper as the senior Navy officer coughed politely.

"Let's not forget the potential threat these armadons represent." Esper's jaw tightened. "And our fallen that we haven't been able to recover."

"Captain Esper is absolutely correct," Norwood jumped in with a greasy smile. "We must return, if only to recover those poor lost souls."

Poor lost souls, Campbell thought sourly. *Right, that's why you want back on Aurora.*

"My *recommendation* is as follows," McCoombs said, holding up an open palm. The tiny movement was far more effective at calming the growing storm in the wardroom than anything else and perfectly displayed the power the man held. "The *Perseverance* shall return to Mars Primus with the civilians. Once they are back on the ground and secure, we shall move to recovery ops. This is what I'll be presenting to both Admiral Livingston and General Poitras, as well as General Grayson of the Home Guard. Unless someone has an objection?"

Mitzi opened her mouth to object, but Norwood smoothly overrode any further protests.

"That sounds perfectly reasonable to us, sir. If you don't mind, though, I would love to have an extra day or two for the poor legionnaires of 4th Squad and their courageous Ravens to rest and recuperate at my hacienda on Mars Primus. As a... *gesture* of respect for their sacrifices. Of special note, I will be submitting the necessary forms to recognize the heroic actions of a few." He smiled. "Including one Lieutenant Astra Eliassen. Granddaughter of Shava Turnien."

McCoombs features froze for a second before he nodded. "Yes. Yes, that sounds acceptable. Please do so at your earliest convenience."

Cold swept down Campbell's spine. This was the political fallout to Blue revealing her familial connections and forcing Norwood to back down over her flying the evacuation mission. Fallout he wasn't about to let her face alone.

Campbell locked his gaze on Norwood.

This isn't over.